Life Without Living

Life Without Living

SC ALBAN

Published in the United States by Creative James Media.

www.creativejamesmedia.com

978-1-956183-01-6 (trade paperback)

First U.S. Edition 2025

For Brian Stephan

Anything is possible, if only you try.

Prologue

or as long as I can remember, I've had nightmares. Sometimes these nightly torments flew by, and I barely remembered what they were about—blurs of greens and browns, reds and blacks. And sometimes they'd seem to drag on forever, a never-ending labyrinth of ghastly obstacles waiting for me, a subconscious gauntlet.

When I was a little girl, I would run into my parents' bedroom after one of these episodes and beg to sleep in their bed. They, being the hippies they were, would toss the sheets back and welcome me in. I'd fall asleep in less than ten seconds. From the instant my feet touched the fabric, I was whisked away to a happier place. A sleep that held me tight until the day pushed the night away.

For the first ten years of my life, I'd run from my room to this haven; fear, an icy wet blanket wrapped around me threatening suffocation, was unable to penetrate the safe barrier of my parents' bedroom.

My mother told me they were just dreams. She'd stroke my hair and assure me they wouldn't hurt me. Even at the age of ten, I wasn't convinced, but I listened and tried to suppress the absolute terror that crept into my head each night. I would burrow down in the blankets until my head was covered and there was just a small hole for air to flow.

By the time I was a teenager, I was able to control these horrific scenes, or at least my response to them. Just as my mother trained me, I would repeat over and over what was to become my mantra: *It's just a dream, it's not real, breathe . . . breathe . . . breathe.*

If only I'd known then what I know now, I could've saved myself a whole bunch of trouble. I could've saved myself a whole lot of regret. Hell, I could've saved myself.

But I didn't.

So, I lived with my fears. I lived with my nightmares. I accepted they were a part of my life and conceded to them. That was how it was supposed to be. My only hope was that the gruesome terrors lurking in my mind were truly what I convinced myself they were—just dreams.

One

KATE

The dream started the same every night.

I was running. Running fast among the trees, my feet bare as I trampled over the wet ground. My breath sliced the air with rapid urgency and my lungs burned for me to slow down. My throat was raw; my heart pulsed to its max. Still, I ran faster.

I was in a forest. The lush greenery that comprised most of the northern California coast flew past me as I raced faster and faster. The monstrous redwoods that flanked both my left and right sides were a blur as I ran in earnest. The spongy moss gave just a little as each foot fell heavily on its furry surface.

As I flew to my unknown destination, I knew there was no alternative to failure. I'd make it on time. My conviction was strong, and I *would* get there. I had to. And yet, in the back of my mind, I knew how this would end. I'd been here before.

No matter how fast I ran, no matter how much I wanted to get there, the simple truth was that I would not make it. What I had would not be enough. I would be too late. I'd never reach him in time and there was nothing I could do about it.

I never would, but I had to try.

~

"No!"

I sat up with a start. The room was black. Sweat poured down my brow; my breathing was labored. How long had I slept? Five minutes? An hour? Six hours? Time eluded me. I glanced over at my bedside table peeking at the red digital glow of my alarm clock. It was 3:23 a.m. Good, I still had time before I needed to get up.

"Honey? Angel?" Alex sat up slowly, rubbing his eyes. "Are you all right? I heard you scream."

As my eyes adjusted to the darkness, I was able to see him. Even at 3:23 a.m., my husband resembled a Greek god. His lean build accentuated the solid muscle of his physique. My eyes wandered across his bare chest and up toward his face. His features were dark, with a strong jaw line and a face that held perfect symmetry. The kind of perfection that would make any woman bargain for a second glance. His longish, obsidian hair stuck up in all directions, commanding attention. He ran his fingers through it as he became more aware of his surroundings. Looking at him, I almost forgot what awakened me in the first place. His eyebrows furrowed as he reached over and gently caressed my arm.

"Jesus, love. You look awful. Are you all right?" The genuine concern in his voice melted my heart, and again I struggled to focus. "Babe, what's wrong? Are you sick? Hurt?" His voice walked close to an edge. He was losing his patience. "Kate, answer me. Please."

The sound of my name snapped me out of my trance faster than being hurtled into a brick wall. Frustration rolled off his body at my non-responsiveness, and I remembered what had started this to begin with. Without hesitation, the images of my dream came flooding back over me like a dark, black wave. Involuntarily, I shuddered.

"Nothing, love," I said offering a half-smile. "I guess I just heard a noise or something."

I wasn't going into the dream again—not tonight. Every time we discussed it, I sounded increasingly crazy while Alex became more and more frustrated. No, I was definitely not mentioning it.

"Are you sure? You look upset." Skepticism played with the tone in his voice. He wasn't fooled. He released a long breath. "What happened in the dream this time?"

Even though I was grateful to have Alex by my side, I didn't want to go through the details with him. Not again. Not tonight. I had to be more convincing if he was ever going to go back to sleep.

"No, love," I replied, my voice soft. "I'm fine. Really. Go back to sleep. It was nothing, just a noise outside—a dog barking or something."

I leaned in and pressed my mouth against his soft lips. His hand rose and brushed the side of my face as he pressed back and I was lost, not knowing who or where I was, spinning alone in a universe untouched by anyone.

Alex always affected me that way. With a simple kiss, my brain turned to mush, and I forgot everything and anything except the wonder of how it happened that I was this lucky. But I couldn't get lost, not now. I had to stay focused if I wanted him to go back to sleep.

"Goodnight, we'll talk in the morning." This time, I almost convinced myself.

I was getting better at hiding the truth from him, though I wasn't quite sure if that was a good thing or a bad thing. I didn't think much on it. I kissed him once more before scooting over in the bed. Resting on my side, my back to him, I pretended to go to sleep.

"Goodnight, love." His voice was soft, sleepy. A fuzzy haze coated his words. He'd believed my lies . . . or was at least resigned to them. "Love you."

It wouldn't be long before he was sleeping again, that I knew. What I was *not* so sure of was why I kept having the same dream over and over again, night after night. And why did I feel this indescribable need to keep it a secret from my own husband?

Alex's breathing returned to the rhythmic inhale and exhale I'd grown so familiar with, and I knew he was asleep.

Not wanting to close my eyes just yet, I slowly slid out of bed and tiptoed to the bathroom. I closed the door as silently as I could, making sure the latch nestled into place without a sound, and blew out the breath I hadn't realized I was holding as I turned on the light.

The bathroom was cold. My feet, surrounded by the soft, warm comfort of my sheets just moments ago, were instantly assaulted by the hard, frigid flooring on which I now stood. I leaned over the sink and looked in the mirror. My forehead wrinkled as I reluctantly recognized the woman looking back at me.

The crease in my brow deepened. I scrubbed my face and inspected my reflection. There was something to be desired in the person gazing back at me.

Dark eyes looked back with indifference. Raven hair framed my oval face. My fair skin, once tight and glowing like a fine piece of porcelain, looked pale and faded. It was during these times, the in-between times—too late to be night yet too early for morning—when I felt I could look at myself and see the true me.

I inhaled deeply and let the air linger in my lungs a few seconds before blowing it out. *When did I get so old?* Even though I'd just turned thirty a few weeks ago, time was taking an express train across my face. Within the past few weeks, laugh lines appeared around my mouth, several fine lines framed my eyes, a large crease streaked across the middle of my forehead, and four gray hairs grew in their own pattern.

The initial shock still hadn't faded from the morning I noticed the sprinkle of grays sitting close to the front of my hairline. Most women wouldn't have even attended to such an insignificant amount of hair, but I did. Against the contrast of my dark locks, those hairs shone brightly and shimmered in a mocking elegance— silver trails meandering through a black forest.

I continued to stare at my reflection. However, it was only a brief respite before the haunting images of my nightmare came creeping back into my consciousness with stealth-like expertise.

The dream. The reason for this early-morning bathroom visit now came flooding back in harsh clarity.

I was running. I was always running. I was running faster this time, faster than any of the other times before. Where was I going? I shook my head in frustration. I didn't know the answer to this question, but I did know I ran to find him. And this time I got further; further than I'd ever gotten before. Yes, I was closer this time. So close. Of that much, I was sure. Soon, I would be with him, and everything would be right again. But who? And why was I so scared? What could it mean?

"Ugh. Why can't I remember?" I grunted at my reflection.

Nothing. My brain was a dark, black vault. I pressed further. All I knew was that I had to get to him before it was too late. My future, no, *our* future, depended on it. It was my destiny.

I closed my eyes and squeezed them tight hoping to wring a memory out.

A flash of light. Dark hair. Blue eyes.

Crystal blue eyes the color of the sea. My heart raced. I swallowed hard and pushed deeper into my brain.

I ran to save him, the one, the man I would give my life for. The man who would save me from what would destroy me; and this man, whoever he was, was definitely not my husband. I pushed further into my brain to capture more details, but the reality slipped away, slick and impossible to hold until it vanished completely.

"Keep it together, Kate, it was just a stupid dream," I whispered out loud trying to convince myself—again.

I took another deep breath and released a sigh. No use staying awake for something I had no control over. I turned out the light and carefully opened the bathroom door.

I peeked into the bedroom. Alex was still asleep; his methodic breathing was instantly calming. With quiet feet, I stole back into bed. I snuck another glimpse at the clock. It was 4:35 a.m. *Shit.* I had taken longer than I'd wanted to in the bathroom, but at least there was an hour and a half before I had to get up.

I lay on my back, contemplating sleep. Anxiety roiled through my body. My stomach twisted. If only I could understand why this dream was on a continual loop night after night, I wouldn't be so obsessed. At the very least, I wouldn't wake Alex up with my screams on a near-nightly basis.

As all the ways in which my life would be better by understanding this damn dream flipped through my brain, my muscles sunk into the mattress. I was tired again. And although I would've done anything to avoid the unfathomable feeling of desperate terror from running through that lush, green forest while I rested, I knew if I ever wanted to find peace again, I could only do it while sleeping.

I consciously slowed my breathing and relaxed my body more. Sleep was coming and I'd be damned if I let it pass. It was the only lifeline to what I sought. It took over my body in a warm wash and I knew I should let it. I'd have to rest if I was to make it through work later anyway.

My eyelids became heavy, and my breathing fell in time with Alex's. My chest expanded with one last deep breath before I allowed my eyes to fully shut. I'd welcome sleep. It wasn't the answer I was looking for, but it was the only one I had. And although I was able to justify its significance, it wasn't comforting in the least.

Two

GIO

I often wondered what I'd do if I ever found her.

It's always been her, even when I didn't know it—she's the one to complete me, make me whole again, and return my mortality. I'd been searching for a long, long time. Around every corner, under every rock . . . everywhere. Desperate to make her mine once more.

There were times when I thought I'd never find her again, but in those times, I searched for my patience and held tight to the belief she was out there waiting for me.

It was exhausting.

I'd been wandering around the world for over four centuries—never resting, never content, never knowing when she would be mine, again.

Sometimes she was right at my fingertips, right there . . . so close. I could feel her, or at least thought I did, and it was the strongest sensation of goodness and beauty. Then, in an instant, it was swept away, leaving me nothing but a numbness in my bones. I cannot count the moments I almost had her, touched her, felt her skin against mine. Each time, she was so close.

Yet, I was still alone.

For centuries, I awoke and prayed we'd cross paths. In those tiny moments, breathless wishes, thoughts would come easy and my soul—if I'd ever had one to begin with—yearned to return to my body. Something I hadn't felt for hundreds of years.

In those moments, when I closed my eyes, I could almost feel alive again, almost imagine what living was. I'd walked this earth far longer than anyone ever should; although, I looked no more than twenty-three, the year I stopped aging.

When I thought back to it, and I mean *really* put some effort into the memory, I could still recall my youth. I grew up in a small village just outside of Florence, near the Arno River. Every time I thought upon my homeland, I was overwhelmed with longing, with grief, with loss. My heart, hardened like an old clay ornament embedded in my chest, was heavy with what could have been but was not.

I could never go back. Never would. Not, at least, until I found her.

My father worked the land, a simple man, making a simple living. Although he didn't have much wealth, he was respected among the townspeople as being a generous, honest, and honorable man.

Honor. The concept meant a great deal to the people of my time. Not like today. Back then, men lived to achieve it, fought to defend it, and died to maintain it. It was the moral code that shaped life. But it wasn't everything it promised, and it wasn't until much later that I realized honor doesn't make or break a man. It's the people who value the ideal that determine its worth, and not everyone plays by the same rules.

When I was fifteen years of age, my father decided I was old enough to learn a trade. At the time, I wasn't sure I was ready, but both my parents encouraged me that it was time to make my own future, to make a good life on my own.

I remember the day so well. It was the day my life changed trajectories and began a much different course. One that not even the most astute fortuneteller could have predicted. One that I'm not even sure I would've chosen, given the option and the outcome ahead of time. One that continues to guide my existence to this very day.

It was a cool spring morning when we headed out; my few belongings were wrapped in a cloth and tucked snugly under my arm. We were headed to Florence, where my father was determined to bargain an apprenticeship for me.

Though it took hours, we walked in near silence. As the city got closer, my steps became slower, my feet getting heavier with each progressing stride.

"Gio," my father said as we neared the city entrance, "what's bothering you?"

"Nothing, father." My gaze shifted down; my head heavy.

"Do not be afraid, son. It will be all right. You will work hard and make us proud. We know you will do your best." He placed his hand on my shoulder.

"Father"—a tremor of doubt wavered through my voice—"what if I can't do it?"

"Do not cloud your future with doubt. Life is simple. Follow the honorable path and everything else will fall into place."

I can still remember quite vividly the way in which he said those words. The tenor of his voice told me he'd never spoken words that held more truth. Though a great many things I've forgotten as the centuries have passed, those words still ring clear in my thoughts.

'*Life is simple.*'

Simple my ass. It was the greatest lie ever told.

Looking up at my father and seeing his sheer conviction, I could do nothing but believe he was right. I repeated the words over and over. *Do not doubt. Follow the honorable path and everything else will fall into place.*

The honorable path. It seemed easy enough, and it served my father well in his life. What could go wrong? I took a deep breath and was determined to show him that I, too, would be a great man.

I was fifteen. What did I know?

As we entered the city, my eyes drank in the activity. It was hard to believe such a busy and bustling place existed. It was so close to home, yet it felt part of a different world.

It wasn't until my father entered the shop of Rinato Cobisino, a local sculptor, that the doubt I'd felt earlier returned threefold and then turned into complete astonishment as I watched my father negotiate my future.

Rinato's face was red and swollen, the aftermath of a night of drinking. I smelled the alcohol as it leached out of his system through his sweat and wondered how my father didn't notice. I listened in silence as a place for me with this drunkard was agreed upon. A head of livestock and my complete disbelief later, a deal had been struck.

And so began my apprenticeship. I worked for Rinato for several years before he even let me touch stone. Even then, it was solely for his benefit. My main duty was to clean up his shop after he finished work for the day. Though in all honesty, I could hardly complain. It was an upgrade from the house chores with which I had begun. I spent the formative years of my adolescence fetching him ale, preparing his supper, doing his laundry, and cleaning up after his personals.

My life was beleaguered with irate commands that were responded to by a symphony of "yes, sirs" until it became quite apparent that I'd never be more than his servant, not an apprentice at all.

But what could I do? What choice did I have? I couldn't go home. My father had risked his reputation to get me here, to give me a chance at a better life. Failing to complete my apprenticeship would bring him great shame and embarrassment. It would strip him of all he believed in.

And so, the few times he came by Rinato's workshop to see for himself the great gift he'd given me, I looked him straight in the eye and lied.

"I hope he is not too much trouble?"

"He is no trouble at all. You should be proud to have a son like Gio. I wish I were as blessed as you," Rinato replied, slipping me a sly look that told me what might happen if I spoke up.

My father beamed, so proud. Who was I to rob him of that? It would hurt him to hear his negotiations with Rinato not only cost him one of his best livestock, but also earned his only son the status of a servant. It was an embarrassment I could save him from.

Besides, I wasn't technically lying to my father. Though not being instructed directly, I was a very observant young man. Even though Rinato rarely spoke to me beyond an order, I was listening. When he worked on a sculpture, I watched out of the corner of my eye memorizing each movement and every motion he made. I branded the name and shape of each tool to memory. Every night I would visualize how to use each tool— how I would use it to sculpt *my* masterpiece.

If that time ever came.

Then a funny thing happened. Though Rinato never knew it, I was learning to sculpt. And I was quite good. At night, after he'd passed out drunk, I'd sneak into the workshop and collect the fist-sized bits of stone that were lying about waiting for me to dispose of. But I wouldn't throw them away. No, I'd take them back to my cot and quietly smooth out the rough edges, silently carving out their shape.

I was surprised at how natural it came to me. I'd hold the

stone in my hands and feel its inner form. My hands would work the hard surface with a chisel and pick, and slowly, methodically, the stone would cease being just a rock, and emerge into a work of art.

I was becoming a master of the human shape, and my collection of miniature men and women was growing so that it was becoming difficult for me to hide them.

When I had about ten figures hidden away, I decided to take them to the marketplace to sell. I wasn't sure if such insignificant items held any worth to anyone other than myself, but I had to try.

It was a cool autumn morning when I approached Rinato. He was just starting on an uncarved piece of stone, which was to become an angel commissioned for the city gates.

"Master Rinato."

"What is it?" He didn't look up from his work.

"Today is my day off."

"I am aware. What is it you want?" Annoyance edged his voice.

I suppressed a smile. This was what I had hoped for; for him to be so concentrated on his work that my presence would be too distracting to have around.

"I was hoping for permission to venture into the marketplace."

"Fine, fine. Just be home by nightfall. I'll need you to clean up this mess and prepare supper."

"Thank you."

"Now leave me in peace." His eyes never left the stone in front of him.

Quickly, I gathered up the small satchel filled with my tiny village of people, some bread, and a small flask of water, and headed out before Rinato changed his mind and came looking for me.

The city was a bustling place. I walked until I found an out-of-the-way spot near a side street between a tavern and a book vendor. I opened my satchel and took out my pieces. Every stone man, woman, and child were a labor of love. The lines of their bodies and the shapes of their faces emerged from the stone like granite snowflakes, each was different; each tiny sculpture was a distinct person. I wondered if there was anyone else in the world who'd find as much joy in them as I found in making them.

As I studied my work, a shadow blocked the sun shining on me. I looked up to see an older gentleman looking down.

"Excuse me, son. May I?" he asked, extending his hand toward the figurines.

He was a tall gentleman with a friendly face; the kind of face that was easy to trust. His clothes were mismatched and not typical of the men of Florence but clean enough and in good shape. I wondered where he was traveling from, as I handed them over without hesitation.

"Amazing," he said as he held a figure of a woman close to his face, inspecting the stone. "I don't believe I've ever seen anything so small and realistic as this. Quite a talent, this artist." His face was reflective as he studied the piece. He looked down at me when he finished his appraisal. "Son, could you tell me where you bought them?"

"I didn't buy them, sir. I made them."

The gentleman eyed me carefully as if he wasn't quite sure if he should believe me or not. "You made these, did you?"

"Yes, sir. I made them. With bits of stone that I found lying around." I wasn't sure how much information to divulge. If Rinato found out what I was up to, I'd have bigger problems than being named a liar.

The gentleman gazed into my eyes as if searching directly into my mind, rooting around for the answer to an unspoken question.

As uncomfortable as I was, I met his stare. My chin lifted and my heart pounded in my chest as I held my ground. Would he take it as a challenge? Then, suddenly, as if the answer to his question magically appeared across my forehead, the gentleman's face relaxed, his eyes lit up, and his face held that friendly look once more.

"Interesting, very interesting," he said to himself, his voice cryptic. "All right, then"—a smile spread across his face— "are you selling these pieces, young man?"

I blinked several times. What did he say? I wasn't sure how to answer. Though I'd made this trip with the sole intention of selling my sculptures, I didn't think I would. I should've been eager to give them all up to any buyer that crossed my path. But to him? Why did this man give me the feeling that selling to him now was not just a simple exchange, but the beginning of something I wasn't sure I wanted to be a part of?

"I . . . I'm not sure," I replied.

"Understandable. It must be hard to part with something so beautiful." He held one of the young girls in his hand. "And the time it must have taken you to complete such work . . . well, I can't imagine. But, you see, it's my daughter's birthday and she would love them."

He looked at me, his eyes a deep shade of brown, flecks of green and gold sprinkled throughout the irises. I sat there, looking up at this strange man, nearly mesmerized. How it was possible for any human to have eyes such as these? It wasn't natural.

And then I understood. This man wasn't a commoner; he was Stregheria—witches that traveled throughout the country buying and selling their goods and magick. A small shiver ran up my spine.

I wasn't certain if I should conduct business with such a person, but the thought of spending the rest of my life as Rinato's servant was the only motivation I needed. I nodded and smiled. I heard myself speaking, though my voice didn't quite sound like me.

"Of course, I will sell them to you."

"Ah, excellent," he said as he reached into his bag and pulled out a small satchel of coins. "My daughter will be more than pleased to receive such a gift. It's not everyday you receive a present from your future."

"I'm not sure I understand."

"Nothing, son, nothing," he said waving his hand, and then quickly adding, "Now, how much would you like for the entire lot? Will four gold coins be sufficient?"

My response became stuck in my throat, I was stunned. Just moments before, I wasn't sure there was another person alive who'd give a second glance at my work, and now this strange man was offering me more money than I'd ever imagined.

"It is too generous, sir." Even though I was tempted by his offer, it felt wrong to accept so much for something that cost me nothing.

"Nonsense," he replied. "It is barely enough for the number of hours you must have spent creating them. My daughter's smile is worth more than twice as much."

I carefully handed him the rest of the figurines wrapped in a piece of cloth. "Thank you, sir. I'm indebted to your generosity."

"Don't think too much upon it," he said. "Besides, I have a feeling our paths may cross again. If they do, and you still feel indebted to me, you may repay me at that time."

"Yes, sir."

He paid with four gold coins and packed up the rest of the figurines in his bag.

"One more thing, son, if you don't mind."

"Not at all, sir."

"Do you mind telling me your name?"

"Giovanni Rossi, sir. But most call me Gio."

A smile spread across his face. "Gio." He sounded amused. "Of course, of course. Well, goodbye, then, Gio. Good luck." He laughed as he walked down the road and wandered gracefully through the crowd until he was eventually out of sight.

I sat on the side of the road, gold coins in hand, contemplating the bizarre exchange between the gentleman and myself. A gift from your future? Our paths may cross again. The more I thought of it, the less it made sense. I sat there in wonder until the sun was well past overhead. It was time to make Rinato's supper, and to clean up the workshop.

THOUGH THE EVENTS occurred lifetimes ago, those memories are as vivid as if they had just happened. At times, my father's ignorance in selling me into servitude was, at best, more than I could comprehend. For years, I carried anger and resentment with me, a heavy burden to bear.

And yet those same thoughts of anger carried me to memories of her—pain peppered with absolute beauty. Pain found on the journey to obtain such a gift. Beauty of a love so pure it transcends reality.

Still, even in my moments of doubt, when I found myself questioning whether I should've pursued such a gift, I discovered I wouldn't have changed anything. I held on firmly to the belief that everyone has a purpose.

That through these moments of doubt we must push through the pain, push our limits to the brink, and hold on to the faith that the truth and purity of love will lead us to the path of ultimate salvation—the day we become part of the eternal cycle.

This was my strongest belief. My greatest truth. And with

that conviction I knew I'd overcome the evil that was there to stop me. I would find her. We would be together. And life would continue once more.

Three

KATE

So, there I was in all my glory, standing in the kitchen, a sleep-deprived haze surrounding my head. My flannel pajama bottoms were two sizes too big as they dragged beneath my feet, the drawstring pulled as tight as it would go around my hips: my thin white tank donning a small stain on the front.

I should've cared more about my personal appearance no matter what time of day, but it just seemed completely unreasonable to make breakfast every morning in silky lingerie or whatever it was a more put-together woman wore to bed. I tugged up my pants. The least I could've done was find pajamas that fit.

I was awake before Alex most days, weekends being the exception. If it were Saturday or Sunday, I would've been sleeping in. It was nearly impossible for me to drag myself out of bed on those days. Alex was usually up running or surfing or doing something that required way too much energy for a non-workday, while I'd be basking in bed until noon, sometimes one. He'd often leave, do whatever, and be back home for hours before coming to wake me up.

It was always the same.

"Are you still sleeping?" he'd say as he opened the blinds, sunlight assaulting my glorious slumber. "Now I could be wrong, but according to Dante, isn't sloth the fifth deadly sin?"

"It's the fourth . . . you know, right after the sin of being freakishly energetic," I'd grumble with my head completely buried under the pillows.

I never quite understood people who got up early on days when they could sleep in. I mean, sure, I was up early Monday through Friday, but only because I had to work, certainly not by choice.

I tilted my head to the side to listen as Alex started the shower upstairs. The clock on the microwave told me it was 6:40 a.m. In approximately twenty minutes, Alex would head out and I'd have to start getting ready for work.

I opened the cabinet above the toaster and reached for the coffee. My nose quickly caught the fragrant aroma of the deep, rich French roast. I closed my eyes for a moment and took a deep breath. I absolutely loved the smell of coffee. It reminded me of my grandmother's house and childhood, the innocence I never knew I had until it was lost to me forever.

I had spent most of my youth at my grandmother's during the summer, helping her cook and tend to her garden. Quiet and peaceful, it was an oasis from the consistent insanity that came with the territory of having two hippie activists for parents. Growing up in my house, day-to-day life was a balancing act defined by who happened to be saving the whales or protesting the injustice of the corporate concentration camps of factory farming. So, it was only natural for my grandmother's house to become the eye of the storm, an unwavering calm surrounded by chaos.

When I was young, maybe five or six, I began my lifelong love affair with the earthy aroma of coffee. My grandmother would sit me on her counter each morning while she made breakfast.

"Katie, love," she'd say, her cream-colored apron tied snugly around her waist. "Give Nonna the coffee."

I'd hand her the square brown canister on the counter, two birds eternally tending their nest etched in its side. I had always thought those birds looked so happy; two parents' content to stay close to home watching over their children. I loved how the canister made a metallic popping sound as she pulled the lid off in one quick movement.

As soon as the lid lifted, the air would fill with the thick scent. Even as a child the smell was intoxicating. We would talk and laugh while we made breakfast. She'd tell me stories of the old days. Stories of how my great-great-grandmother Mathilda ran a boarding house near the lake, and how her brother Salvatore would take his boat up the California coast north to Alaska to fish. I was enraptured by the words that came so easily from her tongue, the stories of our family.

It was our time, our special time.

"Hey, babe. Do you think you can start the coffee for me, please? Thanks, love."

I shook the memory away when I heard Alex's voice call down the stairs from the shower. I imagined his soapy hair, water dripping from his forehead into his eyes and mouth, gooseflesh forming over his body, as he shouted his question from behind the steamy curtain. As if he had to ask. It was quite possible I'd been making coffee for him every morning, or close to it, since the day we married.

I grabbed his mug from the cabinet and set about the task.

We met in college. Although, I think I felt him before I met him, if that makes any sense. It was my fourth year at university. I was working as a barista in the campus commons. I'd bent down to pick up a stack of cups when a soft breeze caressed my back. It was an odd feeling, the breeze. Like fingers tapping lightly up your spine. I slowly stood.

He immediately caught my eye as he walked into the commons and approached a table. The table was already crowded but the people sitting there didn't even hesitate to make room. I could tell he was the type of person who always got what he wanted and never accepted no for an answer. What was it that made certain people so confident and self-assured? Whatever it was, it skipped me. I inspected him from my place behind the counter.

Mother of God, he was gorgeous. How had I never seen him before? This school wasn't that big. Surely, I would've noticed. My eyes drank in his every movement, thirsting for more. I watched him through my long bangs, my gaze glued to him. Never had I been so mesmerized by one individual. He had my full attention.

His longish, dark hair hung loosely to the left side of his face. It looked as if he'd either not combed his hair at all that morning or spent hours making sure it hung perfectly—beautiful chaos. How would it feel under my hand? How would it smell?

As if he knew he was being watched, he glanced over in my direction. For an instant our eyes met, and his lips curved up. His face was chiseled perfection; angled and smooth. My lungs burned. It felt as if I was breathing twice as hard, though I held my breath. I was lost in the curve of his smile as I stood there breathing and not breathing, trapped in a dimension that transcended time and space.

How long had I been staring? Seconds? Minutes? Hours? Heat crept up to my cheeks. I had to regain my composure. This was so unlike me. All those feminist meetings my mother dragged me to ensure I'd be my own person, that I'd never fall under the spell of a man, were instantly forgotten as he casually ran his hand through his hair in one quick motion like some sort of magic wand.

He came up to the counter and ordered a coffee.

"This is good." He smiled after he took his first sip. "You made it?"

"Um, yeah . . . thanks." My God, he was breathtaking. Be cool. Be cool. I tried to sound casual but ended up barely whispering the words. Super.

"I'm a sucker for good coffee."

Silence.

He lifted an eyebrow indicating it was my turn to speak. I struggled to compose myself; my head began to swim.

"I'm Alex," he said when I didn't respond.

Again, he flashed a brilliant smile—perfection. My heart nearly collapsed. *Speak, dammit!*

"Nice to meet you," I choked out reminding myself to breathe.

More silence.

My thoughts were frozen, unable to move backward or forward. A sudden fleeting thought about indecision flashed through my mind; that inability to make a choice was what it must feel like to be under some strange spell. I made a mental note to cut those fairytale princesses more slack in the future.

Still, silence.

My brain argued with itself. *Should I say something? What does one say to a living, breathing God? For Christ's sake, do something.* I continued to stand there, frozen to the floor, struggling with my internal dialogue, completely aware of every movement or rather, non-movement, I made. I implored myself to say something, to say anything.

More silence.

"Well . . ." His voice led me to a far-off place. "Will I be seeing you tomorrow then . . . Kate?"

His eyes sparkled. Had I ever seen such amazing colors in

eyes before? They were a kaleidoscope of green, blue, gold, and . . . was that red? They were completely unique and compelling. They were so clear, so brilliant, and so inviting, like a still lake on a hot summer afternoon.

As images of skinny-dipping in those eyes colored my thoughts, my heart began racing. *Breathe, Kate, breathe*—my mantra in full effect. I concentrated on the air that was supposed to be rhythmically flowing in and out of my body. A few moments passed until I realized he was waiting for an answer. If only I'd been listening to the question.

"Excuse me? How'd you know my name . . . what?" I fumbled, frustrated with myself for not paying better attention to what he was saying. Damn you, oxygen.

"Tomorrow"—he pointed at my nametag and held his cup up as if to remind me that I worked at a coffee bar— "for coffee?"

Answer the question, Kate. My brain was moving at dial-up speed.

"Uh, yeah, I mean, I guess." Smooth.

"Good. Look forward to seeing you. I hope we'll have some more time to get to know each other a little better." He paused and looked around the commons. "I'm fairly new around here. It'd be nice to make a friend." He flashed another dazzling smile and was back at his table before anyone really knew he was gone.

Oh my God, Kate. You are such an idiot!

Could I be any more ridiculous? What in the hell had happened to me? I'd always been so practical, so level-headed. I wasn't one to believe in love at first sight. But what else could explain my behavior? Could I be in love with someone I'd just met? Never in my life had I been so affected by another individual, let alone some random guy with a pretty face.

Okay, more than just a pretty face. Amazingly perfect features would be more appropriate. Still, how was it possible

I could be transformed into some mindless schoolgirl in a moment?

The next morning, Alex came back. He ordered a coffee and stuck around to chat. He was funny, charming, and smart, and I couldn't believe how simultaneously soothing and unsettling it was to be around him. No one had ever made me feel so delightfully nervous.

Day after day, shift after shift, Alex kept coming around. He appeared to only have eyes for me, and I didn't look for nor need a reason for all his attention. Life as I'd known it was drastically altered, never to return to what it'd been before—if I could even remember life before Alex. It just didn't seem to exist anymore.

But since that moment, that very first day, I've made Alex his coffee every morning. And despite that truth, he shouted the same question down to me from the shower almost daily.

I filled the coffee pot with water and filled the well as I mulled over what was for breakfast. I didn't have to start getting ready for work for another fifteen minutes; I could afford the time. And it'd been a while since I cooked. Pancakes, bacon, and eggs were one of his favorites. I didn't even mind cooking it, though I chose a vegetarian lifestyle. I could surprise him. I'm sure he'd love it.

If I'd only gotten more sleep.

After careful consideration and a long line of excuses to justify my laziness, I decided on cold cereal. He'd live. As I reached for the bowls, I was taken off-guard by a warm pair of hands slowly wrapping around my body. I started with a jolt, the bowls nearly toppling to the floor.

"Did I ever tell you how beautiful you look in your pajamas?" The hint of irony in his voice, made his real feelings about my pajamas evident.

"You scared me."

Alex frequently moved about the house in total silence.

The way his body flowed in movement, so graceful, so elegant, as if noise itself was afraid to offend his gait.

I tried to sound put-out, but he wasn't fooled. He rarely was. His lips brushed softly against the back of my neck. I could feel his warm breath on my skin as he spoke.

"I'm sorry, love." His voice was soft velvet. "I can't help myself when I'm around you."

He pressed his nose up against the crook of my neck. His damp hair felt good against my skin. I could smell his cologne; the subtle musky scent tickled my senses and lured me closer until I was pressed back into him. We began to gently rock back and forth. He never released his grip from my waist as I turned around to face him, ready to pout some more.

My jaw slacked. God, he was handsome. The kind of handsome that forces you to continuously wonder how in the hell you ended up with someone so out of your league. His intense kaleidoscope-colored eyes drew me in. His smooth, radiant skin was clean-shaven and flawless. His lips curled upward in that playful smile I knew so well. I didn't stand a chance and he knew it. Damn, why'd he have to be so good-looking? I would definitely get sexier pajamas.

As I leaned in closer, excitement rose from deep within me and tighten in my stomach. Gently, he bowed his head toward mine.

"Good morning," I said in a soft tone, acknowledging surrender.

"Good morning, my angel."

My angel? Was he kidding me? Alex was my angel from the moment I saw him.

Our lips grazed against each other's. The barely-there touch ignited sparks instantly and a fire grew between our bodies. I pressed my lips harder against his as he pulled me close, his hands firm and commanding. Our breathing grew rapid as we became lost in the kiss. Time stood still. There was only us. Everything around us was simply gone.

His hands traveled up the length of my torso. He didn't relent but wrapped his arms tighter around my body, urgent, demanding. I yearned for more. He brought his hands to the front of my pajamas and played with the waistline, sticking his thumbs just inside in my pants and pulling me closer still.

My hands traced his broad shoulders. They found their way to his shirt buttons and began the slow, meticulous work of undoing each one with a flicking motion.

"Do you have to be on time today?" I asked, hope spilling from my lips.

"I suppose I could be a little late," he replied as he kissed my neck.

His tongue traced a line down to the top of my tank. His strong hands grabbed my ass and lifted me up onto the counter, his mouth never leaving my skin. His lips worked my neck in a slow sucking motion, his teeth grazing over my pulse.

My stomach muscles tightened, and my center clenched. God, I needed him.

A loud knock on the front door cut through the moment. Simultaneously, we pulled away, our eyes opening. Silence. For a moment, I convinced myself I imagined it. I closed my eyes and leaned in to find his lips again, to fall into his soul. However, the moment passed quickly as another knock ascended upon the door followed by the doorbell.

Repeatedly.

"Kate! Hey, Katie! I know you're in there, I see the light on. Hurry up and let me in, it's freezing out here!"

I sighed; the moment gone.

There was only one person who had such impeccable timing and a shrill voice. Though, even if he hadn't spoken, I could've figured it out by the incessant knocking.

Dave and I met eight years ago, when I started my job at

Billows Publishing. And even though he was close to twenty years my senior, we hit it off immediately. Often cynical and a bit crass, Dave was the male version of me, or so I liked to think. I instantly connected with him.

"Just a minute, Dave," I yelled in response.

He would have to wait as I stole a few more seconds. I looked at Alex and raised an eyebrow. He held my stare, his eyes lit in a smile.

"As much as I'd like to continue, it's back to reality, Mrs. Martins. The sewing circle has arrived."

He released his arms from around me and began re-buttoning all my hard work. The distance between us felt cold and lonely. Still, I couldn't help but smile at my husband's reference. Always engaging, there was never a lull in conversation when Dave was around. If there was a person who could dish out the latest dirt on everyone and anyone, at any time, it was him.

"Don't you want any breakfast?" I asked as Alex headed toward the door.

He eyed the cereal bowl for just a split second. "Uh, thanks, but I think I'll pass on breakfast today. Before you lured me into your arms, I *had* wanted to get to the office early. Looks good, though." He gave me a wink. He grabbed his thermos, filled it, and returned to kiss me once more before heading to the door.

"Oh yeah," he said as he turned back toward the kitchen, "I forgot to tell you I cancelled the appointment with the cable guy tonight. They couldn't get here until six-thirty, and that's just cutting it a little too close for me. Especially if we're going to be out of here by seven."

"Oh . . . that's fine," I replied casually, trying not to sound too confused.

Cutting it close for what? What did I forget? A work

party? A birthday? I racked my brain, hoping I would catch my mistake before he did.

He stalked toward me, a knowing look on his face. It took him only a few steps, his legs graceful as they moved across the wood floor. He bent in for one last kiss.

"Be ready by seven," he whispered in my ear. His lips sent a volt of electricity through my body. "Happy ninth, Mrs. Martins. I'm looking forward to tonight."

He stole out of the kitchen before his words fully processed and the reality of what he'd said fully set in.

"Shit! Shit!" I couldn't believe I'd forgotten. It was our ninth anniversary. How could I have forgotten it? It didn't make any sense.

"Damn it! Damn it! Mother fu—"

"Well, good morning to you too, sunshine." Dave sauntered into the kitchen, threw his bag on the table, and took a seat on the nearest barstool.

"I know I've said it before, but your husband is totally hot. I swear, if we weren't friends, I would definitely put the moves on him. I mean, you never know, maybe he could like a guy like me."

"Dave," I said in a flat tone, not even looking at him. I was not in the mood for small talk. "Why're you here so early?"

"Geez. Grumpy much? What's your problem? Here I was thinking I'd be doing you a favor carpooling to work, the nice guy that I am, and what do I get upon my arrival?" He sounded irritated.

"Shut up a minute, will you?" As much as I wanted to pacify him, I really didn't have time for his drama. "I've got a serious problem." I felt dizzy. How could I have been so oblivious?

Dave's eyes narrowed. "What's up with you? You really don't look good."

I had no idea what I looked like at that moment, but if it

was close to anything like how I felt, I didn't need to see a mirror.

"I forgot . . ." I choked out. "I forgot our ninth anniversary." The tears were beginning to form as the anxiety crept up on me.

"Ouch."

Classic Dave. Providing the greatest amount of impact by saying as little as possible. I just looked at him. Neither wanting to talk to or ignore him, I hopped down from the counter and groaned.

It was hard to believe just moments ago my morning was headed in a completely different direction, but here I was, recent recipient of the world's worst wife award and proud owner of the guiltiest conscience known to human existence.

"What am I going to do? We planned this night weeks ago. A romantic dinner, the symphony, drinks, presents, you know . . . an anniversary. I can't believe I forgot. Alex pulled major strings to get these tickets, to make this night perfect, and I haven't even gotten him anything. Do you know how hurt his feelings will be if he thinks I didn't put any thought into this? I'll tell you; he'll be totally disappointed." My voice took on an edge of panic. The anxiety was hitting hard. "You know how he *loves* these types of things, Dave. They're majorly important to him. And how good of a husband is he? A great one, I tell you that. I feel so bad. I don't deserve him. What am I going to do?" I plopped down into a chair at the kitchen table and let my head fall face down on its surface.

"Whoa, slow down there, Katie. You're gonna give yourself an aneurysm."

I lifted my head, my eyes searching his face. He was a handsome man with soft features and a gentle smile. His eyes were the first things anyone noticed when they looked at him. Trust me, I'd know. Even strangers made comments about them. Light crystal blue and sparkled like diamond. But not in a harsh way. Just like his smile, his eyes were kind. He sat across from me and smiled, his two pieces of topaz piercing through my negativity, the perpetual silver lining to my dark cloud.

"Now, I know you probably feel like the worst person in the world. That would be just like you, but this is not the end of existence."

"But—" I started. He held up his finger.

"Let me finish." He waited until he was sure I was going to stay quiet. "Now, the way I see it, *we* have approximately ten hours to make sure Alex never finds out you forgot about this day. So, you'd better get dressed, pull yourself together, and for God's sake, Katie, put on some lipstick. Oh, and you'd also better hurry or we'll be late for work." He sat there, his eyes speaking volumes. Those blue orbs told me everything I needed to know about our friendship without saying one word.

"But, wha—"

He immediately stopped me. "Not another word. I mean it. Now hurry up and get dressed, or we really will have a problem."

He turned around on his barstool and pulled a newspaper out of his coat pocket. He spread it out on the counter and began flipping through the front section. I walked over to him and placed my hands on his shoulders, my head resting on his back.

"Thanks." I was so grateful to have him in my life.

"Why are you still downstairs? I thought I told you to get ready?" His voice had fallen back to its playful, sarcastic tone and I knew he'd forgiven me for being so rude earlier.

I smiled and turned around without another word. A quick peek at the clock as I headed for the stairs revealed it was four minutes after seven. Hardly any time had gone by at all, I was still on schedule.

"Don't forget the lipstick," Dave yelled once more as I ran up the stairs.

I grabbed a new towel from the linen closet and tried not to be too hard on myself. Everyone forgets these types of things occasionally, right? Yeah, sure. Everyone except Alex. But I was just human, wasn't I? Humans aren't perfect. Certainly not me. I had the right to make a few slip-ups every now and again. If I fixed them before they caused too much trouble.

I continued to justify myself as I walked into the bathroom. Turning on the shower, I began to undress. I stood in front of the mirror and stared at the reflection looking back. Again, guilt crashed over me in a wave.

What the hell was my problem? Why did I always feel like such a mess? Why couldn't I get it together for one second in my life and not have to depend entirely on everyone around me to hold me up?

Absolutely pathetic.

I continued berating myself until the tears began to silently slip down my cheeks in thin streaks and the steam completely fogged up the mirror.

Carefully, I stepped into the shower. As the hot water hit my skin, I took a deep breath and let the heat wash away all the negativity, all the guilt. That's it. Enough. I was going to make everything okay. I had to. With a renewed sense of purpose, I closed my eyes and took one more deep breath. It was time to get ready for the day.

Four

GIO

Present day

As I walked through the small downtown, a crisp, autumn chill sliced through me like a razor. I took a long, deep breath. My skin tingled. A flicker of hope shot through my body. I was close. I could feel it. Without a doubt and with every inch of my being, I knew I was close. I closed my eyes and tried desperately to organize my thoughts.

After years of searching, after so many missed chances, I shouldn't have believed I'd find her again and get another chance so soon. After all, I'd been given so many opportunities through the centuries and had been defeated over and over. No, I'd been more than repeatedly defeated. I had repeatedly failed—completely and totally failed.

How could I even begin to believe that now, after so many lifetimes, that I'd be given another possibility at happiness? And so soon? Even though reason itself couldn't justify why, I always believed one day I would get one. I couldn't help but hope.

Hope. So pure. So raw. So uninhibited. A feeling I couldn't afford to be with or without. Hope kept me searching when everything else told me to stop. It also crushed me with the immense weight of disappointment as she was yanked from me time and again. And yet I could not concede to hopelessness.

I could have, no, *should* have, ignored the brief flicker flashing in my heart as I stood there on that chilly autumn morning in that quaint downtown. After all, through the decades, I'd become a master of denial as my hopes were continually dashed.

Denying that it was my weakness that began this never-ending cycle of torment and pain. Denying I was good enough to deserve peace. Denying I should continue to search for the one soul whose existence would allow mine to continue instead of remaining in this eternal holding pattern. I was a master at using denial to shove hope back down in the deep trench within my slowly-rotting shell.

And yet, after all these years, after so many missed chances, here I was, again, believing that same small flicker of hope and igniting a sensibility that did not seem so sensible at all.

I just couldn't give up on her. Goddess knows, I wouldn't give up on *us*. I'd never give up on us. It was the only thing keeping me halfway close to believing I still had a soul.

I opened my eyes and slowly glanced around. The entire downtown couldn't have been more than four blocks. Small shops lined the streets, local shops that had been there since the town's beginning, no doubt.

I automatically reached into my pocket and pulled out my phone. I didn't have to dial, there was only one number in the memory. I hit the button and hit Send.

"Hello . . . Gio? Are you there?" The thick Irish accent was a familiar sound to my old ears.

"Yeah, Willem. I'm here." Emotion threatened to spill out. I centered myself and took a breath. "Listen—I think I'm close. No, I *know* I'm close. I can feel her."

I knew what he was going to say, but I just didn't have the time for his doubts. He had to believe me.

"So soon? You really think she's back after such a short time?"

Willem was my voice of reason on most days. If I didn't believe in my heart he was trying to shield me from disappointment, I would've hung up the phone right then and there. But I knew him better than that, and when all was said and done, thirty years *was* an exceptionally fast turnaround.

In truth, without Willem, I would've given up centuries ago. Completely resigned to the fate I'd been dealt and still lying in the hole I'd dug for myself in a remote cave deep in the cliffs of Moher, had he not come.

The memory flooded back like a tsunami . . .

"I'VE BEEN LOOKING FOR YOU," he had stated in a matter-of-fact voice.

I'd not heard such a thick accent in centuries. I almost didn't understand what he'd said. It was old world. *He* was old world, from an ancient time. He carried an accent that the people had long ago abandoned for the softer dialect one hears today.

I didn't move my body, just merely looked up at him from my dirt coffin. Who was this man standing over me? Why was he here? If I hadn't tried to kill myself over and over with no success, I would've feared for my life. If I hadn't been lying there praying for death to somehow find me, the sight of him would've terrified me.

"Get up." His voice was deep and powerful. It vibrated in the cavern. I felt it in my bones. "We don't have much time."

"Go to hell."

"You have to hurry, they're close. They speak of the man who does not age. They're coming here now to destroy you." He spoke swiftly, each word falling into the next.

"Then they come to give me peace," I responded, my eyes closing.

It was true. I hadn't aged in centuries; however, my soul was old. I didn't know of whom he spoke, but if they came to kill me, I'd welcome them graciously.

After wandering for days on end, the pure physical exhaustion coupled with the continual mental anguish had taken its toll. A great wash of relief flooded over me as I began to realize it would soon be over.

"You don't understand," he insisted. "They don't come to kill you. They plan to put you in a place where you will never rest. A place where you'll be trapped with the same torment you live with now, but with no chance of escape. You must come with me if you ever want a chance at peace."

He paused; I could feel his stare boring through my head. I turned my back on him facing down on the wet cave floor waiting for my long-awaited sentence to be delivered. The moist coolness of the earth felt good against my dry lips.

Near silence blanketed me, save one thing. I could hear the stranger's breath echo in the space between us. I lay a second more in the almost quiet before his voice rang loud and clear through the cold air.

"If you ever want to be with Katarina again, I suggest you come with me . . . *now.*"

My heart froze. The sound of her name shot through me

like an arrow. In my head I heard her voice: *Gio, amore mio, per favore.*

My eyes flew open, and before I decided what I'd do, I was on my feet glowering at my strange visitor.

"Who are you?" I demanded through clenched teeth.

"I don't have time to explain, not now. We have to go." There was urgency to his words that made me think he'd be in just as much danger as I if we didn't leave soon.

"I know this may be hard for you to do, but trust me, please. I'm here to help." He took a few steps deeper into the cave and motioned for me to follow.

I stood for a minute, and then I heard several feet just outside the entrance of the cave. For an instant, I was stuck. I didn't know what to do, but the sound of her name called to me and assured me I could trust this stranger. With haste, I followed him deeper into the cavern.

We walked in silence through the narrow passageways. It was blacker than the darkest night as we ambled through the cave, the only reprieve from the darkness was a small light the stranger held in front of him.

"Quickly," he whispered in a gruff voice. "And try not to make any sound. I'll explain everything as soon as I can . . . once we're safe."

We moved forward in haste, the sides of the cave becoming narrower and narrower until it was quite impossible to walk straight. Both the stranger and I turned sideways to effectively navigate the path. A chill ran through my body and the temperature continued to drop further in we ventured.

It was so quiet. The only sounds were the water dripping from the ceiling onto the floor below and my own labored breathing. The stranger was silent. If I hadn't known he was there, I would've thought I was alone.

We continued for what seemed to be no less than an hour. For most of the time, I had the sensation of walking downward, but I wasn't in a state of mind to care. I collected my thoughts in silence, suspicion of him growing with every step.

Who was this man? How did he know about Katarina? How did he know where to find me?

I mulled over these questions as we walked. Then, two things happened simultaneously. First, after hours of treading downhill, it caught my attention that we were now headed uphill at a steady pace. And second, after hours of a steady pace, we were now moving at a considerably slower rate.

After many minutes passed, I tried to look past the stranger at the rocky duct ahead. Though I couldn't see much, I did see that we'd reached a dead end. My mind began to panic. What had I followed this man into?

When this stranger found me, I'd given up. It was true, I was trying to kill myself or get close to it, but it was my decision, on my terms. Was it possible this man led me now to a fate worse than death?

Considering I was already living a fate much worse than death and had been for a little over two centuries, I managed to calm myself. If this man wanted to lead me to an underground hell, I'd welcome it. Nothing could be worse than my current fate.

I stood behind the stranger in silence, waiting. He didn't speak, at least not to me, but lifted his hands and placed both palms flat against the wall.

"Goddess, give me strength," he whispered.

He pushed against the wall with what looked like immense effort while reciting an incantation I didn't understand.

I heard the movement before I could see it happening, the scraping of rock against rock, bits of rubble and dirt falling down the cavernous wall in a miniature rockslide.

The dust rose around me, moist and stale. It settled further in my chest with each inhalation. I coughed violently, my chest heaving, the grit coated my tongue as it descended to my lungs.

A blinding light seared the darkness. I winced, placing my hand in front of my face. For a moment I had no idea where I was, my senses assaulted by my surroundings.

The dust settled and my eyes adjusted revealing a doorway where a wall of rock once stood; beyond the door was an expanse of lush green field. The stranger took no time in walking through. He grabbed his hands above his head and bent backward, stretching his massive body out from the recent journey. When he finished, he turned around and looked at me.

"My name is Willem," he said. "I'm sorry it came to be this way that we met, but you're harder to find than I had originally anticipated." He smiled as I stood there in the doorway, motionless. "Well, don't just stand there. Let's go. We've got much to discuss." He turned toward the rising sun and began walking with great strides that looked to be double of any other man.

Without thinking, I took one step out of the stone doorway, then another, and then another until I found myself following Willem in great earnest, heading in the direction of the sunrise, toward what looked to be a small village on the distant horizon.

The sun was almost directly overhead, or so it seemed behind the cloud cover, by the time we reached the small village of Doolin.

Willem led me to a small tavern just off the square. The door was made of thick, knotted wood and made a loud, measured creaking sound as he opened it letting everyone within the tavern know people were entering.

It was dark inside. Not entirely dark, but with limited window light and only a few torches lit, it was an inconspicuous space. My nerves settled. I liked inconspicuous.

But as of late, it seemed inconspicuous didn't like me. There was a brief silence as we entered, and every set of eyes turned to look at us. I had the feeling not too many visitors frequented this establishment, but when they did, they were given the space they needed.

Willem found a table for us in the back corner and signaled for the maid to bring us something to drink. The table was constructed of a block of wood and looked to be from the same tree as the door.

My eyes adjusted to the dimness, and I took the opportunity to really survey the room. I quickly shifted my gaze across all four corners of the tavern. It was just the sort of place I'd expect to have a conversation with a mysterious stranger. I took inventory of the scene around me, which included a red-haired man behind the bar, two men near the fireplace singing songs, and three men sitting at the table in the far left corner huddled together speaking in hushed tones. Before I was able to complete the survey, the clanking of mugs on our table interrupted me.

"Well, I can't imagine what must be going through your mind," Willem said after taking his first swallow of ale.

I looked at the mug in front of me. The thick, brownish liquid swirled around. I'd never really liked the taste of ale, I preferred something much stronger, but after a day like that day, I didn't care. And honestly, it looked delicious. I put my nose to the edge of the mug and inhaled deeply. Its rich yeasty scent woke me up.

How did I get here? Though each thought rapidly fell into the next and memories began to blur into one long event, I was coherent enough to know that two days ago I'd made the decision to find a secluded space and spend the rest of my personal hell there to rot.

I'd given up. Just as committed as I was to my love, I was committed to perish, my conviction unwavering. I'd gone to the cave to spend the rest of my existence, useless, weak, and lifeless. Lifeless, but not dead. That was my curse.

I remained there offering up my soul to the universe—quiet, tired, motionless. No food. No water. Nothing. Experience dictated I wouldn't die, but I was hoping to become so close to death I'd barely notice my own existence, that some sort of divine intervention would take place, ease my suffering, and free my tortured soul.

I wasn't sure how long I would've continued before I found my resolve again. And then, as if answering my innermost prayers, divine intervention did occur, though not in the form I'd expected. It arrived as a massive six-foot-four tall man with long hair and a rough voice. Or at least I assumed he was a man, though he very well could've been otherworldly.

Sitting in the tavern, I had much to contemplate. But time was something I had more than enough to spare. As I considered my next move, the stranger, whom I now knew as Willem, stared at me from across the table, waiting patiently for me to say something. Best to be forward.

"Who are you?" My voice was flat from exhaustion.

A sly smile pulled at the corners of his mouth. "Go ahead, drink up. We've lots of time now and I suppose you'll be wanting the full story, not the abbreviated one, eh?" His words were light. They didn't match the gravity of his tone.

I took a long pull from the mug in front of me. As I swallowed, the smooth ale flowed down my throat. It tasted good. It tasted real. I took another long swig before I set the half-drunk mug back down on the table in front of me.

"Time, I've got." I felt my body immediately relax as the ale began its journey through my system. I opened my hand palm up to indicate I was ready for his tale. "So, if you wouldn't mind . . . from the beginning."

Willem nodded. He ordered another round of drinks. As

the maid placed them on the table, he leaned back in his chair, stretching his legs out in front of him.

"You and I are not so different," he began. "We are both outcasts, of sorts. Everyone we've ever known has lived and died long ago. We both know what it is to truly love. And what it means when that love is lost."

"You know nothing about me or what I've been through," I spat out, irritated by his little prologue.

"We'll see about that." He ran his fingers through his unkempt hair. "Let me tell my tale, and then you can decide if you want my help or not."

I stared back at him coldly but did not speak.

"May I continue?"

I couldn't tell if his overly polite tone was intentional or not, so I simply answered by nodding my head once.

"Very well. I suppose I should start by telling you my name is Willem." He put his hand up toward me as I began to protest. "My name is Willem . . . *now*. But it wasn't always. My first name, my given name, was Dominici. My mother gave me that name, Goddess give her peace. I changed my name, changed my life . . . gave up my heritage when I was cursed. I settled here and transformed who I was. I've lived here in this beautiful land for longer than anyone should have to live, moving from place to place, as to not cause suspicion." He hesitated as he reflected upon his last words. "But I'm sure you know all about that. After all, we are both immortal."

My head snapped up. "You're immortal," I whispered. "How?"

A small, bitter laugh escaped his lips.

"All in good time." He drank from his mug and wiped his mouth with the back of his hand. "Before I made myself into the person you now see, the person you now hear—I was not so different from you." His eyes flashed.

"Believe it or not, I grew up in many small towns along the

Mediterranean coast of Italia, long ago. Longer than I'm sure you would believe. My people were outcasts. Wanderers traveling from village to village until we had outworn our welcome. But most knew exactly what we were. We were Strega Onesto."

My eyes widened. The Strega Onesto. I hadn't heard the name spoken out loud in centuries. My heart raced hearing it now. My thoughts immediately flashed back to the night of our attempted escape. The night my life had ended. If we had only made it to the Strega Onesto camp before he found her, my life . . . *our* life . . . everything, would've been very different. If we hadn't been separated . . .

No, it was my fault. If I hadn't let her go back. If . . . if . . . if . . .

"Gio, relax." His voice was still. "It's okay. Breathe. Let me tell my story. All you need to do is sit, drink, and listen." He paused briefly.

He was cautious, his words steady. My eyes met his and I could see that behind the calm, there was a glint of alarm. I must've looked a wreck. I couldn't speak. I couldn't think. I couldn't do anything. I was very near the edge of that treacherous slope called insanity.

So, I did the only thing I could do in that moment. I took the advice of a mysterious stranger who seemed to know more about my life than I cared for anyone to know. I sat there, took another pull of my ale, and listened.

"Gio? Gio, are you listening to me?" His voice snapped me back into the present.

"I agree, Willem, thirty years isn't enough time, it makes no sense whatsoever. But I know what I feel, and I followed the signs. I know this is the place. This is where she'll be." I could hear his breathing on the other end of the line and waited.

"I don't know." He paused, drawing a breath. "I just don't know. It's just that—I mean, if you're wrong, we'll have to start from scratch. You don't want to miss this lifetime. It would be . . . devastating."

"Please, you have to trust me on this."

More silence.

"Okay, I'll give this to you, but *if* she's there," he said with skepticism still lingering, "he's not far behind, if he's not already with her. I'll get started on the serum. It may take me a few weeks, so please be inconspicuous. Nothing out of the ordinary, okay? Get a job, find a place to live, set up shop. The usual, you know? I'll be there as soon as I can."

"Thanks. I'll see you soon."

"And one more thing." His voice was quieter now, hesitant. I could tell he was choosing his words carefully, though I already had a feeling of what they'd be. Like Willem, I'd never forget how Alessandro ended it last time. I closed my eyes as the images flashed like a silent picture in my memory.

She'd looked at him, confused, for just a moment before she realized he meant to kill her. The sheer terror in her eyes as he slit her throat with a broken spoon handle, a twisted smile etched on his face, haunts me still.

Everything had been in slow motion. There was no sound other than the struggled gargling of her choking on her own blood. A stream of tears flowing over her lashes, tracing translucent lines down her cheeks.

Her eyes widened and darted around the room frantically. Our gaze met, and I held her still with my eyes. It was the only comfort I could provide. She stilled as I held her with my eyes and watched her life dim until there was nothing.

Frozen with horror, sickened with the physical pain only true and utter loss can bring, I'd collapsed to the floor in agony. Alessandro had tossed her body to the ground and walked away.

Again.

I had crawled across the floor, sticky with death, until my arms scooped her up and I buried my head into her chest, her blood soaking into every one of my cells. It'd taken weeks before my skin was no longer stained.

My heart is still stained.

It hadn't been the first time I'd seen him sacrifice her to spite me. And even though I knew her soul would again walk upon the earth; I woke up nightly in a cold sweat from the pure terror of his brutality.

To him it was a game. A game he never tired of. One that never ended. His smug grimace would be branded for all eternity in my mind, forever a reminder of the evil he was capable of.

Willem released a long, slow breath and continued in a somber, strained tone. I wasn't the only one whose memories were catching up with him. "If you see her . . . *when* you see her, try to remain . . . hidden. Wait for me, and we'll do this together. Don't be a hero, Gio. Be smart. Cautious. And please keep your eyes open. We both know what Alessandro is capable of."

"He deserves to die—slowly." Poison boiled from deep within me and gradually rose until it bubbled over every inch of my body.

"Please, Gio. Just keep focused. Think of Katarina. She must not suffer again. We *will* save her this time. Please, just give me your word that you'll be inconspicuous, that you'll remain calm if you see him, and that you'll do everything in your power to stay off his radar."

"You should know me better than that."

"I do. Which is why I'm asking for your word."

Damn. He did know me too well. Even though I'd like to

think I'd never jeopardize my fate intentionally, my hatred for Alessandro had taken on a life of its own. Alessandro would suffer. One way or the other, he would pay dearly for the pain he'd caused.

"Gio? Your word." Willem waited for my reply.

"I won't engage Alessandro. You have my word."

The tension cleared from his voice. "I promise I'll be as quick as I can. I'll call with updates. Talk soon, my friend." He sounded a little more like my old friend.

"Thank you," I said as emotion suddenly overwhelmed me.

I meant it. With everything that I was, I was thankful. Thankful and honored. I had no idea why I was given Willem, and I couldn't even begin to fathom what my existence would be like without his help, without his drive helping me reach my destiny—my Katarina.

"Yeah, well, we all have our parts. Talk soon." The soft beep on the other end of the line indicated he'd hung up.

I slipped the phone back into my coat pocket. How did I end up here? When I got off the train, I'd no idea what I'd be facing in the hours ahead. I had no idea that today could be the first day of the rest of my life.

I surveyed the town once more and a sense of familiarity swept over me. Of course, it'd be here. With its small shops bustling with their regular customers and vineyards in the distant rolling hills, alive with a comfortable energy, it felt like home. Of the place where we first met. First kissed. First fell in love. And I couldn't stop the smile from spreading across my face, finally admitting, in that moment, things were definitely looking hopeful.

Five

KATE

As I ran out of the house that morning, I had a really bad feeling. Not the kind of feeling you get when you think you forgot to turn the oven off before you left the house, or when you can't remember if you locked your car door at the airport parking lot, but the kind of foreboding that you just can't shake off. It's that bad feeling you get when you know something eminent will happen. That feeling something big is about to change, and you're not sure what it is or when it will occur, but you know only that it will, and there's nothing you can do about it.

"I can't believe you forgot the lipstick," Dave said in a flat tone. His long legs carried him quickly to his car.

As I raced to keep up with him, briefcase in tow, my cell went off. It was Alex. I knew before I even looked at the caller ID because he had his own special ringtone, an alternative rock ballad that got major airtime the year we first met.

"Jesus, that song has got to go," Dave complained as he dug his keys out of his front pocket.

"I like it." I immediately defended. "It makes me think of love and . . . regret, I suppose."

He rolled his eyes. I could tell I wouldn't be changing his mind any time soon.

"I swear to God, if I didn't absolutely love you to death, I couldn't stand to be around you." He hit the unlock button on his keychain and opened the car door. Leaning forward, he looked over the roof of the car at me with serious eyes. "Are you going to pick that up, so I don't have to listen to that crap anymore?"

I glanced at the phone in my hand.

"And be quick about this, we've got things to do." He slid into the driver's side of his black BMW, but not before I caught the corner of his mouth curling upward. That was the Dave I knew, tough on the outside, soft in the center. I didn't know what I'd do without him.

As the ringtone neared its end, I quickly picked up the phone. I initially hated the idea of getting a cell phone, but Alex insisted he be able to always reach me. Call me old-fashioned, but I loathed the idea of being so accessible. Whatever happened to privacy? Personal space? But I suppose a cell phone made sense. And I really couldn't argue with Alex, especially after the incident.

Three years ago, I was driving home from Los Angeles alone when my car broke down on the Five. I was heading home after three days of helping my friend Jamie move into her new loft. About midway through the drive, somewhere between Coalinga and Santa Nella, my car took its final wheezing breath. It was all pretty uneventful, but, with no cell phone, I had to walk a mile and a half along the interstate shoulder until I found a call box that worked. Then, I had to wait by my car on the interstate for assistance.

By the time the tow truck arrived, and I was able to get a rental, I just wanted to get back on the road. I didn't even think to call Alex. I just wanted to get home.

When I didn't return at the expected time, Alex started to

lose it. He called Jamie, and then he called the highway patrol. Then Jamie called Dave to see if he'd heard from me, and then she called the police too.

When I pulled up to our house, five and a half hours after I was expected, and saw a police car parked in the driveway, my heart fell straight down into the pit of my stomach. It was one of the first times he raised his voice at me.

"What in the hell were you trying to prove!" he yelled from his side of the closet, as we got dressed for bed that night. "I know you weren't thinking of your safety, that much is obvious." He spit out the words like venom. "But did you even, for one moment, think of *me*?"

"I'm . . . I'm . . . I'm sorry." My voice came out cracked. "Look . . . I'm fine, really. I mean, cars break down, right? It's no big deal. You know how I hate to make a big deal out of nothing, I just wanted to get home, and everything worked out . . ." My voice trailed off and I tried to smile, but the look on Alex's face was enough to make me think twice about what I'd just said.

At that moment, I was afraid of my husband. His eyes were bloodshot, crazed, and reminded me of the eyes of a rabid wolf I'd once seen in a video. All those colors—green, blue, gold, and red—swirling around together in a furious storm and firmly nested in his face made his olive-toned skin look sickly and was enough to stop my defense in its tracks. His expression was maniacal, absolutely terrifying. I was speechless.

"No. Big. Deal." His voice was calm. It contrasted with how he looked and sent shivers up my spine. "Do you have any idea what it was like for me? Sitting here, waiting, expecting you to walk through the door at any moment and when you didn't, thinking that you were . . . were . . . gone!"

He said the last word with finality and a hint of disgust. The air thickened. My brow furrowed as the room spun around and then righted itself again. I refocused on his face. In that moment, he looked more accusatory than distraught. Panic set in.

My body began to shake. I didn't want it to, but I couldn't stop myself. My God, he was going to leave me. I could see it in his face. The storm in his eyes became a fierce monstrosity, a violent battle of color against color, and I knew if I didn't make things right quickly, my life, as I knew it, would end. Tonight.

"Alex, I'm so sorry," I choked out the words with every ounce of sincerity I had. I was breathless from fear. "Please, love . . . please forgive me." I was begging now. The thick air pressed against my body. I fell to the ground on my knees near the corner of our bed.

"It was stupid of me to fight this cell phone thing for so long. And I should've called, that was just plain irresponsible. I was selfish and stupid. I can't say it enough. Please, love . . . please. I'm so sorry."

I couldn't hold on any longer. I broke down. I couldn't speak. I sobbed through hiccups. What was going on? How had things gotten so intense in such a short time? There was only one explanation. He was right—I was a selfish, horrible person.

His body jolted. He blinked his eyes and shook his head, as if snapping out of his rage, and came to where I was crumpled. He wrapped his arms around me and buried his head in my hair. He kissed my head over and over.

"Katie, love. It's okay, it's okay," he cooed. "I'm sorry I yelled. Everything's okay, Katie. Shh." He rocked me in his arms, and I immediately hated myself more for having to be comforted. I should be the one comforting him and here he was trying to make me feel better.

We spent the rest of the night nestled together, his arms

around me, his hands occasionally stroking my face, his lips gently caressing mine with soft kisses.

For days afterward, I was sick with guilt that the person I most loved in this world had thought I was kidnapped, had left him, or was dead. It was at that moment that I not only conceded to a cell phone, but I also promised to always have it on, just in case.

I shook the memory far away, pushing the uneasiness it left behind down as I answered the phone.

"Hey, babe, what's up?" I tried to sound as normal as possible, which was a tremendous feat.

"Nothing, love. I was just wondering if you were going to be available for a late lunch today?"

I knocked on the window of the BMW.

Dave rolled down the passenger side window and mouthed the words, "What's up?"

I mouthed the word "lunch" back at him.

Dave gave me a stern look and vigorously shook his head no.

He knew me well. He knew I rarely said no to Alex. All right, I never said no. It wasn't that I agreed with everything he said or did; it was more like I was physically incapable of saying no when he made a request. Like some greater force willed me to do anything to make him happy.

Dave called my inability to refuse Alex a lack of assurance. To me, it was just the opposite. It was complete and total conviction. It was an addiction, and Alex was my drug. I swallowed and searched for a sliver of strength.

"Today? I'd love to, but I'm up against deadlines at work." I prayed that my voice sounded believable enough. If he insisted, there was no way I'd refuse. "Actually, I was thinking of skipping lunch altogether, so I could get home early, you know?"

"Me too. I guess I was just hoping we could finish what we

started in the kitchen." His voice was smooth velvet, and the implications of his words sent an instant surge deep down to the core of body. My stomach grew tight, and I had to concentrate on my breathing.

"Oh, um . . . I . . .," I began to falter.

Dave slammed the dash with his palm. I snapped out of Alex's spell and looked at him through the open window.

"Katie, we're going to be late for the topic meeting. Let's go." He spoke a little louder than necessary. Subtle.

"I understand, love," Alex said right on cue. "I'll just have to wait, though I have to admit, the thought of my lips traveling down your body . . . maybe we can get off early together." He left the sentence hanging in the air over the phone.

I felt faint. The thought of his lips anywhere made my breathing shallow.

"Oh, um, okay—love you, bye." I squeaked out the words with my remaining breath.

"I love you too." I could hear the smile on his face.

I hung up and opened the passenger side door just in time to fall into it. Dave sat there and stared at me. He was silent, for all of two seconds, before he started in.

"I swear to God, Katie. You really need to get control of yourself."

"I know."

"I mean, whenever he asks anything of you, anything, you do it no matter what."

"I know."

"Now, don't get me wrong, you know I like Alex. He's a pretty good guy. A little controlling at times, but a good guy. He's cool, totally hot, and apparently a genius between the sheets. But do you really want to spend the rest of your life jumping through hoops to please him?"

"Are you finished?" My voice fell into my throat. I looked straight ahead, my temper teetering between anger and guilt.

"Sweetie, I just want you to be happy with yourself. I see you slipping further and further away from that sharp, spunky, independent woman I met years ago." His voice was intentionally steady, as if he knew where I stood and didn't want me to fall off that line.

"You don't understand. He's not just my husband, he's . . . he's something more," I blurted out before I could stop myself.

"What is he, then? Explain it to me, please." His voice was gentle. I'd always been private about my innermost feelings, the ones I was sometimes ashamed of, but I sensed that if there was ever time to try to explain how and what I felt about Alex, now was it.

"I don't know how to exactly explain it, except that it's more than just I'm in love with him or that we're married. It's almost as if I . . . *owe* him, you know? It's a feeling that somehow, I've yet to repay something, or repair something, and I'm not sure how to do it." An overwhelming sense of atonement began to creep its way up through my consciousness.

"You're not making any sense. What could you possibly owe him? And repay him for what? No one's *that* good in bed." Even though I didn't quite agree with his last statement, I smiled at his attempt to lighten things up.

"I know, I know. I'm not making any sense. I don't quite understand it myself. Sometimes I think I'm going crazy."

He looked at me patiently, waiting for me to continue. I decided to go for broke. I took a deep breath. I might as well tell him everything. He already thought I was a stone's throw from being committed anyway.

"Okay, how about this. For example, when I woke up this

morning, I was dead tired. I'd slept like shit and was just feeling out of it, you know."

"So? You're always half-dead before ten," Dave said.

I shot an annoyed look in his direction.

"So, I was zoned out, total zombie, right? And my mind wandered. I started thinking about how Alex and I met. And then, for a brief instant, I tried to think about what life was like before him, but I couldn't, not really. I mean, I remembered a few general childhood things, but nothing of detail. It's as if life didn't happen before I met him. Or that somehow, some way, most of it got erased or something. The only life I can really remember is the one after Alex. Since he's come into my life, I've never been more blessed. But the thing that keeps coming back to me, and I don't know why, is that lately I have this feeling that I shouldn't be grateful he came into my life, but more that I should be grateful that he's letting me be part of his."

Dave was silent. His eyes gave no emotion away.

I was dangerously close to sounding totally insane, but I continued, "I know this sounds bizarre. But please, just listen to me a little longer. I don't know when this started, but I've had this feeling for a long time now. I think . . ." I hesitated and took a deep breath. "I think my subconscious is trying to tell me something, you know, give me a sign, but I have no idea what it could be. I've been having these dreams, almost nightly. It's like they're not even dreams. They're too real for that. It's like I'm living these scenes . . . or remembering them. Actually, it's just one scene that I see at night. There's this guy, it's not Alex, and I have to save him, I can't say for sure, but I think the dream is trying to tell me something about—"

"Slow down," Dave said in soft voice. "Don't do this to yourself."

"Do what?"

"It's so obvious. Here you are, the wife of someone who,

in your eyes, is practically a perfect individual. Someone who never forgets a birthday or anniversary, who wakes up early to squeeze in a workout, eats healthy, rarely drinks, has no obvious bad habits or vices, and is one hundred and ten percent committed to you. Plus, he has an undeterred confidence that is, to say the least, intimidating. He's probably never second-guessed himself in his whole life, am I right?"

I nodded. I had to admit, he pretty much nailed it.

Dave held my gaze. "And here you are, a caffeine-addicted sugar fanatic who would forget her head if it wasn't attached. Someone who enjoys a cigarette every now and then, a strong drink or two, and who would never, ever consider waking up before ten o'clock in the morning if she didn't have to be at work. But here's the thing. Nobody's perfect. Not even Alex. And the fact that you continually compare yourself to him, it's as if you're trying to convince yourself that you can't possibly deserve him. That if you're lucky enough to have him, you should have to give yourself up entirely to him to make him happy. Not to mention that you don't work best when under pressure. And after this little anniversary slipup, it's no wonder why you went immediately into self-destruct mode."

I thought about Dave's words. Could all my feelings of self-doubt and reparation simply be a by-product of my own lack of self-esteem? Was it possible for me to believe from my core that I didn't deserve Alex, and therefore create this amalgam of thoughts and feelings to justify what I viewed as my own personal inadequacies?

It was a valid possibility, but I wasn't buying it. I knew what I felt, and I knew what I saw in my dreams each night. But I didn't want to talk about it anymore with Dave. I was ready for this conversation to be over.

"Maybe you're right," I said with rehearsed resignation. "Maybe I do put way too much pressure on myself to be like him instead of just being me. I'm sorry. I didn't mean to have a full-blown breakdown."

"Hey, sweetie, no problem." He seemed to have bought my lie. God, I was getting good. Either that or he was just as ready to end this conversation as I was. At that point I really didn't care what the reason was, I was just glad it was over. "Now, how about we get to work sometime this century, so we can cut out early and do a little shopping? I have some great ideas for you that I think Alex will die for." He turned the keys in the ignition and smoothly pulled onto the road.

"Sounds great." I smiled at him with little effort.

My mind was still not in the moment, but it was getting there by the second, and besides, I was ready to move on to solving other issues.

At Dave's break-neck speed, the drive to work took less time than I'd hoped. I sat in the leather seat half-listening to Dave's retelling of his most recent dating disaster saying "really?" and "no way!" when appropriate. I leaned my head on the car window and absently gazed out taking in the view.

The soft rolling hills were beautiful this time of year. The vineyards were close to harvest, and, with the change of weather, their colorful leaves created streaks of bright reds, browns, oranges and yellows. I followed their linear pattern with my eyes against the soft curves of the natural land as Dave drove.

As much as I appreciated the beauty now, I probably never would've moved to California's wine country if it hadn't been for Alex. I've always been a die-hard metropolitanite, but Alex had insisted I check it out when we were looking for a place to settle down after the wedding.

"It reminds me of home." He sighed wistfully as we walked through downtown Freestone during a weekend getaway.

"Home? I thought you grew up in Philly?" I asked.

"What? Oh, I just meant it has a peacefulness I remember from my youth," he answered, barely missing a beat. Barely. For one quick instant, I noticed he looked a little frazzled, like he'd been taken off-guard. Strange.

"So, what do you think?" He eyed me in anticipation.

"I love it, of course," I replied. "It's hard to explain, but it's as if this town has been waiting for us our entire lives. Does that make sense?"

He wrapped his arms around my waist, interlocking his hands across my stomach, and nestled his face in my hair, his lips touching the back of my neck.

"It makes perfect sense," he whispered.

As he held me, I knew I'd made the right choice. It felt so right. This was home. Everything fit perfectly together like the threads in an intricately woven piece of cloth.

As I sat in Dave's car, I longed to try to grasp that feeling once more. What was happening to me? Surely it wasn't because I loved Alex any less. If anything, I loved him more now than I ever had. Being with him was the only thing I could imagine.

But slowly, something was changing inside me. Something had begun to tug on a loose thread. Gradually, cautiously, so that I didn't even know it was happening, something pulled the strands apart, unravelling the cloth.

After nine years of marriage, how could I still be second-guessing myself? It just didn't make any sense. No, I refused to believe that. There had to be another explanation. Some force, whatever it might be, was trying to tell me something. Or maybe I was just trying to justify what a crappy wife I was. No, I couldn't believe that either. My heart sat heavy in my chest. What was my problem?

"We're here," Dave said in his most falsely upbeat tone. "Ready to kill some dreams?" His voice was oozing saccharine. I looked at the sturdy brick building standing in front of us.

When I first went to work for Billows Publishing, I was hired as an assistant copyeditor. It was my first real job. I was officially a grown-up. However, I quickly learned that management found me more useful as an assistant to the assistant. My dream of working in the faced-paced, tight-knit world of publishing was quickly readjusted as I began to comprehend I'd accepted a position as a glorified errand girl. I was two seconds away from quitting when I bumped into Dave one morning while fetching coffee for my boss.

It didn't take me long to realize Dave was a kindred spirit. I decided that even though my job was less than desirable, I could stick it out. Surely, once they saw my potential, they'd have no choice but to promote me. Right? Well, sort of.

Eight years later, here I was, in the passenger seat of my friend's car, looking up at this small, brick building and preparing to dive into the slush of the hundreds of manuscripts that found their way to my desk each day, most of them ending in rejection. From coffee girl to dream dasher in just eight short years. Terrific.

"You know it," I replied, my voice lacking the sarcastic emotion that Dave was hoping for.

"You are *too* fun." Dave rolled his eyes at me and got out of the car. He grabbed his briefcase from the back seat. "Come on, let's go."

As I opened the car door and got out, my purse slipped from my grasp and dropped to the ground, its contents spilling out over the parking lot.

"Shit," I muttered, as I bent down to pick up my belongings. "Dave, go on ahead, I'll catch up in a minute, okay?"

"I'll see you inside," he said. "Hurry up."

I kneeled on the ground. My shins ached as the bumpy asphalt created depressions in the soft skin. I picked up my things and placed them in my purse, one by one. When I had gathered everything, I sat back on my heels and was about to rise when a cool wind picked up.

It blew straight through me, clean and crisp. Taken aback, I gasped, and then closed my eyes letting it wrap around my body. It flowed under my hair and clothing, and I allowed it to overtake my senses. Its long arms curled over and around my naked skin, leaving a tingling sensation in its wake. It felt good, too good, not like the wind at all.

In the distance, I heard the morning train blow its whistle. I looked to the north toward the expanse of rolling vineyard and waited for it to appear. The wind became stronger, more intrusive, and I took a deep breath as it hugged me, letting the chilled morning air fill my lungs. Then, as if materializing from nothing, the train appeared in the distance and slowly made its way closer to where I was still crouched down in the parking lot.

It was traveling much faster than it looked from my vantage point, but I was still startled at how quickly it approached and, just as swiftly, headed in the opposite direction toward the Third Street Station for the morning commuters. The stop after that would be Freestone Central, and then Cotati Plaza, Petaluma Main, San Rafael North *and* South, and then a straight shot to the city.

As the train barreled along, I instinctually raised my hand in its direction. The wind grew stronger and, for one brief second, I had the strange wish for it to lift me up and place me on that train.

"Please . . . come back," I whispered, as it headed in the direction away from me. I didn't even know where the words came from, they were simply there and out of my mouth before I even knew I was saying them.

"Who are you talking to?" Dave was suddenly at my side.

I blinked hard. *Oh God, did he just see me do that?*

"I didn't say anything," I responded curtly, pulling my

hand close to my body. "What are you doing here anyway? I thought I said I'd catch up."

"You did," he said flatly. "But then I got to thinking what a total head case you are today, and I thought I'd come back to see if you'd actually make it into work without having a nervous breakdown." He looked at me with a neutral expression. "I'm glad I came back."

Wholly aware of what I must look like to Dave crouched on the ground by my purse, arm yearning for the train, speaking to nobody, my cheeks flushed hot.

"I can see my intuition was right." He leaned down and offered his hand to me. I took his hand and helped myself up. Throwing my purse over my shoulder, I grabbed my briefcase from where I had stowed it and nonchalantly brushed myself off.

"Thanks," I said as I stood.

Dave eyed me the way one might eye a flying cat.

"What?" I said, trying to sound as innocent as possible. "I swear I wasn't talking to anyone, just myself. Honest. Geez, stop being so serious."

"Are you sure you're all right?" I could tell by his voice he wasn't buying it. I didn't blame him, of course; I wouldn't have bought it either.

I looked him straight in the eyes and said with every ounce of sincerity I could collect, "I'm fine, really. Now let's get to work before Eva has a conniption. You know how she gets."

I started walking, fighting the urge to look back in the direction of the train as it headed south. I quickened my stride, closing the distance between the building and myself. Just one hundred more feet and I'd be through the front door, away from the stupid hugging wind, away from the train, away from the unexplained, and unsubstantiated, feeling that something important was being taken from me.

I picked up my pace. In just fifty more feet, I'd be in the

sanctuary of work. Dave was just behind me. We walked in silence as the entrance to the building came into view. Twenty feet. Ten feet. Just a couple more steps and I'd be at the door. Dave reached from behind my back and held it open for me.

"Shall we?" He nodded his head at me. I could tell by his tone he was beginning to reconcile my earlier behavior and was trying to move on. I was right there with him.

"Thank you, sir." I gave him a slight smile as I swiftly passed him and walked into the building ready to get on with the day. After all, I had a manuscript deadline to meet, an anniversary night to save, and only nine hours to do it in.

I was suddenly overcome with the determination to make it through the day without any more distractions or strange occurrences. I would not let myself be consumed by my own neurosis. Somehow, though, I knew that no matter how determined I was, no matter how focused, I would, without a doubt, be sorely disappointed.

Six

GIO

Just as Willem instructed, I began to set up shop. I grabbed my luggage, one large rolling trunk and a hefty backpack, and headed down the quiet street in search of accommodations. I hadn't walked far before I came upon a small vintage clothing store nestled between an eclectic independent bookstore and an herbal apothecary. A "studio for rent" sign hung in the window.

I opened the door and walked into the shop. The store was empty save for a salesgirl sitting in front of the counter rearranging earrings and bracelets. She looked up upon my entrance, responding to the soft tinkling of a tiny bell on the door, her eyes a little too wide as her gaze met mine. Her expression unnerved me. I pushed the feeling aside and walked up to where she was sitting.

"Excuse me, miss, I was wondering if I could get information about the studio for rent?" I propped my trunk against the counter and looked at the young woman.

She was small. Her petite features were framed by short blond hair that had streaks of fuchsia woven throughout. She was cute, with a pixie face, and no more than nineteen or twenty. She stared at me through green eyes and, after some contemplation, offered me a smile.

"Uh, sure." Her voice wavered as she hopped down from the stool and walked around the back counter. She was wearing a short jean skirt, with black and white striped leggings underneath. A black T-shirt that had the sleeves cut off hung loose against her thin frame. She briefly glanced over her shoulder at me, and then grabbed a set of keys off the wall.

"Follow me," she said heading out through the front of the store. "You can leave your stuff here if you'd like." She flipped the sign on the door to closed and walked out. On the sidewalk she took an immediate left and stood under a small eave at the doorstep of a dark purple door that was almost unnoticeable next to the apothecary.

"My name's Claire," she offered. "The building belongs to my mom, but I'm the one who's always here. You just get into town?"

"I'm Gio. Just this morning," I responded.

Claire took one of the keys and unlocked the door. We walked up a steep flight of steps until we reached a narrow landing where one small table with a mirror stood. She found the key she needed, a long brown one that looked a little like a skeleton key and slid it into the lock of the door just to the right of the landing. She opened the door to the apartment and looked back at me.

Her eyes seemed to travel just at the edges of my body up to my eyes. I couldn't decide if she was looking at me or around me. Whichever it was, the intensity of her gaze made me uneasy.

"Have we met before?" she asked suspiciously.

"I don't see how. I just arrived this morning," I replied calmly. The muscles in my shoulders tightened; her behavior set off all kinds of alarms.

Claire shook her head and murmured something to herself I couldn't hear. She drew her attention back to the apartment.

"It's kinda small—and dusty. No one's really lived here for, like, a couple years. But it comes furnished, so that's a plus." She looked me up and down. "And it's got a nice view. And a pretty good price. Go ahead, check it out." She motioned for me to enter. "When you're done, just come back down to the store and we can move forward, if you're interested."

As I walked past her in the doorway, we brushed arms. The instant my skin touched hers she jolted backward. Her eyes widened and again she seemed to trace the space just around me rather than at me with her gaze.

"I hope you decide to take the place." Her voice was barely audible. "I think . . . I think it would be good for you. Just consider it."

She eyed me through jade eyes, and then turned around and headed back down the stairs, leaving me standing alone at the doorway of the apartment.

What the hell? I wasn't quite sure what to think about our exchange as I listened to her bound down the stairs and out the door that led to the street. She had suspicious written all over her. Why did she look around me, not at me? Why did she recoil from the casual touch of our arms? It didn't make sense. I walked into the apartment still considering the strange interaction.

The room itself was not terribly large. Altogether it was no more than five hundred square feet, but the high ceiling made it appear spacious. There was a small entryway area with a storage closet just inside. Standing at the door, I could tell the kitchen was to the right and the rest of the living space to the left. Though I couldn't see it, I anticipated the bathroom to be past the main living area in the far corner of the studio.

As I took a step further into the apartment, a strong,

musty smell hit my nose. I crossed the room to the windows overlooking the street. I pulled the shade down and let go. It snapped as it retracted, making a flapping sound as it hit the top of the window. I went through the entire apartment, opening all the shades until the room was drowning in the day. I immediately relaxed. When it came to accommodations, I wasn't very picky save for one stipulation —light.

After so many centuries of darkness, both physical and psychological, I found comfort in the way light furled itself around me like a warm mantle, keeping me safe, pushing all the bad things away, a protector of everything it touched.

I took off my coat and laid it on the floor. I lay down on top of it in the center of the room drinking in the warmth of the sunlight and stared at the ceiling. I closed my eyes and tried to feel out a reason why I shouldn't stay here. I pushed my thoughts out into the universe and waited for a sign, a vision, a dream, anything that would hint to me staying here would be bad.

When nothing came, I stood in the center of the apartment, considering my next move. That I'd get the apartment was certain. However, despite my good luck in finding a place suitable to my needs so quickly and the fact the universe didn't give any reason to warrant worry, I was still a bit unnerved by the young woman. Claire.

Her behavior was so odd. What was I missing? After living decade after decade, I thought of myself as a pretty good people reader. As time progressed, it became second nature for me to separate the good from the not-so-good to the bad to the deplorable. And what I read in Claire was that she was . . . different.

Something about her was familiar and yet not familiar. Very unlike most people I encountered. No, she was unlike *anyone* else I'd ever met. For some reason, the way Claire looked at me made me think she knew that I was just an ancient soul hidden in the shell of an ageless frame.

Instinct told me she heard the wind blowing through my hollowed body and knew I wasn't what I pretended to be. Impossible. Yet somehow, I felt she knew. I was torn as to whether I could trust her.

But trust or not, I needed this apartment. This was the place. I felt it in my gut. I would be safe here, without chance of being exposed. After pulling all the shades, I went back downstairs, closing the doors as I went, to inform Claire I was interested in the apartment and wanted to move in as soon as possible.

I entered the store, this time hesitating as I approached her.

"So, when do you want to move in?" she asked as she began to fold a pile of sweaters, her eyes focused on her work.

"How do you know I want the place?" I asked.

"Oh, just a guess," she replied, never looking up from her sweaters. "Let's just say, I'm *very* good at reading people."

"Is that right?" I replied, studying her.

"That's right," she returned as she looked up from her work. The hairs on the back of my neck rose. Those green eyes held something older than she was in them and stared at me with a hot intensity leaving the atmosphere of the store thick and heavy.

I shrank back slightly; her gaze was so direct. It was odd to be intimidated by such a young woman, but I was, and I didn't like it. Something about Claire was raising every red flag I had, yet I didn't feel threatened. I tried to lighten the space between us.

"Well, you must be, because I'll take it." My words were balanced, guarded. I didn't want to say too little or too much, just enough to get what I needed.

"Like I said, when do you want to move in? There's some

work to be done up there, and typically I'd hire cleaners before you moved in, but if you don't mind a little cleaning, you can take the keys and start getting your stuff settled." She went back to folding sweaters.

"Today would be best," I replied carefully.

She reached into the front pocket of her skirt and fished out the set of keys she'd earlier grabbed off the wall. She tossed them in my direction. Instinctively my hand flew out and caught them.

"I set up the utilities while you were upstairs, so everything should be ready to go. Hope you don't mind." A small smile lifted from the corner of her mouth.

"Thank you."

I stepped past her and reached for my trunk. A million questions raced through my mind, but I pushed them down for another time. My questions could wait. They would wait until I spoke with Willem. Right now, I had an apartment to set up, a life to create. I had a future to begin.

I grabbed the handle of my trunk and turned toward the door. The bell tinkled as I walked out onto the sidewalk, leaving Claire alone with her folding. I found the key that opened the purple entrance and propped it open as I tugged my trunk inside. I stood just inside the doorway in a quiet dissonance with myself; a mixed bag of emotions spilled over in my stomach.

What was it about the mysterious Claire? I couldn't quite put my finger on it, but I knew something was up. I decided I'd call Willem once I was situated. Maybe he'd have some idea as to why I was having apprehensions toward her. I was still standing inside the doorway mulling through the possibilities as I watched the door creak shut, leaving the busy street behind.

Seven

KATE

"Are you ready?" Dave peeked around the wall of my cubicle.

"Almost, just give me two . . . seconds," I said, reading over the final chapter of one of the hundreds of submissions my house received daily.

"What you got there?" Dave leaned on my desk looking over my shoulder.

"You know, what I can't believe is that someone, somewhere, actually told this writer it would be a great idea to write a book about an army of flying armadillos that take over the planet and destroy all mankind." I threw my pen on my desk as I painfully finished the last agonizing sentence and turned the final page over.

"I don't know why you have to read every word." Dave picked up the manuscript and flipped it over. "Just do what I do. Read the first couple of pages. If you have an inexplicable urge to vomit after reading, file it in the circular file." He picked up the entire manuscript and tossed it into the trash bin in the corner of my cubicle.

"Dave, seriously. Someone here requested the full. It was the least I could do." I fetched the stack from the garbage.

"Hey, I am serious. This is a tough business, and I can't be wasting my time with rocks when there are gems to be discovered. No harm, no foul." He flashed one of his classic Dave smiles.

"I know you're serious. That's one of our major differences. I just can't do that, even if they never find out." I wrapped a rubber band around the manuscript and stuck a post-it to the cover page—rejected.

"Even if it's total crap you and I both know will never see the light of day?"

"Even if it's total crap," I replied, "I just feel that if someone spent the time to creatively produce something, *and* it was requested, then if for no other reason, I will read it just so that they can honestly say it's been read by someone in the industry."

Dave rolled his eyes. "Whatever, Katie. This conversation is getting real boring at a distressingly fast rate. Are you ready?"

"Ready?" I looked at him, my nose crinkled.

"Are we on the same planet? Hello!" Dave stared at me with disbelief. "Did you or did you not have a major meltdown this morning? Oh, I don't know, something about an anniversary and you forgetting it. Ring a bell? Anything?"

I gasped. It was just like me to get so wrapped up in the present that I forgot about this morning. Every muscle in my body tensed, as if I was mainlining panic.

"Oh, shit! I totally forgot. What time is it? We got to get out of here." I grabbed my coat, my purse, and Dave's arm as I flew past him and headed toward the elevator.

"Whoa, slow down. Deep breaths, Katie, deep breaths. Don't freak out, we have plenty of time. An entire afternoon, in fact. I told Eva we were collaborating on an exciting new project and that we'd be working off site for the rest of the afternoon." Dave looked exceptionally pleased with himself as he slowed down our pace and placed his arm across my shoulders, something he did quite frequently. Given our height difference, I made the perfect armrest.

"I was thinking we'd head downtown, grab a little something to eat, a drink or two, and then do a little shopping. What do you think?" He waited for my answer.

"I don't know. I think it would be better if we found a gift first, and then, if there's time, grab some food."

"Katie," he said, tsk-tsking me, "you'll never make it without something to eat. And if I know you, and I think I do, you'll be useless without a drink." His eyes held mischief. "Trust me on this, will you?"

I shrugged my shoulders and reluctantly agreed. Who was I kidding? No matter how much I wanted to not mess it up with Alex tonight, the thought of a nice lunch and a couple drinks did sound like a good idea. Anyway, if my behavior today was any indication of my sanity, well, then maybe I shouldn't be making decisions for myself.

"All right," I said. "You're in charge. Lead the way."

"That's my girl," Dave replied. "I promise you that by the end of the afternoon, you'll not only be well fed and relaxed, but you'll have the perfect gift for Alex."

I smiled at his enthusiasm. Though I wondered what qualified in his mind as a perfect gift. The last time I put Dave in charge of planning, I ended up more than half in the bag, dancing for my life, at a BINGO event hosted by drag queens. Was it fun? Most definitely. Did it increase my reputation as an upstanding citizen in a small town? Not necessarily, but I'd live.

We reached downtown just a bit after one-thirty. The air was crisp, though the sun was bright in the sky. It was the perfect autumn day. I loved how the leaves fell off the trees lining the street like red and gold rain.

We made our way to one of our favorite bistros. Dave held the door open for me as we entered the quiet restaurant. Out of all the cafés Freestone offered, Bleu Moon was one of my favorites. Its creative menu and private atmosphere had a city feel. Plus, it was the only restaurant in town that served meals on a second-story balcony. As a fervent people watcher, I'd found no better spot from which to observe society than a second-story balcony while dining.

"So, what were you thinking about for Alex?" I asked as we sat at a table near a window that overlooked the street.

"Oh, no, you don't," Dave warned. "First, we have a little fun, and then we get down to business. Trust me."

I took my seat and waved my hand. "Fine, fine, whatever you want. Just tell me one thing. You're not trying to get me drunk on purpose just to convince me to get some crazy gift, are you?"

"Katie! I'm truly offended." He sounded a little too put out. Borderline sarcasm was never a good sign with Dave. It usually meant he had something up his sleeve. If we hadn't been such good friends, if I hadn't trusted him completely, I might've gotten up and left, terrified at what kind of trouble he'd get me into this afternoon.

However, I did trust him. Completely. He'd never hurt me. He always had my best interests in the forefront of his mind, more so than I could say for myself. Sometimes I disgusted myself for being such a needy friend. But when it came to it, Dave was the only friend I could trust to help me in my times of need. I often wondered, no, *hoped* he was just as needy, but in the opposite way: that he needed someone to look after.

It wasn't until after my first drink that I decided not to obsess about our afternoon schedule. Whatever happened,

happened. However, it wasn't until three-quarters through my second that the knot between my shoulders loosened.

As Dave kept up light conversation, I leaned back in my chair and gazed out the window. From my seat I could see the main downtown intersection. The street was busy. I glanced down at the shoppers hustling along the sidewalk as they moved from store to store and the pedestrians crossing the street. Dave was chatting about the latest movie he'd seen, asking if I was interested in catching the independent film festival in a few weeks. I was.

I floated half in the conversation, half out. My mind wandered as my eyes moved from person to person down below. A young woman with pink streaks in her hair glided into my frame of vision. I blinked twice and my stomach clenched. It wasn't the girl who caught my attention; it was the young man following her. Though I could tell they were together, they didn't seem to be friendly toward each other as they walked. They weren't unfriendly, either. They just . . . were.

I sat up in my chair and leaned forward to get a closer look at him. His movements were elegant, each step a specific choice rather than an automated task. His eyes focused on the girl in front of him as they made their way across the street. His shoulders were broad enough to make the black sweater he wore look as if it were on a hanger. Jesus, he was gorgeous. His hair was dark, and I could see curls poking out as they played with the tops of his ears.

Physically, he looked young, maybe twenty-two or three, but it wasn't his stunning youthfulness that made him so mesmerizing. It was the way the expression on his face didn't match his physicality that drew my eyes to him. He looked serious, far too serious. Serious to the point of discomfort. He looked pained.

A fleeting thought wisped through my mind. Someone so

beautiful shouldn't be in that much pain. My heart jolted with emotion. Surprised by my adolescent reaction, I shifted uncomfortably in my chair. I really should've stopped at that first drink. I looked in his direction again. My fingers tapped against my glass. His anguish called to me, and I had an instinctual urge to go to him, comfort him, as if somehow, I could ease his immense pain. I couldn't explain it, but I had to get closer. I excused myself to the restroom.

It took all the self-control I had to not run until I was out of Dave's sight. Once I reached the stairs, I shot down to the first floor. I stumbled out onto the sidewalk, bumping into a neo-hippie guy with blond dreadlocks. His clothes smelled of patchouli and musk. Frantically, I scanned the passers-by but saw nothing. Where was the young man? Where had he and the girl gone? My eyes shot along the street in search of the mysterious stranger. I don't know how long I stood there before a familiar voice came up from behind.

"Katie?" Dave came out of the restaurant carrying my purse. "You all right? You just kind of took off." Concern sounded in his voice.

"I'm sorry. I didn't mean to bail," I replied as casually as I could. "I just wanted to grab some fresh air before coming back up. I think that second drink did me in. Are we ready?"

I raised an eyebrow at Dave with a look of anticipation, though more from wondering if he was buying my cover-up than from the thought of shopping. I must've been getting better at smoothing over my erratic behaviors because Dave returned a sly, almost devious smile.

"Am I ready? Are *you* ready? Let's go." He took my arm, wrapped it through his, and led me in the opposite direction down the street.

I fought my instinct to turn my head and glance back. I sighed and fell in step with Dave resting my head on his arm.

"Please try to remember that I do have to live with Alex." I tried to sound as present as possible, but I was miles away. My mind kept wandering to the young man I'd seen just moments before. Something about him called to me. Something . . .

"Here we are," Dave proudly announced.

I looked up at the building standing in front of us.

I should have known.

The red velvet curtains inside the tinted windows hid merchandise often the talk of many disgruntled Freestone citizens.

"Oh, Dave," I groaned. "This is your great idea? You know how I feel about these types of things. Is this why you insisted on having drinks beforehand?" I felt a little dizzy standing in front of The Sensual Shoppe, Freestone's premier, and only, adult store.

"Come on, loosen up a bit," Dave goaded. "You're way too young to be so prudish. Besides, we're not here to get leather harnesses or a spiked slave collar, just a little lingerie. A safe, simple, sexy beginner's purchase. It's about time you show off that hot little package; I know it's dying to reveal itself. Besides, when was the last time you wore something like this for Alex?"

"Never," I answered.

"Exactly," he snapped back. "Your husband will flip when he sees you in something like this. This is the perfect way to show him you're willing to push the limits with your relationship."

"By looking like a porn star?"

Dave shot me an evil glance. "No, smart ass. By showing him you're willing, after nine years of marriage, to go the extra mile to find out what he likes, *and* to show him that even if it's out of your comfort zone, you're willing to give new things a try." He spoke with confidence, as if he was making the most convincing argument in the history of arguments.

"I don't know. I mean, how do you know that he'll even like something like this? What if he's not that into it?"

"Please. He's a man. And that means two things. One, he's into looking at amazingly beautiful things. And two, um, he's a straight man. No straight man would ever turn his wife away dressed in something like that."

Dave pointed to a mannequin posed seductively just inside the entrance. The tall statue wore a matching purple and black barely there lace panty and bra set, fish net thigh highs, and stilettos. Of course, stilettos would be involved. I wondered if the charges would be worth it if I stabbed Dave in the back with one of them. No sooner had the thought formed, I felt horrible. I really wasn't myself today.

I wasn't totally sold on the idea, but my guilt let Dave lead me further into the shop. After all, wasn't I just wishing I had sexier pajamas this morning? I was pretty sure this was a big step past new pajamas, but it wouldn't hurt to look around.

Maybe it was Dave's convincing argument, though I still wasn't ruling out the drinks, but somewhere between the corsets and . . . ahem, handheld devices, I decided it just might be the perfect present. If nothing else, Alex would be totally surprised.

After an hour or so of trying on several different unmentionables, I decided on a black, silk, lacy panty with garters and little pink bows, some sheer thigh highs, and a matching low-cut bra.

"Well, I have to admit," Dave said as we exited the store, "I didn't think you had it in you. If I was into women, I'd be all over that. Alex is going to love it."

"I'm still not sure."

"Trust me, I know men," Dave said with a little laugh, and I could tell he was thinking of something he wasn't going to share with me . . . yet. I smiled and let it go as we walked down the main street; satisfied tonight was looking better.

As we approached the intersection, a light breeze picked up. My thoughts wandered back to the young man I'd seen earlier crossing the street. He'd looked so familiar, though I was certain we'd never met. Perhaps it was his expression, such intense anguish, which made me feel for him with such conviction.

"You want to go to the bookstore?" Dave asked as he pushed the button to cross the street.

"Um, sure," I half-heartedly responded. Dave noticed.

"What's up?"

"Nothing, really. I was just thinking about something that happened earlier."

"You want to talk about it?"

"Not really. Maybe later. Do you mind if we stop for a coffee? I'm desperately in need of a caffeine fix."

"That makes two of us."

We walked briskly against the breeze, the smell of jasmine and lavender wafted by from the north and a sensation of contentment ran up my arms. How was it possible to live in such an amazing corner of California? Moving here was quite possibly the best decision Alex and I'd ever made.

I fell into a daydream. A montage of moments starring Alex and our life together in this beautiful little town swept through my mind. And then, it changed. Sudden and unexpected, my thoughts strolled their way back to my mysterious stranger.

A twinge of guilt crept up on me and I cringed as the image of the stranger pushed thoughts of the man I was married to out of the way. What was it about the stranger that intrigued me? My memory memorized and traced over every line of his face. It started at his hair and made its way down to his chin, lingering at his lips. My heart pounded in my chest. My expression must've shown my conflict because it wasn't long before Dave questioned me.

"Okay. What's up? That's the second time you've had that look on your face in the last five minutes, so 'fess up. What are you thinking of?"

I walked over to one of the benches on the sidewalk and sat. "You're going to think I'm a horrible person."

"No, I won't." His eyes were intently looking at mine. "Just tell me, already."

"Well . . ." I hesitated, not wanting to admit out loud I was becoming borderline-obsessed with a complete stranger. Okay, fine. Fully obsessed.

"Go on," Dave encouraged. "Please, give me some credit, will you? Have I ever judged you before?"

"No, but I've never done anything quite like this before either," I said miserably.

"Like what?"

I took a deep breath. Might as well. "Well, um, when we were having lunch today, I was looking out the window—people watching, you know?"

"So, what's the big deal about that? We do that every day."

I bit my lip. "Okay, I'm just going to say this, and it's going to sound really bad and a little crazy but here goes. I saw this young guy . . . . maybe twenty-two or three. He was walking with this girl, well, more like behind her, like he was following her."

"And . . ." Dave's forehead crinkled. I wasn't making any sense.

I rolled my shoulders back and lifted my chin. "And I couldn't take my eyes off him. At first, I thought I knew him, he was so familiar, but I know I've never seen him before in my life. Then, I thought it was the look on his face that made me stare; he had this expression, you know, I can't describe it, but I knew exactly how he felt. It was loss. Loss and pain. It was like I could feel what he felt." I paused before making my final and most difficult confession.

"And then"—my voice got quiet— "just now, I was thinking of Alex one minute, and before my thought had finished, there he was, this guy, in my thoughts, taking Alex's place in my head." I dropped my eyes to the ground. "I saw it. I felt it. How it would feel to run my hand through his hair, how his lips would feel against mine." I came to a stop; the last words were barely audible.

My stomach clenched. Dave stared at me, examining my face. I shouldn't have said anything. I'd done some questionable things in our time together, but I was sure even Dave had his limits on sanity. One thing was clear. Whatever he thought about my confession, good or bad, I one hundred percent wasn't going to admit I actually tried to find the stranger when I pretended to go to the bathroom. Some confessions are best left buried. After a long, and excruciating, silence, Dave's face relaxed.

"Is that all?" Dave laughed loudly.

My eyes shot up to examine his.

"I just told you I was having lusty thoughts about a man, much younger than me, and not my husband, on my anniversary, no less, and your response is 'Is that all?'"

"So you saw a good-looking man and you had a little fantasy about it. So what? You wouldn't be human if you weren't able to recognize what was aesthetically pleasing to you."

My frown burrowed deep on my face, unconvinced.

He continued, "Look, did you really run your hand through his hair?"

"No."

"Did you actually kiss him?"

"Of course not."

"Then what're you feeling bad about? That you found another man attractive? Please. You're making a big deal out of nothing."

"You think I'm being absurd?" I asked.

Hearing him say it out loud, I did feel I was blowing things way out of proportion. Still, my conscience nagged. It wasn't just that I was thinking about an attractive man. I'd *wanted* him. I felt it. And I wanted him to want *me*.

"Definitely." He looked at his watch. "Now, we should hustle. It's getting late."

I nodded and stood. The rest of the afternoon was uneventful. After grabbing some coffee, we perused the bookstore, and hit a couple other shops before heading back to Dave's car. As we approached the parking lot, we passed a street vendor selling jewelry and trinkets.

The woman was older, perhaps in her late sixties, and wore a long flowing skirt with a bright multi-colored scarf. Her long, braided hair was pulled away from her face and reached past her mid-back in a thick, silvery rope. She sat in a lawn chair with her merchandise displayed on the sidewalk.

As I passed, a glint of silver caught my eye. I stopped and took a step back to get a better look at what had grabbed my attention.

I stopped and leaned over the box of jewelry. "You go ahead, Dave. I'll catch up."

"You sure?"

I nodded. "Yeah, I'll just be a sec."

Dave shrugged his shoulders and headed to the car.

"See something you like?" Her voice was smooth and songlike.

"Yeah, I think so," I said as I bent down and reached for a delicate silver necklace with a small charm.

"This is interesting. What's this?" I asked.

"That's a Goddess symbol," she said.

I inspected the small circular charm. It was solid silver with an intricate picture of a tree with its bare branches reaching upward and its roots reaching down. A simple star was superimposed over the trunk.

"Goddess symbol?"

"Yes, a Goddess symbol," she answered patiently. "Some practice Christianity, some Judaism, but there are religions and traditions far older than those. They are . . . less conventional religions. Earth based. Nature based. When the stars and the sun and the moon were looked to for answers, and the paths of the cosmos revered. Old traditions."

When I didn't respond, she continued, "To these people, these worshippers of the old ways, the Goddess flows through everything, a nurturing spirit in every man, every woman, every plant, and every animal. She is life. She is death. She represents the universe and is represented universally in several ways. What you have there in your hand is just one of her many symbols, but it is my most favorite."

I cocked my head to the side. "What does it mean?"

The woman smiled. "There are many interpretations, but I'll tell you the one I learned. The tree there is the tree of life. It represents the connection of the three worlds. The branches reaching up are stretching toward the oversoul, where followers of the Goddess hope to travel to after natural life has ended. Those long roots stretch deep down to the underworld, a place where those who are lost belong. And the trunk is the earth connecting them both. It is the glue between the two and the balance that keeps the others in place. The star you see is called a pentacle. Its five points represent the four elements—earth, air, fire, and water—and the fifth point, the one pointing up, represents the soul, the energy of a person."

"How interesting. Did you make it?"

"Yes, I did," she replied. "In fact, I'd just placed it in the case moments before you passed, almost as if it were meant to be. Curious how those things work out, isn't it?"

"Yeah, curious."

Though not exactly my style of jewelry, something about the necklace intrigued me. I asked the woman if she'd help me put it on. The tiny bauble felt at home around my neck, the charm dangled and glinted in the late afternoon sunlight. I had to agree with the woman; it was made for me.

"A perfect fit and very befitting of you," she said as she smiled.

"Thank you," I said, paying for the necklace and then hurrying to Dave's car.

"What'd you get?" he asked when I was fastened in my seat belt.

"Just a necklace." I pulled the front of my shirt down to expose my new piece of jewelry, the charm dangling slightly. Dave lifted the charm with his fingers inspecting my recent purchase.

"Very witchy," he said sarcastically. "Wait a minute. You're not going to join some cult now, are you? Or start making potions in a cauldron?"

"Shut up." I laughed, pushing him away. "Can you just imagine what Alex would think if I suddenly started casting spells and stuff? He'd think I'd lost it for sure."

"Oh, my dear, you've already lost it." Dave teased as he started the car and threw it into reverse.

I smiled. Lost it? After today, it was probably true, but I wasn't going to let it bother me right now. I rolled down the window and let the wind cleanse my face, its wispy fingers playing along the contours of my cheeks. I stuck my arm out, letting my hand ride the wind as Dave accelerated in the direction of my house.

The necklace shone in the autumn light, reflecting prisms onto the car's interior and I could honestly say I was happy. Funny how something so little can do that.

Eight

GIO

I spent most of the afternoon cleaning the studio. It was apparent no one had been there in quite some time— the dust created a thin fog throughout the apartment as I ran a cloth along the surfaces. I walked to the windows overlooking the street. It took some work, being that they were painted shut, but I managed to open one of them. I inhaled deeply as the crisp autumn air swept through the space and peered out onto the street below.

Unhindered by the dirty glass, light spilled in. I squinted at the suddenness of it, my eyes slow to adjust to the brightness. The street was busy. Afternoon shoppers bustled along the sidewalk, bags in tow. I took a moment to enjoy the scene. A young man with hair past his shoulders, carrying a guitar case, came out of a music shop. A couple of skateboarders flew past pedestrians in the type of authoritarian disregard common among youth.

I inhaled again, letting my chest expand and welcomed the chill of the autumn air as it filled my lungs. The air drew down, spiraling deep into the depths of my body, filling every crevice, every space available. A sense of peace overcame me, and I was reminded of something Willem once said. *You'll feel like your life has been returned.* Every cell in my body vibrated. Yes, this was the place. It had to be.

I settled into a sense of deep satisfaction when I was startled by a knock at the door.

"Gio?" I spun around to see Claire standing in the doorway.

"Claire, what're you doing here?"

"I was just . . . I mean, I . . . sorry, I didn't mean to startle you. I hope you don't mind me just barging in; the door wasn't closed all the way. Sometimes in these older buildings you need to give it a good tug." She had one earbud in, the other dangled in front of her shirt, the device they were attached to mysteriously hidden somewhere on her person.

I let my shoulders fall. No sense in going into high alert —yet.

"It's no problem, really. I was just enjoying the view," I replied. "What's up?"

"Uh, yeah. Well, I'm just about to close the shop for an hour or so and wanted to give you this." She fished into her front pocket and pulled out a small silver key. "The key to your mailbox. You're 1A. You can drop the deposit and first month's rent in the slot mailbox to the left of yours." She hesitated, and then added, "Can I ask you something?"

"You may." My words were careful.

"You're not from around here, are you?"

"Not exactly," I answered, waiting to see where this conversation led.

"You've come far," she said. It was more of a statement than a question.

I eyed her cautiously and waited for her to continue.

"What I mean is, and you don't have to answer if it's too personal, but I was wondering if you were from around here —as in America."

"No, I'm not. I'm actually from—"

"Italy," Claire interrupted as if she'd known it all along.

If earlier I'd been feeling a bit unnerved, it was nothing to the complete apprehension I felt as she spoke now. My heart pounded with such ferocity I thought it would jump out of my chest.

"How—" I began. She didn't let me finish.

"I . . . I know . . . about you, about what you've been through. I know about her, and I know . . . I know about . . . *him* too." Her voice was both soft and strong, and it didn't quite match the body it was coming from. It was too experienced. It knew too much. "You have to be careful. Freestone is a small town, you know. Everyone knows everyone, and if they don't, they know someone who does. But there are places that even *he* will never go. Safe places. Places like here." She gestured to the apartment. "And other places close by. I'll show you if you'd like." She looked around the room avoiding eye contact.

"Who are you?" I whispered, taking a step back. The frame of the windows pressed against my back. "What do you want?" My mind raced. Who was this girl? Was she a witch? Something else I'd yet to discover? I didn't want to begin this trip with violence, especially since I wasn't sure as to what I'd be fighting, but I wasn't going to go quietly, and if it came to a fight, well, it wouldn't be the first time.

Claire suddenly looked up at me. Her green eyes were filled with surprise and then cleared as panic filled the rest of her face. "No, no, it's nothing like that. That's not why I'm here, I mean, it's just that—this is coming out wrong—look, I don't want anything. It's just that I . . . I . . . that's not what I wanted to say . . ." She broke off.

"What's the deal then? Experience tells me I should kill you. Kill you now and get the hell out of here, away from whatever you are. But my instinct tells me differently. It tells me I'm safe here. And"—I paused— "I have to go with that." I held her gaze. "Besides, I can't leave. I have unfinished business to take care of. I need this place. So, against my better judgment, against my experience, I'll listen to whatever it is you have to say, but you'd better start talking before I change my mind."

My voice was firm, and I spoke clearly, so there'd be no confusion between us. Goddess, where was Willem when I needed him? What was she? Or what did she belong to? The two questions were at the forefront of my mind. I needed the truth. I didn't have time for deceit. I'd been waiting thirty years for another opportunity, and I wasn't going to take any chances with accidental oversights.

"No, please. I'm sorry. I didn't mean to alarm you. It's just that sometimes, not always, well, at least when I don't ignore it, but sometimes I have . . . I have this gift, sort of. It's kind of hard to explain, and I know we've just met, and the only thing I really know about you is your name . . .," she stammered. "It's actually more of a curse than anything—my mother and grandmother have it too."

I didn't know if it was the troubled expression on her face or the way she tripped over her words, but, in that moment, I felt sorry for her. I knew her frustration. I knew what it was like to have a part of yourself you loathed. A part of you that, for no better words, freaked you out.

Though she was still a mystery, she no longer unnerved me. On the contrary, I wanted to ease her pain, make her feel comfortable. Call it instinct, call it stupidity, but something about her screamed safety and it radiated strong and deep in my core. Claire was someone I could trust.

"I have no clue about any of that, but how about we start again?" I stepped away from the window toward her and held out my hand. "My name's Gio." I waited for her to accept the gesture. She looked at my hand for quite some time before she answered.

"Yeah, okay. I can do that. Hi Gio, I'm Claire." Her voice held sadness. I let my untouched hand drop to my side.

"Well, Claire, I think it's time we got to know each other a little better. You think you can show me one of these safe places where we can grab a drink? You are old enough to drink, right?"

Claire smiled. "No, not legally," she said. "But that's never stopped me before. And I know just the place."

I eyed her carefully as I grabbed my coat. "Someplace out of the way, not too—"

"Conspicuous," she finished softly.

I didn't try to hide my surprise. "Exactly."

"Yeah, I do."

"Then let's go." I pulled on my coat and motioned for her to lead the way. Though I no longer felt the immediate alarm I'd felt moments before, I wasn't taking any chances. If I'd learned anything after four hundred years of mistake after mistake, it was how to exercise caution.

Claire walked out into the hallway and waited. I turned off the lights and tugged firmly on the door, locking it behind me.

"Shall we?" I said as I offered her my arm. She looked at it briefly, and then tucked her hands firmly in her pockets. She offered a half-hearted smile.

"If you don't mind, I'd prefer if, for now, we kept our space."

She promptly turned and descended the stairs, jumping over the last one to the ground floor. She was out on the street in a minute and waiting for me to catch up.

"This way," she said as she briskly walked down the street toward the intersection. I followed intently, my eyes scanning the area out of habit.

"You'll like this place," she said. "You'll be out of sight. *He* wouldn't be caught dead there—*if* he even noticed it."

As she approached the intersection, the light turned green. She continued across the street, never breaking stride. I followed silently, watching her with curiosity. When she reached the other side, she abruptly turned right to cross again, never slowing as she stepped into the street.

"Wait . . .," I began, warning her of oncoming traffic, but I stopped when I realized the signal had changed. I hesitated at the corner and wondered how the lights could've changed so quickly. Claire kept her pace until she reached the other side. Once firmly planted on the sidewalk, she turned to look at me.

"Are you coming?" she yelled from across the street. A slight smile broke out of the left side of her mouth.

I snapped out of my thought and glanced at her from my corner. Without hesitation I jogged across the street to where she stood.

"How—" I began.

"Let's just get off the street and into the bar. Less eyes, you know?" she interrupted scanning the edges of my body again.

"Okay, what's up with the look?" I asked, unwilling to let her glances slide any longer.

"Nothing," she said hurriedly.

"Look, Claire. I want to trust you, I do. I need to trust you. I need you to tell me the truth. My purpose for being here is far too important to screw up again. I can't take any chances, and if I feel you're a liability, please believe me when I say I won't hesitate to get rid of you."

Her eyes widened and for a moment I thought she would scream. But she didn't.

Instead, she opened her mouth and, in an unusually calm voice, said, "For what it's worth, I give you my word I'll tell you the truth. For now, I just need you to hold on a little while longer. Please come with me. Once we're off the street, I promise everything will be explained."

I swallowed hard and let her request sit between us in silence. After a minute, I nodded and followed her down the sidewalk a few more buildings until we reached the outside of a lacquered wooden door sunken in a few feet from the street. Claire stopped and turned to face it. She took a deep breath and mumbled some inaudible words.

"What're you—"

She held up her hand to me in a signal to wait.

I had a moment to reflect upon the situation. How'd I end up here? I wasn't certain I was making the best choices at present. The thought of being so close to *her* had distracted me in the past, aided in bad choices, left callous regrets, and I hoped I wasn't on that road again. I wish I'd taken a private moment earlier to phone Willem before I found myself standing in a strange place, about to walk into an inconspicuous building that could very well be a trap. After all, over the centuries, there'd been plenty who'd sought to destroy me; this wouldn't be the first time.

Alessandro himself had come perilously close to doing the deed. Though he cannot physically kill me, he's killed her repeatedly; a sick and twisted game of cat and mouse that has destroyed me far more than death ever could.

But Claire? A danger? As strangely as she acted, my instinct insisted she wasn't a threat. The universe screamed she could be trusted.

Earlier in the apartment, I'd sent out my energy. At that time, I'd received no ill feelings, no feelings of dread or doom. Nothing that warned me of any danger. On the contrary, I'd felt continued assurance that this was my time. From the moment I stepped off the train, I'd felt certain about this place, I was so sure this was where everything would end, or begin, or continue, depending on how you looked at it.

Whatever Claire was, she wasn't here to cause trouble and she wasn't here to destroy me, not intentionally anyway. Though I was unsure of her purpose, I was certain she had a purpose to this journey. If I'd only spoken to Willem, he could've told me how to proceed.

As it was, I was thinking on my feet, and so there I stood in front of an ordinary wooden door leading into what I could only assume was a bar, watching this young woman mumble to herself words I couldn't quite catch and praying to the Goddess above I wasn't walking into a major ambush.

"Look," she whispered, her eyes directed to the door in front of us.

I looked. At first glance, I merely saw a door. I turned my attention back to her. Her eyes were intently gazing upon the seemingly empty space in front of her. When I realized she meant for me to copy, I stood next to her shoulder to shoulder, refocused my energy, and gave the door my undivided attention.

After a minute of staring, the air between where Claire and I stood condensed and wavered, and a shape began to emerge from the air. Floating in front of the wooden door was a symbol of the Goddess encircled by a halo of white energy. My breath caught in my throat. It'd been centuries since I'd seen such a clear sign in broad daylight.

I reached my hand over and touched Claire's hand. This time she accepted my touch. I was afraid to look at her, afraid to take my eyes off the symbol, but I couldn't stop my head as I longed to see the woman who'd called upon this energy. She was already looking at me.

"Let's get out of here," she said as she wrapped her hand around mine and squeezed.

Overcome by emotion, I was unable to move. My breathing became rapid. Trust was no longer an issue; I no longer questioned her motives. If Claire could pull a pure Tree of Life image out of thin air, in broad daylight, hell, I'd trust her with my life. No, it was something else keeping me frozen, something inside me.

I shuddered. I just couldn't bring myself to face the centuries of pain I'd caused, the pain I'd brought upon others. Everything came flooding back with unstoppable force. Everything I'd fought for and lost, repeatedly, came back to me the instant I saw that symbol. The rush of memories turned over and over, crashing like waves in my head.

~

Rome, 1602

SHORTLY AFTER MY father passed away, I decided to take the money I'd been saving from selling my statues and leave Rinato's service. I was twenty-two at the time. As my mother had passed years before, I'd no other family, no friends, and very few prospects, thanks to my master. I was a grown man but held the status of a glorified servant. There was nothing left for me in Florence except a sour taste in my mouth. I was ready to leave the city behind and begin a new life far away.

Thanks to my secret side-business, I'd accumulated quite a bit of wealth over the years, enough to give me a good head start. I left Florence during the night. Silently, I stole out of the workshop and headed south toward Rome on foot, never looking back. I walked all night, sometimes running; trying to gain the greatest amount of distance I possibly could between Rinato and myself before the sun rose.

When the sun did rise the next morning, I was entering a small village just outside the Province of Perugia. I quickly acquired a horse and continued my journey south.

For weeks, I traveled alone, keeping to myself, stopping only for food and drink. Most nights I camped in the woods, making a shelter with what I could find. I washed my clothes only when I happened upon a stream and picked up work when it was available. Always moving. I was a man with nothing to his name, a wanderer, but for the first time in my life I was free.

Free from Rinato. Free from the expectations of my father. Free from the lies I'd been telling for years. It was during that time, on that journey, in those days spent in solitude, that I became my own man. I'd never been happier. I couldn't imagine ever needing anything else in life. I was complete, or so I thought.

A year later I finally stumbled upon Rome. I was twenty-three. If I'd thought Florence was a large city, Rome was immense with stone buildings sprawling over great distances. The feelings of awe I'd had as a boy entering Florence flooded back, this time with an excitement blossoming from the knowledge that here, in this glorious city, I would not be a servant; I'd be what I wanted here. I could even make a living as a sculptor if I chose. Anxiously, I walked through the city gates.

The streets were crowded with people. Hungry, I found my way to a fruit stand in the open market. As I was about to bite into a pear, a strange feeling came over me. A chill started at the base of my spine and traveled upward to the nape of my neck. I shivered. My heart raced, my breath came fast. For a minute I thought I'd pass out. A sudden urge to turn around struck me. I looked behind me. What had caught my attention? What was pulling me to turn around? I had to see. My eyes searched through the people for only a moment before I saw her.

Her hair was dark like a raven's feathers in the night. Her skin, smooth and creamy, was an untouched canvas of flawless features. I watched as she moved from booth to booth, closer and closer, each step gracefully over the gravel-lined street, though she wore no shoes. Her skirt curved nicely around her hips, leaving images in my head that'd never been there before and my stomach tightened.

Her top lip came together in a perfect bow and flattened out as she looked up at me and smiled. My heart stopped. What would her lips taste like?

Her eyes were a familiar shade of dark green with flecks of gold that left me struggling to remember where we'd met before.

Everything went silent as the world stopped. The very air around me became dense as I struggled to catch my breath. Who was this woman? I had to get closer. If I hadn't felt my legs moving underneath me, I would've thought I was floating. Seconds passed like hours, minutes turned to years, until I was standing just a few steps from her, and still it was not close enough.

"Hello. My name's Giovanni," I greeted her.

"Hello, Giovanni," she responded in a voice reminiscent of a sinewy thread of silk.

"May I help you?" I motioned to her basket of items.

"Thank you, that's very kind, but I don't think—" she began.

"Please, I wouldn't think much of myself if I knowingly let you go about your day with such a heavy burden."

"It's no trouble, really. Besides, I'm not sure you want to be seen with a person like me."

"Please," I insisted again, dismissing her last comment. A person like her? Who wouldn't want to be in the presence of a goddess? I tried desperately to muster every bit of confidence I had. "Allow me." This time I reached down and placed my hand on the handle. She let me take it with a smile.

"Where to?" It was difficult for me to not sound nervous when I was so close to her.

"I'm actually heading back to my camp. They'll be waiting

for me. It's a bit of a walk. We're a couple miles outside the city gates," she said.

"Then we'd better not keep them waiting." I offered my arm and waited for her to take it. She eyed me thoughtfully, and then slid hers through mine.

Our skin touched and the energy between us materialized. It sizzled and sparked. I shuddered. My eyes grew wide, and I was forever changed; something inside my consciousness shifted irrevocably. I knew I'd be unable to live one moment without this woman.

"Thank you, Giovanni." Her voice was breathless, as if she was trying to recover from what I knew we'd both felt. "I'm Katarina."

"Katarina." The name slid off my tongue like honey.

"You're not from around here, are you?"

"No, is it that obvious?" I laughed at myself.

"Not really," she answered, "well, it wasn't until you offered to walk me home. Then, I began to have my suspicions."

"And why's that?"

"Well, it's not every day a man such as yourself would venture to the outskirts of the city with someone from the encampment."

"And what kind of man would that be?" I asked.

"A gentleman, of course."

"And how do you know I'm a gentleman?" Lust slipped off my lips. I immediately pulled it back with a cough. "What I mean is, how do you know I'm not a commoner . . . or a servant, escaped from his master, with nothing to his name, and not a gentleman at all?"

She smiled. "A gentleman is not measured by what he has, but by how he acts, by the pureness of his intent, the goodness of his heart. Those are the qualities that make a gentleman."

Her beauty distracted me as she spoke. I tried to recover,

though I was clearly sidetracked. "And why would a gentleman not offer to walk you home?"

Her face got serious. "There are some people who believe my people are born from evil, that we're an abomination of God. They call us Strega Ilmalo, witches of the darkness. There are even some who would rid us from this earth, if they weren't afraid of what might become of them if they harmed us."

My heart crushed at her words and my hackles rose. The pain in her voice drew anger up from deep within and an instinct of protectiveness reared. How could anyone think such thoughts about such a beauty? I blinked, startled at how much I wanted to become a part of her life. Was it possible to fall in love within moments? My heart seemed to think so. We walked a bit in silence before she spoke again.

"Do you believe in signs?"

"I believe things happen for a reason and that sometimes we might not even know what those reasons are."

She smiled, her shoulders relaxing. She loosened her arm from my hold and let her hand find its way to mine. The softness of her fingers wound their way around my calloused roughness and held fast. I stopped walking and stared at the connection. My body buzzed with excitement.

Katarina's gaze met mine and then drifted down to our entwined fingers. She brought them up to eye level and rubbed her cheek against them. I was mesmerized. Her cheek brushed against my fingers and every muscle in my body was at attention. She pulled back, her lips slightly parted. The wind picked up and lifted the ends of her hair off her shoulders. Placing the basket down, I reached out with my free hand and tucked a wayward strand behind her ear, my thumb grazing her cheek.

I shivered.

"We should keep walking," I whispered.

"We should."

Neither of us moved.

My hand caressed her cheek again, my thumb tracing the outline of her lips this time. My God, she was exquisite. Her eyes closed as she inhaled deeply. Once more the wind picked up around us. Temptation called me to press my lips to hers. Would she kiss me back? Again, the world around me stopped. Everything was motionless. Her eyes opened and I recognized the desire in them. It was a mirror of how I felt. An invitation.

I leaned in and gently pressed my lips to hers. Hesitantly. She tasted delicious, like pears dipped in honey. My chest filled. The air pressed us together. Closer and harder as time stopped.

Her hand released mine and she wrapped it around my neck, pulling me to her, devouring me with her soul, leading me toward a towering cliff from which there'd be no return.

I willingly fell. I grasped her hips and pulled her into me and fell deep and long with her to a place where there was no one except us.

From the moment our lips met, my destiny was sealed. I took an oath with that kiss. There was no way I'd ever be without her. Until the day I took my last breath, I'd give Katarina my soul.

Reluctantly, she pulled away, her chest heaving, flush and swollen. She examined my face, her eyes wide with surprise, as if she hadn't expected to feel what passed between us. "I . . . I felt you looking at me before I saw you. In the marketplace." She was breathless. "I thought to myself, *If I look up right now, I will see him, the one I've been waiting for.* I almost didn't look up in fear of seeing someone else, but there you were, looking right back at me, and I knew, Gio. I knew. I knew it wouldn't make a difference to you where I came from or what I was. I'd asked the Goddess for a sign, and there you were, looking at me like you'd been waiting for me since forever." Her voice was a whisper.

"Katarina," I said, my eyes drinking in every inch of her face, "I'm not sure I understand what you mean."

"Come with me." She picked up the basket and tugged me further away from the city gates into the surrounding forest. I followed without protest. Our bodies still thrummed with our recent connection and as we walked deeper into the forest, I longed to touch her, to kiss her once more. When we approached a dense gathering of trees, Katarina led me through it to a small clearing in the center. I looked around at this secret forest room.

"Sit. I'll explain everything," she ordered in a way that was neither a request nor a demand but could have been either or both and I would've listened. I sat near the base of a tree while she sat across from me on the ground, our bodies facing each other. She was too far away. I reached out and pulled her close. She melted in my arms.

"I know this sounds insane," she began, "but I've been waiting for you my whole life. And . . ." She hesitated.

"And what? Tell me."

"That kiss . . ." Her voice trailed. "Goddess above, Gio. My blood is still near boiling after that kiss."

I leaned down, my lips pressing against the top of her head. "I'd like to kiss you some more."

Katarina squirmed at the touch, lifting her chin to look up at me. "I'd like that too. But if you do that now, I'll never tell you what I need you to know. What you should know before we go any further."

My heart pounded in my chest. It didn't matter what she said, I was already hers. Instead, I nodded.

She took a deep breath and blew it out slowly. "I come from a long line of Strega—witches. True creatures of nature, creatures of life and death. For us, everything in life is a cycle and we pray to our mother, the Goddess, to help our journey here on the earth to complete our cycle until we die and become part of the oversoul."

"I've heard of the Stregheria before," I replied. "My father warned me of your kind. He said the Strega sold their souls to the devil to gain powers humans shouldn't have. He believed anyone who fell into their company would fall into the devil's snare."

"And what do you believe?" She looked at me intently.

I opened my mouth, then closed it again, reflecting on my father's words. Life was so much simpler for him than for me. Had I lived my life as he had lived his, I probably would've believed his words as the ultimate truth. However, my life was woven from a different cloth, and I knew that things weren't always what they seemed.

"What do I believe?" I ran my fingers through her hair. "My father was simple. I believe a person's heart is what determines their goodness."

Katarina smiled. She leaned toward me and whispered, "I knew you'd find me. I felt it in my soul."

"I'd be lying if I told you in the moment I first saw you I didn't feel the same way." I shook my head. "It was like I'd been waiting to find you, though I didn't know I was looking in the first place." My voice reflected my struggle with the intensity of my emotions. "Seeing you, touching you, it seems so natural, as if I've been doing it forever. Like it's meant to be. As if I'd been put on this earth to be with you." I released a soft laugh. "Now I sound insane."

Her breath caught and my eyes found her mouth. I leaned down until our lips met. Katarina twisted in my arms, the kiss never breaking, until she was straddled on my lap. My hands held her hips firmly in place, keeping her planted across my thighs. Just where she needed to be. A small gasp escaped her lips, and my breathing became frenzied. Hands and mouths and lips and tongues feasted. The energy between us grew and built and grew some more, until I became nervous about where it would lead. I'd never wanted anyone like I'd wanted this woman. And now, I wanted to make her mine.

A far away bell echoed in the trees. Katarina pulled away.

"I have to go." She scooted back and took the basket.

"Wait, when will I see you again?" I called, grasping her hand. Electricity.

She glanced at our hands, and I knew she felt the same pulse I had. How could she not? "Can you be here tomorrow midday?"

My heart exploded in happiness. "Of course. I'll be watching every hour pass until I see you again."

She closed the space between us and kissed me again. This time her lips pressed hard on mine, her body flush against me. The stirrings of arousal twisted and twirled my insides and every muscle in my body clenched.

Again, another bell rang through the trees.

"I have to go, but I'll see you tomorrow."

My heart ached as I watched her turn and leave, disappearing through the trees out to the main road.

The next weeks, Katarina and I met nearly every day. Stolen conversations and kisses wound us tight together, like the twine in a hemp necklace. My desire for her grew. We were becoming inseparable. Parting became torture.

On the third week of our secret meetings, Katarina was unusually quiet.

"My love, tell me, what's wrong?" We sat under the largest tree in the clearing, she leaned against my chest.

She sighed. "I have something to tell you and it's not good." A tone of seriousness shadowed her words and nearly stopped my heart. "It's something that could make things difficult for us to be together."

"Stop. It can't be that bad. Besides, now that I've found

you, nothing can keep me from you. Are you still concerned about what other people will think? I don't care what others say. I'll become part of the Strega if I have to." I pressed my lips to her hair and inhaled deeply. The soft smell of jasmine curled around me. "It doesn't make a difference to me as long as you're mine and I'm yours. No matter what, we'll face it together." My voice rose as the thought of being apart from her threatened my existence.

She placed her hand on my cheek. "This isn't about what you would do to be with me." Her eyes were filled with fear. "It's about what others would do to keep us apart."

My brow furrowed. "I don't understand."

"It's not the outsiders I'm worried about. It's the insiders that are making me uneasy. My people." She paused. "It's no secret that the Strega Ilmalo likes to keep to themselves. As a result, we're bound together in every aspect of life. There are no secrets, no jealousies, at least no open ones, and very few rules among us. In fact, there's only one rule that must never be broken."

"What's that?" I asked, though somehow I already knew the answer. It crept up on me like a predator.

"That we never bring outsiders into our lives on a personal level."

My jaw clenched. I didn't like where this conversation was headed. How could a group of people just decide who you could and couldn't fall in love with? How could anyone but Katarina know what she desired in a partner? What she needed?

Though I couldn't explain it, I knew I needed her. And I had the distinct feeling she needed me too. The way she spoke, the way she held her head with her chin slightly lifted, the way she knew herself were only a taste of what urged me to want to be with her forever. I wanted her to be mine in body and mind and soul and me to her, a circle of completeness and no one, not even the Strega Ilmalo would stop us from being together.

"Why?" I asked, my voice low.

"In order to keep our lives peaceful, we stay to ourselves as much as possible, only venturing out for the most basic needs. Everything else is done within the camp. We dance together, pray together, eat together, sell our goods to each other, *everything*." Her eyes grew dark as her voice lowered.

"One time my father had returned from a wandering across the countryside with some small figurines he'd purchased for my birthday. He told me he had a surprise for me, something only I could know about. He took me into our tent and unveiled my special gift. He told me they were exceptionally special. That he'd bought them from my future, from someone whose heart was of the same material as mine. I didn't understand what he meant by that. Still don't. But the figurines? They were perfect. Who could create such beauty? I adored them. I promised my father I'd guard his secret gift. And I did. For a while. But I was young, and I wanted to show off my new possessions. It wasn't long before others in the camp knew about it and felt my father should be punished for bringing the outside in, especially when there were several within the camp who he could've commissioned to sculpt."

As she told the story, my heart stopped. I knew where I'd seen her eyes before. My mind flickered back to my youth to the odd-looking gentleman with green and gold-flecked eyes I'd met long ago in the Florence marketplace. It felt like a lifetime ago, but there was no mistaking those eyes. It was his gold coins that helped me believe I'd one day make a new life for myself. What was it he said to me that afternoon?

I have a feeling our paths will cross again.

How could he have known? I swallowed hard as the truth set in. Katarina continued her story.

"When word got to Stephano, our leader, he wasn't

pleased. He called my father to the council. There, the elders decided my father was in the wrong; he'd broken one of our most important rules. I cried as the council's judgment was rendered." Tears made her eyes shiny. "And I nearly died as my father suffered his punishment as an example to others all because I couldn't keep my mouth shut." She shuddered. "I begged them to stop such merciless beating. They just pushed me aside." Katarina took a slow, steady breath. She continued, her voice holding onto a slick edge.

"One of the more powerful Strega in the camp, Benito, approached me. I didn't know him well; my father had always told me to keep space from him and his own as their ideas were radical and dangerously close to conceding to the darkest forces. But Benito told me he could advise the council to stop my father's punishment if I were to promise my hand to his son, Alessandro." Her eyes closed.

I listened intently, captivated by her story. She opened her eyes, continuing.

"What choice did I have? I so desperately wanted to help my father I would've done anything. I didn't love Alessandro when I agreed to the arrangement, but I liked him well enough. What did I know? I was a child; I would've agreed to anything if it meant my father would be released." Her eyes fell again, dark clouds stealing away those golden flecks. "But a promise is a promise and I agreed to the bargain. And even though I do not truly love him, I'm to be hand-fasted to Alessandro on my twenty-fifth birthday . . . next week."

My throat began to close and made breathing difficult. "Hand-fasted, but— "

"That's why I cast a spell to Goddess to show me the way. To prove, if only to myself, that the arrangement was a mistake. I prayed to be shown the right path toward true love. Was I destined to marry Alessandro? He has some redeeming qualities, but I don't believe he truly loves me, and I don't truly love him. He loves me as his possession, his grand prize. And there's something else about him that my feelings run from, something hiding, something deep, dark, and treacherous. Something that truly scares me."

Angry fire exploded in my stomach and left me ruminating on these last words.

"A hand-fasting to Alessandro is my debt. I understand it. The promise of this marriage is what saved my father. It makes sense. But just because something makes sense doesn't mean it is right. I refused to believe the Goddess would allow me to live in a marriage out of debt. So, I cast a spell to reveal my true love, the love I should spend the rest of my days with, the person whom I'd love with intense passion." She lifted her hand and ran her fingers through my hair. "I can't explain the feeling I had as I stood in the marketplace that morning and felt the Goddess around me. I knew it'd worked. All I had to do was look up and see whom she intended for me.

"Would I see Alessandro staring back at me?" She shuddered. "I hoped not. I forced myself to look up. And there you were. My true love, my destiny. The man I'd die for a thousand times over." She got quiet. The only noise was a rustling in the brush below and the far-off call of a bird. The wind blew around us in a warm, gentle breeze.

"Katarina," I whispered as I leaned toward her, "my life was nothing before we met. It will be nothing without you. I'm a changed man. I don't fully understand how it happened, but I believe to the depths of my soul that you and I were meant to be."

I leaned forward and pressed my lips softly to hers. Her response was immediate as she crushed her body against the growing hardness of mine, her breasts were soft as they molded against my chest.

My hands followed the lines down her sides, stopping at her hips and pulling her onto my lap. Her chest heaved against my chest as she straddled me. She rubbed slowly against me, and I recognized my intense desire, my want for her. It was instinctual and raw. My body responded to her every movement. My mind wanted to know everything about her. My mouth yearned to taste her. I wanted to consume her physically, intellectually, and emotionally.

My lips traced down her neck and played along its base, leaving my tongue to trail the line of her collarbone. She let out a small gasp. My eyes found their way to her face.

Her eyes were closed, her lips parted, just barely. I pulled her closer and my mouth covered hers. Her face leaned toward mine and her lips found my mouth with a slick wetness. My fingers found the hem of her blouse and slowly began to lift it. The soft skin of her torso was hot and smooth. My hands held her sides and traveled up to just under her breasts. My thumbs rubbed over her hard nipples and every muscle in my body tensed. I became hard with desire. She moaned into my mouth and pressed her body against mine. I grew harder with each passing moment.

"Katarina!"

The voice echoed through the forest and pierced my being like a knife. Katarina's eyes shot open, terror-filled, as they turned toward the sound of the voice. She shuffled off my lap and put her finger to her lips.

"We've to go! It's Alessandro," she said in a barely audible whisper. "If he finds me with you, there's no telling what he is capable of." She stood and began backtracking to the main road.

"Wait. What if we confront Alessandro, explain that the Goddess has brought us together? Surely he couldn't deny it." I tried to make a case to defend us, but my mind was still reeling from her touch. She stopped and turned to look at me.

"You don't know him like I do. When Alessandro sets his mind on something, there's no diverting him. Even if the

Goddess herself spoke to him directly, I'm sure he'd still do what he wanted. And as a descendant of a very long and very powerful line of Strega Ilmalo who have a mixed reputation, luck doesn't bode well in our favor. Please trust me when I say that when the Strega Ilmalo feel they are wronged, they'll stop at nothing to avenge themselves. Please, Gio. There's a very thin line between being wronged and feeling as if you were wronged. And I'm not completely sure which side of the line Alessandro will come out on."

"Wait," I whispered as I held her from walking further. "Why don't we just circumvent Alessandro? We can just go to the council. We'll tell them everything we've just told each other. When they see true love has bound us together, by the Goddess herself, they couldn't possibly hand-fast you to Alessandro, not when I'm alive."

"That's what I'm afraid of." Her voice was flat. "Don't you see? The Strega Ilmalo, when necessary, will use force when their lifestyle is threatened. You won't know what's happening to you and then, before you know it, it'll all be over."

"So, there's no hope?" For the first time, I began to comprehend the severity of the situation.

"No," she said with resolve. "I've just found you. I won't be giving you up just yet. All I ask is to please don't give up on me." She threw herself into my arms.

"I've never thought I'd ever leave my people. But to be with you, I'd give up everything. You're my hope. You're my life."

"Katarina! Where are you?" The voice was closer.

She looked over her shoulder, and then back to me. "Go back to the city. Wait for me at the tavern on the east side of the marketplace. I'll be there after dark. I give you my word. Then we'll leave together. Tonight." She kissed me once more before rushing to leave. The sight of her walking away was too much for me to bear.

"Wait! Where are you going? Why can't we just leave now?" I called in a hushed tone.

She shook her head. "There are a few things I cannot leave behind. But I promise, we'll leave the city tonight, and then we can start our life together." She took another step away, hesitated, and then came back to me. "Here, take this." She placed a circular pendant in my hand. "It will bring you good thoughts."

She kissed me once more and my head swam with emotion. When she pulled away my lips were throbbing from her touch. She turned back and headed to the main road. I watched as she left and thought of nothing but the next time I'd be with her. Later that night. Soon.

I looked down at the pendant she'd placed in my palm. A bare tree reached toward the sky and branched out; its roots firmly planted in the ground. In the forefront, a perfect star, carved of silver, pointed up.

My hand closed around the pendant. It was the first time I'd ever seen such a symbol, but I knew it was a symbol of the Goddess. The pulse of life she left behind on the metal radiated against my skin. It was strong. It was beautiful.

It was real.

~

PRESENT DAY

"GIO . . ." I felt a gentle tug on my arm. Through a tear-filled haze, my eyes shot in the direction of the voice.

Claire stood there, empathy radiating from her face, as if

she'd just experienced the entirety of what I'd relived through my haunted memories.

"Gio," she said with care, "trust me, it'll be all right. Come with me. You're not the only one who's been waiting. We all have."

"What?" I choked out.

"Come inside with me, please," she pleaded. "There's much to explain and there's someone I'd like you to meet." She tugged at my arm gently again.

My mind was blank. I didn't know what to say or how to respond. I didn't know what to do. What was I supposed to do with the information Claire shared with me? One would think after existing for so long, I'd know how to handle any situation.

However, often, I found myself unprepared for most things I encountered. It was a constant reminder of how horrifyingly inadequate I was. A reminder of how I'd never been good enough. A nagging voice in the back of my head telling me I should've let her go because she would've been better off without me.

But I couldn't let myself believe that. I couldn't let those doubts permeate the surface. I refused to let myself believe those doubts over the one thing that was pure and true and good in the world—love.

I believed in love like my father believed in honor. My love for Katarina was pure. I knew her love for me was equally chaste. It was this unadulterated belief, this knowledge, that I wholeheartedly knew would lead me in the right direction.

I only hoped I wasn't blinded by it, unable to see as I gave way to Claire's tug and let myself be led past the glowing symbol, through the wooden door, and into the unknown beyond.

Nine

KATE

I arrived home earlier than I'd anticipated. Dave dropped me off, wished me luck, and made me promise to tell him all the dirty details Monday at work. As he drove away, my cell phone rang. I retrieved the device from my coat pocket and answered.

"Hey, Alex. What's up?"

"Hey, love," he began. "Nothing good, unfortunately."

Disappointment sat in my stomach. I knew that answer well enough. Either he'd gotten caught up at work or he had forgotten an appointment he'd made earlier in the week. Given the tone of his voice, I was betting on the appointment.

"What's going on, hon?" I tried to sound casual.

"I messed up, love. I told my boss that I'd take the latest environmental report over to my connection at the museum. I completely forgot until he just dropped it off on my desk about ten minutes ago. I'm sorry, but I've got to do this before I get home."

"No big deal. What time were you thinking?"

"Not long, I promise. I'll be home well before we need to

leave for the restaurant. I swear; I just have to follow up on this one thing."

"No problem. Actually, I just got home myself."

"Thanks, babe. You're the best. I'll be home soon, I promise."

The line went dead as he hung up the phone. Sliding the phone back into my coat, I walked up to the house. Once inside, I threw my purse down on the counter and went into the kitchen to grab a beer.

I sat at the counter and opened the bottle. Taking a long swig, the thick coolness slid deliciously down my throat. I waited and let the beer contribute to my afternoon buzz and thought maybe it was a good thing he was running late; I'd at least have more time to drink up the courage to put on that ridiculous outfit for him later tonight.

How easy was it for Dave to convince me sexy lingerie was definitely the way to go? Such a simple idea, yet I would've never thought of it on my own. Why could Dave always, with very little effort, talk me into doing things I'd never think of?

I spent just a few more seconds of thought on Dave and his inexplicable powers of persuasion, before hopping off the stool, and beer in hand, walking up the stairs to find a hiding place for Alex's gift for later that night.

The bag was small enough to hide just about anywhere; there was hardly any clothing in it at all. I placed it neatly in my bathroom drawer and then took it out again, deciding to try it on once more.

As I stood in the bathroom looking at my reflection in the full-length mirror, I concluded I liked what I saw. I wasn't a breathtaking beauty, in the contemporary sense, but I was satisfied with what I did have in the looks department. My grandmother had always commented on my classic beauty and in the afternoon light, it showed.

All those the curves I'd so longed to be rid of in my

twenties were a bit more welcomed by me now that I was officially in my thirties. Was this newfound self-appreciation a product of becoming more confident in myself, or the numerous cocktails I was now digesting? My guess was the latter, but I was feeling too good to care.

After one more inspection in the mirror, I carefully placed the outfit back in the drawer and started a bath. Sitting on the edge of the tub, I reached in to test the temperature. My new necklace bounced at the base of my throat. My fingers reached up and found the silver charm. I held it delicately before undoing the clasp, removing it, and placing it on the tub's ledge for safe keeping.

When the basin was full, I lit some candles and slid into the hot water. My muscles, already relaxed from the alcohol, soaked in the heat. I leaned back and closed my eyes. Steam swirled around my head, moistening my skin.

My mind wandered over the day's events. This morning seemed a world away. In my alcohol-induced state, I could appreciate that all my insecurities, all the drama that played out this morning were just byproducts of an intense overreaction. I laughed. Of course I overreacted. As little as I wanted to admit it, I tended to be an overreacting maniac. I always had.

My mind flipped through its Rolodex of memories back to all the times I'd taken things over that edge. It stopped at the worst memory of all. My wedding day. I cringed internally as I thought about how it'd almost not happened.

My body sank deeper, seeking the comfort of the hot water as my stomach twisted. I remembered the moment like it was yesterday.

~

SAN FRANCISCO, *9 years ago*

. . .

I STOOD ALONE in the dressing room, staring at myself in the gilded full-length mirror. My feet peeked out from underneath the hem of my dress; a tiny golden ring glinted from my middle toe. My wedding dress, a vintage piece with bohemian influences found in the lacework, flowed loosely to the floor. A wreath of baby's breath was woven through my long, dark hair.

I looked into the mirror, stared into the reflection of my eyes, and asked myself why I was doing this. My insides froze in terror. This wasn't a case of cold feet . . . it couldn't be. I'd never felt such an intense feeling of apprehension in my life.

A secret inner voice whispered in my mind. *Get out of here! Run! This isn't what it seems! He isn't who he says!*

Where did that come from? I shook my head as my voice of reason argued. *What? I can't run. We're getting married.*

The voice was insistent. *Please. This isn't what it seems. Something's wrong.* My reflective eyes pleaded with me as I stood there, a human statue.

My nostrils flared and my brow furrowed as my voice of reason grew impatient with its antagonist. *No. Stop this. Nothing's wrong. Don't do this.*

Do what?

You know that second-guessing thing you always do to talk yourself out of doing what you should do. It's so classic. My voice of reason did have a point. Since I'd met Alex, my second-guessing ratio had hit an all-time high.

The secret voice persisted. *Are you listening to yourself? Something you should do? Are you seriously going to marry him because you think you should? Really?*

Anger began to rise. *Stop it, dammit! You know very well why I'm marrying him.* The voice of reason became short with ire as the secret voice refused to let this go.

No, I don't. Please refresh my memory. Mock innocence played on the secret voice.

I'm marrying him because he is the most wonderful man I've ever met . . . and he loves me. Why did my voice of reason sound unsure just then?

That may be true, but you didn't answer my question. Are you marrying him because you want to or because you think you should?

I'm marrying him because I want to, maybe, I think. Shit! What am I doing? I've got to get out of here! The voice of reason folded into panic.

I frantically glanced around the room for a method of escape. A large open window leading to the back of the building beckoned me. I could easily catch a cab and run far, far, far away. My body made a movement toward the window just as there was a knock on the door.

"Kate? You ready? Can I come in?" Celia, one of Alex's closest friends, inquired from just outside the room.

"Um, yeah, Celia. I'm just about ready."

Damn it, damn it, damn it! What the hell was I supposed to do? Nothing. It was too late. My internal dialogue silenced.

Celia entered the room. "Oh. My. God." She let out in three distinct breaths as she closed the door behind her. "You look absolutely stunning, Kate. So beautiful."

I smiled at her, wondering if she could tell simply by looking at me that I was, just half-seconds prior, planning my escape. Immediately overcome with guilt, I lowered my gaze.

She approached me and adjusted the wreath in my hair, her fingers combing their way through the long strands and twirling them at the end.

A wave of shame rushed over me. My voice of reason spoke up again. *How could you even think of bolting? Leaving Alex? He'd be heartbroken. Of course you want to marry him. He's the best thing that's ever happened to you . . . ever. Now, stop all this nonsense and get out there. Alex is waiting for you. You will not blow this.* I wasn't sure if I was just telling myself this or if I really meant it.

Somehow, I swallowed, though my throat was dry, and resolved to not let myself stand in the way of something that made so much sense. Of course I'd marry Alex. He was everything I wasn't. He was my better half, right?

I turned to face Celia. She handed me a small bouquet of wildflowers from a side table and led me to the small outdoor garden where Alex stood waiting. He was heart-stopping handsome.

~

Present Day

THINKING BACK TO THAT MOMENT, I remembered every sound, every smell, every detail of what was going through my mind before I walked down that aisle. My stomach involuntarily lurched as my memories brought to light my less-admirable qualities.

The steam from the bath swirled around my head. It was still hot enough to leave moisture on my brow. I opened one eye and peeked out the window. The light from outside told me I could spend a few more minutes in the tub before I had to start getting ready.

A thin ray of sun hit a glint of silver that shone from the ledge of the tub. I picked up the necklace I'd placed there to examine it once more. Such an interesting piece. I played with the charm for a moment before returning it to the ledge.

As I closed my eyes, I sunk down further until my shoulders were submerged in warmth. I let relaxation take over me and let my thoughts drift off.

The sound of cars driving down the road couldn't cover the song of a bird in the distance. And then, before awareness knew where I was going, I was dreaming. *My* dream. Only this time, I wasn't running to find someone.

Someone was chasing me.

"Help!" I screamed. "Please help me!"

Sweat would've been collecting on my forehead had I not been running at full speed, the wind drying it as fast as it formed. I had the distinct feeling that whoever was chasing me was easily gaining ground.

Although my feet were bare, they knew every part of this forest. My steps confidently took me closer to where I needed to be. I felt my pursuer encroaching, though his footfalls were silent, and I knew it would be only a few more strides before he caught me.

I jumped onto the trunk of a fallen tree and heaved my body over it, scraping my arms as I moved. Everything was a blur of green and brown around me. God, would this ever end?

I ran faster through the brush. I was getting closer to where I needed to be. Soon I'd be safe. If I could just make it a little bit further. If I could run just run a tiny bit faster.

My hair hung loose and free. It flew behind me as I ran with greater intensity, pushing myself to take longer and longer strides as I pressed myself deeper and deeper into the forest.

I heard his steps behind me. They sounded twice as fast as mine and seemed to cover double the distance per stride. My heart flew into a panic as I tried, in vain, to pull ahead.

"Help! Please!" I screamed, knowing I was alone. There was no one to help me. Fear closed in around me as I heard his laugh rise over my futile calls for help.

I knew it was too late, but I pushed on still, hoping for a

miracle. I was still hoping when his presence bore down on me.

I shrieked in terror as his large hands closed in around my shoulders and jerked me effortlessly to a complete stop. His hot breath coated the back of my neck. Chills traveled over my skin.

"You thought you could leave, did you?" His voice was an even mix of hatred and rage.

"Please, let me go." I whispered.

"Did you honestly believe I would forget everything? Did you think I'd just let you go as if nothing had happened?"

"Please, please . . . just let me go," I begged.

He pulled me toward him, my back against his chest. I tried to keep the tears from forming, but it was far too late as they slid down my cheeks in thick trails.

"Listen to me, now. Hear my words. I will never let you go. Never."

He quickly twisted me around to face him and pressed his mouth violently against mine. His lips crushed against my lips with the burning of his need, leaving me queasy. He forced his tongue into my mouth. I bit down as hard as I could.

"Stupid bitch!" My faceless assailer screamed as he threw me roughly to the forest floor. "You'll pay for that!"

He loomed over me, shadows blocking his face, before he collected the blood in his mouth and spit it in my direction. I shielded myself with my hands and prepared myself for the attack I knew was imminent.

I brought my legs up to my chest, ready to kick them out at the first sign of assault. I tried to remember anything that would tip the scales in my favor, anything that might give me an edge over my assailant, but nothing came. I wasn't a fighter. The only thing in my corner was the instinct for survival, but even that seemed to prove too little, too late, when it came to physically protecting myself from danger.

His body hovered over mine and held its position, invading my space with his thick presence.

"Don't be scared, little one." His voice vibrated against my skin. His rancid breath was sticky and grimy on my face.

The need to escape was overwhelming. His voice sickened my pores with poison, and I knew if I wanted to live, I had to try and fight.

Any thought of escape was useless. There was no way I could fight him off physically. Even if I happened to land a few good hits, I wouldn't be able to hold him off for long. He was too massive. His body was twice the size of mine, and it held enough contempt for me to fill an entire universe.

This was the end. I could feel it, and surprisingly, I resigned to it. If death were to be my next journey, then I'd no longer fight it. I'd welcome it. I let my legs relax as I uncoiled my body. My breathing, still hurried, was more out of anticipation now, rather than fear.

"What? No more fight left in you?" He sounded disappointed at my reaction.

"Just do what it is you came for and get it over with." My voice was flat.

"You'd like that, wouldn't you?" He was thoughtful, reflective in his detestation. "However, I've got other plans."

Still unable to see his face clearly, my attacker put a small burlap sack over my head and tied it around my neck. The rope was just tight enough to cause discomfort, but not so tight as to completely restrict my breathing. He roughly flipped me over and tied my hands behind my back. Then, with great force, he pulled me to my feet and dragged me in the direction he meant for me to follow.

Tears stung my eyelids and silently spilled over onto my cheeks. In the distance someone called my name.

"Kate! Kate! Where are you?"

I thought it was a delusion until my kidnapper stiffened,

his hands tightening around my arm. The voice was real. My miracle. Though I didn't recognize the voice, it was familiar. Even in the distance, I felt my soul pull toward its sound.

And then, something changed. The voice called my name again, but it wasn't the voice I hoped for. It was different, closer. Panicked? It called my name.

"Kate, wake up. Kate! Wake up . . . please!"

I awoke with a start; not entirely sure my dream had ended. For an instant, I looked into the eyes of my kidnapper. And then, I refocused. A moment more passed before I realized Alex was kneeling at the side of the tub, hands on my shoulders, his eyes intently on my face.

"Alex?"

His chest released a long breath. "Jesus Christ, Kate, who else would it be? Are you okay?" His eyes swirled in a colorful storm.

"I'm . . . fine, I think. A little confused, but fine. Why?" I watched carefully as worry slowly transformed into something a little closer to anger. My chest tightened. I'd seen that look before. He took a deep breath before speaking.

"Would you please tell me what in the hell you were thinking, falling asleep in the bathtub?" His voice was too controlled, scary. Familiar.

Oh, God, please don't let this happen, not tonight.

"Um . . . I guess I just dozed off. You know, maybe a little too relaxed." I didn't mention I'd had a few drinks to help that process along.

"Kate"—his eyes were looking through me as if pulling my thoughts straight out of my head— "how much have you been drinking today?"

My hackles rose. "What? What kind of question is that?" Anger snapped in me immediately, igniting my defenses. Who in the hell did he think he was?

"Just answer the question." He looked at me with emotionless eyes, empty, cold, vacant.

"Not that it makes a difference, but I had a drink with lunch," I lied with perfect ease. I noticed the beer I'd left sitting on the bathroom counter in his left hand and quickly added, "And one beer when I got home."

His jaw clenched. "What were you thinking, taking a hot bath after drinking? Do you know how dangerous that is?"

"I'm fine. You're acting as if I'm some raging alcoholic who is one drink away from an intervention." Perhaps he did have a point, but I wasn't ready to admit it. "I just dozed off for a minute."

"For a minute! You could have drowned! Did you think of that? You could have drowned! And then what? What about me?" His voice walked the line between anger and hysteria.

"I'm sorry. I didn't think that—"

"That's right, you didn't think! You never think about anyone other than yourself! You never have. You never will." He pulled me up by my wrist half out of the tub so I was kneeling facing him, my naked body steaming from the water.

"Alex, you're hurting my wrist." I looked into his eyes. He was almost unrecognizable through his anger.

Oh, God, not tonight. Please not tonight.

"You'll never think of anyone other than yourself, will you?" His accusations cut through me like a knife.

I cringed. Though my actions this afternoon were not the most responsible, I hardly deserved his verbal attack. He squeezed my wrist harder.

"Alex. Stop." I tried to pull my hand away from him, but he held it fast. "You're hurting me."

Tears collected in the corners of my eyes as reason seemed to flicker in his and he quickly released my wrist.

"I'm so sorry, Katie." His eyes fell to the floor. His breathing was heavy, and he looked tired.

I was filled with guilt. How could I be so careless? He was obviously concerned about my safety. Though he wasn't in the right to grab me the way he did, I pushed it aside to deal with later. Right now, I had to fix the mess I'd made, again.

I reached out and lifted his chin. "Alex?" He refused to meet my gaze. "I'm so sorry. I didn't mean to cause you any worry. Please forgive me," I said, bringing my hands to the sides of his face and pulling him gently toward me and forcing him to look at me.

When our lips were barely touching, I felt his hands wrap around my bare torso and pull my body close to his. We kissed, him outside the bathtub, me in it. His hands ran down my back, over my backside, and back up again, exploring every rounded edge of my body. I shivered, and it had nothing to do with being out of the tub.

When the last fringe of shivers tingled away, I pulled back and forced our eyes to meet.

"I'm sorry. I hope I haven't spoiled the night."

He let out a small laugh. "What am I going to do with you? I can't stay angry with you. You're all I ever wanted."

I wasn't entirely happy with his non-acceptance of my apology, but he did seem to be in a better mood, so I forced my discontent aside and concentrated on ways in which I could salvage the night.

I smiled and attempted to stand. "Well, should I get dressed? After all, we have dinner reservations, do we not?"

Alex placed his hands around my waist and held firm. "I don't think that's entirely necessary. Not yet anyway."

My cheeks grew hot as I saw him look me up and down. I was suddenly very aware of my nakedness. His mouth curled up around the edges as a thoughtful expression crossed his face.

"Now correct me if I'm mistaken, but I do believe we have some unfinished business from this morning to address." His voice was throaty. It held an edge that made something low in my body grow tight.

My cheeks burst into flames as I remembered the unfinished business he was referring to.

He placed both his hands on my shoulders and traced the outline of my body, around my breasts, down my waist, stopping again at my hips. My breathing picked up and my heart beat frantically in my chest in response to his touch.

As if guided by an invisible force, I leaned in closing the space between us. He bent his head and brushed his lips against mine, our noses rubbing each other. My insides boiled as I struggled to simultaneously make this moment last forever while moving past it to the next.

Alex didn't make me wait much longer. He found my hands and led them to his shirt buttons, where they quickly took to their duty with unparalleled skills, manipulating each button through its buttonhole in fractions of seconds. At least I got that right.

It only took moments before he was kneeling before me, his chiseled torso exposed between the two sides of his shirt.

My lips found his chest and kissed the bronze skin, my tongue finding the taut part around his nipple and circling it with the tip. His breath caught and he moaned softly as my teeth gently bit the hard flesh that stuck out from his chest. The spot between my legs began to throb and I squeezed my thighs together to alleviate the pressure building.

He quickly unfastened his pants and undressed. He crawled into the tub and, leaning me back, positioned himself on top of me, our lips finding each other again and crushing each other with desire, the lukewarm bathwater splashing around us. Our bodies pressed together, his hard musculature crushing my soft roundness. I marveled at the stark contrasts of our bodies.

He was perfection. His body could've been sculpted from

stone, every muscle proportioned. It often seemed unreal. Mine seemed to be rolled out of Play-Doh, soft and pliable, but it never seemed to matter to him. I was the object he sought after.

His lips played along my neckline while his hands held my wrists firmly. I wasn't much into restraint, indifferent at best, but it was something Alex enjoyed. Once, when I'd asked him about it, he replied it was a turn-on to physically possess me in such a captive way, that he wanted to hold me tight so I wouldn't run away. When I'd asked him where I'd possibly want to run to, his face darkened, and his voice dropped.

'Only you would know that, Katie.'

I'd dropped the subject. It appeared to bother him something fierce and it made me extremely uncomfortable. However, since bondage was neither a turn-on nor a turn-off for me, I continued to occasionally allow him to mildly restrain me during lovemaking. Although if he'd insisted, I would've let him chain me to a tree if that's what he'd wanted. I simply couldn't refuse him.

Now, as his hands squeezed tighter around my wrists, he brought them above my head. I sank deeper into the tub but did not submerge. My breasts hovered just at the water's surface.

I bent my knees and opened for him. He found his way between my legs and paused as he lingered at my entrance.

"Tell me you want me."

My breath caught. "You know I do."

His eyes flashed. "Tell me."

My center pulsed for him. I couldn't wait any longer. I had to have him inside me. "I want you, Alex. My God, I want you. Please."

With one thrust, he filled me with himself. I sucked in my breath as he entered me over and over again with an intensity that'd always touched me deep within my core.

My body clenched. It built up to meet him, rising and rising, squeezing him tight, slowly and steadily edging closer with each movement until I could no longer hold on to my control and felt myself spilling out, pulsing and contracting around his length, gripping him closer and closer with my legs, which I'd wrapped around his torso, though not nearly close enough.

He came soon after, a massive release inside me, his body thrusting with the intensity of each spasm, on and on and on, and then slowly, almost deliberately, he relaxed.

He waited until he became soft inside me and remained there until he lusciously slid out and lay on top of me, both of us breathless and satisfied.

It was quick and dirty and just what I needed. My arms wrapped around his body, my fingertips stroked his back. I could never quite grasp how amazing he could make me feel sexually. It was as if his presence intoxicated me to the point in which I didn't even have a choice in the matter; I would enjoy myself.

"Alex?" My voice was lazy.

"Hmmm." He did not raise his head from my chest.

"Do you still want to go out tonight or are you content to just stay at home?"

"Oh, no, you don't," he said, raising his head to look at me, "don't think you're getting out of it. We're going out tonight. In fact, we'd better get dressed if we're going to make our reservations."

He stood and stepped out of the tub. I watched him dry his body with a towel. If there was a more perfect male specimen on Earth, I'd never seen it. I had to check my hormones as I watched the water droplets glistening on his skin.

No dice. I slowly climbed out of the tub and stood behind him, my arms wrapping around his chest. As I pressed my cheek against his wet back, my nipples grazed his skin. "Are you sure you want to go out tonight?"

He grabbed my hands and pried them apart, turning around to face me. "You, my love, are too easily distracted."

"You say that as if it's a bad thing." My hands made their way down past his waist. He grabbed them as they pulled on his towel and stopped them from reaching their ultimate destination.

"No, not a bad thing, but we do occasionally need to leave the house. What would the neighbors think?" He planted a gentle kiss on my lips.

"Fine, you win, but just for the record, I vote we stay in." I pulled away in defeat.

I watched him leave the bathroom. Taking a towel from the rack I dried myself off in long, even strokes. As the glow of sex began to fade, like a spell broken, my thoughts drifted back to the dream.

Though it was different in many ways, it was the same dream, I was sure of it. I found it odd that despite the terror I felt being chased and caught, it seemed inconsequential to the fact that *he* was looking for me. A warm bubble filled my chest.

I didn't know who he was, but I'd heard his voice. He'd called my name. He was looking for me. And that small, minute detail was what made all the difference in the world.

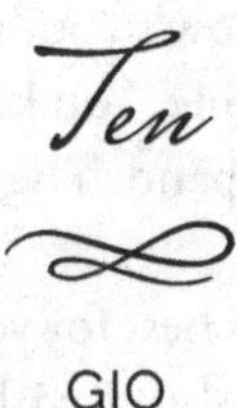

Ten

GIO

I followed Claire into the bar. The smell of stale beer and mold permeated from every corner. The woman behind the counter looked up at us as we walked in, her smile revealed a missing tooth.

The place was relatively empty; not exactly the kind of establishment that would draw a big out-of-town crowd, just the locals, and only a select few at that. A gentleman sat at the bar drinking from a tumbler, his back to us, his body turned in the direction of a television screen on the opposite wall.

"Claire, my girl," he said in a loud, welcoming voice, "it's good to see you poppin' in. It's been a while." He didn't turn around, but I could tell he took a sip from his glass. "I see you've brought company. Who's your friend?"

I narrowed my eyes. How could he tell I was here; he hadn't even turned around. As if answering my silent thought, he spun from the television to look at Claire. I jumped when I saw his face. He looked a few years older than Claire, save for one important feature. Both eyes had been gouged out, leaving rough scars in their place. Claire shot me a glance and swallowed.

"Patrick, it's good to see you too. How've you been?" Claire said as she approached the man and placed a hand on his shoulder. He brought his hand up to hers and held it for a minute.

"It's been too long. How's your mother?"

Claire sighed. "She's fine. You know how she is, always on my case to study . . . to expand. The same old thing. It's rather tiring, you know?"

"She just wants what's best for you, that's all."

"That's what she says, but I wish she'd just let me find my own path, one that she doesn't push me down in a stroller." There was sarcastic defiance in her voice. "But enough about me, how are you?"

"Better now, after seeing you." A strange comment for a man with no eyes. I remained silent, still unable to find words.

"It's been boring around here. You really need to come by more often; I mean it's not like you're in another country or anything." After a minute he furrowed his brow, and then smiled as he turned his head toward me. "However, I have a very strong feeling things are going to get really interesting, really quick. Wouldn't you agree, Gio?"

How did he know my name? We hadn't been introduced yet. I shot a glance at Claire.

"Patrick, stop showing off." She rolled her eyes.

"What?" Patrick said innocently. "I was just including him in the conversation."

"Well, we aren't here for conversation. Not today. We're actually here on business." Claire's voice became tense.

"Does your grandmother know you're here? Is she expecting you?"

"No, it was kind of a last-minute thing. Is she around?"

"Yeah, she's in the back. Go on ahead," he replied.

Claire started walking and I followed.

"Oh, and Claire"—Patrick turned in his chair— "I like

your hair. It's really pink, but pretty. Has your grandmother seen it?"

"I'm not sure. I don't think so. I'm sure I'll find out in just a minute."

"Yeah, well, good luck with that."

We walked past the end of the bar toward the back room. Claire waved casually at him.

"See you later, Patrick."

"See ya, Claire. Don't be such a stranger, okay? Not all of us want to turn you into your grandmother. Some of us just like you for you." He smiled and I had a feeling Patrick hoped Claire would someday be a little more than just a friend.

Claire smiled at Patrick, and he seemed to respond to it as if he had two working eyes with twenty-twenty vision. She turned and again headed to the back room.

"Claire," I said in a low voice as I continued to follow her lead, "would you please explain how your friend over there one, knew my name, and two, appeared to see everything even though his eyes were cut out."

"Oh, Patrick? He's . . . special, I suppose. Not too many people like him around, I guess."

"And . . ." I pressed.

"Oh, and I promise I'll explain everything. But I think it'll go better if you meet my grandmother first. She can tell you more than I can. She's one of our most powerful. The one who protects this space we stand in now."

Protected? As odd as it was, I did feel protected. I let that set in a moment. Even in this dive of a bar, impossibly old and run-down, I knew that when I was in here, I didn't need to look over my shoulder.

"But how?" I asked, unable to stop myself. I wasn't sure which question I was addressing, there were so many, now. I took a deep breath and said, "I'm sorry. I can wait."

"Thank you. I promise it won't be long."

We walked past a pool table and up to a narrow door. Claire knocked and waited for a response. Silence. Just when I thought she'd knock again, she turned to me and smiled.

"Let's go."

She walked through the door down a narrow hallway and into another small area resembling a waiting room at a doctor's office, though less sterile and with a homier vibe. A single door was in the middle of the wall opposite where we'd just entered.

The room was bright, a welcome contrast to the bar outside. The walls were a warm golden hue that gave the impression of a marvelous sunset. A couch and a few chairs furnished the space in addition to a sturdy looking table, and a few floor lamps. Claire walked over to one of the big leather chairs and flopped down in it. She threw her legs over one of the arms looking completely relaxed.

I carefully chose a chair that allowed me to see both the door we'd come from and the one I expected we'd be entering soon. Since it was impossible for me to let my guard down, the best I could do was put myself in the most advantageous position possible.

Claire and I sat in silence, though I had a hundred questions and she, apparently, had the answers. It wasn't long before the door in the middle of the wall opened and an older, attractive woman walked into the room.

"Claire, what a surprise." The woman walked toward Claire with open arms. Both Claire and I stood as she approached.

"Hello, grandmother," she said timidly.

The older woman ran her hands through Claire's hair, inspecting her streaks of pink. "This is . . . nice," she said in a strained voice. "To what do I owe this visit?"

"We need to talk." Claire pulled away gathering her resolve.

"I take it this is business, not pleasure."

"Yes, and of the utmost importance. I'd like you to meet someone." She motioned in my direction and for the first time, the older woman looked at me.

Her eyes widened as she looked around my body in the same way Claire had done a couple times since our first meeting. Irritated, I clenched my teeth. What were they looking at?

"Oh, my," the woman said as she looked at me, and then to Claire, her eyes questioning.

"Grandmother, this is Gio. Gio, this is my grandmother, Rose."

I nodded. "It's nice to meet you, Rose." I tentatively moved toward the woman, my hand out in an offering.

She stood there, hands at her side, not accepting my gesture.

"It's all right. He's a friend," Claire explained in a cautious tone.

I dropped my hand to my side.

"In all my years, I never thought I'd see the day . . ." Rose's voice trailed off.

"I hate to be rude," I interrupted, my patience all worn out, "but would someone please explain what in the hell is going on?" The extended silence that followed was not comforting.

"Claire, I've done everything you've asked. Please." How I wished I'd spoken to Willem.

The two women continued to ignore me.

"Grandmother?" Claire's voice was quiet. "What do you think? Can we provide him protection?"

"What kind of question is that? Of course we will. That's our job . . . the reason why we exist. If you'd paid a little more attention to your mother and me, you would've known that already." She chided, and then turned to me.

"Gio, please excuse my granddaughter, she's not very practiced in our craft." She shot a reproachful look at Claire. Claire rolled her eyes.

"Now, let's make ourselves comfortable, shall we? Claire was right about one thing. There's much to discuss. I imagine you must have quite a few questions." Rose sat on the big couch across from me. She clasped her hands together and placed them in her lap.

The time for pleasantries was over. "Who are you?" I demanded hitting the heart of the matter with my first question.

Rose smiled. "We"—nodding toward Claire— "are the descendants of a long line of guardians placed here on earth. We're most frequently called Watchers. We've been granted the responsibility of tending the lost ones as they pass through our earthly domain."

"I've been around a long time, and I've never heard of your kind."

"No, you wouldn't have." She shook her head. "Our job is undercover, more or less—to live here, to protect our domain and the people within, and to do this without any notice."

"Are you human?" I asked, still not quite sure about the explanation given. I made another mental note to call Willem as soon as I was back in the apartment.

"Oh, very much so. We are born, we live, we die. The cycle of life is very present in our existence. The duty of our people is passed down generation to generation, for centuries, dating all the way back to ancient civilizations."

"So, you're witches."

"I prefer the term Pagan. We worship the Goddess as well as other deities. We cast, we chant, we foresee, and we can make things happen, but we are also so much more."

"Our people have been given the grave duty to look after those in trouble, to protect them, to guide them, but most importantly it is our responsibility to keep our domain free of the darkness that follows the evil arts."

"A responsibility we never asked for." Claire suddenly jumped into the conversation; her tone suggested the arrangement was iniquitous.

"True," Rose said shooting her granddaughter a sharp look, "but a duty we humbly accept. It's who we are, Claire. You cannot run away from that. The sooner you accept it, the sooner your life will fall into its place." Rose's eyes glowed with a white-hot intensity.

Even though it was silent, the air between the two women seemed to carry entire conversations on its waves. Rose's eyes seemed to bring the unspoken discourse to a conclusion.

When Rose spoke again, it was in a gentler tone. "Tell me, why did you bring Gio here? You could've taken him anywhere. You could've ignored him. But you brought him here, to me. Why?"

Claire looked down at her shoes. "I . . . I didn't know what else to do." Her words were quiet.

"Is that all? You brought him here because there were no other options?"

"No." Claire's voice was barely audible. As she raised her head I noticed her eyes were glassy from the tears welling up in them. She looked so young. My heart ached as I saw her struggle with inner conflict.

"No, that's not all," she continued, her voice more confident. "I saw his aura. I see it now; so bright and pure and brimming with love, true love . . . but part of it's missing, and I know that he's looking for the one who will fill it. But I also see it lined with the mark of the dark ones." Her voice lowered. "The same darkness that killed my father. And I thought . . . I thought maybe we could help him find his way."

"Very good," Rose said approvingly.

Rose turned her attention to me. "So, you see, we are

witches, more or less, but with greater responsibility. We don't have the luxury of looking solely after our own. We must tend to the lost souls as well."

I chose my next words carefully. "And what exactly does it mean to tend to lost souls?"

"A lost soul is one who has lost his or her way. One who's been intentionally misguided or led astray or has for one reason or another made a wrong choice and is crying out for help. One who is condemned to wander until some sort of condition is met."

"What makes you think I've been condemned?" My focus was now entirely on Rose.

"The answer is in your aura." Rose looked at Claire, and then back to me. "Tell me, have you ever felt that people are sometimes looking around you, not necessarily at you?"

"Yes, though I have a feeling you knew that," I said shooting an accusing glare at both women. A chill ran up my spine.

"An aura tells a lot about a person. It's the energy of the soul. Watchers look to a person's aura for the first sign of need. When a soul is in need, it will get extraordinarily bright—as if it were trying to send out some type of signal. The brighter the aura, the more intense the need."

"And my aura's bright?"

"Let's just say your aura could light up a runway." Claire piped in.

I furrowed my brow. "How come no one's mentioned this before? I've lived for over four hundred years, and it's never come up." My voice grew louder out of frustration. How could so many centuries pass without any mention of this apparent beacon I always carried with me?

Had I been traveling this road for centuries a marked man? Had I done this never knowing that I could've been sending signals to the very person I was trying to defeat, serving as a warning for Alessandro, and condemning Katarina to death repeatedly?

My head spun. Everything I thought I'd known was convoluted with this new information that I struggled to comprehend. Where was Willem when I needed him? I knew nothing of this Watcher world. My only true encounter with witches was over four centuries ago, the night Alessandro murdered my love. Before I could fall into the memories of my wretched past, Rose's voice brought me back to the present.

"I know all this must be confusing but let me try to help you understand." She leaned forward on the couch, her expression soft, maternal.

I took a deep breath and nodded in agreement as I let my anger subside. For the moment, I was safe. I resigned myself to listening. Besides, I still had questions that needed answers, and I wasn't leaving until I had them.

"First, let me assure you that you're not, and have never been, walking around with a big sign around your neck revealing what you are. That your aura shines bright for me is true. But I'm a Watcher. Only those like us can see what you are. It's what makes us what we are."

"And what am I?" The words came out before I knew they were there. I wasn't even sure I wanted to know the answer.

"You're an agent of the Goddess. She's using you as an example."

A sour laugh rumbled in my chest. "That's all? Just some tool to be used, and then discarded?" My anger was rising.

"Gio, please be patient," Claire said. I'd almost forgotten she was in the same room; I'd been so focused on Rose.

Claire stood, walked over to me, and held out her hand. I instinctively took it. The warmth between our hands built and calmness flowed out of her palm into mine. It wrapped itself around my bones and crawled up toward my chest. I pulled my hand back with a start.

"What was that?"

Claire scrunched up her nose in confusion. "I think that's what you called from me. I can only give you what you ask for—what you need in the moment."

"Are you saying that you felt my anxiety and, in response, your magick created a sort of calming sensation to help me relax like some sort of magical Xanax?"

"Exactly," Claire responded. "You—"

"Claire, not yet. Sit down, please. There's still much for Gio to know," Rose interrupted with the authority only the leader of a powerful group or a grandmother could use effectively. Claire obediently complied.

Rose inhaled deeply and continued, "The Goddess uses us as she sees fit. Your aura tells me of a great love, a love so powerful it could only reflect the Goddess herself. It's not common for humans to possess such love. Yet here you sit before me, radiating it from every inch of your being. So powerful, yet incomplete. Am I right?"

I studied the floor unable to make eye contact. "I had a love . . . long ago." The words were difficult to say.

"Tell us your story."

My chest tightened as my lungs struggled with each breath. I looked up at Rose with tired eyes, and then over to Claire. In Claire's face, I found the strength I needed to continue.

"I haven't spoken of the actual night in four hundred years, but its memory is as clear as if it happened yesterday." I had the feeling this moment was one I'd been waiting for a while. The two women sat silently, waiting for me to continue.

I took a long, deep breath.

"The day I met Katarina, I knew my life was changed. I felt it in the innermost part of my heart. I still feel it today. Her existence moved me from the moment I felt her presence. I knew from the second my eyes fell on her I'd be with her until the day I died, or life would be meaningless. I don't know how I did; I just did. And I'm not sure what it was, but she felt it too. I knew it in my bones. She believed I was sent to her as a sign from the Goddess to prove true love existed, that it wasn't imagined out of the minds of storytellers. We were two souls brought together to form one creature of pure love." I paused.

"We began a secret courtship. Although, at the time, I had no idea of the risk accompanying it. When she revealed she was to be married to another, not out of love, but of obligation, we planned to run away. I didn't know much about the Strega Ilmalo or their powers, but I didn't think they would step in the path of the Goddess. Katarina knew different. She told me if we had any chance at a life together, we'd have to run, that we could seek refuge in another group she knew of, the Strega Onesto. She said they'd protect us until we were safely away.

"That night, the night of our escape, I waited where Katarina said she'd meet me. When an hour had passed and she hadn't arrived, I knew something was wrong. I left and went to the edge of the forest, where we often met.

"I heard two voices in the darkness. One was Katarina. The other was Alessandro, the man she was to marry. They were arguing. I ran."

Guilt overwhelmed me, swelling into my throat and threatening to choke me. I looked at Rose. She waited, uncomplaining of the time it took me to collect myself. When the swelling subsided, I swallowed and began again. My voice grew quiet as the memories of that night sharpened.

~

Rome, 1602

"Did you think you could just leave without a proper goodbye?"

"Alessandro, don't. Let me go, please. It was never meant to be. Don't you want to be with someone who loves you?"

I approached the clearing where I saw Alessandro holding Katarina by the arm.

"Let her go," I demanded.

Alessandro looked at me and smiled. "Is this your precious love? The one you were willing to give everything up for?"

"Let her go." I said louder, as I took a step forward.

Alessandro took out a knife and held it to Katarina's throat. "Not so fast. One more step and I'll slit her throat."

Looking into his eyes, I recognized that he'd actually do it. He'd do it and enjoy it. *Enjoy it.* I froze, my heart dropping down into my stomach. Katarina stood there, helpless, terrified, apologizing to me with her eyes.

"Let her go. Fight me instead. This isn't her fault. It's mine. I was the one who convinced her to leave with me." My voice betrayed. The waver in my tone gave him knowledge of the power he held by keeping that blade to her throat.

"Why?" he asked. "Why should I give you the one thing I've ever loved? The one thing I've ever wanted that was good in my life." His voice was filled with poison. Time was running out. I'd have to act quickly if I was going to save her.

MY VOICE CRACKED and I stopped as the tears came. I let them come. It'd been too long since I'd cried, too long since I'd let myself release the torment that'd been building up inside me for years. I placed my head in my hands and began sobbing, releasing all control.

"But you couldn't save her, could you?" Rose said.

I shook my head as I continued to weep, still so deeply pained after over four centuries. I could hold it no longer. The dam had finally broken.

"He . . ." I uttered between sobs. "He saw what I was thinking, I don't know how, but he knew what I was going to do. He knew I could overpower him. He knew that if I got my hands on him, I'd kill him. He knew. And he did the only thing that would stop me from doing anything.

"His lips . . . twisted into a smile and he looked right into my eyes . . ." My voice trailed off as I closed my eyes and drifted into my thoughts.

"Then what happened?" Rose asked, bringing me back into the room.

"Then"—I could barely speak— "he grabbed a fistful of her hair. He . . . he pulled her head back and slit her throat." I pressed my fingers against my eyelids. "I watched as the blood spilled from her neck. He threw her body toward me, and I fell to the ground with her in my arms. I felt the last beatings of her heart grow fainter before her breathing stopped and the light in her eyes faded."

I sat quiet as the memory haunted me.

Swallowing hard, I continued, "I became crazed in my grief. I screamed for him to take my life as well, to finish what he started. But he didn't move. He just stood there wiping her blood off his hands, staring at me through cold, red eyes. My grief was so strong, images of how I'd take my own life, to be with her, shot through my head.

"And then I heard his voice, a snakebite in my ears, answer my thoughts. He said, '*Why should you get to be with her in the afterlife while I've been left with nothing? That doesn't seem quite fair now, does it?*'

"He laughed and told me I couldn't even begin to imagine what suffering was, but that he'd help me truly understand." I paused and wiped the tears from my eyes. "He cursed me that night. A curse that granted me the opposite of what I'd just wished for.

"It was a torture beyond anything I could've ever dreamed

—eternal life. With Katarina gone, my life had ended. Now Alessandro assured me it would never end. I couldn't imagine it to be true. Impossible for me to die? It didn't make any sense. But with every deathly blow I gave myself that night, to no avail, I became more and more convinced he'd truly cursed me. There was nothing left for me to do but accept I was doomed to this meaningless existence.

"Then, just as I'd conceded, the Strega Onesto found me. They brought me to their encampment. Their magick was pure and strong, and when used as a collective, they were able to alter Alessandro's curse. They couldn't take it away entirely, but they were able to twist it just enough so that I'd only remain on this earth until I found Katarina again.

"The Onesta told me of an old magick that could be used to call Katarina's soul back down to earth and be reincarnated until I could find her and bring her back to me. She'd be returned over and over again until our souls were joined once more."

I paused and took a few deep breaths before I continued.

"Somehow, Alessandro found out what the Strega Onesto had done and became incensed. He cast the same spell of eternal life on himself and vowed that while he was alive, Katarina and I would never be together.

"To this day, he's been successful. Over the course of more than four hundred years, I've battled with Alessandro to free Katarina. And for those same interminable centuries, I've watched him kill her eleven more times." I closed my eyes and rubbed my temples with my hands.

"Because of the Onesta, I remain hopeful. I'll never give up. Each time she's reincarnated, I get a little closer than the last time. Each lifetime, Alessandro's grip on her becomes less and less. I know it does. I feel it. I only hope this time, in this life, that I can save her. That we'll finally be joined and become one once more."

My thoughts grew excited at the possibility, but swiftly became somber as I remembered the adversity that lay ahead.

"Throughout time, there've been some others who have tried to interfere, witches who are frightened of me, frightened of the curse. They've tried to stop me with their magick and trap me in a perpetual hell." I laughed. "As if they knew what hell was." My voice turned bitter from fatigue.

"Then there's Alessandro, of course, who has done everything in his power, quite effectively, I might add, just to prevent Katarina and me from being together. His hatred grows with each incarnation. With this hatred, his power appears to become darker and more malign, though I don't know how it's possible. Sometimes I fear I'll never be able to reach Katarina as long as Alessandro is here to interfere."

I stopped as my story ended and the hard truth of what I'd just said settled into the room.

"Thank you for trusting us with your story," Rose said after a moment. "Since you've entrusted us with a very sacred part of your being, I will now answer any questions you may have."

It took me a moment to switch gears, but the questions I'd had before I began my tale came rising to the forefront of my consciousness. Glad to leave my memories behind, I sat up in the chair. "Before, you said my aura had told you of my struggle, but it didn't tell you my story. What does that mean?"

Her voice was calm. "From your aura, I can get a general feeling of what has happened, but I don't know the details. I needed you to fill those in for me to get the full picture."

I thought about that before I continued my inquiry. "But earlier, when I was in the apartment and Claire touched me, she saw more than just my aura. Her eyes told me that she saw much more."

Rose was cautious as she spoke. "Claire, no matter what

she would like to believe, is a rare talent . . . even among our people." Rose glanced at Claire. "She sees much more than any of us. More than she lets on. But to know what she's seen, you'll have to discuss it with her."

I shifted toward Claire and thought about asking her right then and there but given the sense of strained relationship between the two women, decided it might be better to speak with her outside her grandmother's presence.

I turned back to Rose. "You also mentioned that it's the job of Watchers to help, to protect, to lead a lost soul on their journey. How do you do this?"

"As Watchers, we have special powers given to us by the Goddess to help others. Our protection spells against those who practice the dark arts are quite powerful and almost undetectable. We can channel to help others see the path they must take, and we can foresee the future. I also suspect that some of us"—she shot a deliberate side-eye at Claire— "also bear powers that are beyond my knowledge and understanding."

"And now that you know my story, with all the details, are you able to help me find my way? Protect me? Help me on my journey?"

"Of course we'll help you. Won't we, grandmother?" Claire said.

Rose's voice was steady as Claire stared at her, anticipating her next words. "It is not me who can answer that question, dear. He came to you. He's your responsibility. You must take this on. Protect him. Guide him on his journey."

Claire shook her head. "But" she protested, "I don't know how. I'm not ready."

"You know more than you think. You can do this. Trust yourself. I'll do what I can, here, to make sure you'll always have a safe place to run to, but on the outside—you're the one who must guide Gio on his path safely." Rose's eyes glowed gold as she said, "I believe in you, Claire. I always have. All you need to do is believe in yourself."

Then, as if deciding the conversation was over, Rose abruptly stood and walked to the door from which she came. Just before she stepped through it, she turned back.

"Gio, good luck to you." Her voice was sincere. "Claire, trust in yourself and all will be well. You can do this. *You* are his Watcher."

She left the room; a heavy silence remained behind.

Claire stood. "It's time to go," she said in a voice with more gravity than her usual light tone.

I stood and followed her out the way we entered. As we walked out of the bar, I placed my hand on Claire's shoulder. She immediately recoiled from my touch.

"I'm sorry, I didn't mean to . . ." My voice trailed off as I looked at my hand.

"What do you want?" Her mind seemed a thousand miles away as she turned around to face me.

"Nothing, I . . . I just want to say that you don't have to do anything you don't want to. The only thing I need from you is an apartment to rent. I've done this alone for over four hundred years, well, not entirely alone. Willem has been with me for more than half that time. But still, I don't need anything from you."

I really did feel bad for her. She didn't ask for any of this and yet here she was, right smack dab in the middle of it all.

"You heard my grandmother. It's up to me to guide you. And besides . . ." Her voice trailed off, and then returned with a renewed curiosity. "Who's Willem?"

We stood on the sidewalk in front of the bar. It was early evening now, not quite dark but night was approaching quickly.

I shuddered. I never did like the night. I was most alone

when the dark set in. It twisted around me like a boa constrictor waiting to squeeze the life out of me.

I had the sudden urge to get back to the apartment, and I spoke in haste.

"Why don't we talk more about this back at the apartment?"

Claire nodded, agreeing without objection. As we crossed the street, I couldn't help but ask one more lingering question. "I was hoping you could tell me something about that guy back in the bar, Patrick?"

"Patrick? Uh, sure. What about him?" She continued to walk as she spoke with me.

"His eyes. What happened to them? How'd he know you had someone with you? How'd he know my name?"

Claire blew a deep breath out, as if I should know the answer to that question. "Weren't you paying attention at all to my grandmother?" Her voice was impatient. "I thought you would've picked up by now that you don't necessarily need eyes to see."

She said these words as if all Watcher talents were obvious, though I had to admit as helpful as they seemed to be, I was still a little wary of the gifts some of the Watchers apparently possessed. However, if they were going to use those talents to help me out, well, then, hell, who was I to doubt? I could use all the help I could get.

When we got to the apartment, Claire made herself at home, taking a seat on the couch. She rested her head on the arm and closed her eyes.

"Are you okay?"

"Yeah, I'm fine. I was just thinking about what my grandmother said." She sounded tired. Too tired for a woman so young.

"What do you see when you touch me?"

Claire sat up and looked me square in the eye. She held

out her hands in an invitation for me to hold them. Kneeling on the floor in front of her, I took both her hands in mine and waited.

"I see him. I see his face. Alessandro. He's left a mark of darkness on you, the same mark that someone put on my father. It helps him identify you throughout time. When you're near." She straightened her back and pursed her lips. "I see him, not from four hundred years ago but in today's world. I see hate in his eyes and a determination unparalleled to any I've seen before. He won't let you have her. He'll never give her up. His hate consumes him and poisons his soul."

Claire opened her eyes. She looked at me apologetically. "I'm sorry. I'm not very experienced at this. I've spent most of my life running away from who I am. I . . . I don't know what to do."

"You didn't ask for this." I tried to assure her with my eyes that I wasn't upset with her in any way.

"No, I didn't." She sat back on the couch. "But my grandmother's right. You came to me. Out of all the places in the world you could have found help, you walked into my store. This wasn't a coincidence, that much I believe."

"So now what?" My voice was flat, emotionless. I wasn't sure of where to go with the conversation, and I was tired.

"Right now, I suppose we should get to know each other a little better. But first, let me remove that dark mark from your aura, it's really starting to drag me down. I'll be right back."

She ran out of the studio. I could hear her barrel down the stairs and out the door leading to the street. Within two minutes, she was running back up the stairs and into my apartment, a small pouch in her hands. She opened the bag and removed a small jar of what looked like ointment infused with herbs.

"It's called a pontive. It's like a heavy-duty spiritual

cleanser. I made it myself, my own recipe. If anything will take that mark away, it's this." She sounded proud.

With a hard twist, Claire opened the jar with a pop; I snapped my head back, as my nostrils filled with the scent. It was horrendous, sour and rotten with a hint of rosemary.

"Don't be a baby. Come here, unbutton your shirt."

I gave her a sideways glance. Claire rolled her eyes.

"Yeah, right. I need to put this over your heart," she explained, though I could see she'd turned slightly pink. She immersed her fingers in the sticky goo and motioned for me to come near. She spread the stuff across my forehead and down the front of my neck. She then took great care to mark the place over my heart with what felt like a star within a circle as she spoke.

"I call on the power that binds me to you, remove this mark. I call on the power that breathes life into our souls, remove this mark. I call on mighty Hecate, mother of all, who sees and hears all her children. Grant me this power, grant me this strength. Remove this mark. So mote it be." She looked at me intently.

A slight stinging sensation spread across my chest.

"You're good," she said suddenly. "Keep this on overnight. By morning it will've removed that nasty stain off your aura and, hopefully, make his connection to you a little less strong." She put the lid on the jar, placed it back in the pouch and handed it to me.

"Put some of this on the wall above your bed. I know it smells bad, but it'll help to keep your dreams closed off to others who may want to snoop around."

I took the bag and put it on the small table near the bed and buttoned my shirt before returning to Claire. Though it'd been quite an eventful afternoon, she appeared to be in better spirits, and I wasn't ready to let my questions go unanswered.

"How is it that you were able to touch me now and not recoil?"

She sighed. "I think it's because I knew it was coming. When I'm able to predict when contact will be made, I'm better able to control my magick. I can control the speed in which it travels through me and the intensity in which it flows. I can also control what kind of magick I'm using."

"Like today at your grandmother's, when you touched me and I felt calm?" I asked thinking back to this afternoon.

"Exactly like that. I find that I can call on certain types of magick when I need to, if I have time to mentally prepare myself."

"Do all Watchers have this gift?"

She shook her head. "No, just me. Well, what I mean is that all Watchers have been given different gifts, but there are a few of us who've, for some reason, been given several magical abilities at one time. In the past four generations, I'm the only one I know of. I guess that's why my grandmother gives me such a hard time. She thinks I'm wasting it."

"Are you?"

She shrugged. "Maybe. But I never wanted this life, you know. It's not all unicorns and cotton candy. Sometimes things don't go as planned. It takes some getting used to."

Claire stopped and looked at me thoughtfully. I sensed she was wrestling around with some inner conflict, but I let it go. I waited quietly until she was ready to continue.

"Who's Willem?" Curiosity leaked from her voice.

"Willem? Oh, Willem is . . . kind of like my guardian."

"Guardian? How so?"

"Well, for one, he came to me when I was at my lowest. Which is pretty hard to imagine, all things considered. He was sent to aid me in completing my mission." I chose my words with care as to not let too much information out at once.

"Is he Strega, like Alessandro and Katarina?" Claire asked.

"Yes and no," I answered curtly.

Claire wrinkled her brow. "I don't understand."

"Perhaps, but that's something you'll have to ask Willem to clarify for yourself. Unfortunately, as much as I'm a part of it, it's not my story to tell."

I closed the subject on Willem before it opened too much. It wasn't that I distrusted Claire, at least not anymore, but I couldn't, not in good conscience, tell a story that wasn't my own. I respected Willem too much to reveal his secrets.

As the sun fully set, the sky outside became dark and a chill wind blew in through the windows. I took a moment to close them, pulled down the shades, and went to my trunk. I pulled out a bottle of Glendronach fifteen-year single malt and two glasses, items I'd learned a person in my situation *could* be but never *should* be without.

"How about that drink?" I suggested as I handed Claire one of the glasses.

"That'd be nice."

I sat on the floor, my back resting against the front of the chair. I poured the drinks, gave her one, and held my glass in the air.

"To new friends," I toasted.

"To new friends."

I brought the glass to my lips and let the aroma of the scotch fill my nostrils. The scent was fuzzy as it tingled my nose. I leaned my head back and closed my eyes. I tipped the glass further and let the liquid touch my mouth. It left a warm coating in its wake as the alcohol passed through my lips and traveled down my throat.

Eleven

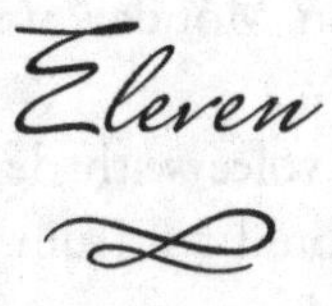

KATE

"Okay, so tell me all the details. Every last dirty little secret."

At least Dave had the courtesy to wait until I'd actually closed the car door before he jumped into a full-on verbal assault.

"Dave—"

"You just better start talking because I cannot handle one of your moods today." He held up his hand just inches from my face. "Now, start from the beginning. I dropped you off and . . ."

I took a deep breath. There was no use fighting over things like this with Dave. He knew he'd ultimately get what he wanted anyway—a voyeuristic journey into my personal life.

Arguing just prolonged what I knew in my heart I'd be doing anyway in just a few short minutes without prompting of any kind—spilling my guts about what was supposed to be a romantic evening with my husband, and what in actuality turned out to be one of the most confusing and disturbing nights of my life.

"C'mon, I'm dying here. I've got to know. I've been

waiting all weekend! I wanna hear all about your trip to Sexy Town.”

“Did it ever occur to you that maybe you should go out more? Get your own damn life? I mean, if this is what kept you coming to work on Monday, well, I hate to say it, but that’s pretty sad.”

I tried to load my voice with derision, though not very effectively. I knew he could tell from my tone I was going to give him what he wanted.

“Puh-lease. You know I always have fun. Don’t you worry.” He gave me a mischievous smile. “But, as the saying goes, there’s a time for work and a time for play, and my playtime is over, so now I’d like to know how yours went before we have to get back to work. And don’t skimp on the adjectives. It’s *so* beneath your syntactic ability.”

“I’m not sure I followed that statement there, but I think I get the point.” I hesitated, knowing the preliminaries were ending.

“Just remember,” I warned as my mind catalogued Friday’s disastrous outcome, “you might not get what you’re expecting.”

“What is that supposed to mean?”

I made eye contact with him for the first time that morning. His blue eyes reflected my image. I saw the distinct outline of myself before it became blurry from the swell of tears gathering at the rims of my lids.

“Oh, honey. I’m so sorry. What happened?” Dave leaned over the center console and wrapped his arms around me. I knew I couldn’t hold out any longer, but I didn’t want to get into this while sitting in his car in front of my house.

“Can we just get going and I’ll talk along the way? I promise.”

Dave released me and started the car as I dug around in my purse for a tissue. How in the hell was I going to get this out?

For as long as I've known Dave, I've never been able to *not* tell him anything. But this? It was so embarrassing in a very non-humorous way. What would he think? What would he say?

As Dave pulled away from the curb, I knew there was only one way to do this.

"All right. I'll tell you everything, but you have to promise to keep quiet until I've finished. If you don't, I'm not sure I can get it out. Then after, you can say whatever you want."

"You have my word." He glanced at me from the side, looking quite nervous. He had no idea what to expect, and I would've bet my next paycheck he'd never even get close to the truth, if given an opportunity to guess.

I dabbed my eyes with a crumpled-up tissue and took one long, solid breath. I opened my mouth and let the words fall out, my mind remembering every detail of the night I wished to forget.

~

FRIDAY NIGHT

ALEX HAD ALREADY GOTTEN ready and was waiting downstairs. Pretty typical. It wasn't until after I slipped on my heels and made my way downstairs that I noticed I'd forgotten to put on a necklace. An image of the necklace I'd gotten earlier that afternoon flashed in my mind. Not thinking much of it, only that I thought it'd look nice with what I was wearing, I ran back upstairs and grabbed it from the tub ledge.

"You ready?" Alex called just as I was coming downstairs.

"You bet," I said taking the last stair. "How do I look?"

His eyes devoured me. After nine years of marriage, how could I still direct such a suggestive look at me? It was instinctual, animalistic. It made the girl inside me nervous and the woman inside wriggle in anticipation.

"Absolutely amazing." He took a step toward me, wrapped his arms around my body, and pulled me close. He brushed his lips against my neck.

I threw my arms up around him and responded with equal want. Every cell in my body was swept away in his kiss. Again, doubt crept up. Why me? What was so special about me?

I was just an average, ordinary woman. Throughout my life, I'd been complimented on my ability to work hard, my determination, and my intellect. But an object of intense desire? Hardly.

Before Alex, I dated occasionally. I'd even had a few boyfriends. In some circles, I was even viewed as quite the catch. But to be treated as if there were no other women on the planet? I just didn't understand it. It was almost unnerving the way he venerated me; it seemed almost unnatural.

His fingers traced along my torso and up the length of my arms. His hands firmly grabbed my wrists from around his neck and brought them back in front of me.

As he did this, his lips kissed down the center of my neck. His mouth found the thin strand of silver and ended at the small circular pendant. He pulled his head back to examine my new bauble.

"What's this?" His voice didn't match what I thought it should sound like. It was hard, terse. It snapped me out of my dream-like trance and forced me to focus on his face.

"Nothing. Just a necklace I picked up today downtown. I got it from a street vendor. Some old lady passing through, I guess. Do you like it?"

"Downtown? I thought you were swamped today. That's the reason we couldn't meet for lunch, right?" His voice began to rise.

I wasn't quite following where he was going with the conversation. I only knew he was getting angry. Red flags waved about wildly. I began to panic, stumbling on my words. "Well, yeah, I was . . . I mean, things just got shuffled around last minute, you know?"

"No, I don't know. Why don't you enlighten me?" He was close to losing it.

"I'm not sure what's happening here. Are you angry that I was downtown today or that I bought a necklace?"

I went to pull my hand away from his, but he held it fast.

"Stop. Please. What's wrong with you?" I asked.

"What's wrong with me? What's wrong with me?" He gave a short laugh. I sucked in a breath. This was the calm before the storm and my heart jumped in my throat in fear. Shit, how did we end up here?

Most days, Alex was very level-headed and calm. In control. However, there'd always been one part of his personality I'd tried never to awaken—his temper. It rarely showed itself, but when it did, it was such a powerful force.

In fact, it happened so infrequently that each time it did appear, it shocked me, like an unexpected slap in the face or a splash of cold water to keep you awake. I'd completely forgotten about the times before and compartmentalized each individual instance as a very specific and isolated occurrence. Of course, I knew this was what I told myself to reconcile with the aftermath of his anger. No matter how unjust his tirades were, I dismissed them as something that only happened every once and a while. Or at least that's what I kept telling myself over and over and over again.

And besides, the in-between times were more than I could've ever asked for in a husband. It was like someone cast a magical spell over us and in those in-between times I was given back my perfect life. I was more than willing to exchange a few horrible hours every now and then for everything I got in between. I owed him that much, didn't I?

But now? Tonight? On our anniversary? I stood there staring at him and hesitated as I thought about the thousand different ways I could approach this instance.

If I could only figure out what he was so upset about. The necklace? No, it couldn't be. Why would he be mad at something as insignificant as that? It must be the whole downtown thing. It had to be. It was the only thing that made sense. He had wanted to meet for lunch, and I'd told him I was busy. I blew him off. It was a small, white lie, but it'd been imperative. I swallowed hard.

"Alex, please calm down. Listen, I'm sorry we didn't meet up today, but I promise things got shuffled around at work last minute and I had a few errands to run, so Dave and I went downtown for a while." I forced my voice to remain calm, though my heart was threatening to beat out of my chest. I was lying and he knew it.

"Do you think I care about your stupid little drunken trips downtown with Dave?" He threw the hate-lined words at my face.

I flinched at the accusation. Even if there was truth behind it, I cringed at his harshness. I lowered my eyes from his stare.

"What? Did you think I didn't know about your little excursions?"

"Stop it." I hated him for doing this. God, why was he doing this?

"No, you stop it! You wanted to know what's wrong with me, didn't you?"

"You don't have to be so mean about it," I whispered. I instantaneously wished I hadn't said it.

"Mean? Ha! You've no idea about what I've had to put up with." He still had hold of both my arms and squeezed tighter.

"Alex, let go. You can't do this every time you get mad at

some little thing. You're hurting me." I spoke calmly and clearly. I knew it was the only way to get him to calm down. Experience told me yelling and getting myself all worked up would do no good, it would just add more fuel to the fire.

"*Some little thing?* You think this is some little thing?"

I looked up at his face. The red flecks in his eyes seemed to glow with fury, leaving a look of menace lingering in his gaze. I flinched.

"Wh—what are you talking about?" I whispered. My mind desperately raced to figure out what it was I'd done that was so wrong. What could I have done to warrant this response? My insides shook with fear.

He pulled me into the living room and sat me down roughly on the couch. He knelt in front of me and lifted the necklace to my line of vision, my right wrist still held in his firm grip.

"What the fuck is this?"

"What? The necklace?"

"Yes, the fucking necklace, Kate. Where did you get it?"

My voice rose and cracked. "I—I told you; I just picked it up from a street vendor downtown. We were walking back to the car and . . . and . . . she was there and there was this box of stuff and . . . and . . ." I was speaking too fast, my words stumbled on each other as they fell from my mouth. Tears formed in my eyes. I couldn't think straight. Everything was so convoluted. My breathing became rapid as my chest became tight.

I looked at Alex, his stare was relentless, his eyes boring through my soul.

"Are you sure? There's nothing else to it?" he asked.

"Am I sure? What are you talking about? Where else would I have gotten it?"

His grip tightened as he pulled me toward him, our faces

just millimeters apart. I could feel his breath on my face as he spoke.

"No one happened to give this to you, did they?"

"What? No, who would give it to me? I swear to you, I bought it downtown . . . I promise. Look, if you don't like it, I'll take it off."

I was finally able to wriggle my hands free from his grip. My fingers fumbled with the necklace's clasp as I frantically tried to remove it from my neck.

"Let me help." His voice was unrecognizably cold as he fluidly slipped his index finger under the chain and gave a sharp tug. The necklace snapped off instantly, stinging the back of my neck. My hand flew to the spot where the clasp dug into my skin. Alex looked at it in his palm before tucking it away in his jacket pocket.

The tears were flowing down my cheeks. I didn't even try to stop them. He looked at me. I didn't meet his eyes; I was much too scared for that. He backed up from where I sat and ran both hands through his hair. The air in the room shifted.

"Oh, God, Kate. Shit, I'm so sorry. I didn't mean to overreact. I . . . I don't know what came over me . . . please forgive me." His voice was drained of all anger. He was Alex again. "Katie? Please stop crying, love. It's all right. I'm fine now . . . everything's fine."

I gathered enough courage to glance up into his eyes. The hard, coldness was gone. His expression was back to the man I'd fallen in love with many years ago. He looked at me with soft eyes and I knew his anger had passed. It was as if with the snap of the necklace, his anger had been released. Relief flooded me. Still, I couldn't stop crying. Tears streamed down my cheeks twice as fast as before.

I didn't know why, but I had an overwhelming compulsion to apologize. Why would I need to apologize? He was the one who overreacted. As I fought to understand this need, the words were already coming out of my mouth. "Alex, I'm so sorry. Please forgive me." Why was *I* apologizing?

I placed my head on his chest, and he immediately wrapped his arms around me.

"Katie, it's okay. It's over. Shh. Stop crying." His voice was the calming, hypnotic Alex of old.

I didn't feel like stopping. In that moment, I felt like crying forever, but somehow I'd already caused more trouble than I could've imagined, so I forced my tears to stop.

He brought his hand up to my face, his thumb rubbing my tears dry. He kissed me full on the mouth gently. I let him kiss me and kissed him back, but it wasn't the passionate response I had from before. But, as our lips met, a warm wave of calm washed over me, and I couldn't resist. I fell into the abyss. His touch, just moments before so violent, was now soft and strangely safe, like a teddy bear or your parents' bed after a nightmare. It radiated through my body. It pulsed through my lips.

The night went on as planned. Emotionally I was exhausted, but I couldn't risk admitting that. Alex seemed in much better spirits and I was determined to salvage whatever I could of this anniversary.

We drove down to the city for dinner and the symphony. He spoke of work, and sports, and the latest news. I smiled, nodded, and added commentary when appropriate, and although I felt more settled, I had trouble truly relaxing and letting go of what had happened earlier in the evening.

My mind just couldn't forget his harsh words. Though a sense of balance seemed to stabilize between us, deep down, my memory couldn't let it go. The words were sharp and pointed and scraped like nails on a chalkboard. What had happened today? Why would something as small as a necklace anger him to the point of such rage?

I smiled at him as he finished a work story about a

disagreement he got into with a colleague in which he came out on top. I marveled at how he drank his wine with such ease. How could he act so . . . so normal? His body language gave no indication he'd completely lost control earlier.

And so I did what any wife who wanted a good night with her husband would do. I pushed my thoughts as far back into my brain as I could shove them and closed the door on them. I'd deal with it later. Maybe.

The drive home was quiet. He drove with precision through the changing landscape from urban to rural. Though the trip took no more than an hour, time was in slow motion.

"You're quiet tonight," he said as he lowered the radio.

"Am I? I'm sorry, I hadn't noticed." I replied, hoping he wouldn't notice my emotional distance and get angry all over again.

"You've barely said anything all night. You're not still thinking about earlier, are you?"

My heart picked up its pace.

"No," I lied, "I was actually thinking about how we've been married for nine years. I can hardly believe it. Time has gone by so fast."

He smiled. Apparently, the wine had marred his perception just enough to believe my lie with ease. He took his hand off the wheel and placed it on my thigh. I fought not to stiffen under his touch.

"I can. I've always known you were mine." He squeezed my thigh. "One more year, love, and we're home free."

I furrowed my brow. "One more year? What do you mean?"

He retracted his hand and placed it back on the steering wheel. "I just mean that ten years seems to be the number most people who end up in divorce can't get past."

"I thought they called it the seven-year itch?"

"Well, it's more like ten where I come from."

He turned the radio up, and then leaned back into his seat. The conversation was over, and I was glad of it. I leaned back into my seat and stared out into the dark night.

When we got home, I headed straight up to the bedroom. I wasn't quite sure how I was feeling, but I was definitely not in the mood for small talk.

"Katie, love?" Alex entered the bedroom with caution, his hands behind his back.

"Yes?" My voice was timid. I felt silly, but I was still nervous. I mean he could get angry, but that's all it was, right? I mean, he would never . . .

"Happy anniversary." He smiled and brought his hands out in front of him. In them, wrapped in light blue paper with a white ribbon, was a delicate box. He held it out to me, and I took it from him in surprise. I'd honestly forgotten about gifts. I sat on the bed and held the package in my hands. I looked at the crispness of the corners and the perfect way in which the ribbon was tightly wound around the sides. He'd probably wrapped it himself.

"Well, aren't you going to open it?" He looked at me in anticipation.

I smiled as we shared a glance. I didn't know why, but my fingers were trembling. I shifted my position on the bed to mask my tremors and hoped he didn't notice.

Carefully, I opened the wrapping around the box. I removed a silver lid to reveal another box inside. This box was black velvet. I pulled it from the outer box and held it in my hands.

I took a deep breath as I slowly pulled back the lid. I gasped when I saw what it held. There, in the center, was a red stone, a little larger than a quarter, perfectly shaped, each facet the same size as the one it neighbored.

"Alex, it's beautiful." I gasped.

"Do you like it?" He sounded pleased. "I know that you're really not into flashy jewelry and all, but it suits you so well."

"What stone is it? It looks like a big red diamond."

Alex smiled.

"It's a ruby. I thought it would look beautiful on you." His voice fell at this last word.

I closed my eyes. Of course! That was why he freaked out earlier. That must be it. He was just anxious about my gift and when he saw my necklace, he just lost it. Of course it was no excuse, a tremendous overreaction, but then he was the type to do everything one hundred and fifty percent or not at all.

Placing the gift on the bed beside me, I threw my arms around his neck and gave him a kiss full on the lips.

"Thank you. I absolutely love it," I said as I pulled away to admire it from the safety of the box.

"Where did you find it? I've never seen anything like it before. It looks like it's glowing." The color of the stone was brilliant, unearthly. My fingers reached out to touch the surface.

"Oh, it's just something I've been looking for for a while. I wanted it to be a surprise. I'm glad you like it."

"Thank you. Really. I don't know what else to say." It was the truth. I was speechless.

He watched me carefully, stroking my hair.

"Thank you is more than enough. That and a promise that you'll wear it always," he whispered, his breath warm against my ear. He took the necklace out of the box and placed it around my neck. I jumped as the stone touched my skin; it was cool and smooth.

"Of course," I said, touching it as he leaned back to see how it looked. My fingers buzzed, like how it feels when a part of your body falls asleep, as I rubbed the stone with their tips.

I remembered the gift I'd picked up for Alex carefully

tucked away in my bathroom cabinet waiting to be put on and then quickly taken off . . . hopefully.

I sat up straight. "Wait here. I'll be right back." I jumped up off the bed and ran toward the bathroom.

"Where are you going?" Alex called as I was halfway out the door.

"Just wait there," I replied over my shoulder.

I locked myself in the bathroom and removed the lingerie from the cabinet where I'd strategically hidden it hours ago. I took my time putting it on, careful not to snag the lacy fabric.

When I had the few parts of the set on, I took a step back and looked at myself in the mirror. Pretty good, but something was a little off.

I pulled my hair down and let it cascade past my shoulders. I grabbed a purple silk scarf from one of my drawers. I folded it into a thin strip and tied it around my hair loosely. Better, but something was still missing.

I continued to search my drawers for more appropriate jewelry. I stopped when I found two thick silver hoops. I quickly exchanged them with the more conservative studs I'd worn to dinner and reassessed myself in the mirror.

Fortune teller chic. I tilted my head to the side. Not bad. I took a deep breath to steady my nerves, and then walked out to where Alex was waiting.

I stood in the doorway for a moment until he noticed my presence. His eyes followed my form from my feet upward, stopping once or twice along the way. It wasn't until his eyes froze on my face that I realized something was wrong.

His face was pale gray; all color draining rapidly from his skin. His eyes looked vacant, like he was in a completely different place, not in his bedroom just feet from me.

"Alex? Are you okay?" My voice was hesitant, careful.

When he didn't answer, I slowly approached him and sat next to him on the bed.

"Alex? What's wrong?"

He blinked his eyes, pushing tears down his cheeks. Now it was my turn to freeze. Was he crying? My heart began to race as I tried in vain to figure out what went wrong and when.

"Why are you wearing that?" It wasn't harsh or rude, just questioning, as if I'd taken him by a sad surprise.

My mind stopped. Of all the things he could've said in that particular moment, that was the least expected.

"I . . . um . . . I . . ." Again, my words tripped over each other as they staggered out of my mouth. "I'm not sure what you mean."

He took a deep breath.

"What I mean is exactly what I said. Why are you wearing that?" A tear dropped from his right cheek and left a small circular mark on his pants leg. Shit.

"I thought, well, I thought you'd like it." My voice grew small. "I thought it would be sexy." Heat flooded my cheeks as the last part trailed off. I forced myself to look at his face. If he didn't say something soon, I was going to panic. This had not gone as planned.

"You look . . .," he began as he brought his hand to my head.

He barely touched my hair as he traced the scarf I had used as a makeshift headband. His hand followed the natural curve of my head and down the side of my cheek hesitating momentarily at my ear, his thumb playing with my earring. I waited for him to finish.

"You look like someone I knew . . . from another time." His voice was strained, but not angry. It sounded sad, hurt maybe. It matched the tears that were still glistening in his eyes.

What the actual fuck?

I didn't know what to do. I didn't know what to say. I was

so confused. So, I did the only thing I could. The only thing I was really good at.

"I'm sorry," I said, standing up and walking back into the bathroom. "I'll go change." I'm not sure what hurt more. The sadness I'd caused, the rejection I felt, or the fact that he let me go.

I changed into the pair of oversized pajamas that I'd left on the floor that morning and took off the scarf and earrings. I pulled my hair back into a ponytail and silently, without too much fuss, went about my nightly routine.

This time I took a long time. Longer than usual. I was in no hurry to return to the bedroom. I would've slept in the bathroom if I thought Alex wouldn't have noticed. When I did return, Alex had changed and had climbed into bed reading what looked like something from work.

He looked up from his work, his smile echoed melancholy. I walked to my side of the bed and got under the covers.

"Goodnight, Alex," I said as I rolled over on my side.

"Goodnight, Kate."

WITH THAT CURT GOODNIGHT, I began the sleepless night I'd been expecting, though the reasons for my sleep deprivation were not exactly what my hopes had been.

When I stopped talking, I realized Dave's car was sitting in the parking lot of Billows Publishing. I'd said everything I'd wanted to and more. If Dave had had any hang-ups before of me leaving out the details, well, those days were over. I'd laid it all out for him, clear as day, and waited for his response.

"Oh, sweetie, I'm *so* sorry." Dave handed me a tissue. "What the hell has been going on over there? I didn't even know you two had any major fights, let alone him putting his hands on you."

I tried to focus on his words, but the steady stream of tears made it impossible for me to do anything. Finally, I blubbered out words. "I don't know what's going on anymore. I used to think he could do no wrong, but lately things have been getting all weird, like they were on Friday. Do you know what the rest of the weekend was like? It was me walking around the house on eggshells, trying to make him happy. I was afraid to talk. I was afraid to leave the house. I was afraid of doing anything that might piss him off or make him cry." My voice caught in my throat. "It was me giving myself to him, so that he'd be sexually satiated and not suspect I wished I could run away." I sobbed into my hands.

Dave leaned over the seat and wrapped his arms around me. He let me cry on his shoulder even though he was wearing his favorite cashmere sweater. I cried and cried and after what seemed like forever Dave pulled back and handed me another tissue.

I blew my nose and sat there, looking out the window at the vineyard-covered hills. It was still early, quiet. Magically, an overwhelming sense of peace could be found on those hills at any given moment. Today, however, I found magick in the sound of a car engine as Dave started his car back up.

"We're getting out of here," he said.

"What? Why? Where are we going?" I managed after a minute.

"First, we are going to get a massage. Then we are going out to lunch, and then shopping. There's too much to unpack right now, but we'll get there, trust me, sweetie. You are not alone in this. I promise. Right now though, you need a break. Besides, there's nothing due today that can't be done out of office and you're caught up on your manuscripts, so—"

"We're ditching work?" I laughed at the absurdity.

"Ditching is such a harshly juvenile word. No, we are simply working offsite today."

He smiled at me with a devilish look in his eye and threw the car in reverse. Before he had a chance to back out, I reached over and placed my hand on his.

Never in my life had I had a friend like Dave. I knew in that moment that our friendship spanned farther than I thought. Tears welled up in my eyes, though this time they were from gratitude.

"Dave," I said, "thank you."

He took a deep breath and squeezed my hand. His hand was large and felt warm and comforting wrapped around mine.

He bent over toward me and kissed me on the forehead. Then with a sudden jolt I was not ready for, the car lurched backward as he drove out of the parking lot.

It was sometime after the massage but before lunch that the feeling that my life was taking a drastic turn returned. For the worse or for the better, I couldn't say, but a change was coming, most definitely. I felt it in my bones.

I was perusing the stacks at the bookstore, my muscles relaxed from a combination of the deep tissue therapy and the champagne that accompanied it when I heard the soft tinkle of the bell on the door and felt a breeze blow through the store. I didn't think much of it, only that the warm chillness in the air was a reminder autumn was in full swing. A sense of peace wrapped around me and the fight with Alex was a world away.

I continued to look through the shelves, my fingers trailed down the titles as I waited for Dave to return with the salesperson who'd taken him to the annex downstairs to claim a book he'd ordered. The sound of a man speaking with the clerk behind the counter caught my attention and I stopped to investigate who had entered the store.

"Excuse me? I'm looking for a book."

His voice was a sinewy melody around the words. It was familiar, like a lovely song played over and over until every part of it was memorized. Though I couldn't quite put my finger on it, there was something about it I instantly recognized.

I peeked around the corner to where the owner of the mysterious voice stood and gasped. It was him. Even though his back was to me, I knew it was the young man I saw from the restaurant balcony last Friday.

I watched from behind the safety of the shelf as the clerk turned to his computer and began searching for the requested title. I held my breath, afraid to make a noise and attract attention and waited.

I watched from my secret spot and longed to be closer. Unexpectedly, and with no rational reason, the intense urge to be near him nagged at me. I had to get closer. I grabbed the first book my hands touched from the shelf and walked to the front counter.

As I neared, the young man stiffened. His shoulders tightened, his posture became a bit straighter. I stopped, not wanting him to turn around yet hoping he would.

My God, please turn around.

Before I decided what my next move would be, the clerk called from behind his post.

"May I help you, miss?" the salesclerk said. His voice was tight and pinched.

"Um . . . uh . . ." I was caught off guard.

"May I help you?" he repeated in his nasally tone.

"Yes." I recovered and said, "I'll take this." I held the book up.

The man waiting placed both hands on the edge of the counter, and then, as if pushing off he stepped back and quickly walked toward the door, never turning around. My muscles twitched to follow him. *Don't go! Not yet.* In his haste he knocked over a display of books. They tumbled noisily to the hardwood floor. He stopped, and then sighed before kneeling and picking up the books in a resigned fashion.

I walked over to where he was and knelt next to him.

"Let me help," I said as I reached toward the closest book to me.

He was motionless as I picked up the book and held it out to him, his back still toward me. I heard him take another deep breath and then, with a deliberate movement, he turned to face me.

Every cell in my body jolted.

What the hell?

His face was exactly as I'd remembered from the other day —anguished perfection. My memory didn't fail me in that respect. In fact, I was surprised at its accuracy.

His skin was a smooth olive tone, creamy with a hint of golden glow that looked as if he'd just come out of the sun, though more natural, not as harsh. His eyes were piercing blue, as if someone had blended a piece of turquoise, a diamond, and the ocean. Like a tropical sea, not the type of ocean water here in Northern California.

"Thank you," he said as he hesitantly took the book from me, avoiding my eyes.

"Not a particularly good spot for a display, if you ask me," I said, trying to lighten the mood.

He said nothing as he continued.

The clerk had made his way over and was helping to clean up the mess. He gave me a slanted look and huffed at my last comment. We continued to pick up the books in an awkward silence. The clerk was as agitated by the extra work he was being forced to do as I was of his presence.

"My name's Kate," I offered, stunned by my sudden boldness and complete disregard for anything other than the visceral and unfounded insistence to know this person.

He looked up and made direct eye contact for the first time since I'd come over. His eyes locked into mine. His stare was intense, making it impossible to look away. Not that I'd ever want to. Quite the opposite, I needed to move closer to him, though I don't know why; he was a complete stranger, and I was a married woman.

But for some unknown reason, he didn't feel like a stranger. Every cell in my body thrummed at his nearness. He felt more like someone I'd known for a long time, like someone I could trust. And as he looked at me with those shockingly blue eyes, something, in some way, changed. My stomach tightened. My heart expanded. My mind raced and I struggled to identify what it was that seemed more important than anything I could remember . . . but almost did.

"Hello, Kate. My name's Gio."

Gio...

Questions flew through my head like darts, each one hitting their mark in my mind. Who was he? Where was he from? How come he was so familiar?

We chatted and I took in his every word. Did he know how my belly clenched each time he looked at me? Did he feel it too? Did he suspect that my heart raced uncontrollably with each smile, with every blush in his cheek, and didn't stop until our conversation had ended, long after he stood to leave and the door closed behind him as he left the store?

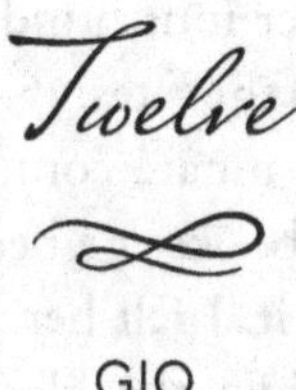

Twelve

GIO

It was always a mystery to me how I found her. Something like a compass needle being pulled in the right direction, I suppose—a natural phenomenon that leads explorers and wanderers alike to their homes, but more.

Long ago, when the Strega Onesta found me, they'd said they couldn't bring her back to life but could instead alter the damage. They cast upon us the thread of eternal love, an unbreakable line of magick that stretched between her and me, tying us together forever. It was the thread that would lead me to her, over and over again no matter where we were. It was always present, always connecting us—my Katarina forever on the other end.

And it was always the same. Once I'd established a sense of where I could find her, I'd settle in, so to speak. Once I was close enough, the thread would lead her to me. My only tasks were to find a dwelling and keep out of sight, maintaining a low profile until Willem arrived with the ingredients for the serum and a plan was developed. It was a process we'd perfected over the centuries. Staying out of sight should've been simple; I'd done it time and time again. How was I to know this time would be so different?

Perhaps I should've known I wouldn't be physically able to resist being near her if the opportunity arose. There's only so much you can do after four hundred years before you just have to resign yourself to the fates.

It must've been the innate connection tying us together that pulled me into the bookstore because before I even knew what I was doing, I felt it. I felt her. Stronger than ever. As I stood there waiting while the clerk fumbled around, the breath of life that completed me grew in my body. It started in my core and slowly stretched out, filling first my legs and arms, and then reaching out to the very tips of my extremities, threatening to spill out my fingernails.

Goddess, she was close, too close. If I turned around, she'd be standing there waiting for me. I stiffened. No, I couldn't interact. It wasn't time. I didn't trust myself to resist the urge to run to her, wrap my arms around her, pull her close, kiss her, tell her how sorry I was, hold her tight . . . forever.

I had to leave. I tried to escape, but the fates stepped in yet again. Damn books. And suddenly, she was there, just inches from me, helping me, introducing herself—as if I didn't know who she was. I knew her better than she knew herself.

You are as lovely as the first time I laid eyes on you. Your raven hair still falls loose over your shoulders, your smooth skin. Everything about you, I've missed for more than eleven lifetimes.

"I'm new in town. It's nice to meet you." I heard the words come out of my mouth and knew they shouldn't have. *Shut up. You know better than this.* I could jeopardize everything, but I couldn't stop myself. Seeing her face, looking into her eyes, having her just inches from me was intoxicating.

I knew what would come next. "Would you like to have coffee with me sometime?" More contact. I had to have more contact.

"Sure, that'd be nice. Thanks." Her smile gave the sun light.

"How about tomorrow? Eleven o'clock? Though you'll have to recommend the place, I really don't know anywhere around here." *Shut up. Don't do it. For her own safety, stop this now.*

"Sure, sounds great. There's this place just out of town right past the farm stand; you can't miss it. Kind of bohemian, very low key, relaxed. I love it there. They've got all this funky outdoor seating and tents. You can sit outside for hours and just chill." Her cheeks flushed as she spoke. Too late.

I didn't want to leave her. Walking away was nearly impossible. But I would see her again, soon. I hadn't entirely blown it. I'd managed to maintain some semblance of anonymity. Who was I trying to convince? When he found out what I'd done, Willem was going to go ballistic.

"I'll see you then." My voice was weighty with anticipation.

As I turned to leave, my heart was torn from my rib cage. I couldn't leave her. I had to. I swallowed hard and tried to focus on the positive. She was here. She was alive and well and as beautiful as ever. I very well could've picked her up and taken her far away from anyone who would try to come between us, but I didn't. I couldn't. Not if I ever wanted the chance to save her. I shook my head. I couldn't dwell on my mistakes. Willem would just have to deal. Right now, I was floating high above the clouds.

As if reading my thoughts, my phone went off the minute I stepped out onto the sidewalk. I took a few more strides down the street before removing the phone from my pocket and answered. How did he do that?

"Willem, what's going on?" I tried to sound casual.

"Gio . . ." He'd heard something in my voice. He wasn't fooled. "What's happened?" His voice was serious, firm. He wasn't going to let up until I told him. Shit. Sometimes I really despised witches.

"There've been some unexpected developments." I tried not to alarm him, but if I knew Willem, he was well beyond alarmed at this point.

"You better start talking."

"Please keep in mind that there's nothing you can do halfway around the world, so you can listen to what I'm going to say and flip out, but you're gonna have to trust me when I tell you that nothing has been compromised." It took great effort for me to believe the words I spoke; I really hope Willem bought it.

"That's why I called. I've collected the ingredients for the serum. It took a great deal of skill and some maneuvering, but luck is with us, brother. I was able to get every last ingredient. I hopped a flight last night out of London. I just landed in San Francisco." He paused and then continued.

"Now, since I'm on my way, would you please inform me what I'm driving into?" I could hear the volatile mixture of anger, frustration, sleep deprivation, and anxiety in the gist of his voice.

"Okay. Calm down, please."

I went into detail about the apartment and Claire and the apparent coven of Watchers that inhabited this area. I told him of my encounter with Rose and Claire's offer to be my Watcher. When I'd finished, there was silence at the other end of the line.

"Willem? Are you still there?"

"I'm here." He paused. "I was just thinking how this presents an interesting twist for us. I've heard of these American Watchers before, but I've never encountered one, let alone an entire homestead."

"Is that all?" I was stunned by his reaction. Maybe I didn't know him as well as I'd thought.

"Well, that and the fact that I have a feeling you haven't told me everything."

Damn. How was he always one step ahead?

"Well, there's just one more thing."

"Oh, Gio, please don't tell me you made yourself known to her." There was a sense of resigned disappointment in his voice. He already knew the answer.

"Please listen. It wasn't my intention to make any contact, but as you well know, some things are out of our control."

"What happened?" His voice held no emotion, just a quest for information.

"Nothing. It was harmless, really. We just introduced ourselves and made plans to meet for coffee . . . tomorrow."

"You're meeting her? Tomorrow? Are you out of your mind? And what if Alessandro has already found her?" Worry was building in his voice as it grew louder and louder over the phone. "What if he's already found her and is her husband or boyfriend or whoever he's pretending to be in this life? You think it will be harmless when she tells him she's going out to coffee to meet her new friend Gio?"

I could feel my face drain of all blood. The world around me began to spin and the surrounding air became dense and unbreathable.

How could I have been so stupid? I was so wrapped up in my own need I completely disregarded the safety of the one person I would die a thousand deaths for. Desperately, I looked back toward the bookstore. I had to go back. I had to get her and take her away. I'd kidnap her if I had to.

Willem must have sensed my state of extreme panic and my immediate plan of action because he spoke quickly. "Stop. Don't do anything else. Go back to the apartment. Find Claire. Tell her what happened and ask if there's anything she can do to assist. Wait for me. I'll be there in an hour. Do you understand?"

There was an authority in his voice that I'd grown accustomed to follow. Still, though I heard the words, I was unable to respond. Trapped by indecision with the phone to my ear, I stood motionless.

"Gio," he repeated, this time with more force. "Do you understand?"

"Yes." The word came out in a whisper as I hung up the phone and slipped it into my pocket.

I ran down the street and burst through the door of the shop, where I knew I'd find Claire. She looked up at me from behind the counter where she was braiding a hemp necklace. Her smile was replaced with fear when she saw my face.

"What's going on?"

"I was so stupid. So damn stupid. She was there, and I knew I should walk out, just ignore her, run away if I had to, but did I? Not me. I couldn't, and then we were talking and I . . . I told her my name, and if she's with Alessandro already and she tells him, then all this will be for . . . for . . ." My mind was racing ahead of my tongue. The last thought refused to come out.

"Whoa, slow down." Claire stared at me trying to make some sort of sense of everything that had just fallen out of my mouth. "Did you say you saw Katarina? Here in Freestone? Today?"

"Kate. She goes by Kate in this lifetime. And yes, I saw her here, today." I placed my face in my hands and didn't try to stop the emotion welling up.

"Hey, I'm here." She waited until I looked up at her. "Tell me exactly what happened? Tell me everything." Claire's voice was soft, non-judgmental. It was a nice change from Willem, though disturbing in its own way.

I pinched the bridge of my nose. How could I have been so irresponsible? This wasn't how it was supposed to happen. "I was at the bookstore down the street. It was like I was pulled there, I didn't even question it, just followed this emotional tug. As soon as I got to the counter, I knew she was there. Her lifeforce was too powerful. Too familiar. I tried to leave before she noticed me, but it was too late. And then it was like being sucked into a whirlpool. Except I didn't want to escape. I wanted to fall into it, fall into her. We started talking and before I could stop myself, we'd made plans to have coffee tomorrow. I couldn't help myself. I just had to see her again." My body was fully numb at this point as I continued to mentally curse myself. How could I be so stupid?

"This is great." Claire's voice held true excitement in it. "Gio, this is amazing news."

I inspected her face before I trusted what I heard. Sure enough, Claire's skin practically glowed. She was truly excited.

"I'm not sure you heard me correctly. I just said I'd made contact with Katarina." I stopped and shook my head. No, that wasn't her name this lifetime. "Kate, I mean Kate. I told her my name. We made plans to meet again."

"Yeah, I heard all that."

"Then how can you sit there? This isn't how it's supposed to go."

"It's actually great news, Gio. You found her! She's here within reach."

"You don't get it. What if Alessandro has already found her? What if she tells him she's going to meet someone for coffee? And worse, I used my real name. How many Gios do you know these days? He'll know it's me and he'll take her away . . . or kill her before she even knows what's happening."

My stomach turned. I was going to be sick. I folded my arms across my middle and tried to steady my breathing.

"I wouldn't be so sure about that."

"So, what? You think she'll go home tonight, not mention anything to anyone, especially a husband or boyfriend, about the stranger she agreed to meet with tomorrow?"

"Yeah, that's exactly what I think. *Especially* if she has a boyfriend or husband."

"And why's that?"

"Are you serious? I mean, come *on*. Have you looked in a mirror the past four hundred years? If what you've told me about Alessandro is true, and they are together, there's no way she'd go home and tell him she's going to meet some handsome guy from the bookstore for coffee. Trust me, she'll be safe. I... I have a feeling. Try not to focus anymore on that. If I were you, I'd be concentrating more on how you're going to gain her confidence and get her to fall in love with you again."

I stared at Claire. Could it be that simple? I hoped so, but I wasn't so sure. Rarely were things so easy.

"How can you be sure? For all we know, she's with Alessandro right now and . . ." I couldn't even finish the thought; acid pooled in my stomach.

Claire reached out and touched my hand. Her skin was soothing against mine. I knew she was using her magick to calm me. Quickly, I pulled away.

"No, don't. I need to stay focused. Willem will be here shortly, and I need to be ready to follow through with whatever he needs me to do."

She looked put off, but her pout quickly turned to interest. "He's coming here? So soon? I thought it would be weeks before he'd be here."

"So did I, but if there's one thing you should never do, it's underestimate Willem. He has ways of getting things done that are beyond my understanding."

She didn't respond. She appeared to be lost in her own thoughts. After a minute, she looked back at me. My face must've revealed I was still concerned about earlier. Her voice cut through my worry. "Please. Don't worry about this too much. I know it's hard, but please trust me. I know everything will be fine. . .well, at least until tomorrow. Past that, I can't really tell, but there's no need to worry about things that are out of our control. For now."

"What do you mean, you know everything will be okay?"

"I just do. It's nothing really, maybe we should wait until Willem arrives. I hate explaining myself more than once. Now why don't you go upstairs and rest? You've hardly slept since you arrived."

I was about to argue. I was about to yell she didn't know what the hell she was talking about. But there was no use in arguing and it was pointless to yell. And I realized she was right. I was tired.

So, I did the only thing I could do. Without another word, I turned around and went upstairs. Mechanically, I put the key in the lock and opened the door. I took off my coat, poured a generous glass of scotch and downed it, and promptly lay down on the couch where I fell into a deep and, thankfully, dreamless sleep.

~

I AWOKE to two silhouettes standing over me. Half asleep, I jumped up and staggered backward, trying to get my bearings on the situation.

"It's okay, it's just me. It's Claire." Her small voice was calming.

My eyes slowly focused on the petite figure that, over the past few days, had become familiar. I thought it strange how Claire had so quickly made herself a permanent fixture in my existence, or perhaps it was strange that I'd so quickly accepted her into my life. Whatever the case, the idea that she wouldn't be there seemed stranger to me than the former.

My head cleared and I glanced around the room; I hadn't imagined two, had I? As I became more aware, my faculties quickly returned and I immediately registered who the other figure was: Willem.

Standing just a bit behind Claire, my old friend watched me fumble with a gentle smile on his face.

"It's good to see you getting rest." His voice was familiar, and it sounded so much better in person than through a phone.

"Willem, it's good to see you. I can't believe you're here so soon, brother." I took a couple of steps toward him and gave him a hug. He returned the embrace and patted my back a few times. I pulled away and looked over at Claire.

"I see you've met Claire. Claire, this is Willem," I offered.

"Yeah, we met downstairs," she said, running over my words as if she had been anticipating what I was going to say. I looked at her, but she diverted her eyes to look out the window.

"Well," I said, trying to ignore her strange behavior, "Claire, have you caught Willem up on the situation?"

"Not yet," Claire admitted. "As soon as he got here, I thought it best to come and get you."

I nodded in agreement, looking back at Willem. Other than a bit tired, he looked good. It was hard to believe that less than twenty-four hours ago, he'd been halfway across the world, and before that had spent weeks searching for the ingredients for the serum. I walked over to the kitchen, opened a cupboard, and took down a few tumblers.

"Willem, a drink?"

"That would be great. It's been a long road to get here." He took off his coat and tossed it over the arm of the couch.

"Claire?" I held a glass in my hand.

"Yes, please. But, um, first let me go lock up the store. I'll be right back." She very agilely made her way out of the apartment, closing the door behind her with a sharp tug. I stood in the kitchen a moment and stared after her.

"What the . . ." My voice trailed off as I continued to look at the door.

"I think I make her uncomfortable," Willem offered as he took a glass from the counter and put it to his lips.

"Uncomfortable? What do you mean?" I asked.

"I don't know if you're aware, but Claire is probably one of the most powerful magical humans you'll ever be in the presence of. As soon as I entered the town limits, I could feel her magick. At first, I thought it was simply the magick of all the Watchers in this area, but as I made my way to the apartment, I could feel the others' power peel away, like ribbons unraveling.

"Except that the others' magick was like embroidery threads wrapped around one thick rope. As I got closer to the apartment, I could feel her magick above all else. It's thick and dense and powerful."

"But why would that make her feel uncomfortable?" The fuzzy headiness of sleep still lingered as I struggled to understand what Willem was saying.

"Because she knows what I am. And not only can I sense her magick, but I can also sense that it's new to her. I get the feeling that when she accepted her mission to be your Watcher, all her magick descended upon her, like a tidal wave. And it's apparent she doesn't know what to do with it all, not yet. Especially when she encounters people like me, who also carry a bit of their own. It can be overwhelming, to say the least."

"I had no idea."

"No offense, but you've never been the quickest at realizing the full potential of magickal energy."

I shrugged. He was right. Other than being cursed, I had no magickal inclination whatsoever. Until I had been thrown into my current malady, I was simply a human.

I sighed at the thought of returning to that clumsy,

awkward, non-magickal being once more. I longed for the day I'd return to being human in every sense of the word. And if I'd ever see that day, would I have my Katarina back? Would we live together in peace? Have children and watch them grow old as we grew old ourselves? It was a dream, I dared not speak of.

Claire's small voice interrupted my thoughts as she knocked twice on the door. "May I come in?"

"Claire"—I broke out of my thoughts— "of course. Come in." I held out a short glass to her as I crossed the studio to where she stood.

She took the glass and walked over to the couch. She sat carefully. I noticed how her movements were deliberate, planned, as if she'd be unable to move if she didn't force herself to do so. Was she uncomfortable to the point of pain?

"Claire," Willem said, "if it's too much, I can stand further back. Sometimes, the pressure is less when there's more physical space."

Claire looked at him wide-eyed. "How did you know?" she asked.

"Gio, haven't you told her anything about me?" This time it was Willem who had a look of wonder.

"I asked," Claire interrupted, "but he said it wasn't his place to do so."

"Well, I suppose that's true, but I would've thought he would've given in. He's never been one to deny a request from a lovely lady." He shot me a look that was both reprimanding and teasing. He looked back at Claire. Her face was flushed. "And I suppose we should get a little better acquainted . . . since I anticipate we'll be spending quite a bit of time together."

Claire just stared, waiting patiently for him to begin. She took a sip from her glass and curled her legs up to her chest.

"Now it's been so long, I can't quite remember the days or

years. Things tend to fade after you hit two hundred years old or so, but the event itself is as clear as day. I remember every detail: how things sounded, how things looked. It could've happened yesterday . . ."

I listened as Willem began his tale. I knew it would be a painful account, a tale of sacrifice, a tale of ultimate loss. I grabbed the bottle of scotch and offered him a refill, which he accepted. I walked over to the couch and sat next to Claire.

She was transfixed on Willem. Her face was still, the glass frozen halfway to her mouth as the words flowed out of him like a siren's song. I leaned back, closed my eyes, and let Willem tell his story.

"I come from a long line of powerful people. 'Witches' is, I suppose, a more contemporary term, though I've come to prefer Pagan. We were Strega Onesta, practitioners of goodness—white magick is the phrase used today. Anyway, long before I was sent to Gio, I lived as an aging creature. My original path was to be born, grow old, and die—the natural way, the way it was intended by the Goddess.

"My mother and father were among the leaders of our group. They were respected and listened to. They were sought after for guidance. Everything about them exuded wisdom. Separately, they were powerful. Together, they were a great force, nearly unstoppable.

"They could've used their collective power and created fear and servility among our people, but they didn't. They were dedicated to the peaceful movement of the natural earth and lived in the way they both believed was the key to truth, light, and love.

"Growing up, I was told that young witches come into their power when the time was right; that most would inherit their gifts through either the mother's or their father's lineage. As I grew, I witnessed many of my friends come into their power. I didn't. But I wasn't concerned. Both my parents assured me that when the time was right, Goddess would provide. I believed them.

"Over the years, I grew and grew and soon, before I knew it, I was a young man, and then, a grown man. My powers had yet to come. Many of the others, power-hungry and bloodthirsty, those who wished for our group to align with the Strega Ilmalo, viewed my lack of gifts as a sign from the Goddess, a warning against my parents. They started rumors that my parents had fallen out of favor with the spirits, that my lack of power was a symbol of their misfortune, and they didn't hesitate to spread their poison throughout our people.

"About this time, I'd become increasingly interested in a young woman I'd known since my childhood. To me, she was the most perfect creature ever created. Her hair was golden, with a reddish tint. Her eyes were crystalline green. She was kind and just, and she showed an inclination to me that went beyond friendship.

"But her family would have nothing to do with me. I was cursed, or so they'd believed. A marriage to me would bring nothing but disfavor. So, it was arranged she would marry another. I knew it was a mistake, that she would never know true love with this other man, but I didn't speak up.

"My parents implored me to follow love. They told me to trust in the Goddess, that when the time was right, my powers would come. They told me love was the truth behind life; it gave life. They beseeched me to not ignore such a powerful emotion. They told me I should trust in them, I should trust in myself, and go to the council to ask for my love's hand."

Willem shook his head.

"But it was too late. I truly believed I was a curse to them, that because of me, they were falling out of favor with the people they'd led for years. If I could do this to my parents, how could I be of any benefit to her? What could I provide? A lifetime of misery? Being shunned by our people? No. I decided I wouldn't fight it. I would let her go."

Willem paused and took another long sip from his glass.

"The night she came to me and begged me to fight for her, I almost broke down. I almost did it. She asked me to go to the council, to explain to them our love for each other, to ask for her to be released from her arrangement. She was confident once the council and her family saw how much we cared for each other, they would grant our wish. They would see the strength of our bond and wouldn't deny such a love.

"I was afraid she was right. All I'd have to do was appear before the council and there'd be no denying our connection. But I was too weak. I didn't want her to live as the wife of the cursed one. I was too ashamed." Willem bowed his head, his voice low.

"And so I looked her straight in her eyes and I told her I wouldn't do it. I wouldn't fight for us because I didn't love her enough. I lied. I lied with everything I had to the one woman that was my whole existence.

"She ran out of my tent sobbing, unable to speak, unable to look at me. I wanted to run after her, to tell her I lied, confess my true love to her, but I didn't. I let her go. I thought it was the only way to save her from me.

"The next morning, my father stood above me, his face serious, his eyes grim. A couple of elders found her body mutilated by self-inflicted wounds and hanging from a tree just outside of the encampment." Tears lingered on his cheeks, but he continued.

"I didn't believe him, and I ran to go find her, but it was true. Her family was preparing her body for its new journey to the place where only the dead could follow.

"I was crazed. Guilt ridden. Destroyed. This was my fault. Her blood was on my hands. I'd made the gravest mistake any person could make. It was at that moment the voice of the

Goddess came to me. I felt the power from the universe flow through me with such strength that there was no mistaking what it was. My powers had come to me.

"The Goddess spoke clearly. She told me I didn't trust her; I didn't trust my parents. I didn't trust myself. But most importantly, I didn't trust in love, and for that, for this most devastating blasphemy, I would now truly be cursed. As punishment for my lack of faith, I'd now live eternally with my powers, only able to use them for others in the name of love. She cursed me indefinitely, until, when the time is right, she'll lift my shackles and my life will continue."

He stopped speaking. His eyes met Claire's and then flicked out the window. He gave a small laugh. It hung sour in the air.

"After I realized what'd happened, what was to happen, I couldn't stand to be near my parents any longer. I was truly a disappointment and a curse. I said goodbye as my mother wept, and I shook hands with my father for the last time. They didn't try to stop me.

"By nightfall, I'd left the camp, never once looking back, never to return. I willingly accepted the punishment given to me and considered the suffering I endured as nothing compared to what I deserved."

Willem was quiet, trapped in his memories before he brought his gaze to mine and revealed a half-smile.

"I suppose it was a century or two later when I heard of an ageless wanderer; a man, who followed the spirit of a young maiden, trapped into perpetual existence living lifetime after lifetime. I was in Ireland at the time; I'd lived there for a hundred years by then. I'd taken an Irish name and adopted an Irish accent. Like a snake shedding its skin, I'd shed my original person and turned into what you see now. In my journeys, I'd stumbled upon many unsavory covens and cursed peoples who played within the darkness during that period.

"When I caught wind of the unspeakable things that some of these witches had planned for this man, I decided it was something I should become involved in. I procured a strip of cloth from this man's clothes and used my powers to read his past, learn his story, and find him before the others who wished him ill did."

"And it's a good thing you did, brother. I don't know where I'd be right now if you hadn't," I said.

Willem nodded and smiled. "To this day, I've dedicated the powers that were given to me to help Gio reunite with Katarina. Although, I admit, I didn't foresee such a struggle. Alessandro, over the years, has grown stronger and quite astute in his ability to anticipate our every move."

As if suddenly snapped out of a trance, Claire said, "Willem, I don't know what to say."

"Don't feel sorry for me," Willem replied gently. "I'm glad to suffer. It's but a small price to pay. Not nearly close to what I deserve. And if I can create good out of my shame, then I'm a willing participant."

Claire nodded in understanding. Then, after some reflection, she said, "You said you didn't foresee such a struggle in reuniting Gio and Katarina—"

"Kate," I interrupted, saying her name with reverence. "Her name is Kate in this life. The sooner we get used to that, the more likely we'll be not to slip up."

Claire looked at me and instantly corrected herself. "Kate, sorry. I was just thinking about why it's been such a struggle to reunite Gio and Kate when it seems as if this union is destined. Willem, do you have any idea as to why Alessandro has grown stronger and appears to anticipate your every move?"

Willem sighed with heavy lungs. "There are some things, Claire, that even I, with all the powers given to me, am not able to foresee." He shrugged his shoulders. "It gets complicated the more players you throw in the game, especially players that have immensely powerful magick. I imagine that there'll be a few more obstacles to maneuver around now that you're in the mix too."

He smiled a friendly smile to show her he meant no ill-will with this last comment. It was simply a statement of fact.

Claire smiled back for the first time since I'd woken up. "Willem," she said, "do you think you'd be able to help me control some of my magick? It's so much, you know? Sometimes I feel like it's going to swallow me whole."

"Of course, I can," Willem answered, "but first, I think we should come up with a plan for tomorrow, and then there's the matter of the serum."

Willem looked at me and then back to Claire.

"Serum?" Claire sounded confused and I realized I hadn't really told her anything.

Willem looked at me disapprovingly. "Gio, I'd at least have thought you would've explained the serum."

I simply shrugged.

"Well," Willem began, "simply put, when the Strega Onesta found Gio, they couldn't help him in the way he wanted them to—they couldn't bring her back to life. There are some things that are irreversible. But since Katarina's body had just recently been robbed of its life, her soul was still near. They were able to cast upon her a spell that connected her soul to Gio's. When the time comes, when their souls find each other once more, they'll be reunited."

"But what does a serum have to do with anything?" Claire asked.

"The serum," Willem continued, "is vital to counteract the curse cast upon Gio. Kate is already human. Her soul is brought back to this Earth over and over again. She is born, she can grow old, and she dies. It's not true for Gio.

"Even if Gio should win her back, she would grow old and eventually die. Gio would never age. He wouldn't grow old with her, he'd be with her until she left him again in death and he would continue forever."

Claire looked at me suddenly and said, "But I thought that once you found her and she fell in love with you again, the curse would be lifted. That's not true?" She sounded offended, like I'd lied to her.

"It's not that simple," I answered. "It's true that once we're together again, the curse will be broken. But the love has to be given by her in her original consciousness, not by the person she is in this life."

Claire looked between us both, confusion dug deep in her brow.

"You see," Willem said, "every time Katarina is brought back to this earth she's given a new existence, an existence that supersedes her original one. Her original soul is there, breathing life into the body she is given, but everything else, her memories, her powers, are locked up and bound deep within her psyche." He took a deep breath.

"In order for Gio to become an aging human again, he has to release that inner part of her soul. Release it, before they . . . are *connected* in the most intimate aspect of love."

Understanding clicked in Claire's eyes as she finally grasped the complexity of the situation. "And all this has to be done before Alessandro finds her, or figures out what you are doing, because if he does, he'll kill her, and it will start all over again." Her words were a confirmation of what she was beginning to understand.

"Exactly," Willem said. "And that's where the serum comes in. To release Kate's inner soul, the one that fell in love with Gio those many years ago, she must willingly drink it before they . . . well, before they . . ." He coughed. For the first time in centuries, Willem stumbled over his words. His cheeks flushed.

Claire diverted her eyes to the floor. "I think I understand," she said, giving him an out.

I wasn't used to seeing Willem embarrassed but figured it was nothing more than having a new person in the room. Up until now, Willem and I had always worked alone.

Claire was quick to change the subject. "And so I take it that this serum is a pretty complex potion. Not something you can toss together at a moment's notice with ingredients from your kitchen cupboard, right?" Claire was looking at me now, giving Willem the space he needed to compose himself.

"Pretty much," I replied. "The serum itself uses over fifty very-hard-to-find components. Willem has not only collected them all and brought them here, but he now has to use the next few days preparing it for the one moment that will define my existence."

"How do you know if it will work?" Claire asked.

A long silence ensued.

"We don't," Willem said at last. "But it's all we've got, and if I've learned anything during my life, it's that sometimes we must simply believe everything is done for a reason and the Goddess has a plan for everyone. Sometimes we must put aside our own doubts, our own fears, and trust that the path we're on is indeed the path meant for us, no matter what may happen."

"That's quite an obstacle to overcome," Claire said with a sort of cynicism appropriate when dealing with the terminally formidable.

"Yeah. There's that," I added, "and then there's also the fact that all this needs to be done before Alessandro has had Katarina for ten years."

"What happens in ten years?" Claire's voice was barely a whisper.

"Well, after Alessandro found out about what the Strega Onesta had done, he cast a counter-curse. Like me, he would never age, never die, but if he found Katarina first and was able to make her love him for ten years, then her original soul would be locked in forever. We'd never be able to recover her . . . ever. She'd be his and his curse would lift, while mine would remain for all time." My stomach turned with the memories of how close that had actually come to happening in the past. I had to take a deep breath to steady myself.

Claire took in my words as they permeated in the silence. I sat unmoving, waiting for her to digest this new information.

"And this has been going on for four hundred years?" Claire asked.

"Four hundred and forty-four." I let the last syllable resonate in the quiet room.

It was Willem who broke the silence. "Well, I suppose we should come up with a plan for tomorrow," he said as he took a seat on a chair near the windows, overlooking the street. "Apparently, you have a coffee date."

Claire and I snapped out of our trance and looked at each other. It was at that moment I realized in less than twenty-four hours I'd be in the presence of my love once more. My heart pulsed through my ribcage. I instinctively brought my hand to my chest and held it there, trying to hold in what was so blatantly trying to escape.

"Don't worry," Claire said. She put her arm around my shoulders. "Tomorrow will be fine. I know what coffee shop she's talking about. I'll go before and cleanse it. I'll make sure there's nothing there that would leave any mark on you or Kate."

"I'll go too," Willem offered.

"You probably shouldn't," Claire responded. "I can perform a basic cleansing and protection spell on my own. Besides, if Alessandro did leave something lying about, it would probably recognize you, or at least tip him off that there's old magick about." She sounded confident as she spoke. "Also," she added, "even if my magick were sensed, it's the magick of a Watcher, not a Strega. It's also pretty new, and there'd be no way he'd associate it with the two of you. Let me take care of this," she said as she stood to leave. "You know, this stuff may be new to me, but I'm not a complete newbie."

She headed toward the door, her movements light and graceful. "Good night," she said. "I'll need my rest if I'm going to do my best for you tomorrow."

I watched her as she opened the door and quickly exited. Again, she seemed to be in hurry to leave the room. Why? Probably information overload.

Everything about her seemed a little off tonight, not necessarily in a bad way, just different. More uncomfortable, perhaps. I knew from my brief conversation with Willem earlier that she was still adjusting to her magical talents, but it seemed like there was something more. Something strangely familiar. Something I couldn't quite put my finger on.

I didn't quite know what to think of it until I noticed, just before she left the room, when she thought no one was looking, the way she looked over her shoulder to spy one last glimpse at Willem before she left.

My mouth opened in surprise. Her nervousness. Her shy smiles. Her darting eyes. It all made sense now. Everything always seemed to be crystal clear, if you stood on the outside and looked in.

I only hoped it wasn't too late for an old Pagan like Willem to fall in love too.

Thirteen

KATE

I wasn't quite sure why I was so nervous, okay maybe I did, but I couldn't eat all morning, and I almost jumped through the ceiling at the sound of Alex's voice as he called down from the shower.

How could meeting someone for coffee jumble my thoughts and make it impossible to calm down? What was the big deal? It was perfectly okay to meet up with a friend for coffee. I mean, I was just helping a new person in town. It wasn't as if it were my idea or anything. Still, I couldn't help but think that if Alex found out, he'd be more than a little irritated. Scratch that. He'd freaking destroy me. I thought it funny, in a very serious way, how I was willing to take that risk, even though the accompanying guilt that played with the edges of my coherent thought began to fray my sanity.

Honestly, I really didn't know why I was going. It was as if I was pulled to him in the bookstore by some otherworldly force and I just couldn't refuse. Or maybe I was just making excuses because I was still hurting after my disaster of an anniversary and attention from a handsome stranger just felt good. Dave had found me just after Gio left, and I didn't bother mentioning it to him at the time, which was further indicating that I knew I shouldn't go. But now I was dying to tell someone. I was dying to release my conscience on someone and spill my innermost secrets. Less than twenty-four hours had passed since I met Gio, and I felt as if part of me was fading without him. How was that possible? It wasn't. It didn't make sense. There was only one exaplanation. I was a terrible wife.

I cursed at myself and went back to making Alex's coffee. As the rich, dark brown liquid percolated through the machine, I felt a twinge of guilt at the lack of care I held for my husband's feelings in this. I knew in my core his feelings would be hurt, he wouldn't like it one bit, but the hard truth was I didn't care enough about them to cancel my plans. Besides, he'd probably just flip out like he did this past weekend, and I'd avoid that at all costs.

It's just coffee. Nothing more...right?

After Alex left, I went about my morning as normally as I could. Shower? Check. Cute outfit? Check. I hesitated before grabbing the small bottle of fragrance and walking through a perfume mist. I rarely wore fragrance. *Would it be too obvious? Would Dave suspect?* I grabbed my work bag and a tube of lipstick before heading downstairs to answer the door for Dave, who leaned casually against the frame.

"You ready?" he asked, looking around the room as I opened the door.

"Yeah, let's go," I said as I pushed past him.

"Whoa, whoa, what's the hurry? Is everything okay?" he said as he caught his footing.

"Yeah, everything's fine. I'm just ready."

He furrowed his brow as he intently inspected my face digging for information.

"Where's Alex? Are you okay?" There was concern in his voice.

"He's already left for work. Why?"

"Oh," he said as he instantly relaxed.

"Why?" I insisted.

"No reason," he replied. "Just trying to figure out what the big secret is."

"What secret? There's no secret. Why do you think there's a secret?" I shot back, a little too quickly. Shit, I was already blowing it. Earlier this morning I'd been dying to tell Dave every detail about Gio, but now all I wanted to do was to keep it to myself. Something inside me screamed to keep things to myself.

"Sure there's not." He paused. "Are you sure everything's all right?" He looked me up and down again.

"Yes, I'm fine. Alex is fine. Everything is fine. There's no secret. I just want to get to work. Unlike you, when I miss a day, I need to kick things up a notch to catch up." I was grasping for straws. My cover was glass; Dave saw right through it.

"No secret? Okay. We'll go with that." He raised an eyebrow. "Whatever it is, I'll figure it out, you know. Whether you want me to or not, I *will* figure it out."

He relaxed his shoulders and casually walked past me to his car. He got in and started the engine. I was barely buckled up before he took off. He reached toward the stereo and began searching the stations.

"So, what'd you do last night?" he asked.

"Nothing much, really. Just hung out. You?" I tried to keep my tone as light as possible.

"Oh, nothing," he answered back. "You know, just the usual. Dinner, shower, TV." There was a short pause. I knew him well enough to know that he was calculating his next move. "So, did you and Alex have a good night? He hasn't had any more psychotic episodes, has he?"

I sighed. "No. Everything's fine. You know, if you keep driving this slow, we'll never get to work."

I'd noticed he was driving ten miles below the speed limit, very unlike the Dave I knew. Most days he drove so fast I barely had time to realize we'd left the house before we were already at work. My only guess was that he was trying to prolong our time in the car so he could pump me for more information.

I didn't know why I was being so secretive with Dave. It felt odd, keeping things from him; he was my proverbial partner in crime. I should've been excited to share my secret.

However, as soon as Gio had left and Dave met up with me a few minutes later, a hot orb in the center of my stomach urged me to keep everything on the down low. I couldn't bear to keep things from him. He was my best friend. He was what kept me sane. Call it guilt, call it shame, call it whatever, but I just felt like I couldn't tell him . . . not yet.

He drove the rest of the way in silence, and I knew he was put off by my apparent lack of interest in divulging to him, but I was too high-strung about my impending meeting to remedy the situation.

When we got to the office, I didn't wait for the interrogation to continue. I got out of the car quickly. He got out and we headed toward the building. I was relieved we walked in silence. I wouldn't be able to focus on conversation, anyway; my thoughts were miles away.

The morning dragged on. I wasn't actually watching the second hand move around in a lazy circle, but I might as well have been, my eyes sought out the clock on the wall no less than fifty thousand times.

Dave seemed to notice the attention I was giving the time and every ten minutes or so would appear over my shoulder and casually ask me a mundane question.

Repeated questioning was a tactic he used when I tried to

hold out on him. If Dave was anything, he was predictable in his persistence. I knew he would continue to ask me random and meaningless questions over and over and over, letting me get nothing done, until I broke down and confessed. Childish? Possibly. Effective? Most definitely. But this time I wouldn't give in, and it was starting to get on his nerves.

Besides, I was pretty sure I'd have to give in sooner rather than later, due to the one little problem I hadn't thought about until just a few minutes prior. How was I going to get to the coffee shop?

As usual, Dave had picked me up for work. I was so nervous and in such a hurry to get out of the house that I didn't realize I'd need a car. I'd spent the majority of the morning worrying about how I was going to handle that detail while avoiding Dave's questioning every ten minutes.

It was no use; I'd have to fold. Just as I was about to break down and fill him in on everything, I overheard one of the managing editors ask a small group of interns if one of them would pick up an order at the annex downtown. Her mentioning the use of the company car was all I needed to decide. My personal prayer had been answered.

I jumped from my desk and accepted the errand, claiming I was heading that way and could stop by and be back before lunch was over. A small lie, but hey, I seemed to be getting better at those by the minute.

Dave's mouth dropped open in what I can only assume was pure and utter shock as I graciously accepted what we both considered to be grunt work. He stared at me; his narrowed eyes laden with suspicion. I avoided direct eye contact as I took the keys from the editor and, with her thanks, hurried to my desk to collect my belongings. As I grabbed my purse and coat, the tube of lipstick I'd snatched from the bathroom that morning tumbled out of one of the pockets.

It rolled, in slow motion, across the floor and came to a stop right at the tip of Dave's shoe. With an exaggerated movement, he bent over and picked it up. The tube was small in his hands as he turned it around in his fingers.

"What in the hell is this?" he questioned as he removed the top—a deep red revealing itself as he twisted it.

"Red? Really?" Dave's voice was beyond patience. He sounded quite fed up with my unwillingness to talk. He took a deep breath and asked once more, "Katie, what the hell is going on? I know something is up. Why won't you just tell me?"

I looked at the clock once more. It was quarter to eleven; I didn't have a moment to spare. I walked over to him and held my hand out for the tube. "Please. I promise I'll explain everything when I get back. I just have to go right now." He continued to hold the tube hostage in his grasp. I pleaded, "Please, Dave. When I get back. I promise."

He must've seen the desperation in my eyes because his expression softened, and he willingly handed over the lipstick without another word.

"As soon as you get back." I heard him call as I hurried toward the elevator.

Miraculously, I arrived at the coffee shop before Gio and strategically chose a table in the patio, off to the side. It was the kind of spot where you could see everything happen around you but still be hard to be seen. I must've been there no more than three or four minutes before I heard his voice.

"Kate, you came." Again, I was taken aback by the way his voice was oddly familiar.

"Gio, hello." My muscles relaxed. How could a complete stranger make me feel so comfortable?

He sat and placed two coffees on the table. "I hope you like Americano," he said as he offered me one of the beverages.

"Um, yeah. That's amazing. It's my favorite. How'd you know?" I stared at him in disbelief.

"Just a guess." He smiled and made himself comfortable as he took a cautious sip from his cup. Even his most simple movements intrigued me. I caught myself staring at his lips for no particular reason other than that was where my eyes led me.

"So," I began, not quite knowing where the conversation would take me, "you're new to Freestone. What would you like to know?"

"Well, I thought you could just kind of give me a rundown about what kind of place this is. I just landed here by chance and am still feeling my way around."

He leaned back into his chair, his arms folded across his body. The long sleeve cotton shirt he was wearing was tight around his biceps and shoulders. Not too small, just perfectly snug. I forced myself to pull my eyes away from the smoothness of his chest and looked at his face. It was boyish in a very manly way. He had no facial hair, and I was glad of it. A beard would just cover his amazing, olive-toned skin. He had to be no older than twenty-two or three. My God, what was I doing here?

"You arrived by chance? That's interesting." I smiled at the thought. Could someone actually happen upon this town? Freestone was nearly impossible to happen upon, it was so far north of the city. Sometimes it seemed so far north of *anything*.

"Interesting? How's that?" he pressed.

"It's just that this is such a small town, and it's so out of the way. It's not exactly a tourist attraction." Sometimes it still amazed me that I lived here.

"Well, that can be a good thing. I was looking for something a little more permanent." The fire behind his eyes forced excitement to run through my body as he spoke.

It must've been a minute before I realized I was staring

again. I diverted my eyes away from his as I tried to continue casually.

"So, here we are." I listened to the playful voice that came out of my mouth and knew it was wrong. Was I flirting? I shouldn't even be here. I studied my coffee. I should leave. He's so young. I'm married. This isn't right.

Gio shifted in his chair. "I really appreciate you meeting me. What else can you tell me about Freestone other than it's a little out of the way?" He gave a brilliant smile. It was warm, inviting. I felt it vibrate through me and relaxed. It took me a second to realize he was waiting for an answer.

"Oh, um, it's a great little town . . . kinda artsy. Really mellow but still pretty progressive, you know? Though, at times it can be a little too low key." I sighed. "I really do miss the city, though I suppose I'm happy I don't live there anymore. I've been here about eight years now."

I stopped short of mentioning the small fact that I was married, though I knew it was just a matter of minutes, perhaps seconds, before I would have to mention it anyway, considering the gold band currently wrapped around my finger like a banner. I hated myself for not wanting to tell Gio about Alex. What was I thinking?

Up until just recently, Alex had been the man I'd always hoped for. Despite his short bursts of anger, he was everything I'd ever dreamed of. I felt horrible and guilty for just being there, yet not guilty enough for me to leave. What kind of a person did this make me?

How was it possible I'd justified my meeting Gio for coffee? My voice of reason told me my behavior over the past twenty-four hours was disgusting and vile and completely unacceptable. Too bad I wasn't listening in the slightest. In fact, it was almost as if my other secret inner voice was telling me it was imperative I not only meet with Gio this time, but at every other chance I got, as well.

And then he asked the question I knew was inevitable, though I was hoping somehow it could've been miraculously avoided.

"So why'd you choose Freestone? How did you end up here?"

I knew it was coming. I almost wished it'd come sooner. Then, I reasoned, I wouldn't have had this unwarranted feeling of hope that somehow, Gio and I would be able to get closer.

"Well," I began, looking him straight into his eyes, "it was Alex's idea to move here."

That was it. I'd led him on long enough. At the very least I owed him the courtesy of eye contact, though I'd rather have crawled in a hole, as I revealed I'd accepted a date with him while married. Was it a date, though? It was just coffee, right? My hands began to tremble, and I had to grip my cup tighter in order to mask the tremors.

I swallowed once more before I continued. "Alex, my husband, found this place just after we married nine years ago. He's always loved the country. The rolling hills, he said, reminded him of home. Though I'm not sure how similar the hills of Philadelphia are to here, but who knows, right?"

I saw something flicker in his eyes, though I couldn't quite place what it was. His smile twitched for just an instant when I had mentioned Alex's name, but faded almost as soon as it had appeared, his composure immediately regained.

I threw myself into apology mode. "I'm sorry. I should've mentioned I was married earlier. I hope this isn't awkward. I didn't mean to lead you to believe this could ever be more than just coffee. I . . ." I faltered in embarrassment. My cheeks burned.

"Kate," he interrupted. His voice was smooth and caressed my feelings of guilt. "Please don't think anything of it. You've done nothing wrong. If anything, I should apologize to you for making you feel uncomfortable. I hope this hasn't caused any strain between you and your husband . . . Alex, did you say?" He chose his words carefully, his voice gentle.

"Yeah, Alex. But it didn't come up—our plans—so no harm, no foul." Well, unless you considered it harmful that I'd intentionally kept my little rendezvous a secret from my husband and had no intention to mention it ever, even if directly questioned. Then, I suppose, one could argue there might be irreparable harm done to my morality or lack thereof. I gave an embarrassed half-smile.

Somehow, Gio's eyes appeared pleased, no, relieved, that I hadn't told Alex about our meeting. His pleasure seemed to confirm that this entire situation was definitely in the wrong.

"Look, I'm not sure why I'm here. I'm not sure of a lot of things lately. And I'm not sure why I didn't tell my husband. The more I think about my recent behavior, the more I wonder about the kind of person I am." I spoke the last part more to myself than to him. I shook my head.

"But that's beside the point. The point is I'm sorry for misleading you in any way and if it means anything, I'm glad we did meet, even if just for today. I don't know why or if this makes any sense whatsoever, but I kind of have this feeling that I really didn't have a choice in the matter anyway."

"You don't have to—" he began, but I didn't give him a chance to explain.

"No, I owe you an explanation. I want to. I'm not the kind of person that acts so selfishly. It was wrong of me to lead you on like that. I'm sorry." My shoulders felt instantly lighter as I said all I'd needed to say. The silence that followed edged in from around us and seemed to create a bubble that encircled where we were seated.

It was as if external sound did not exist at all. Everything in the background faded to nil and there we were, sitting in the eye of a silent vortex, our eyes fixed on each other, neither willing to pull away first.

As it appeared that he was not leaving, in light of my recent confessions, I became aware once more that I was staring. True to form, I dropped my eyes nervously.

"So, what do you do?" I desperately tried to change the subject.

"I'm a writer," he answered, never breaking his gaze from me.

"A writer? Really? I work at a publishing company. What do you write?"

"Fiction, mostly, though I've dabbled in poetry and some freelance, but I like to push myself into new genres. In fact, my most recent book is a nonfiction."

"Nonfiction, that's quite a jump. What's it about?" I asked as I leaned closer toward him.

"It's a history of two lovers. A romance, of sorts." I could tell by his face that he was very serious about his subject.

"Really? And it's nonfiction? Who's it about? Anyone I know?" I pushed, completely absorbed in his every word.

"I'm pretty sure you'd know them if I told you, but I don't think I'm ready to reveal my subjects just yet." He smiled.

"I'm sorry, I didn't mean to pry. It's just that you don't find too many nonfiction love stories these days. Would you at least tell me if it has a happy ending?"

He took a deep breath and hesitated before he answered, his gaze trailing off into the distance. "With all my soul, I hope so."

He seemed sad, almost in a guilty way. I wasn't sure if it was my questioning or something else I'd said, but I got the distinct feeling his sadness was directed toward me.

"I didn't mean anything by it," I began, trying to erase any error I'd unintentionally committed during the conversation.

There was no use trying to save all the intentional ones committed thus far, there were just too many of them.

"Kate, you've done nothing wrong." He laughed lightly before he continued. "I was just thinking, wondering, really, would you mind helping me with my book? I could really use a person with some experience in this arena to throw ideas back and forth with. Especially a woman, who would have a different viewpoint."

"Sure, that'd be great. I'm flattered," I answered with enthusiasm. I should've said no. I should've gotten up and left. Instead, I sat there and couldn't help but agree to meet again.

More time with Gio? Of course I'd help him, despite the fact that every fiber in my being told me I'd have to be very careful, that I was dangerously close to something that would alter life as I knew it. Surprisingly, I found I was willing to risk that possibility. Hell, I'd be willing to write the damn book myself and give it to him just so he could ask me to work on it with him.

"Thank you," he barely spoke, almost breathless. He sounded more sincere than I'd heard anyone sound before, and I wondered what I'd done to deserve such a sentiment. "I'm in need of someone to help me read through what I've got. You know, for pacing, flow . . . coherency." He flashed a brilliant smile.

My cheeks pulled at the corners of my mouth as I returned the smile. Something about him just felt—I couldn't put my finger on it, but it just felt like it was supposed to be.

"So, do you have anything currently publish . . ." My voice trailed off and I froze as my eyes wandered to the entrance of the patio. There was Dave, leaning nonchalantly against a heat lamp, watching me, a look of unreserved smugness spread across his face. As our gaze met he raised his eyebrows at me, his lips upturned in a too sweet smile. Oh, shit.

"Kate? Is everything okay?" He was staring at me trying to make eye contact.

Before I could take time to think, I went into a semi-panic. "Oh, I'm fine. I was just thinking about something I forgot to do at work. Gio, I'm so sorry, but I have to go." I stood to leave.

"Kate, wait. When can I see you again?" he pleaded.

"Oh, um, soon, I hope. Listen, I really had a good time. Thanks for the coffee," I said, full panic setting in.

Dave was threatening with his body language to approach us. It was the last thing in the world I wanted to do, but I had to get out of there. I seized my purse and took a step away.

Gio's hand grabbed mine. His touch fired through my body with the speed and accuracy of an arrow hitting its mark. I stopped and turned to look at him, the air sucked from my lungs.

Again, the world ceased to exist for anyone but us. There was no movement. There was no sound. There was nothing but the two of us and that in itself, was everything.

A warm wave washed over my body and tingled from the inside out. I staggered back, my eyes widened. Gio pulled his hand back. This time, I didn't drop my eyes from his gaze. I held it and gave back in my look what I felt he'd given me in his touch.

I grabbed a pen from my purse and pulled a clean napkin from the holder on the table. I quickly wrote down my direct line at the office.

"This is my work number," I said. "Call me when you want to meet again. I'm there most days."

"I'll call you. I promise." He sounded like he truly meant it.

I don't know why those last two words struck such a chord in me, but they were the words that gave me permission to walk away. Although I didn't know him well—hell, I didn't know him at all— *somehow* I knew he was a man of his word and if he said he'd call, I'd get a call.

I walked right past Dave at the edge of the patio and straight to the company car. As I fumbled in my purse for the keys, his voice came from behind me.

"Kate, I thought we were friends." Disbelief and hurt made their way to my ear.

Why'd he have to sound so sincerely upset? It would've been easier to be mad. He did, after all, follow me, and who knows how long he'd been spying. But he was probably counting on the fact I'd never been able to hold a grudge when his feelings were hurt.

"Dave," I replied, "we *are* friends. Best friends."

I turned to face him. The distress in his eyes alone was enough to send me into a spiral of despair.

"Then why won't you tell me what's going on? Maybe I can help. Who is that?"

I took a careful breath before I spoke. "I told you I'd tell you everything when I got back to the office. This isn't exactly what it seems. I'm sorry you felt the need to spy on me to find out. Truly, I am. But I said I'd tell you and I will."

I felt as if I'd been apologizing all morning and nothing seemed to be getting any better. Every time I thought I was past the guilt, a new reason popped up and the whole process started all over again. God, what was my problem? I wanted to kick my own ass.

"Look, I'll meet you back at the office in thirty minutes. Let me just do the shit errand I was supposed to be doing in the first place, and then I'll head straight back. We can talk then, okay? I swear." The office wasn't my ideal place to confess to quasi-adulterous behaviors, but it would have to do for now.

"Dave, please." I reached out and put my hand on his shoulder.

"All right, fine," he said, "I'll go back to the office and wait, but I'm only doing it because I love you and I'm worried about you. You're not yourself lately."

He turned and walked back to the car that had driven me to work so many times before. I watched as he drove off, and then jumped into the company car and sped out of the parking lot.

As I left, I shot a quick glance in the rearview mirror. A petite woman, who looked as if she were barely out of high school, ran across the parking lot, her shockingly pink locks blowing in all directions.

Though I'd only seen her once, I recognized her as the girl I saw walking with Gio the very first time I laid eyes on him. I wondered if it was coincidence I saw her now, or if it were something else. I was startled as a pang of jealousy shot through me like cold steel.

I knew I'd no reason to feel the way I did about Gio, but the thought of him and this strange woman having some sort of relationship struck a sensitive chord within me. I felt jealousy deep within my core and had to force myself to focus on the task at hand.

I pushed the girl out of my mind and drove out of the parking lot. I'd deal with my neurosis later. At the moment, I had an errand to run, a marriage to rethink, and a friendship to save. The day was certainly filling up.

I walked into the office and made my way to my cubicle. I sat in my chair and stared at the growing pile of work that had been accumulating while I was apparently living in another world.

What was happening to me? For as long as I could remember, my life was built upon order and sanity. I'd never missed a day of work, let alone willingly ditched one. I'd never *not* finished an assignment. I was one of the few who stayed late at the office. I was the one who could be counted on to do what no one else would do.

I lived for order and organization and, most of all, took pride in my work. However, as I stared at the tower of papers and folders I hadn't even touched over the past few days, I realized something was changing inside me, though I hadn't the foggiest as to what it was.

I tossed my purse under my desk and covered my face with my hands. I closed my eyes and let out a heavy sigh. I sat there motionless and waited. I knew it was just a matter of time before Dave made his way over to me.

Four minutes later he walked into my small space. He pulled a short stool next to my chair and sat.

"Kate?" Dave's voice was soft, careful.

I should've trusted in him more than I had, and I honestly felt horrible about how I'd treated him, but I couldn't do anything about that now. I brought my hands down and opened my eyes.

"I'm sorry. I should've told you." I kept my voice low so as to not attract unwanted attention from anyone who might be in the area.

"Yeah, you should have." His voice sounded hurt.

"I really don't know where to start, but—" I began.

Dave put up his hand to stop my words. "Wait. Grab that stack," he said, pointing to the mountain of unread manuscripts precariously piled next to my keyboard. "I know somewhere we can go through those and talk while we work that's a little more private."

I nodded and without question grabbed the stack and followed him to the second-floor conference room.

The room was small and stuffy. The one small window on the west wall had a reasonably amazing view of the surrounding vineyards, but had been broken for months now and, therefore, unable to let fresh air in. Because of that small detail, the room was rarely used, and when it was occupied, it was by those who wanted to hide while they worked. There were only a few regulars, Dave and I included, that used the room. On this day, I was grateful we were the only two there. As soon as we were both sitting at the table, he started in on me.

"What the hell is going on? And don't try to bullshit me. I knew you were keeping something from me this morning, but I was going to let you work it through." He barely took a breath. "And then, you volunteered for that shit errand, and then the lipstick. My God, Kate. Red lipstick! I knew something was up then, and . . . how could you not tell me you're having an affair? How can you not trust me?"

"Whoa. Slow down. I'm not having an affair." I was almost shouting to be heard over his ranting.

"You're not having an affair?" He looked confused. "But I saw you with that hot, young guy. And the way the two of you looked at each other—well, it was something, let me tell you. I thought for sure you were having an affair."

I let Dave's explanation settle. Holy shit. I was so enraptured by Gio's every action I didn't even begin to consider what we must've looked like to others around us. What if someone I knew saw us? What if someone who knew Alex saw us? My throat tightened. God, what was I doing?

"I'm not having an affair. I was just having coffee with someone I met at the bookstore yesterday while I was waiting for you."

He wasn't fooled.

"Oh, I see, you were just on a date with an amazingly handsome man you met while at the bookstore. That's all it was, my mistake." His sarcasm was thick. He took a deep breath and brought his hands to his face. "Please, talk to me." He was almost pleading now.

"Yes, I mean, no, I mean, sort of." I let out a frustrated

sigh. "Look, I'm sorry for not filling you in on what was going on, but if you want to know now, then just hold on for one second and listen."

His silence was all the answer I needed.

"Yesterday, when I was waiting for you at the bookstore, I met Gio. He knocked over a stack of books and I helped pick them up. We got to talking and I found out he was new in town. He asked me to coffee, thought I could tell him a bit more about Freestone, and that's it."

I gave him the edited version, of course. My mental fingers were crossed. Lies by omission aren't quite as bad, right? I'd figured I'd have my hands full explaining myself, without the added layer of the completely unexplained enchantment Gio held for me.

"And when he asked you out, did he know you were married? I mean, granted, I know Alex has been completely out of line lately. I know that. But did you even bother to mention that you were married before this guy asked you out?"

"No," I said quietly, there was nothing else I could say. "But he knows now. I told him today."

"And . . .?" he led.

"And what?" I replied.

"Did he even care that he was on a date with a married woman?"

"Dave, it wasn't like that," I lied . . . again. Sort of. "He honestly just wanted to know a little more about Freestone. He's also a writer. He's working on a nonfiction book now, and it actually sounds pretty intriguing. He's asked me to take a look and toss ideas back and forth."

"I'm just concerned about where this could lead. I'm concerned about you. Lately you've been so . . . *not* yourself. And Alex. I mean, if Alex ever found out—"

"Found out what?" I challenged. "That I'm working with

a writer whose book I'm editing? Besides, there's nothing to find out because there's nothing going on."

"I just hope you know what you're doing."

"I do. And I'm not going to stop seeing him. He knows I can never be more than just a friend and he's fine with that. Besides, I like being around him. He's interesting. I like him." I'd never spoken with such unabashed confidence before. I saw Dave look at me in surprise. I tried to lighten the tone of the conversation. "Don't worry so much. It'll give you wrinkles."

He looked at me and then a smile broke out across his face. "It's amazing," he said.

"What is?"

"How I've been trying everything I know to get you to wear lipstick for who-knows-how-many years, and all I needed to do was to get some hot kid with some lips to die for to ask you to coffee." His voice slipped back into his normal tone and I knew he'd forgiven me—for now.

"He *is* pretty hot," I conceded with a smile.

"You think? Geez, Katie love, you sure can pick 'em."

He reached over the table and went for the envelope at the top of the pile that was strewn over the table. He shook his head to himself as he tore open the deep golden cover and pulled out the manuscript.

My shoulders felt lighter and all was better as I grabbed the next package from the pile. I ripped it open and looked at the manuscript inside. Single-spaced. The only manuscripts I didn't read were those that didn't conform to our guidelines. I pushed it aside and went for the next envelope as Dave tossed the one he was reading into a rejection pile. We continued in near silence, only making a random comment here and there, until the stack was down to practically nothing.

"Shall we head back?" I asked collecting the manuscripts I thought could use a more serious read.

"Let's go," Dave said, grabbing the rejection pile.

We headed up to our floor and made it just in time to catch my phone ringing. I ran to pick it up.

"Good morning, Kate Martins."

"It's a little late for the morning, wouldn't you say?"

My heart gave a shock as Alex's voice came through the receiver. I don't know who I was expecting, but Alex was not the one. He rarely called me at work, and when he did, it was planned.

"Oh, yeah, I guess so. I've been working straight since . . . oh, hours ago." I peeked at the clock on my desk. He was right; it was almost four. Where had the time gone? Today was flying by.

I realized he was waiting for me to acknowledge him and though I was still feeling wary from this weekend, I didn't want him to think I was holding a grudge. That would be all I needed. I was already feeling a little guilty about my meeting with Gio this morning, but I'd live. I didn't think I'd be able to live through another one of Alex's fits of rage. Not yet, anyway.

"Hey, Alex," I greeted as I struggled not to reveal the soreness of my psyche. "What's up, love?"

Dave gave me a sideways glance as he put his armload of papers on the corner of my desk, probably musing over the hypocrisy between my words and my actions of this morning.

Funny, I understood them as two separate entities. My meeting with Gio had nothing to do with the relationship I had with my husband. I could just imagine, though, how Dave viewed them as one and the same. I decided to ignore him.

"Oh, nothing," Alex replied. "I was just calling to let you know that I'll be home late tonight. I'm behind schedule and as if things couldn't get any more hectic, I had to bump up a meeting scheduled for tomorrow to late this afternoon. I'm sorry, love. It looks like I won't be home until ten or eleven."

"That's okay. I've got a lot to do, as well. Not as much as you, it seems, but I'll probably be staying a little late myself."

"All right, sweetheart," he said.

There was something about his voice that bothered me. Did he always use this many terms of endearment when speaking to me? I'd never realized it before, but he seemed to be laying it on pretty thick. Maybe he still felt guilty about this weekend. Or maybe it was this weekend that had smeared a bit of his image for me.

Since the moment I met him, he'd always been a portrait of perfection. A brand-new canvas painted with flawless strokes, a masterpiece.

But recently the image seemed different, almost distorted. It was like someone had left the masterpiece unprotected in a damp garage, the moisture in the air corroding the colors and bleeding them slowly.

"Love? You still there, baby?" He interrupted my thoughts.

"I'm still here." I scrambled to come up with an excuse for not listening to what he'd been saying. The words came with ease. "I'm sorry, I just got distracted by some work. You were saying?"

"No big deal, I was just saying you shouldn't wait up for me. Be a good girl tonight without me." There was something to his tone that was different.

"What is that supposed to mean?" I snapped back, offended by the insinuation. I mean, sure, I'd been acting questionably lately, but he didn't know that. And after all, wasn't he the one that just recently flipped out on me?

"Nothing, love." He chuckled, and said, "I'm just teasing you . . . unless there's something you're not telling me?"

"Don't be ridiculous," I replied. Lies. I was filled with lies. "Listen, I'll leave a plate in the fridge for you. I was planning on making pasta tonight."

"Don't bother. I'll just grab something out here. I've gotta go, love. I'll call later."

"Okay. Bye."

He'd already hung up by the time I reached the last syllable. I put down the receiver and felt relieved I wouldn't have to deal with him later tonight. Surprisingly, I wasn't my usual emotional self.

True, this morning I'd been a wreck. But after meeting with Gio, I felt recharged . . . no, *grounded*. Like I'd been waiting for something to bring life into focus for me. It just so happened that something came in the form of a handsome, twenty-something wandering writer.

I smiled to myself.

Dave cleared his throat. "So that was Alex?" he asked, already knowing the answer.

"Yeah," I responded, my smile fading. "He just wanted to let me know I shouldn't wait up for him tonight. Slammed at work, or something."

I thought a moment about the conversation I'd just finished, and then called Dave just as he had turned to leave.

"Hey, Dave? Has Alex always used an absurd amount of endearment terms when speaking to me?"

Dave rolled his eyes. "Don't tell me you've never noticed it before," he replied. "It's quite over the top, actually. You know, when we first started hanging out, I couldn't handle it. It was like he was trying to prove something, but I pushed it aside. I thought it was because you were just married and all that. Newlywed syndrome. Then, as the years went by, it just never stopped. I realized that was how he always spoke to you. A bit much, if you ask me."

"Why didn't you mention it, if it bothered you so much?"

"Well, honestly?" he asked.

I nodded. I was tired of the screen I'd been living behind. I was ready to look at the truth straight on.

"Honestly, you really seemed to need it. I mean you've never been a poster child for confident women, at least not as long as I've known you. And besides, after a while, I was just able to kind of tune it out."

"Really?" I asked.

"I'm sorry. I didn't mean to hurt your feelings."

"No, you didn't. It's the truth. Thank you for being honest."

I really had some thinking to do. Had I changed so much over the past nine years that even when my best friend described me, I didn't recognize who I was anymore? Was I really so much different since marrying Alex?

"Look, we're still planning on heading out around six-thirty, right? I'll check in with you a little later, okay?" His voice was gentle; even when dealing a painful blow to the ego, he was gentle about it.

He smiled once more, and then headed back to his office, meandering through the cubicle maze.

How bizarre it was to hear I was lacking in self-esteem. When did all that start? Throughout my childhood and adolescence, I'd always had a strong grip on who I was. Even during my awkward teen years, I remember being happy. I couldn't have imagined that, could I?

When did things begin to change? It didn't take long to guess when my life had taken a sweeping turn. At the time, I'd thought it'd been for the better, but now I wasn't so sure.

I immediately shook those thoughts out of my head. What was happening to me? Did Alex's behavior this weekend resonate so deep within me that I was beginning to question our ever meeting?

Or was it my own actions that had set my discontent into motion? Was it possible I'd been lying to myself for over nine years? Was it possible that somewhere deep within my heart,

I'd always known Alex wasn't the person I was supposed to be with?

I shook my head. But how could that be? He was everything I'd ever wanted, or at least that's what I'd been telling myself repeatedly.

No, something was wrong with me, I was positive.

I knew I shouldn't make comparisons, but I just couldn't help myself. Couldn't or wouldn't, I wasn't sure, but my mind insisted that I compare how I felt when I was with Alex to how I'd felt this morning, when I was with Gio.

I cursed myself for even going there, but it was too late, and the comparison was no contest. By far, I'd never felt more complete than I had this morning at coffee. So complete, in fact, that it rattled my core and had me second-guessing every decision I'd made for almost a decade now.

The grass is always greener . . .

Even if Alex's behavior was unacceptable, I should cut him some slack. He deserved better than my quick judgments. He had been with me for nearly ten years. One hundred percent fully committed. He deserved everything I had to offer: love, patience, kindness, and much more.

My brain reiterated that Alex, whose only apparent flaws were that he loved me too intensely and had an occasional bad temper, was indeed my husband, the man I'd chosen to marry. The man who above all else, would look after me and take care of me until death do us part. He deserved my commitment.

Or at least that was what I kept repeating to myself as I picked up the receiver of my ringing phone to a voice I didn't realize I'd been waiting to hear until I heard it and a sudden wave of relief washed over my heart.

"Hey, Kate. It's me, Gio," he said, reservation in his voice. "I hope I'm not bothering you much. I can call back another time."

"No, I'm not busy at all," I replied offhand, as all the

reasons why Alex deserved my very best got tucked neatly away into the recesses of my brain.

"Great. I just wanted to know if we could schedule a time to meet again. You know, for my book?" I could tell he was tentative, as if by calling the same day, he was breaking some unspoken code of conduct when dealing with people you've just recently met.

"You know"—I heard myself speaking the words though I had no idea of where they were coming from— "I actually have some time tonight. I'll be here at work for another couple of hours, but I'm pretty much free from seven to about nine thirty. Does that work for you?"

"That would be perfect," he said, quickly adding, "but I wouldn't want to interfere with anything you and your husband had planned. I don't want you to feel obligated to make it tonight or anything."

"First of all, tonight Alex is working late, so I'd just be hanging out, watching reality TV or something. Second, I don't feel obligated to do anything. I want to help out. And believe me, tonight is perfect for me too. The only question I have is where?"

"I think I've got that covered." His voice was more confident now. "I may be new in town, but I have the perfect meeting place. Do you know the conference room on the second floor of the bookstore? No one is using it tonight. What do you think?"

"That sounds great. How about I meet you there around seven?" I offered.

"I can't wait."

There was silence on the other end and for a moment I thought he'd hung up.

"Gio? You still there?" I asked.

"Yeah, sorry." His voice was quiet, raspy. "Hey, Kate, I just want you to know I really am looking forward to seeing you tonight."

A pang of guilt shot through my body, and it wasn't for Alex's sake. My brain told me that if I were smart, I wouldn't meet up with Gio later tonight. I wouldn't if I didn't want to hurt him later on.

I knew I didn't, but I just couldn't will myself not to see him. I couldn't explain it, but I knew the instant I saw him again later, my life would be changed even more, like I was merely waiting for this to happen. That I was supposed to make this change.

"Yeah, me too."

I heard the line click on his side and I gently placed my receiver in the holder. I looked at the clock. I still had a couple more hours of work, but my mind was ready to leave.

After sitting and staring at the clock for another five minutes, I came to a conclusion. Although it appeared I was willing to make a complete mess of my personal life, I didn't want to shatter my professional one.

It disturbed me that my career took precedence over my marriage, and even though I hoped I wasn't actually the horrible person I was becoming, I was able to reconcile it to myself. Because no matter how I turned it over in my brain, I just couldn't see myself *not* being a part of Gio's life.

As I worked into the early evening, I mulled over the recent developments in my life. Distracting as they were, I was able to make significant progress in reducing the mountain on my desk.

I was still deep in work and thought when I heard a small knock on my cubicle wall. I swung around to see Dave leaning against the side of the entrance.

"You just about ready?" he asked.

"Yeah, just let me finish up this one thing and . . ." I stacked the papers in a neat pile and stuck them in the return envelope, addressed it and stamped the return address in the top left-hand corner. "There. Ready."

I grabbed my purse and jacket and followed Dave out to his car, wondering if I should casually mention I needed to be dropped off downtown instead of my house or if I should just have him drop me off at home and then drive downtown myself.

Dave started the engine. I looked at the clock on the control panel. It was almost seven. If he dropped me off at home first, I'd risk being late to meet Gio. That wasn't an option.

I didn't give him a second to back up before I decided keeping him informed was probably the best option I had anyway. He'd understand, I knew he would.

"Hey, Dave," I began casually, "would you drop me off at the bookstore today instead of home? I'm going to be working with Gio on his book for a couple hours."

I gave him my most innocent smile. Dave just looked at me.

"I really don't feel good about that. Do you think that's such a great idea?" My glare made him retract. "Not that I don't trust you to know what you're doing. It's just that this guy is still a stranger. You don't know that much about him."

I rolled my eyes at him. Still, he did have a point. I really didn't know all that much about Gio, only an approaching conviction I could trust him with my life, but I wasn't quite sure I could articulate that to Dave and have him believe me without sounding like a hormone-driven lunatic.

I decided to go for a compromise that just might get him off my back. "How about you come with me for a couple minutes, meet him, feel him out, and then take off? Would that make you feel better?" I offered.

Dave eyed me. Whether he liked it or not, I was going to

the bookstore. I could tell he conceded to that fact as his shoulders dropped.

"Don't think for a minute I agree with what you're doing." Then resigned, he said, "But if you're going to do it anyway, well, I'll take what comfort I can get."

He looked as if he were going to add something else but thought better of it. Just looking at his face I could see the conflict about who I was. Somehow between yesterday and today, I'd shown him a side of myself I didn't know existed, let alone one that I was proud of.

I hoped he'd be able to forgive the person I was turning into. If he'd just hold on, if he could just trust in me for a little while longer, I'd show him all of this was happening for a reason.

I wasn't a bad person. I knew that from the bottom of my soul. Dave might've begun to think so, the conflict in his face revealed that much, but I would fix that.

All I had to do was just hold on to what I had and let it all play out. My only hope was I'd be able to keep up this mess long enough to prove him wrong.

Fourteen

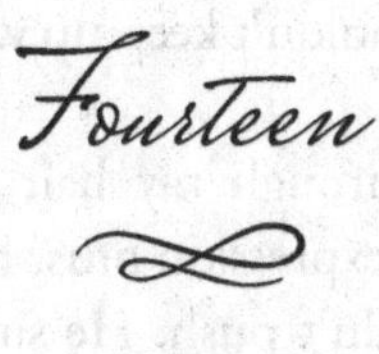

GIO

When I entered the apartment, my hands were almost in full-fledged convulsions. I dropped the keys at the door and walked straight to the kitchen where I proceeded to search for something hard to drink.

Willem appeared from out of nowhere with two full glasses in his right hand and my keys dangling in his left.

"I thought you might be needing one of these," he said as he placed the glasses on the counter.

I took the glass closest to me and downed it in one swing. I slammed the glass back onto the counter where Willem was waiting with the bottle for the refill he'd anticipated.

"Are you okay?" he asked.

I closed my eyes and took a deep breath. I couldn't quite speak, not just yet. As I downed the second drink, I felt my body slowly become a bit more sedate. Not much, but enough to begin to dull the sharpest part of the edge.

I didn't know if I was capable of being okay. Was there some sort of protocol for people to ask if someone was okay after they just experienced a massively significant event in their life?

And how was I to answer? I didn't know if I had an answer to give. Was I okay?

I searched deep within to find any answer that would adequately communicate what it was I was feeling on the inside, but my brain couldn't keep up with all the information I had to relay.

I ran my hand through my hair and exhaled loudly. I looked at Willem. My expression must have clued him into my feelings because he didn't push. He simply waited for me to speak.

"I'll be okay," I managed, though at that moment I wasn't quite sure if I believed it myself. You'd think after hundreds of years, I'd be used to seeing her.

But it wasn't so. It became more difficult for me to be in her presence as the years slowly passed; each successive year became a more vicious reminder of how I've failed her, like a deeper wound in my flesh.

Willem nodded as if understanding that what I really needed was some space; just a couple more minutes to let the scotch settle and fully dull the razor's edge shredding my nerves.

"Where's Claire?" I said looking around the empty room.

"She's coming," Willem replied. "She stayed behind at the coffee shop to clean up any sign of the protective spell she cast. I'll admit, for someone who's just come into her power, she's quite astute."

"How do you mean?"

"It all comes so naturally to her. It's almost as if that by finally accepting who she really is, by accepting her duties to protect you, not only has her magick come to fruition, but it's done so with a grace I've not seen in centuries." He stopped speaking and seemed to lose himself in deep reflection.

"And you find this especially intriguing?" I asked, though I already knew the answer. I was just hoping he'd continue to talk and keep my mind directed on topics other than Kate.

"Yes, extremely," he answered, as he looked at me in disbelief, and then shook his head. "I forgot. I'm sorry. Though you're cursed as I've been, *you* did not deserve it. You were never one of us. You should've lived and died a long time ago, never knowing about what can really happen in this world.

"But for the rest of us," he said, as he looked up toward the ceiling, "the rest of us know what happens when the Goddess is displeased, or pleased, with the decisions we make here on Earth." He gave me a crooked look.

"And the Goddess is *pleased* with Claire?" I took a guess at where he was headed with his story. When he smiled at me, I knew I was right on track.

"Very much so. At least, that's what I'd conclude. You see, even though Claire is new to the craft, she behaves as if she's known what to do all along. Sure, the intensity of such power can be quite overwhelming, but it appears the magick is being guided through her. That is, as long as she is willing to let it flow.

"I've only heard stories of those rewarded by the Goddess so graciously, and they are few and far between. Hers is no small gift. She's definitely a unique one, that's certain."

His voice lingered. It sounded in the same way my eyes felt every time they caught a glimpse of Kate. That fleeting thought focused my mind back to her.

Willem saw the change in my demeanor and knew exactly where my mind had gone.

"Are you ready to talk about it?" he asked.

"He better be." Claire's voice broke my hesitant silence. "I've been rushing around for the past forty minutes, trying to clean up the mess he left behind. Geez, Gio, next time, try not to leave such an auric mess, please."

"A what?"

"An *auric* mess." Claire rolled her eyes and smiled as she overemphasized her words. "Basically, it's quite simple." I could tell she was being patient with me, though she'd rather get on with what I had to say. I listened carefully so she'd only have to explain once.

"Okay," she began, "everyone has a specific energy surrounding them, you know, an aura. It's very distinct, kind of like a fingerprint. As we move through life, we meet people, we interact with them, our energies touch, bounce, mix; you know, intermingle.

"But, when we're especially moved by a person or an event, we can leave bits of our energy behind. Little pieces of us, like little fingerprints scattered everywhere." Claire sighed. "I've only heard of it happening. I've never actually seen someone's aura scattered like lost pieces of a puzzle . . ." Her voice trailed off.

She shook her head and looked back at me, her eyes filled with meaning. "You must be really connected to her." She watched me through sad eyes. She shook her head. "Don't worry though, everything is back to normal at the coffee shop."

I stared at her, my mouth agape. In four hundred years, I'd never once heard of a person leaving their energy behind. Questions began to emerge that I'd never dreamed of before.

I shot a heated glance toward Willem. "Did you know about this?" My voice was on edge.

"It is not of my people's traditions. I've heard of it happening before, but we're not ones who can see such things. My people were of the earth's energy. We didn't fool around with the energy of the physical form." His voice was defensive. He probably didn't like my accusatory tone.

"I didn't mean anything by it. I'm sorry." I immediately recoiled.

"I understand. I'm just as taken aback by this as you." His face was full of concern.

I turned my attention back to Claire. "So you're telling me I left these little pieces of me?" It was hard to imagine I'd unintentionally be leaving evidence of myself behind.

"Yes," Claire said.

"And these pieces," I pressed, "these pieces are very specific. They're identifiable to me, correct?"

"Yeah," Claire answered, and then added thoughtfully, "but unless the person who saw them could first, see auras, and second, know your specific aura, then I don't think anyone could identify you."

"But it is possible?" I pushed.

"Yes, of course it is."

"So, for the past four hundred years, it's possible Alessandro has always been one step ahead of us because I could've been leaving these markers behind?" My voice rose.

"Impossible," Willem interrupted. "Alessandro doesn't have that kind of power. His people were Strega Ilmalo, but not the kind known to possess such gifts."

"But that doesn't make sense," Claire said, almost to herself. "He was able to place the dark mark on Gio's aura that I removed. I knew it was his, I saw him do it in my vision. You can't place a mark on something you can't see."

"But . . . how?" Willem looked from Claire to me, momentarily lost in his thoughts.

"Gio, relax," Claire said, "I've cleaned the coffee shop. There's not one speck of you back there, I promise. Even if Alessandro goes in there right now, I'm confident he'd have no idea any magick had been cast there at all. It's clean. Relax."

"But Claire—" I began.

"I cleaned everything you touched. It's like you weren't even there."

Dread shot through my body. *Touched*. My memory shot to the moment in which Kate stood to leave.

"Claire," I whispered, "is it possible to leave these bits of energy on people?"

Her face turned white as she quickly put my question into context, and I instantly knew the answer. My only hope was that I'd be able to see Kate before Alessandro did.

"Tell us everything that happened. And quickly, please. We don't have time to waste if we're going to stop Alessandro from stealing her from you again," Claire said.

I glanced at Willem who nodded in agreement. And then quickly, with as steady of a voice as I could assemble, I told them everything.

After I'd finished, it was decided the sooner I saw Kate again the better. I took the napkin from my pocket and held it before me. My fingers trembled as I dialed the number.

"It looks as if the stars are in our favor, for now," Willem said with relief as I hung up the phone and told them of our meeting later that evening.

"That's perfect," Claire said. "I'll go with you to the bookstore and see if there's anything else I need to clean up."

"I still don't know how I'm going to explain you. I've already told her that I don't have any friends or relatives here," I replied. "What should I say? Oh, hey, Kate, by the way, this is Claire, my Watcher. She's just gonna check and clean your aura real quick. Don't move, okay?"

Claire just shook her head as she mostly ignored my sarcasm. "Or we can just pretend to bump into each other at the bookstore and you can introduce me as your building manager," she offered matter-of-factly, looking at me as if I should've figured this out myself.

"I don't know . . .," I started.

"It's perfect," Willem interjected as he took a seat on one of the chairs that faced the street window. "What's important is that Kate doesn't track any of you back with her when she goes home to Alessandro tonight."

I cringed at the thought of Kate spending the night, in the same bed, no less, with that monster. My stomach hurled. Anger began to build deep within. It was only a matter of time before it swelled and flowed over. Goddess help anyone who was in its path when it finally decided to crest.

Willem recognized the emotions flying through me and tried to talk me down. "It does no one any good to get this upset. Alessandro will pay for the wrongs he's committed, but right now, you must focus on Kate. You must begin to *win* her over. Remember, if she doesn't come to you willingly, then all is for nothing."

"Gio," Claire offered, "do you need my, uh . . . assistance?"

She held out her hand to me. I knew if I took it, I'd experience the wash of calm I'd felt before. It was hard for me to believe that was just days ago; it felt like a lot longer. My blood felt like it was on fire.

Desperate, I stretched out my hand and took Claire's, her petite fingers intertwined with mine. I closed my eyes and felt the warmth emanate from her skin and caress each strand of sensation against my palm.

Instantly, I was calm. I opened my eyes and looked at Claire. Her smile was wide, and I was glad that by trusting her, I was able to make her happy. Eventually her smile gave way to concern, and I searched the rest of her face to discover the source of her worry.

I followed her eyes.

Willem, quiet for the past few minutes, sat on the chair staring at Claire with a strange, disturbing look on his paler-than-normal face.

"Willem," I asked, "what is it? What's wrong?"

My voice shook him out of his trance.

"She's . . . a healer." His voice was ragged, breathless; he could barely get out the few words that he did.

"What?" Claire said.

"You. Are. A. Healer." Willem said each word clearly, this time, with an accent I hadn't heard from his throat in a long while. He recognized that neither one of us knew what he was talking about, so he continued, "You touched Gio and made him feel better, right?"

"Yeah. So?" Claire said.

"Ha!" His booming laughter caught us both off guard as we jumped at the initial shock of it. "So, when you touched him, you altered his mental state. You fixed it, so to speak." He continued to look at us as if we should've caught on by then. When he realized we hadn't, he continued, his voice rising with excitement as he looked intensely at Claire. "So, you are aware that this gift can also be applied to the physical, aren't you?" He waited for her to respond.

"What? No. You mean . . .," she began.

"Yes, that's exactly what I mean." He didn't let her finish.

Claire looked at her hands as if she expected them to sprout extra fingers. She stared at them for a couple minutes more before she spoke again. "Willem, I'm not so sure about this. I mean, I don't think that—"

Willem didn't give her a chance to continue. Before we knew what he intended he knelt in front of Claire, his left palm up near her face, his right hand searching for something in his pocket.

He pulled his small silver pocketknife out. My stomach turned; it didn't take me long to put two and two together, though it was longer than it took for Willem to take the knife and make a deep, thin slice across his hand. A thin red line surfaced across his palm and gradually became thicker.

Claire jumped at the quickness of the movement but

didn't make a sound as she watched Willem bleed from his self-inflicted wound.

"Claire," Willem said confidently, "heal me."

"I can't." Her voice was quiet. She moved to stand. "Hold on a minute and I can go get a bandage—"

"Forget the bandage, I won't need it if you heal me."

"I don't know how."

"Just trust your feelings. I know you can do it." He stared directly into her eyes, excitement pouring out of his, unable to be contained within his body. "All I'm asking is for you to try. See what happens."

Claire took a deep breath and lifted both her hands over Willem's bloodied one. Then, as if changing her mind, she dropped her right hand so that her hands were hovering both above and below the wounded body part.

I watched in silence, as Claire's eyes closed and then fluttered. Her hands appeared to glow, first golden, and then white. The white light seemed to collect in the top hand, becoming brighter and growing thicker with each passing second. I sat in silence, unable to pull my eyes away.

The white light grew and grew into a ball around Claire's hand until it looked as if it could grow no more. Then, slowly, deliberately, it traveled through Willem's injured hand and into her waiting hand below in thick, curling ribbons.

I continued to watch, mesmerized, until the light faded into the hand below and Claire brought both hands down to her lap.

She dropped her head and breathed heavily. Sweat had collected on her brow. It dripped down the side of her face.

"Are you all right?" I went to her side and placed my hands on her shoulders.

"Yeah," she said between breaths, "I think so. Just tired." She leaned back on the couch.

"Look." Willem stood and held his palm up for us both to see.

Where just seconds before the four-inch cut had bled, there was a now smooth palm. I looked back at Claire.

"How did you do that?" I asked, amazed.

"I . . . I don't really know. It just kind of happened." She stumbled over her words, and I could tell she was just as amazed as I was. "It was like . . . like . . ."

"Magick?" Willem offered, a smile spread across his face, and he held out his hand to her. She took it hesitantly.

"Claire, in all my years here on this earth, and there have been far too many, I've never come across someone quite like you. I sensed your power when I first met you, but I'd no idea you were blessed with such gifts.

"My mother was a healer, you know," he continued. "She was very powerful, but she couldn't heal by touch. She relied on what the earth provided for us to create cures, and she could cure anything. She was a most amazing woman.

"I've always believed she was given her gift because the Goddess only bestows the most powerful gifts to those that most closely resemble her, and my mother was as close to a goddess as anyone could get."

He paused momentarily and looked as if he were thinking about whether he should continue or not. It seemed his reservations about continuing were wiped cleanly away because he leaned toward Claire and whispered two words, "Until now." I heard the words distinctly as he spoke them and knew he'd meant them with all his heart.

For the first time since I'd met her, Claire looked truly startled. Her eyes grew round, and her skin turned an ashy white. Her breath quickened and with each successive breath her complexion grew more and more gray.

"Calm, Claire. Breathe." Willem continued to whisper in

her ear as he stepped closer and supported her tiny frame in his arms. "It's all right. It'll be all right. Just breathe."

"Is she going to be okay?" I asked.

"She'll be fine, I promise," he answered, though his concentration seemed to be elsewhere. He gently placed her on the couch. "She's just in a little bit of shock right now. From what I've heard, physical healing can be a difficult and exhausting magick to perform as it is, but to find out you can do it, actually perform it, and realize what a truly unique gift it is, all in the same hour—well, it must be a bit overwhelming, as I'm sure you can imagine."

"Is there anything I can do?" I offered. "I just can't sit here."

There was a general uneasiness to my body as my insides coiled about underneath my skin. I hated not having any magick of my own. I hated being the only . . . *human without power* in the room.

"How about a drink?" Claire's voice was cool and easy over the chaos of my thoughts. It brought my attention back to her.

Her face had some color in it now. A rosy pink pushed the ashy whiteness to just the edges of her features. She still looked uneasy but managed to sit up straight and push her hair back off her face.

I immediately went over and poured her a drink. By the time I returned to her side, her complexion appeared to be back to normal. She was calm and poised, and I wondered how such a young woman could master what I'd been working on for centuries—utter composure.

I handed her the drink and she took a deliberate sip from the glass. She sat quietly and shifted her gaze between Willem and me. When I realized she was waiting for us to speak, I began with my questions.

"Do you have any idea how that happened? Can any other

Watchers do that? Do you think Rose knows?" I was still amazed by the potency of the healing spell cast from within her body. Images of the white light were vivid as they lit up my mind.

She was still silent, but I could tell she was thinking. "I honestly couldn't tell you. I have no idea. It was almost like I wasn't moving the energy myself, but more like I was just giving way to a greater force moving within me." Her face was filled with wonder. "This is too unreal," she gasped. "Unreal—and yet, it makes perfect sense. And no Watcher I've heard of can do that. But now that I think about it, I'm pretty sure my grandmother has always suspected."

Her gaze met Willem's.

"What are you thinking, Willem? Please tell me. Out of everything that's happened today, I believe the most unnerving is that you're so quiet." She tried to sound casual when she spoke, but her words trembled just a little and instantly gave her away.

Willem was still in front of her, staring. His mouth opened to speak, and then closed again, as if he thought better of what he was about to say. He opened his mouth once more, and finally said, "If I'd any doubts in you or your abilities, I can safely say they've been quite eradicated. You are a force that defies all I've believed to be true. I see now why you've always been so reluctant to be a part of your clan of Watchers. You're so much more than they can ever be."

Willem took a seat on the left side of the couch. His frame took up most of the space. He looked like a giant sitting on children's play furniture, the exact opposite of how Claire looked as the couch threatened to eat her up in one gulp.

Willem looked more relaxed than I'd seen him in a long time. He stretched out, his limbs extending over every inch they could find.

"With a little training, I cannot comprehend the powers

you will possess. And your recovery time—it took you less than five minutes. Quite unbelievable, really. There's no limit to what you may be able to accomplish," he continued, his voice rising again with excitement.

"Perhaps, but all I care about right now is refocusing and figuring out how I'm going to keep Gio safe." Claire's voice was firm. "I'm Gio's Watcher. It's my job to keep him safe and alive, right now. I just wish I could've learned about all this before I met him. Then, at least, I'd feel as if I could give him the protection he deserves. Especially since Alessandro appears to be stronger than either of you anticipated." Her voice was certain as she reminded us we didn't truly know the extent of Alessandro's powers.

"But, Claire," Willem protested, quickly recovering from the sting of Claire's accusation, "you should really spend time getting to know yourself all over again. If you could harness some of your energy, manipulate your skills just a tad more . . . well, let's just say it could help Gio later on."

A small whisp of energy rippled from her body, and I sensed the frustration as it built up from her core and prepared to leap from her skin. I decided to step in.

"Willem's right." I placed my hand on her shoulder. "You should take the time to explore your gifts. You never know when we might need them." I felt guilty for saying it, but I knew this was something she had to do. I had the feeling that, as my Watcher, Claire was bound to take my words seriously.

Claire looked at me like I'd betrayed her, daggers flying in my direction. Then, slowly, the anger gave way to resignation as her expression softened. "You're right," she said. "I should spend some time honing my skills. But I won't do it when Gio needs me. I'll do it only when there's down time, and from what I had to clean up at the coffee shop and from the planned meeting later on, down time doesn't appear to be happening tonight. Will you at least give me that?"

Willem stared at her with a mixture of reluctance, pride, and awe. It was the kind of look a mentor gives his star protégé.

"Of course," he responded, as his eyes continued to explore every aspect of her face.

"And, if everything goes well tonight," Claire continued, a slight smile playing on her lips, "as I suspect it might, then I should have a little down time."

"What does that mean?" I asked.

"Tell me, Gio, have you ever heard of a name-erasing spell?"

"Excellent idea," Willem chimed in.

"Is that when you put a kind of block on a specific person's name that makes it difficult for someone to remember it?" I suggested.

I could tell they were both impressed by my answer.

"What can I say?" I shrugged. "After four hundred years of hanging out with a witch you're bound to pick up a thing or two here or there . . . even as a human." I smiled, pleased with myself for once.

"Very good," Claire responded. "I was thinking that tonight, I could cast that spell on Kate. That way, if she's not in your presence, she will literally forget your name. We won't have to worry about her accidentally letting it slip when she's with Alessandro, you know?"

"Great idea," I said. "But won't Alessandro be able to sense a spell on her? I mean, he does seem to have more power than we'd initially thought." This time I directed my question to Willem. We both had underestimated Alessandro's abilities in the past, with tragic consequences.

"I was thinking about that too," Claire answered, "but I'm hoping to cover my tracks as well, with a protective spell."

"Hoping is one thing, Claire, doing it for sure is another. If you have any doubt about this, I'd rather take my chances with her not mentioning it rather than have Alessandro sense a spell and"—I swallowed so hard it hurt— "do away with her when there's nothing I can do to stop him." I was trying to keep my voice even, but it was hard to keep the emotion at bay. I just hoped Claire didn't get the wrong impression.

"I don't think Claire would—" Willem began, but Claire didn't allow him to continue.

"He's right, Willem, it's too risky." Her voice was matter of fact. There was no evidence I'd hurt her feelings and I was glad for that. "I'll just go there tonight and clean what I can if I need to. I'll have time to practice my skills later. Tonight is not the night to take chances."

"Okay," Willem conceded, shaking his head. He smiled to himself, and then brought his gaze to meet mine.

"Well, brother, it seems I don't have to worry about you as much this time around." Relief and sadness lined his words. "It seems the Goddess has sent you someone else to do that job."

"Perhaps she sent someone to help you," I answered, hoping he'd catch my double meaning, and then quickly added, so Claire wouldn't, "so that you could focus on the serum."

"Perhaps," he said. I wasn't sure if he understood what I was trying to say. "And perhaps not. Only time will tell, and that's something that we always seem to be running low on."

I laughed at his comment. Funny how time always eluded me. There never seemed to be enough of it, yet I was cursed with far too much. How I longed for time to hold meaning once again.

Willem coughed and gestured to the clock. It was almost seven. Again, time seemed to be disappearing from my reality the closer I got to getting Kate back. It was time to go. I had to be at the bookstore, ready for my next act. The book. After all, we were meeting on the pretense that I was a writer needing some expertise.

"I should get ready," I mumbled to myself as I ran to my trunk and threw it open to search for my journals.

They filled up most of the case. I didn't have a manuscript to produce, but I did have hundreds of years of journals to select from. If I was one thing, I was meticulous in my notetaking. When you have no magick, when you're not graced with powers other than what every other human is given at birth, you're at a tremendous disadvantage when going up against those with supernatural abilities.

It wasn't until after I'd met Willem that I found my writings could shed light on dark places. Writing helped me become more observant. It helped me find more patience. And it helped me level the playing field between Willem and myself, if only in my mind. Deep within my soul, I was convinced my writings would come in handy someday. Was it possible that day was today?

When Claire first saw the books, she was amazed at how many there were. It was her idea I use the guise of a writer. It was just luck that Kate happened to work in publishing in this life. Or was it? I was starting to wonder about my little Watcher. There was no way she could've known, was there? I'd have to remember to talk to her about that. Later. Right now, I was running late.

I'd told Kate I'd written a nonfiction love story, and a love story I would produce. I grabbed the thinnest leather-bound journal from the bottom of my trunk. I opened the book and blew into the pages. Dust flew out in a small poof. The binding was coming unglued and half the pages could have easily fallen out if it were a dry, hot day. But it wasn't dry; there was wetness in the air.

I flipped through the pages and revisited some of the writing. It was one of my oldest journals. The one that memorialized the day I saw Alessandro set my love on fire when I was but a few feet from her touch. That time we were too late. It was the first time Willem came face to face with Alessandro, the first time Willem saw his true evil. I read and remembered the hot, melting pain of failure, smelled the charred resin of her soul as it spirited away. I read and remembered the black, abysmal sorrow of loss, the things that should've been stopped but were not. Yes, this one would do.

I sat there reading and remembering for a few more minutes before I closed the trunk and set the book carefully on top. I brought my hands to my eyes and wiped away the tears. Some things were better left unread.

My mind raced as I finished gathering my stuff for the night. I changed clothing and sat quietly for a moment. It was no use. I couldn't relax. My mind just couldn't shake the horrors the journal held. All the "what ifs" and the "could haves" floated around in the self-negating whirlpool that was my brain.

I tried to focus on the task at hand. I couldn't fail Kate again. I *would* not. My mind took no notice of my resolve. It continued to race as I stood to leave. It raced faster as I reached the front door. And it continued racing as I wondered if my nonfiction story was, perhaps, a little too fiction for Kate to believe.

Fifteen

KATE

I never thought I'd ever be as glad as I was when Dave left the bookstore. It hadn't been easy to convince him to drop me off there in the first place, and I didn't think his behavior was stellar, but he was cordial and polite, and most of all, satisfied I wouldn't end up chopped into a million pieces by the end of the evening.

It also helped that I gave him my most absolute promise that if I didn't tell him everything from now on, he could have full rights to go to Alex and expose my secret.

Not that he ever would. Dave may have been uncomfortable with what I was doing, but he valued our trust above all else. Short of my unexpected disappearance, the last person Dave would go to would be Alex. At least, that was what I was hoping.

"Your friend seems nice," Gio commented nervously as we watched Dave leave the store.

"Dave? Yeah, he's great. He's my best friend." As the words left my mouth, I couldn't help but think how completely corny I sounded. I wasn't sure why this made such a difference since I wasn't there to impress Gio. I mean, it wasn't like we were on a date. But still . . .

I briefly rechecked to make sure I was still on the right side of the adultery line I drew in my head. I hadn't crossed it yet, but I was getting damned close, and I wasn't a very good tightrope walker.

I decided to refocus on the purpose of the meeting.

"So, I'm dying to hear about your book. Shall we?" I felt a bit sheepish as I began heading toward the stairs leading up to the conference rooms above the stacks.

"Let's go." He flashed a smile so familiar I flinched. Where had I seen that smile before? Quickly, I tried to recover, but he'd already noticed.

"What's wrong?" he asked.

"Nothing, really." I tried to decide how I was going to explain how familiar he was to me and then decided against doing it altogether. I didn't want to be branded crazy before he knew me. I wasn't quite sure why, but it was important.

"I just remembered something I have to do tomorrow. No big deal." I smiled back and continued toward the steps.

I was nearly to the first step when I almost tripped over a small figure leaning over a stack of books on the floor near the walkway.

"Excuse me . . .," I began, and then stopped when I noticed the shock of pink hair framing the face of a young woman looking up at me.

"Claire, what are you doing here?" Gio asked.

I turned to look at him. I didn't even try to hide my astonishment as he addressed her. In the seconds that passed since he'd greeted Claire, my mind scrambled to piece together all the different ways in which they could know each other.

Again, I shocked myself when I realized how much I didn't want Claire to be his girlfriend or lover. A pang of jealousy ran through my body, poisoning my thoughts as it traveled. I tried to shove it away.

What did their relationship matter to me? I was a married woman, I repeated to myself—again. It shouldn't matter whether Claire was his sister, cousin, girlfriend, or lover.

It shouldn't have made one bit of difference to me, but it did.

"Kate, I'd like you to meet Claire," Gio said, and then added, "Claire's the building manager where I'm staying and the first person I met in Freestone." His stance was as casual as his words, and I knew I'd begun to make a big deal out of nothing.

I immediately stuck out my hand. "It's nice to meet you," I said, hoping that my relief wasn't too obvious.

Claire looked me up and down carefully, as if she were examining every aspect of my person. I began to feel uncomfortable as she continued to stare.

Seconds felt like minutes under her observant eye and just as I was about to pull my hand back, her face turned warm, eyes gentle, and a wide smile spread across her face exposing a set of brilliant white, perfectly straight teeth.

She stood and clasped my hand between both of hers. They were warm, and when they wrapped around mine, I had that strange sensation of closeness I'd been feeling so often recently. Then, under all the warmth and closeness, a distinct streak shot through my blood. Something was moving through me. Or around me. No, away from me. It peeled from my body in thin layers. I gasped.

I glanced at Claire, unable to identify the feeling, yet knowing I was feeling it and that she knew I was. It pulled at those familiar parts, and I wasn't happy about it at all. Not quite painful, just uncomfortable, like someone pulling the sheets off you on a cold night as you lay snuggled in your bed, sleeping. I opened my mouth to say something when she spoke.

"Kate, it's so good to meet you. And it's nice to see Gio meeting some people in this small town." Her voice commanded attention in a light, fairy-like way.

I became so distracted I forgot what I was going to say.

"Claire works in the vintage shop down the street and manages the building, including the studio above," Gio said.

"Well, I only manage it as a favor while my mother is out of town, which is pretty much always. I should probably start charging her a fee for all the extra work I've been doing lately," she added, smiling at Gio.

He smiled back, but it had an edge. Was I missing something?

"I can't imagine the amount of work it takes to keep an entire building up and running," I responded automatically. Honestly, I was just being polite until I could have some time alone with Gio.

My God, I was going to hell.

"Oh, it's not that. The building pretty much takes care of itself these days. It's all the riffraff that stumble in that can make things tricky." Her eyes were practically on fire; they were so bright with amusement. Again, I wondered what it was that I was missing. Before I could think about it further, Gio spoke.

"Well, Claire, it was good to see you, but we're actually here to do some work. I guess I'll be seeing you later," he said, as if trying to get rid of her. "Did you get everything you were looking for?" he asked as he stepped aside to let her pass.

"Yep. Every last bit," she said, though she held nothing in her hands. Then she turned to me and said, "You should come by the shop sometime. We've got loads of clothing I think would be just perfect on you. I'm surprised I've never seen you there before. Anyway, we could spend an afternoon playing dress-up. What do you say?"

"Um, sure. Thanks, that would be great." I wasn't quite sure what to say, but I had to admit the thought of hanging out with another woman, even one that looked at least ten years my junior, seemed pretty appealing. I couldn't even remember the last time I'd hung out with a girlfriend.

Plus, there was something else in her presence that drew me in. It wasn't the bright pink hair or the punk clothing or the way her face was friendly and inviting. It was hard to pinpoint, and extremely frustrating to explain, but it was the way she felt that instantly called to me and told me she was someone I could trust; she was someone I'd enjoy being with and could even be close to.

Did she have that effect on everyone she met? Some people are just lucky that way, the quintessential "people person." I'd never been that type of person. Friendly, yes, but I could never walk into a room and own a crowd. I didn't quite have the touch.

Yet here I was with two strangers and feeling as comfortable with them as I was with people I've known for years. Strange. No, not strange, just . . . different.

"All right, Claire," Gio said through his teeth. He seemed a little agitated she was still there.

"Oh, yeah," Claire said, with a beaming smile. "Have fun, you two. Kate, again, it was a pleasure."

She brushed past Gio and almost skipped out of the store. I watched until I saw her fly past the window and out of sight. When I brought my attention back to Gio, he was staring at me.

"Claire seems nice," I offered. Despite the fact I'd been insanely jealous of her just a few minutes ago, I didn't want her to catch any flack if Gio thought she'd interrupted us.

Quickly, I erased the thought from my mind. What was

wrong with me? Why would he care if our meeting were interrupted? It wasn't as if he were Alex? Besides, it was just a casual meeting to discuss his book. Nothing more, right? Sure.

I mentally scolded myself as I continued to edge closer and closer to that invisible line between what was right and what was—not right.

I couldn't even bring myself to say the word wrong, though I fully knew I shouldn't be there with him, no matter how I twisted reality to justify my cause. But, in all honesty, it just didn't seem wrong to be with Gio. It actually felt better than anything had in a long time.

"You ready?" he said as he motioned toward the stairs. "I promise, no more interruptions tonight."

He held his arm out in a sweeping motion as if to clear the way for me. I smiled and walked up the stairs to the second floor.

The room was the first one to the right along the hallway. The door was open and there was a large table up against the windows, overlooking the street. The desk lamp attached to the table lengthwise was turned on, and its soft glow was the only light in the room. Two large chairs were at the table.

I walked in and took a seat in one of the chairs, throwing my bag on the ground. Gio followed and took the seat across from me without a word.

He took his bag off and placed it on the table. I watched as he rifled through papers, searching for something specific. His hair, the darkest black I'd ever seen, fell in his face in soft waves. He absently ran his fingers through it as he continued to look through his papers.

I hated to stare, but I couldn't look away as I noticed the light purple circles beginning to form under his eyes. Did he sleep well? Or were his nights filled with fitful dreams, like me?

He must've felt me staring because he brought his eyes up to meet mine like he'd been expecting them to be there waiting. I tried to pull my gaze away but couldn't. No, I *wouldn't*.

I held his stare. His eyes were unlike anything I'd ever seen before, bright like a perfect afternoon in late September. They welcomed me like a warm embrace.

He smiled, the edges of his cheeks pushing up against those perfect blue spheres, making them more absolute, if that was possible. I felt myself falling into those impossible eyes. They were a true turquoise. Or were they more teal? They shifted somewhere in between the colors with a mesmerizing subtlety.

"Kate?" he said.

"Mmmm, yes . . .?"

"Do you want to talk about the book now?"

Was he actually giving me a choice? We could either discuss the book or we could . . .

"Of course," I said suddenly, shaking my head, embarrassed at my behavior. I forced myself to look away, no easy task. I cleared my throat. "You mentioned earlier that this is a nonfiction, right?" I fell into my professional voice, nothing but business here.

"Yeah," he said as he grabbed a leather-bound journal from the top of the pile. I waited for him to continue. "It's a love story. More like a history of the relationship between two lovers, I suppose."

"Really? Who are you writing about?" I was definitely intrigued. "No, don't answer that. Start at the beginning, please. How'd you first decide to write this story? Where did the idea come from?"

He smiled as he unwrapped the leather cord from around the book he held.

"Well, years ago, I was in Italy, traveling on my own, trying to find a new life for myself—"

"Years ago?" I interrupted. "How old are you? You can't

be that far past twenty." I wasn't trying to be rude, but it came out in a heap. And almost as soon as the words had come out, I immediately wished they hadn't.

He raised an eyebrow at the barrage of words that fell out of my mouth, an amused expression on his face. My stomach turned, nauseated by my social ineptness.

"I'm sorry. You don't have to answer that, either. I wasn't trying to be rude. Please, continue," I stammered hoping I hadn't offended him to the point where he'd consider leaving for the night, or worse, not wanting to see me again—though I knew he wouldn't.

"It's fine. No big deal." His face was completely composed again as he flashed a warm smile and my insides squirmed. God, it was amazing what his smile could do to me. "I know I'm pretty young looking, but I've been on my own for quite a while, now. It's kind of aged me, inside, beyond my years."

I nodded my head understanding perfectly, though I was unsure if he was speaking the truth or just teasing me. I decided to let it go.

I nodded. "Please continue."

"Anyway," he said, "I was traveling through Italy when I came across some old writings. It was just a bunch of old letters and notes from decades ago. Their owners had most likely passed on a long time before, and they were in Italian, but there was something about the notes that made me hold on to them.

"I speak a little Italian, but it still took me a while to translate the writings. When I was finished, I discovered the notes were written from a young man to his lover. The letters chronicled their relationship: how they met, the intensity of their love, the hope for a forever together, and how it all unraveled to an end.

"Well, needless to say, I became fascinated with their love, obsessed really, and I thought to myself what it'd be like if I ever found a love like that. I thought about how it'd feel to be affected by a higher power. What if I found my greatest love?

"So, I decided to write this story. Not your traditional nonfiction, I know, but true as any true love story is." He paused, as if reflecting on the secrets he'd found in these personal notes and letters.

"It's definitely a unique story, and the research you must've put in to find out about these people's history, it must've taken a lifetime," I said.

"You have no idea." His voice was serious and his gaze steady as it held mine, totally and completely, strong and unwavering, gentle and safe.

A shiver ran the length of my body, and still, I didn't pull my eyes from his. Did he feel as equally transfixed by mine?

"May I read some of your manuscript?" I asked, though our eyes seemed to be having a different conversation altogether.

"Of course," he responded, "but I thought we might first . . . um, spend some time tonight getting to know each other a little better." He broke away from my stare as he ran his hand through his hair in a nervous gesture, adding, "You know, since we'll probably be working closely, it might help to know a little more about each other, um, your work style, that's all."

I was pretty sure that wasn't all, but I was beginning not to care. Something strange was happening to me. Being near Gio *should* feel inappropriate, it *should* feel dirty and wrong and against every word of my wedding vows, but it didn't. It was a visceral feeling, a gut instinct, a distant memory remembered, and I was confident it had everything to do with the handsome man sitting across from me. Being together was right. I wasn't going to give that up anytime soon. That much, I knew.

"Okay," I said, smiling. "Let's get to know each other."

It felt like minutes passed when my cell phone went off. I

wasn't sure why the ringer volume was at the second to the loudest tone, but it was, and I jumped out of my chair at the first few notes of Alex's song. I glanced at the clock on the wall. It was nearly ten o'clock. Three hours had flown by. Where did the time go?

"Shit. Excuse me," I said, apologizing to Gio as I searched through my purse, looking for the source of the noise. "I've got to get this."

"No problem." His face looked the same as his voice sounded: blank. I glanced at him curiously as I answered the call.

"Hey, Alex, what's up?" I said, irritated that Gio and I had been interrupted.

"Nothing, babe. What's up with you? I tried calling the house, but you didn't pick up. Where are you?" His voice had the beginnings of the accusatory tone that was really starting to get on my last nerve.

I took a deep breath and stood. I walked toward the hall, instinctively trying to put as much space between Gio and Alex as I could manage without walking too far away.

"I'm still working. Where are you?" I tried to sound normal, but my voice was short.

"It's almost ten o'clock and you're still working? What's so important that it's keeping you from home?" he said completely disregarding my question.

"Are you home?" I asked innocently, ignoring his pointed accusations and trying not to sound too shocked that nearly three hours had just slipped by without me noticing. "If I would've known you'd be home this soon, I would've had dinner ready. I guess I lost track of the time. You know how absent-minded I've been lately. I'm sorry, hon."

My jaw tightened as the apology came out. I didn't feel like apologizing. He didn't deserve one, at least not for what he was condemning me for. But I knew it was what he wanted, and I didn't feel like getting into it over the phone with Gio sitting just feet from me.

"I forgive you, love," he said, and I had to force myself not to lose my temper. Was Alex always this predictable and overbearing? How was I just noticing it now?

"Anyway, I'll come pick you up, I'm on my way home. Okay?"

The words jolted me back to the present. I snuck a peek at Gio from the corner of my eye. He was intently writing in the journal, his hand moving fast over the page, his fingers gripping the pen so hard his knuckles were white.

"Oh, that's okay, Dave's giving me a ride. I have to clean up and reorganize for tomorrow, but I'll be home before eleven." I wasn't sure if he'd go for that, so I added, "Hey, maybe if you want, when we get home, we can watch that movie you wanted to stream yesterday."

There was a long silence as I bit my lip waiting for his response.

"Sure, that sounds nice." His voice was neutral, but there was a distinct air of suspicion surrounding his words. Oh, well, I'd deal with that later.

"All right, well, I'd better hang up if I'm going to be home before eleven," I said as I tried to end the conversation.

"Bye. I love you."

"Love you too." I rushed through the sentiment blending it into one word.

I hung up and let out a breath I hadn't known I was holding. Shoving the conversation back until I could later deal with it, I turned around. Gio was standing as close to me as he could without touching. I caught my breath.

"I hope I didn't keep you from your husband." His voice was low.

I swallowed hard. "No, you didn't. Alex just likes to know where I am—at all times. He says it makes him nervous when he doesn't." The lack of space between us was making my heart race double-time and the words came out in a breathless puff.

Gio raised a brow. "A bit controlling, I suppose. Can't say that I blame him, though. If you were mine, I'd keep you in my sight, always."

"That's very bold," I whispered.

Not that I minded, of course. As each word had come out of his perfectly shaped mouth, blood flooded my heart and whooshed out with such powerful force it was as if I were traveling down a never-ending chasm, free of gravity, as I floated more than fell.

"I'm sorry," he said as he immediately backed off, going to the table and collecting his books.

"I didn't mean," I struggled, "it's not that . . . it's just that . . ." I had a vocabulary of over a million words and I couldn't think of a thing to say. Typical.

"Kate," Gio said, and smiled as he looked up from his bag, "you're right, it was bold. Sometimes I forget myself, but don't worry; I don't have the wrong idea about us. I'd be very much appreciative if you'd forget that little slip and please continue helping me with this." He held up the journal in his left hand, and then placed it in his bag.

What could I say? That I didn't mind he'd said it? That I liked it? Again, words seemed to evade me. I settled for simplicity.

"Of course, I will. Consider it forgotten."

"Wonderful. Now can I call you a ride home?" he offered.

"Thank you, but I've got that covered," I said as I took out my phone and hit the speed dial. The phone only rang once before it was picked up.

"Hello, Kate? Are you all right? What's going on?" Dave's voice was on edge.

"Hey, Dave, it's me. I need a huge favor. Do you think you can give me a ride home?"

When we pulled up to the curb, Alex was out front watering the plants.

"Does he always water at ten-thirty at night?" Dave asked.

"No, he doesn't." My voice was flat, unemotional. I knew Alex was outside just to see if I was hiding anything. "I think he's just pissed I wasn't home to answer his call."

"Are you sure you're going to be all right tonight? Want me to come in for a minute?" Dave's voice was a whisper even though we were inside his car and the windows were rolled up. "I mean, look at him. I don't know what it is, lately, but there's just something about him . . . something different. It scares me."

"Don't worry about me. I'll take care of Alex. I've been doing it for nine years, now."

"Call me if you need me." Dave placed his hand on my hand as I turned to open the car door. He squeezed it urgently. "I mean it. Anytime."

"Thanks. I will. I promise. But please, don't worry about me anymore. I can take care of myself." I was impressed as I realized I meant it.

Then, suddenly, a bright light illuminated the darkness surrounding me for so long and everything was clear. I *could* take care of myself. I didn't need anyone to take care of me. I was a smart, strong, intelligent, independent woman who could take care of herself. I was not a victim.

With every step forward, with every passing minute, I was becoming more aware of myself than I'd been in years—the self I thought I'd lost, the self I thought had abandoned me. I was my own person, and I would not be controlled by anyone.

But there was something about the way Alex greeted me as I walked up to the house that warned me not to test this revelation tonight.

"Well, hello, there." His eyes were incensed; the tints of red appeared to be sparking in his iris. He looked me over intently. "Did you get everything you needed done tonight?"

In my heart I knew I should stand up to Alex. I didn't deserve this treatment, this tone. Sure, I'd nearly crossed the line of faithfulness—nearly. But I hadn't. And as far as he knew, I'd been at the office all night with Dave.

However, self-preservation told me to play this night smart. No sudden movements, no drastic changes. Just be good, old, predictably pathetic Kate. Just smooth things over until I had a chance to calmly think things through.

"Hey, love," I said in my most girlish way, ignoring the ire in his voice. "Yeah, I guess so. I'm still behind, though. God, sometimes I wonder if I should be doing this job. I feel so inadequate. Maybe I should find a different career."

A little self-loathing never hurt anyone. If I knew Alex, and I was pretty sure I did, he'd want to be right there to pick me up, acting the part of the knight in shining armor.

I could see it working as Alex turned off the hose and walked over to me arms open. The anger in his eyes was fading as the red flecks gave way to more gold tones.

"Come here." He sighed. "What am I going to do with you?" He sounded as if he was talking to a child. Why had I never noticed this before? Just as Toto pulled the curtain back to expose the Wizard for what he truly was, something was pulling the curtain away from Alex and I was seeing him without all the smoke and mirrors. I leaned into his embrace.

"You know, you had me worried tonight. From now on, I'd like you to be home before nine o'clock." He continued to hold his patronizing tone.

My stomach turned and fury whipped through me, but I shoved it deep down and ignored it with my entire being.

"Do you really think that's necessary?" I asked in a casual tone.

"It'd make me feel better, okay, love?" He looked down at me from his embrace.

I didn't want to push him over the edge, but I just couldn't swallow the way he was treating me. "But there was no need for worry. I told you earlier I had some work I might do. You had some stuff you needed to get done, and I really didn't want to be home alone all night, so—"

"I'm serious," he interrupted. "I don't want you working that late anymore. Understand?"

"It doesn't seem I have a choice, does it?" I tried to push the hurt away, but I couldn't quite disguise it. Damn it, I wasn't some teenager who needed a curfew!

"Oh now, sweetheart, don't be mad. You know I love you. Just do this one little thing for me, please?" He wrapped his arms tighter around me and pulled me close. I didn't want to be close to him, but he was much stronger, and then there was something about his touch that always seemed to get him whatever he wanted.

I closed my eyes and tried to resist him, but his smell was intoxicating. He lifted my chin so our faces were just inches apart; I could feel his breath on my lips. I couldn't help but give him what he wanted. I just *couldn't*. How did he do that?

"Of course, I can do that for you. I love you too. I'm sorry I made you worry." I heard the words come out of my mouth and they almost seemed to not be mine, but they were. I didn't intend to give in, but I had.

He closed the space between us and kissed me, his tongue barely touching the opening of my mouth, his lips catching my bottom lip and tugging it gently as he pulled away. My body relaxed into him, but something inside me stirred, though it wasn't telling me what I thought it would.

Instead, it shouted a warning and urged me to pull away. I tried to listen, but the warning was no match for Alex. It was almost as if he'd put a spell on me, a spell activated by his touch.

His hands wrapped around my waist and squeezed tightly. I edged closer to him, pressing my body flush against his. His hardness pressed against me, ready. My insides tightened and throbbed for him. I angled my hips closer to him.

The voice inside me became louder and louder. *Pull away, Kate! Pull away! You'll see!* Where did that thought come from? I'd no idea what it meant, and I didn't care as I fell deeper and deeper into Alex's touch. I was dizzy, drowning in his arms. I knew this touch. It was enthralling, complete in its power. My lips pressed firmly against his yearning to taste him. He was entirely in control and there was nothing I could do except kiss him hard and touch him, feel him, close my eyes, and smell his smell and . . .

Far away, my phone rang. It was miles and miles away. Even if I'd wanted to answer it, I probably couldn't. It was too far away for me to care, too far away for anyone to care. Two rings . . . three rings . . .

"Who's calling you this late?"

I blinked and tried to focus but was still dazed by Alex's kiss. "What?"

"Your phone, Kate. Who's calling?"

I shook my head and rummaged around in my purse digging for the phone. Pulling it out, my heart stopped as an unknown number flashed on the screen.

"Answer it." Alex's voice was cold. Demanding.

I shuddered as my finger automatically hovered over the green accept button. I paused, panic flying through my mind. Who was calling? It couldn't possibly be Gio.

"Answer. It."

My lip quivered as I hit the screen and brought the phone to my ear. "Hello?"

"Hey, Kate, this is Claire. I was . . ."

Claire's voice jolted me out of the last bits of Alex's haze and I was instantly back in the present.

"Claire!" It was all I could manage as I responded. My heart was practically spasming in my chest. Why on earth was she calling? Where had she gotten my number? She was too close of a link to Gio to be calling me.

"Oh, hey," she continued. I fumbled with my purse and tried to take a step away from Alex. Before I could accomplish the feat, Alex's hand was over the phone at my ear and slowly pulling it down. Keeping his eyes locked on mine, he hit the speaker button on the screen.

I let it be, sighing in resignation. If this was how Alex found out I'd lied to him tonight, well, then so be it. I'd have to fess up sooner or later, and what was the worst he could do to me? A cold shiver ran straight into my core. I held my breath as my conversation with Claire continued.

"I was wondering if you'd want to come into the shop on Friday night and help me out? We could meet up at the store. I'm getting a bunch of new inventory and I was going to close up about an hour early." I listened without speaking, waiting for the moment when she mentioned the bookstore or Gio, but it never came.

"So, what do you say? Do you think you'd mind coming in and helping me organize? I have no one to help me, and I promise you can have first dibs on anything you like. What do you think?" She finally paused and waited for me to respond.

My eyes darted to Alex's and then back to the speaker. "Oh, well, I don't know. I'd have to check with my husband to make sure we have nothing going on Friday. How long do you think it'd be?" I wasn't sure what was going on, but I followed her lead. Hopefully, I could get through this conversation without incriminating myself.

"That's the thing. It will probably take a while. You see, I've got over sixty boxes coming in, and I have to get everything out on the floor by Saturday. So, I was thinking maybe from six until . . . I don't know, maybe midnight?" Her voice was a perfect balance of calculating innocence and persuasion. What was she up to? "Please, Kate, please. I know we're kind of new at the whole friend thing, and this is a really big favor, but I wouldn't ask you if I wasn't absolutely desperate. I'll even buy you as many coffees as you can drink. *Please*."

My heart pounded the entire conversation. Now, I gathered up the courage to meet Alex's gaze. I raised my eyebrows giving him a *What do you think?* look.

"Hold on, let me talk to my husband really quick." I hit mute.

"What do you think?" I said.

Alex paused. "Who's Claire?"

"Just a woman I met in the bookstore. She and her mother own a vintage clothing shop downtown. We got to talking and kind of hit it off, I guess." I thought we'd gotten along okay when we met, but I'd no idea we had gotten along *that* well. Was there something to this I wasn't quite seeing?

Alex's eyes narrowed and my heart stopped beating. Shit. He wasn't buying it. He blinked twice and smiled. "Sounds good to me. I'll actually be in the city Friday for a business thing," he responded.

My heart resumed its rhythm, and I unmuted the phone. "Sure, Claire. That sounds good. I'll be there at six."

"Great. Thanks a lot. You're helping me out big time."

"Okay, see you then." I ended the call before she had the opportunity to bust me. I stared at the phone for a minute in disbelief, the shock slowly settling in around the confusion.

"She sounds harmless, a little too talkative maybe, but harmless." He took a step closer to me and ran his hands up the length of my body, trying to pick up from where we'd left off.

I stepped away and ran my hands through my hair. I was completely and totally drained. I was confused, hungry, and most of all, sick to my stomach with nerves. Adulterous thoughts had taken their toll on my body. I wasn't in the mood for what Alex had planned for the rest of the evening.

"Look, I'm sorry, but I think I'm just going to head upstairs for the night. I'm exhausted." I could see he wasn't going to take no for an answer, so I added, "You're right, I shouldn't work so late. From now on, it'll be nine o'clock at the latest."

This seemed to appease him as he leaned back, examined my face, and then let me go.

"Sleep tight, love. I'll see you in a bit."

I could feel him watching me as I walked toward the stairs. I had almost escaped before he called me back.

"Kate?"

"Yes?" I answered hesitantly, trying to sound exceptionally tired, though after tonight, I was so wound up, I could've run a marathon.

"I'm glad you're making new friends. I'm not sure Dave's such a good influence on you." He looked me up and down and licked his lips. "Don't fall asleep too quickly. I'll be up to bed soon."

I gave him a half-smile and nodded my head. It'd be a long night if I refused him. With great care and much guilt, I retreated to my room, resigned to what the rest of my evening held, and waited for Alex to come to bed.

Sixteen

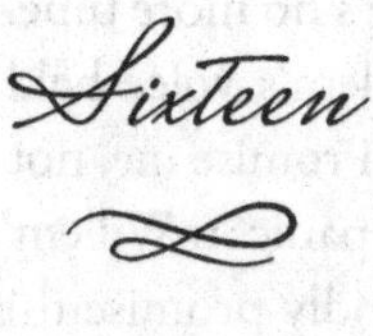

GIO

"What were you thinking, Claire?" My voice was on the edge of real anger.

Willem must've sensed the desperation in my voice because he stood from the table at which he and Claire were sitting and deliberately put his body between her and myself.

"Gio, you really need to calm down. I have no idea what you're talking about," Claire said in her casual, small voice.

"What about inviting Kate out to play dress-up sometime? At the bookstore earlier? Ring a bell?" I had to crane my neck around Willem's immense presence to see her sitting comfortably with her feet propped up on the table.

"Oh, that, well . . . I'll get to that in a minute, but first I've got to make a phone call." She looked at her watch and pulled a cell phone out of the inside pocket of the worn army jacket hanging on the back of the chair she was sitting on.

"Trust her," Willem said as he took a step toward me. "Whatever happens in the next few minutes, promise me you'll not make a sound. Kate's life may depend on it."

"What the hell is going on?" My mind felt heavy, everything moved as if it'd been dipped in thick, dark syrup.

"I'm telling you to trust Claire."

"*Willem* . . .," Claire pleaded as she looked at her watch one more time. "There's no more time. I must call now."

"Gio, please." Willem's voice held a frantic urgency that caught my attention. "Promise me, not a sound. Swear it!"

Just looking at the panic in Willem's eyes, I could see it was real. Of course, I'd blindly promise this to him. I knew it and he knew it, though he now held my arm tightly awaiting my answer.

"I promise," I said as I walked around Willem and fell down on the couch. I looked over at Claire. She'd already dialed the number and was patiently waiting for someone to pick up the other end.

The moment she started speaking, I was thrown into a state of semi-hysteria. Goddess above! She called Kate. Since we both knew she wasn't at work, I could only assume Claire was calling her cell. Where had she gotten the number?

My heart almost flew out of my chest as I jolted up and advanced toward Claire. Willem was there before I could even take a complete step. Damn, he did know me too well. Before I knew what was happening, he had one arm around my chest and the other around my mouth.

A cloth was between his hand and my mouth and I knew that I probably shouldn't take a breath in, but the instant I thought it, my brain craved air and I inhaled deeply, taking in both oxygen and a strange, metallic smell.

"Shh." His voice was barely audible in my ear.

I didn't want to believe Willem would drug me, but almost instantly I became more relaxed, and I knew he had. Honestly, I couldn't blame him. On most days, Willem knew what I'd do before I did. He'd probably anticipated my reaction and knew he'd have to be ready to intervene at any cost. Goddess, help me. After four centuries, I guess some things never change. Was it his fault I was not only predictable, but also reliable in my predictability?

I stopped struggling and thought about Kate. I let myself become intoxicated with whatever Willem had put on the fabric. I didn't fight it one bit. I reminded myself that whatever Claire and Willem were up to, it was solely to help bring Kate back to me.

Willem held me up and carefully sat me back on the couch. My vision blurred and my head swooned, but I could still hear Claire talking in the background. Her voice was far away, but it was there. I was still conscious, barely.

I focused on her voice. It sounded like she was talking underwater. If only I hadn't been so damn impulsive, I could've heard the entire conversation.

"How did you know?" Claire's voice was suddenly right on top of me.

Damn, I missed the entire phone call.

"I've been with Gio for more decades than I care to count. I know him better than he knows himself." Willem didn't say this with any emotional tag. There was no disappointment or chiding in his tone. He simply stated it as if it were fact. True, undeniable fact.

"Well, what now?" Claire asked.

"He'll be out of it for a good twenty minutes. How about you fill me in on that call and I'll make you something to eat?"

In the distance, I heard the clattering of plates and utensils, drawers being opened and closed, and voices murmuring in the background too far away for me to make out.

I knew I'd made an ass of myself tonight. I practically forced Willem to drug me, but there was no way in hell he should get to know what Claire and Kate had talked about before me.

I tried to force myself to come around. I turned my head, or at least thought I did, and willed my body to stand, but it was completely useless. I couldn't move. I was completely incapacitated. Damn, Willem.

When I could finally move again, both Willem and Claire were sitting in front of me, anticipation in their eyes. I brought my hands to my face and rubbed my eyes and forehead. I didn't feel all that bad; there was seemingly no after-effect to whatever Willem had given me. I'd have to remember to thank him for that. *After* I ripped him a new one.

I didn't even get the chance to say a word; Claire already started in on me.

"Look. I know you're probably pissed off right now, but I need you to focus in on what I'm saying to you, okay?" She didn't wait for me to respond. "I need to know any information on Alessandro you can give me. Anything Kate mentioned, anything you noticed in her behavior when she talks about him, anything."

"Whoa, whoa, slow down. I don't think the drug has entirely worn off yet." I shot a heated glare at Willem.

"Don't be mad at Willem. You're the one who acted like you were going to do something crazy," Claire scolded. I wasn't sure how I felt about being reprimanded by a twenty-year-old who looked like she was sixteen, but she did have a point.

"Fine." I wasn't going to apologize, but I wasn't going to press it any further. "But can you please fill me in on what the hell is going on? I feel like I'm missing something huge here."

Claire and Willem exchanged a look. It became painfully clear I'd indeed missed out on something, and moreover, their look told me they were debating whether to fill me in on this new information.

"Somebody better start talking." I tried to make my voice

sound threatening, but it came out more like a kid trying to make his parents tell him what they got him for Christmas. What did Willem put on that cloth?

"There've been some . . . developments, since Claire left the bookstore." Willem's voice was careful not to give anything away before he was supposed to.

"And . . .?" I waited.

"And please don't freak out but we've got some problems. Mostly with Alessandro and the amount of power he apparently has, specifically over Kate. He's marked her." Claire spoke quickly as if it'd be less of a shock, a bandage ripped quickly from the skin.

Unfortunately for Claire, I had no idea what she was talking about.

"What does that even mean?" Maybe I should be panicked, but I wasn't. Maybe it was the drugs.

"Alessandro's marked her. Just as he marked you, he's marked her. His mark carries a certain power. Look, in the past you said Alessandro always seemed to be one step ahead of you, right?" I concentrated on Claire's words as she spoke in haste.

"It was as if he knew you were there, right? Well, the mark he cast on you, the one I removed, was alerting him to your presence. He's done a similar casting on Kate, though it's so much more complex.

"When I saw Kate in the bookstore, I almost didn't know where to begin. She was surrounded by this terrible energy and there were all these little bits and pieces of you stuck in it. It was tricky, but I managed to clean her up and not disturb the other stuff. This isn't just your everyday, run of the mill magick. We're talking evil of the darkest kind here, really serious stuff. I was shocked to see she could even function. I mean, with that much magick clouding a person's aura, well, I'm surprised she remembers her name."

"Are you telling me Alessandro has been energetically drugging Kate?" Heat stirred in my blood. Of course he'd resort to magick to have her, it was the only way she'd ever be with him.

"Yes, I am. And not only that, but this is powerful, alive. It responds to his voice, his touch, his scent. It lets him know when it grows weak and needs to be recharged. It clouds her mind, makes her doubt herself, intensifies her need for him, all by a word, a touch, or a smell." Claire's face was still.

"I didn't think Alessandro had that kind of power. I mean, I knew he held power, but nothing like this." My voice echoed her expression.

Again, Willem and Claire exchanged a glance. This time it was Willem who broke the silence.

"We think he's raised old magick. Pure evil. Power that could not only destroy us but would do so willingly, that grows with every drop of blood spilt, every scream, every death. Power that can create things more horrible than anyone can imagine, that, I wish beyond all wishes, didn't exist."

"But if he was so powerful, he could've killed us off a long time ago and had Kate all to himself . . . forever." I swallowed hard as I tried to fathom what we were up against, as fear was finally starting to get the best of me.

"That's the thing. I don't think he'd kill us." Willem's voice held an edge of disgust. "This is too much of a game for him. More than he enjoys her pain, he enjoys *yours*. If he wins, the game is over."

My stomach turned. I'd always known Alessandro was truly a monster. Hearing the words out loud was a different story.

"Is there anything else?" I asked.

Claire looked at me earnestly. "Well, just two more things. First, you have to be very careful about not touching her when you're together. If you do, I need to clean her before she leaves;

otherwise, Alessandro will know. Secondly, once you think Kate is ready to take the serum, she must do it immediately and the two of you need to, um . . . you know . . ."—Claire's cheeks tinged pink as she looked for the right words— "you know, get *on* with it because I sensed that one of the spells Alessandro cast was to help him locate her. The thing about the spells is that I'm pretty sure once the serum is taken and the process of her original soul being released begins, all the enchantments Alessandro is using will be broken. At least temporarily. So, he'll know. And thirdly—"

"I thought you said there was just a couple more things." My human brain was having trouble keeping up with all the information.

"Well, this is more about me than Kate, really, and I think it'll give us an advantage," Claire answered. "I've discovered a new power. It seems to be pretty accurate, though it's extremely draining; I'm probably not strong enough to handle it, just yet. Anyway, it seems I've a flair for seeing the future. It comes and goes, and I'm still getting control of it, but if I concentrate hard enough, I can almost will my psyche to see certain paths, follow certain people."

I looked blankly from Willem to Claire and back to Willem. Everything was spinning in circles and I hadn't even made it to what was said during the phone conversation. I decided to test my comprehension.

"So, let me get this straight. Alessandro has brought back old magick to make sure I'll never be with Kate again. Like really evil shit. He's used this magick to drug her so he can coerce her into doing what he wants. And after fighting for what seems like eternity, I now have a good chance at getting her back but can't touch her for fear of setting off the equivalent of supernatural booby traps.

"And, *finally*, not only do I have to convince Kate to take a serum without explaining what it is—which is going to be no easy feat in itself—but then we have to move on with our . . . our *business* as soon as possible because Alessandro has put some sort of psychic GPS on her. Does that sum it up?"

I was close to a breakdown. I'd always known it would only be a matter of time. A man can only take so much failure, so much guilt, so much pain and loss before something inside him snaps. I felt that point edging closer and closer, but I pushed it down. I may have deserved this pain, but Kate didn't. I refused to fail her again, but it was close.

"Yeah, that's pretty much it. Well, except I can apparently see the future," Claire said.

"Of course, how stupid of me to forget." I spit out a laugh. "And how is the future looking now, Claire?"

"Well, actually," Claire said, "no one really knows the future for sure; it's always changing. But the immediate future, the one that's happening just minutes and hours from now, is much more predictable, and that's what's going to help us. That's what we need to talk about now."

"The phone call."

"Exactly. And I think I've found a way to buy us some time while Willem's finishing up the serum."

She immediately broke into what had transpired over the course of the night. I sat and listened intently as she spoke, hoping more than I'd ever hoped before that I wouldn't fail Kate again. It's funny how hope seems to creep in on you when you least expect it, a sliver of light shining under the door into a dark room leading you to freedom.

I waited until Friday afternoon to call Kate at her office. It was a nearly impossible feat to accomplish, but I managed. I couldn't imagine being without her, now that she was so close, but both Claire and Willem had convinced me the extra time apart was imperative if everything was going to go smoothly.

The plan was simple, really. Claire was adamant I follow her directions and I decided not to fight it.

Simply put, I would ask Kate out for later that night, knowing that she'd already made plans with Claire. When she mentioned this to me, I would suggest spending the afternoon together. After, I'd drive her to Claire's shop where Claire would cleanse her of anything left by me and breaking down some of Alessandro's lesser spells, while hiding what she'd done with her own magick. At that point, Willem would be completed with the serum, and I would then have approximately forty-eight hours to convince Kate to drink it and spend the night with me.

It sounded ludicrous because it was. But I'd done things my way for four hundred years, to no avail. Maybe it was time to do things differently.

I pinched the bridge of my nose with my fingers and took a deep breath. Just thinking about the plan made me nervous.

"What if Alessandro notices something isn't as he left it?" I asked.

"With both Willem and I working on different types of shielding spells, he won't get the chance to notice." Claire was confident in her words.

"But you said wards like this only last for about two or three days before they begin to break down, before flaws may be visible, right?" I responded, still not convinced this was the way to go.

"That's right," Claire said. "That's why once things get set into motion, there's no going back. We do it and keep moving forward."

"I don't know. What if it's not the right time?" I protested. "What if Alessandro senses something? You said he was more powerful than you'd thought. What if Kate mentions my name? What if something tips Alessandro off to us and he simply does away with her? What then?"

"I can't imagine what you're feeling right now," Willem said, placing his hand on my shoulder. "But think about Kate.

Think about what she must be going through right now. Think about all the vile and horrific things that Alessandro has done to her in past lives with a smile on his face. Think about him living with her in this life as her husband and tell me that it's not the right time to save her from his wretched grasp.

"I know you must be nervous, thinking about going through this again, but everything is different this time. Alessandro won't notice. I'm confident. Between the two of us"—he motioned to Claire and himself— "there'll be so much magick to confuse him, he won't know what is what. We *will not fail*." He looked straight into my eyes as he spoke and it was clear he wholeheartedly believed in his words.

I had to believe him. We couldn't fail. Kate would be finally free of Alessandro, and, if she should choose, be mine once more. I took my phone out and dialed her work number.

"Kate, how are you?" I tried to sound calm, though my insides were balled up with tension.

"Gio. I'm so glad you called." Her voice sounded genuine.

"Did you think I wouldn't?" I asked.

"Well"—her voice dropped— "it's just that, I thought after the way things ended last time, you were . . . I mean, I thought that I might've said something wrong."

My heart broke three times over. I closed my eyes and kept my breathing even. Here I was, thinking about what not seeing her was doing to me, and all this time she'd thought I was blowing her off.

Damn it! Damn it! No matter what I did, I couldn't manage to *not* hurt her.

"I'm sorry," I said, my heart falling into my stomach, the acid boiling it and turning it over again and again as I gritted my teeth and began my next lie. "I've been so busy lately with moving and everything. I didn't mean to give you that impression."

"It's no big deal, really," she said. "I'm just glad you called. I was hoping we could get together, you know, to discuss your book again." She added the last part quickly.

I smiled. She wanted to be with me. The feeling of being wanted is something every human craves. But to be wanted by the one most desired? Well, it was indescribable.

However, I couldn't let myself get sidetracked. I was given specific orders from both Claire and Willem. Willem was just hours from finishing the serum. Even as I thought it, it was hard to believe. I couldn't remember a time when Willem had completed the potion in such a short period. Even he was amazed at the fluidity of his ability this time around. But then again, everything about this time was so different.

I closed my eyes, took a deep breath and knew the words said next would be the beginning of either a liberation or a death sentence for my love. Funny how liberation and death can sometimes go hand in hand.

"I was thinking the same. How about tonight? I know it's kind of late notice, and a Friday as well, but I was hoping to see you as soon as you could manage it. What do you say?" I waited.

There was a short silence on the line.

"Unless you have plans, that is." I knew she did.

"Well, actually, I do. But I'd much rather spend the time on the book. I can call Claire and ask her if—"

"Oh, I would hate for you to do that," I interrupted. "It's no big deal. We can meet up another time, okay?"

"I'm sorry." Her voice was sad. I hated myself for putting her through this charade.

I swallowed hard and continued, "Well, what about this afternoon? No, never mind, you're probably exhausted from work and—"

"No! That's a great idea. I'm actually close to wrapping up

here. I could be finished in about an hour. The only thing is that I carpool with Dave, and I don't have a ride."

"That won't be a problem. Just give me the address and I can pick you up." I pictured Billows Publishing in my mind from when I scoped it out yesterday.

I felt bad, leading the conversation the way I did. It felt wrong and conspiring, but it was a necessary manipulation. I'd have to remember to apologize for all the little things, once we were together again.

Once.

I arrived at her office at three o'clock on Claire's motorcycle. Kate's eyes were beaming as she saw me pull up, and her smile lit up her face.

She seemed to move in slow motion as she walked closer to me, her dark hair blowing in the warm autumn breeze. She threw her bag over her shoulder so that it hung diagonally across her body.

"You know, I've never been on one of these before. I think I'm a little nervous," she said as she examined the bike.

"Well, first things first. This is imperative," I said, handing her a helmet.

She grabbed the helmet and put it on her head, "Okay, what next?" Her voice was muffled under the protection of the headgear.

"Well, hop on," I said.

She placed her hands on my shoulders and threw her leg over the bike. It was a little difficult for her in her skirt but not unmanageable. I struggled to keep my thoughts chaste. That was pointless. All I could picture were her thighs spread open behind me. I grew hard and shifted on the seat. She bounced up and down on the seat twice before she spoke next.

"All right, I'm ready. Let's go."

I cleared my throat. "Um, I was thinking about that. I really don't know where. I mean we could go back to the bookstore, but it's such a nice day. Do you know anywhere outdoors where we could enjoy the weather?"

I didn't want to say work because I'd no intention of working. My only motivation was to spend time with Kate and somehow convince her I was the love of her life.

She was silent for a moment. Then, hesitantly, she spoke. "Well, if you don't mind a short drive to the coast, I know the perfect spot. Just head west and keep going until you see ocean."

"Let's go," I said, chills running through my body as she carefully placed her arms around my waist.

I kick-started the bike and looked over my shoulder.

"Hold on tight," I said, over the roar of the engine and smiling as her careful arms turned into a firm grip wrapped completely around my waist.

I had to keep extra focus on the road; I was too aware of the closeness of her body to mine. About five minutes into the ride, she placed her helmeted head against my back and kept it there for the next ten minutes.

My body trembled with anticipation, with excitement; I had to remind myself to keep breathing and to focus on where we were going. After living lifetimes in a hell-spun purgatory that didn't exist anywhere but in my life, those ten minutes with Kate holding tight to me were heaven on Earth. Unfortunately for me, there was no such place as Heaven. I'd have to hope the Goddess would find a place for us together if we were ever reunited.

But I couldn't think like that. I had to concentrate on driving. We hit the coast and headed north as Kate led us to a place where there was an abandoned schoolhouse; old and weathered, its white paint of years past was just an impression.

We parked the bike off the side of the road, just past the tree line into the lush green forest. Kate led the way as we hiked a short distance behind the schoolhouse.

"Are you ready?" she asked over her shoulder as she climbed the massive trunk of a fallen redwood.

"Ready? For what?" I asked back, my curiosity aroused.

"My secret spot." She stood on top of the trunk and looked down at me.

I climbed up and stood next to her.

"Well, what do you think?" She held her hand out and gazed to her right. I followed her gaze. My breath caught.

The clearing was amazing. It was far enough away from the road that you couldn't hear any cars that might pass. A small space, no bigger than a backyard, it was surrounded by fallen trees and heavy moss. The sun streamed in through a break in the foliage above, giving the place magick.

"It's amazing," I said as I looked back at her. "How did you find it?"

"Come on, let me show you my favorite part." She jumped down from the trunk and headed toward a fallen tree, near what looked to be a ledge.

"Sometimes, I just sit on this trunk, look out and get some of my best ideas." She climbed the tree and took a seat on its worn surface.

I walked over to where she sat and stood behind her.

My initial assessment had been right. It was a ledge, and a steep one at that. The tree was positioned at the edge of the forest and looked out over the Pacific Ocean. From this spot, the rush of the water was clear and powerful. I looked down over the edge. The drop was about a hundred feet and was met by jagged rocks continuously beat upon by powerful waves.

"Take a seat," she said, patting a space on the trunk next to her.

I instantly sat next to her, though I would've rather grabbed her and whisked her as far from the edge as I could manage. Sure, the view was amazing, but my stomach turned having her so close to something so potentially dangerous.

"So, tell me, what do you think? Have you ever seen anything as amazing or beautiful before in your life?" She looked expectantly into my eyes.

I stared into her eyes and held her gaze.

"No, I've never seen anything as beautiful," I whispered as my eyes held hers, my voice low, "or amazing."

Her chest rose rapidly, though I knew it couldn't have been as fast as my thrumming heart. I wanted to reach out, to pull her close. I wanted to crush my lips against hers, my mouth tasting her tongue, my breath hot on her skin. I wanted to grab her and tell her how sorry I was for failing her, over and over again. I wanted her to know I was the reason she'd been forced to live this four-century nightmare.

My throat tightened and I swallowed. Even if she wanted to be with me, I didn't have the serum and the rules about that were very clear. She had to drink the serum before we could join physically. Instead, I continued the conversation.

"You never did tell me how you found this place." The change of subject brought a flush to her cheeks as she quickly turned away, toward the ocean.

"Um, I actually found this place by accident, when I got a flat tire. About six months ago, I was checking out this bookstore up north, in Mendo, and on the way back I got a flat. While I was waiting for the tow truck, I don't know what it was, but I felt this urge to walk around." She furrowed her brow. "It was really weird, 'cause I'm not much of an adventure-type, but there I was, hiking out in the woods. I just felt it was important to check things out, even though it was almost dusk by that point.

"Anyway, I climbed up over that same trunk just as the sun was setting. It was like nothing I'd ever seen. The colors were so bright. Everything was an amazing shade of green of course, and then there was this dazzling pink and red and purple tint streaming in from this break in the trees. I've never felt so settled . . . I can't explain it, but it was almost like I was *supposed* to find this place."

Her lips twisted and she chewed on the inside of her cheek.

"It sounds insane, but the moment I stepped over that tree trunk, I felt safe. Protected. Like something led me here for a reason, though I still couldn't tell you what that reason is. I know, it's weird. I'm not sounding too crazy, am I?"

"No, not at all." I was barely able to answer her; my head was swimming with emotion. A soft vibration in my soul pulsed and the distinct feeling that this place was important reverberated throughout my body. It couldn't have been just coincidence that Kate had simply happened upon this place right before I came into town, could it? No. It went deeper. This place was key.

"Do you visit often?" I asked, trying to regain my composure.

She shrugged. "Not as much as I'd like to. It's kind of a place that I come to alone, and lately I haven't had much alone time . . ." Her voice trailed off and her expression got dark, as if her thoughts were leading her far from where we sat. She blinked once, and then continued, "Anyway, nobody else knows about it, and I kind of like it that way." She cocked her head. "Well, now *you* know, but I don't mind. It feels right that you're here."

"Thank you," I said.

"For what?" She offered a half-smile.

"For sharing this piece of you with me. I can see it's important to you and that you don't share it lightly."

"You know, it's strange. I know we just met, but there's just something familiar about you. I can't quite put my finger on it, yet, but I . . ." She looked away now, her cheeks completely flushed. "Now I'm starting to sound crazy to myself."

"You don't have to worry about sounding crazy with me," I said as I reached out for her. I knew I shouldn't have, but I just couldn't help myself, it was pure instinct.

My hand barely brushed against her arm and a jolt of energy flew between us. Kate jumped, startled by the contact, and then looked at me, her eyes wide, the dark irises staring at me intently. Far behind the darkness of her eyes, I could see just a hint of green and gold. Somewhere, deep inside, Katarina waited for me. My breath caught.

Neither one of us spoke, the silence around us was absolute, yet a thousand words flowed between our touch. I edged closer to her, closing the small space between us.

Kate brought her hand up and touched my cheek. My eyes closed at her touch, her fingertips softly caressing my hot skin. My breathing sped up as her hand traveled up the side of my face and ran through my hair.

I could feel each finger as they made their way to the back of my head and stopped. Her face was close to mine; I tasted her breath on my tongue. It was soft and sweet and tasted of pears and honey.

This couldn't get out of hand; I didn't trust myself to stop at just one kiss. But I also couldn't imagine not letting it continue. Everything in my body pulled me toward her, and I knew, by the quivering of her fingers against my neck, she felt it too. I let her move closer.

Her cheek pressed against my cheek. She rubbed it against mine, her skin softer than I remembered, the friction between our skins electric. It sent bursts of stardust into the atmosphere.

"Do you feel that?" she whispered.

"Yes," I whispered back, "I feel it."

She breathed in deeply. Her chest rose and fell against me, and I couldn't resist her touch any longer. I was falling into her. Her energy was warm and inviting. She was my safe clearing.

I held my breath as I brought my hands up around her body. My hands found the small of her back. I drew her closer, waiting for the moment when she would stop me, but knowing it'd never come.

I pulled my cheek away from hers and looked at her face. Her eyes were closed; her lower lip was quivering. She was the most amazing creature my eyes had ever beheld. Be it the seventeenth or the twenty-first century, her beauty remained constant. It flowed from her being and coiled itself around me. I brought my face toward hers; my lips hovered just above hers, my hands trembling in anticipation, our lips so close air could barely pass between them.

The piercing melody of Kate's phone cut through the moment. Alessandro. I immediately recognized the ring tone from the other night. Kate jumped. Her eyes snapped open, the connection holding us together, broken instantly.

She fumbled through her jacket pockets until she found the phone. Taking one deep breath before answering it, she got up and walked toward the center of the clearing.

"Hey, Alex, what's up?" Her voice sounded strained.

Panic rose in my body. If Kate were to convince Alessandro into believing nothing was going on, she'd have to calm down. Alessandro had been playing this game for far too long. He'd recognize the strain in Kate's voice. He'd recognize it and find her, I was sure of it.

I shuddered at the thought of what he was capable of if he found her before I could give her the serum. I sprang from the trunk and ran to Kate's side. I stood in front of her and placed my hands on her shoulders, my eyes searching hers for a sign she was all right.

"Breathe," I mouthed the word to her while gesturing it with exaggerated movements of my body.

She nodded as she took a deep breath.

"No, nothing's wrong. Why?" The high tenor in her voice had faded. She was talking with more ease.

I stayed with her.

"No, the phone just startled me, the ringer was up all the way, that's all"—she looked anxiously at me— "I was just waiting for Claire to pick me up . . . Should be any minute now . . . You'll be gone how long? . . . Overnight? . . . Oh, I don't know, Claire mentioned having girl time after . . . no, it won't be late . . . no, that's okay, you don't have to call, I'll call when I'm home . . . no . . . no . . . Alex, I don't think it's necessary . . ."

She was arguing too much. I could tell by the way her body began to tremble Alessandro was getting angrier and angrier. I could sense it through her. If he got angry enough, he might act on impulse. I caught her attention with my eyes once more.

She stared back, tears filled her lids and threatened to spill over. I nodded. She understood exactly what I was trying to tell her.

"You know, you're right," she said, "what time will you call? I just need to know so I can be certain to be home . . . Okay . . . Talk to you then. Bye."

She slid the phone into her pocket and looked down at the ground.

"I really don't know what kind of person I am." Her voice was quiet. Her tears flowed freely now.

I grabbed her face between my hands and lifted it so she could see my eyes as I spoke.

"Listen to me." My thumbs pushed the tears away. "You are an amazing person. This is my fault, please, *please*, don't blame yourself."

"No, it's not your fault. It's mine. Don't try to make me feel better. I have to be responsible for my own actions. How can you look at me like that, knowing what I was about to do? Knowing that I'm married and that I was still going to kiss you? That I wanted to, practically yearned—no, still yearn to kiss you." Her eyes were searching, questioning.

Goddess, she was going to kiss me. We almost did. My lips throbbed. "Stop. This is my fault. I knew what I was doing when I asked you to hang out. I told you we'd be friends. You've done nothing wrong." I felt a new rip in my heart as each tear fell from her lashes down her cheek. "Please, stop crying."

Something in my voice must've gotten through to her, as she nodded once and sniffed, her tears slowing.

As we looked at each other in the early evening light, her eyes wet with what I could only assume to be guilt, my eyes wet with the helplessness one feels when one realizes one has very little control in life.

The minutes passed us by quietly.

"We should go," she said. "Claire will be waiting."

I nodded and turned to head back.

As we walked back to the motorcycle, she was silent. She seemed lost in her mind, far away from where we'd just been. She put on her helmet, and I grabbed mine. We got on the bike and my muscles tensed as I noticed her hands were tentative as she held on to me. There was space between our bodies. Distance. I wanted to die.

We rode back to Freestone, the scenery a blur. I couldn't remove the image of Kate's tears from my head. I struggled with not stopping the bike on the side of the road and explaining everything to her, right then and there. I was so tired of hurting her, so tired of making her cry.

But I kept driving. If I stopped now, I ran the risk of blowing everything. I'd already come too close to blowing it in the clearing. Having her lips so close, I couldn't resist. I cursed my stupidity. I wouldn't fail her because I was weak.

Back in Freestone, I stopped the bike in front of the shop. Claire stood on the other side of the window; she was opening boxes and unloading clothes. She looked up from her work when she saw us pull up and gave us a friendly smile and wave.

Kate got off and removed her helmet, handing it to me.

"Look," she said, studying her feet, "I just want you to know I don't regret the afternoon. And I meant what I said about it feeling right you were there, for what it's worth." She kicked the ground in distraction. "But maybe we shouldn't see each other anymore. Its painfully obvious that I can't be your friend and I just don't think it's fair to you."

Then she was gone. Before I had time to take off my helmet, before I could respond to her, before I could even call out her name, she was gone. She walked into the shop, Claire standing up to greet her in an embrace.

I didn't know what to do. I laughed. It was a tight, corrosive laugh; I choked on its poison. Since when had I ever known what to do? Pathetic. I was a weak, useless, pathetic excuse for a human being.

I stood on the sidewalk outside of the window and watched as the love of my life walked into the arms of my Watcher and did everything I could to not run after her. Stick with the plan. Above all else, I must stick with the plan. Claire led Kate to the back of the shop until they disappeared behind the counter, and I prayed I'd see her again soon.

Seventeen

KATE

I walked into the shop, fighting tears. I couldn't cry . . . no, I *wouldn't*. I wasn't sure how I was feeling; I just knew that it was like nothing I'd ever felt before.

Guilt. Yes, but not for Alex. I felt guilty I couldn't be to Gio what he wanted me to be, what I knew I wanted to be. There was sorrow. Sorrow for the loss of opportunity. Anger. I was so angry with Alex for calling. Why did he have to call? Why hadn't I turned off my ringer? And then there was the humiliation. God, I was humiliated I'd cried in front of Gio.

But what bothered me most of all was the feeling of rejection. Gio had nodded at me, silently telling me to do what Alex wanted. To make amends with, to appease my husband when I was more than willing to be with him.

My heart crushed, but it was more than that. It was the feeling of utter rejection. Gio hadn't wanted to carry on with me. And for some reason that knowledge alone cut something deep inside me, deeper than I thought was possible.

I saw Claire stand up and walk toward me.

"Hey, Kate. I'm so glad you're here." She gave me a hug.

It was strong and warm, not at all what I thought a hug

274

from Claire would be like. I let her hug me and found myself wrapping my arms around her and returning the gesture.

"I'm glad to be here," I said into her shoulder, my voice muffled by the thick sweater she wore and by the tears I let drop.

"Is everything all right?" she asked, still hugging me.

"Maybe I'll tell you in a little bit. Right now, I just want to put my stuff down and then please put me to work," I answered, pulling back and wiping my eyes with my sleeve.

She studied me for a moment, I assumed to make sure I wasn't about to have a complete breakdown.

"Of course," she said grabbing my hand. "Follow me. You can put your stuff in the back."

We walked past the counter and through a doorway decorated with strings of beads. The baubles hung loosely from what looked like fishing wire, but shinier, almost silvery, like they were made of some exotic metal. As I brushed past them, I noticed that between every few beads hung small silver charms. The charms glinted in the light, catching my attention, and I stopped to get a better look at them.

I pulled my hand from Claire's as I took a charm between my two fingers and brought it into my line of sight. The charm was the same as the one on the necklace I'd bought from the street vendor. I gasped.

"Where'd you get these?" I asked.

Claire stopped and looked back at me. "The beads? Do you like them?"

"Yes, I do. I actually bought a necklace that had this exact same charm on it, but I don't have it anymore." I shuddered. My free hand touched the base of my throat. The huge ruby Alex had given me hung heavy and uncomfortable, like a pair of wet jeans, underneath my blouse. Its weight pulled down on me.

Claire eyed me carefully, her eyebrows drawn down, her mouth crunched up.

"I see," she said, her voice low, penetrating. Her tone caught me off guard, and for a moment, I wasn't sure if she'd actually seen what had happened to the necklace. I shook my head. Nonsense. My imagination was working overtime again. There was no way Claire could know what happened to my necklace. She wasn't a mind reader.

I examined her expression. Within seconds, her face smoothed out and the dark clouds cleared from her expression. She walked over to me on light feet and smiled. Carefully, she grabbed a strand and pulled it off the line. She unstrung the beads until she came to a silver charm.

She held the charm in her palm and then squeezed her hand around it, closing her eyes.

"I call on the goodness and pureness of life and love, live in this vessel and protect all who hold it." She opened her eyes. "My mom used to say that when I was little. You know, for good luck." She took my hand and placed the charm in it, then closed my fingers around it. "I want you to have it. Promise me you'll keep it with you."

I held the charm tight in my fist. It emanated warmth into my hand. "I will. Thank you."

"You know, I think we have more in common than you know," she said as she started toward the pile of boxes stacked in the storeroom. "Here, grab a box and follow me."

I threw my stuff on an old table in the corner and grabbed the nearest one, then followed Claire out to the front of the store. I made myself comfortable in a display chair, placing the box at my feet.

"What do you mean we've more in common than I know?" I wasn't just going to let a comment like that go. And I was genuinely curious.

"Well, for starters," Claire began, "we're each an only child."

"How did you know that?" I interrupted.

Claire shrugged. "Oh, I can just tell. You know, personality type stuff. Anyway, there's that, and then I can tell you're an extremely intuitive person. Everyone's always telling me the same thing too." She waved her hand dismissively.

I scoffed loudly at that one. "Yeah, right." Claire may have been right about me being an only child, but I definitely was not intuitive. And yet, recently I couldn't help but feel things were going to dramatically change soon.

Claire ignored my jab.

"And then there's Gio . . ." she continued leading with her voice.

My heart stopped and sped up at the same time. I tried to act casual, trying not to tip her off to what had happened earlier.

"What do you mean?" I croaked. It sounded strained, even to me. Smooth, Kate. Smooth.

"You know. I've only known Gio for a short time, but what I do know is that he has the purest soul of anyone I've ever met. I think you know that too."

My heart sank. I did know it. I knew it the first moment I saw him as I sat on the balcony and lunched with Dave. God, that felt so long ago. I marveled at how he'd become such an important part of my life in such a short amount of time. And for some reason, I thought he'd felt the same about me as well. I blanched. What the hell was I thinking? I was a married woman. Nothing could ever come of my feelings for Gio. I felt like such a fool.

"I hardly know him. I don't know what I know."

"I can tell you've had an impact on him. You know more than you think."

She grabbed some clothes from the box she'd brought out

and began laying them on a display table. She was quiet, thoughtful, as she folded, smoothed, and straightened.

We worked in silence, and I felt the energy between us grow strong. I could trust Claire. Maybe she could help me sort out what had happened this afternoon with Gio. I opened my mouth to tell her everything that happened that afternoon when a man stormed through the shop and rushed straight toward the back room.

"That's Willem," Claire said, and then yelled, "Willem, don't be rude, come over here and meet my friend Kate."

I watched as Willem came through the beads again and walked over to me. He was a tall man and handsome, in a rugged way. But what stunned me the most was how amazingly graceful and light he was on his feet. He appeared to glide through the room and stopped just before me.

"Kate," he said in an Irish accent, "it's my pleasure to make your acquaintance." He held out his large hand to take mine. I placed it in his and he brought it lightly to his mouth.

"Nice to meet you too," I said. My words seemed awkward in comparison to his gallantry. I noticed Claire was watching his every move, her eyes beaming. Eyes of a woman in love.

Willem dropped my hand and turned to Claire. "I hope you two ladies won't be too busy tonight?" There was the sense that he wasn't just talking about the clothes we were supposed to unpack, but what he was referring to was beyond me.

"Oh, we'll be plenty busy, all right," Claire responded. Again, I had the distinct notion they were talking about something altogether different.

"Well then, I shouldn't keep you any further. I just came to get the last thing I need to finish up." He started to walk out, and then turned back. "Claire, will I be seeing you later?" There was anticipation in his eyes and butterflies erupted in my stomach. He felt the same way about her as she did him.

"Of course."

Willem smiled and left the shop in a bustle. Just before the door swung shut, a warm autumn breeze blew through and settled in my bones.

"Willem seems nice. Are you two, you know . . . together?" I asked.

It wasn't until after I'd said the words I wished I could take them back. I barely knew Claire and already I was nosing around her personal life. Claire smiled back at me. It was the sort of smile that belonged on a Cheshire cat, the kind that hinted she knew a whole lot more than she was going to reveal, a whole lot more than the rest of us.

"No . . ." She left the word hanging in the air.

"I didn't mean to pry. I just wasn't sure. It's just that he just looked so much older than you and I was curious. I mean, it's just that you're so much younger . . . no, that's not what I . . . um. Shit." I cringed as I repeatedly shoved my foot down my throat. I finally had the decency to stop talking and just apologize. "I'm sorry. It's none of my business. I can just go if you'd like?"

Claire eyes lit up, amused by my uncomfortable, stumbling monologue. She came over to where I sat and touched my shoulder.

"You'd probably like to escape all this work, but you can forget it." Her eyes were a warm October day, the kind that'd always made me feel happy to be alive. "You really need to lighten up. It's no big deal. Yes, Willem is a bit older than me, but we're adults, and love, true love, knows no age." She bent down until we were eye level with one another.

"I firmly believe that there is one person out there made just for you and you for them. That everyone has this person out there, but only a fraction of us will ever find them. Sure, we can love others and live happy lives and everything, but it's nothing compared to living that same life with the person who was made for you." She took a deep breath.

"Willem is that person for me. He may not know it yet, but he is. Men always take longer to figure these things out, though. His age makes no difference . . . to me, anyways. You know?"

I studied her face; she had the knowledge and confidence of a woman twice her age, which was about three times more than me.

"Yeah, I do know," I said. Gio flashed in my mind. Was it possible he was the one who'd been made just for me? I clenched my jaw. No, I couldn't think like that.

"Kate," Claire said, "may I speak candidly?"

"Sure. What's up?" What could've brought on her somber tone?

She took a breath and then spoke slowly and clearly. "I noticed how you and Gio interacted with each other the other night at the bookstore, and I wanted—"

I didn't let her get any farther. "You don't have to worry about protecting Gio. I should've known better. I mean, *I'm* the married woman, *I'm* the one who's supposed to be more responsible and more mature, and I acted like a complete idiot. A selfish idiot. I've just been so confused lately. It's really not like me. I just don't know what's wrong with me lately. And Gio, well, he's just . . . he's just . . ." I couldn't continue. I felt nauseous.

I felt foolish as tears welled up in my eyes again. What was I thinking? I hadn't even gotten this personal with Dave, and here I was spilling my guts to someone I'd just met.

Claire placed her hand on my shoulder. "I was just going to say no one is here to judge you. I wanted you to know that I saw you and Gio together. Really saw you both. It was beautiful. That's all."

I gave her a crooked look. "You mean you don't think I'm horrible and ought to be ashamed of myself?"

"I believe everything in this universe happens for a reason. Beauty can be found everywhere, and darkness can affect all. But everything happens because it is *meant* to. We just need to listen to ourselves, I mean, *really* listen, to figure out if we'll live in the beauty or the darkness."

I considered her words carefully. There was something in the way she said them that struck a chord within me.

For thirty years I'd lived on this earth and never realized something was missing. I'd lived with Alex. I'd been his. But what ate at me was the distinct feeling that even if I hadn't chosen him, it wouldn't have mattered in the slightest. I'd still be married to him because he was going to make me his, at all costs. I couldn't deny it any longer. There was something about our relationship that was wrong, toxic. I hadn't realized it until Gio came into my life. Like light illuminating the cave revealing shadow puppets, Gio's presence made me aware of Alex's falsity. It didn't make any sense at all, but I just knew being with Alex was wrong, that *he* was wrong.

"Oh my God," I gasped as the epiphany hit hard.

"Are you okay?" Claire asked.

"What time is it? Do you think I can get a ride home a little early? There's something I need to do. I promise to make all this up to you." I waved my hand around at the stacks of boxes that we never even got to.

Claire studied me; her eyes dove deep into mine. She seemed to be searching for an answer to a question I'd not heard. Then, suddenly, as if finding her answer, she nodded her head, and said, "Let's go."

∿

I TOLD Claire not to come in, I had some things to do by myself. It took some convincing because for some reason she didn't want to leave me alone at my house, but I finally got her to trust I'd be fine as I headed inside.

Everything was turned off; the house was dark. Alex wasn't home. At least I'd have a head start. I opened the door and ran upstairs to my bedroom in the darkness.

I flipped on the bedroom light and headed straight into the closet. Grabbing a couple of duffle bags, I threw them on the bed. I ran into the bathroom and opened my drawer. I scooped fistfuls of the essentials and hurriedly threw them into the bags.

My heart was racing. I was leaving him. I couldn't believe it. It was the most frightening, anxiety-ridden decision of my life, but I knew I couldn't stay with him. I couldn't explain what had helped me make that decision. All I could think was that if being with Gio felt right, then Alex was wrong—very, very wrong.

It seemed ridiculous to try and reason with myself that if Alex was so wrong, why had I spent the past nine years of my life with him because, in truth, I didn't have an answer. It was crazy, I knew it, but I also knew it was important to follow my instincts and get the hell out of the house as soon as I possibly could.

When I'd enough clothing to last a few days in the bags, I grabbed the stash of cash I kept hidden in my bedside table and stuffed it into the pocket of my wool skirt along with my car keys.

I quickly snatched the small three by three photo taken of my parents and grandmother at my college graduation and shoved it into the closest bag. It was one of the last times I saw them alive. Shortly after, the three of them were in a fatal car accident.

When it'd happened, all I could think about was how my father would never have the chance to walk me down the aisle. How my mother would never help me ease into marriage. How my grandmother would never get to see me grow to be like her.

What would they have thought if they could've seen me at that moment, standing in my bedroom, bags packed and thrown over my shoulder, no longer willing to sacrifice myself for him?

"It's now or never," I said determined. Taking a deep breath, I turned around, and hit the light as I ran down the stairs, never once looking back.

Exhilaration ran through me, ecstatic. Yes, this was the right decision, I'd bet my life on it, I was so sure. A small part of me felt a little bad for Alex. He'd come home later and I'd be gone. I didn't have time to leave a note, the urgency to escape was too great, but I'd call him later. I'd call him as soon as I knew where I was headed, to let him know I was okay, and that I wasn't coming back.

I bounded down the stairs and grabbed the front door handle. It was locked. Strange. I didn't remember locking the door when I ran in. In fact, I didn't even remember closing it behind me when I got home. A fraction of a second passed before everything stopped. I was paralyzed, standing in the blackness of my house, terror winding icy hands around me. I heard a slight rustling to my right just before the small click of a lamp switch flooded the room with light.

It was an instant before my eyes adjusted, but when they did, I wished they hadn't. Alex. He sat unnaturally upright, arms on both armrests of the black leather recliner, his face a portrait of stone. There was no expression.

"Now tell me, Kate"—his voice burnt my skin— "where the *fuck* do you think you're going?"

"Alex," I said, my voice barely audible, stifled by fear. "Alex, I . . . I . . ."

His eyes were dark. His voice betrayed the lack of expression, and something told me to get out of the house as quickly as possible. Again, instinct screamed at me to run, and run fast. Quickly, I flipped the latch on the door and pulled it open.

I was one step out of the door when I felt his hand grab the back of my shirt and savagely pull me back in the house while the other slammed the door shut, the frame missing my head by millimeters.

Alex whipped me around to face him, his body cornering me against the door, both arms on either side of my head. His breath was thick, heavy. I could see saliva gathering at the corners of his mouth.

"You didn't answer my question, love." I flinched as his voice charred my skin. "Where. The. Fuck. Do. You. Think. You're. Going?" He said each word as a separate sentence, getting louder and louder until he was yelling in my face.

"I'm leaving," I said it quietly, but with conviction. I was leaving. I was still leaving. Nothing had changed.

"Oh, I see. You're leaving." I was unprepared for the hard slap that ended his statement like a punctuation mark across my face. "And where, might I ask, are you leaving *to*?"

"I . . . I don't know." My breathing was more uneven now as my hand touched my cheek. He hit me. My God, he hit me. He'd never hit me before. I was losing composure. My thoughts jumbled. "I . . . I just needed some space, some time to get my head together. Time to think, that's all." I was blubbering; tears choked my throat, stopping the fluidity of my words.

Alex ripped my bags from my shoulder and threw them across the room.

"Looks like you were planning to be gone a while." He took a step back from me and I was able to breathe better.

"Sit down." He wasn't asking.

I thought about protesting, but when I didn't move, his eyes flared, and I decided to listen. I walked over to the chair next to the fireplace and sat quietly, waiting for him to speak. Waiting for him to do anything.

"So, here we are . . . again." He didn't sit, just paced in front of me. "What to do, what to do? This is a quandary now, isn't it? We were so close this time, Kate, so close. Just one more year. That was it."

Close to what? One more year till what? I wasn't following what he was saying and was about to point it out. *No! Don't say anything! Just stay still and let him talk.* I watched as the emotions ran over his face: sadness, anger, betrayal, rage. I didn't listen.

"Alex." I stood and brought my hand to his cheek. "I'm sorry."

He brought his hand to cover mine and pulled me close to him. Had my apology given him the wrong impression? Did he think I was apologizing for trying to leave, not thinking I was still intending on doing so. I pushed against his chest.

"Alex, look," I said, my voice was stronger now. The fear was still there, but just playing at the edges of my psyche, not running amuck within it. "I'm sorry you're hurt, but I'm still leaving. I need some space."

His eyes burned with what I could only assume was pure hate, and I skillfully stepped out of his immediate reach toward the fireplace.

"I should've figured as much." Spit flew from his mouth. He'd fallen back into his rage. "You never were one to stick around."

"Look, I know you're angry, but this isn't going to help us.

Why don't you just let me go, we'll have the night to cool off, and we can talk about it in the morning, okay?" I desperately tried to calculate a way out of there, but with Alex blocking my path to the door, my options were limited.

"I'm sorry, that's just not going to work for me." His voice sounded strange. Different. It was Alex, but it wasn't. The voice I heard was completely disconnected from his body. What was happening? Who was this person? I stared, my chest rising and falling in double time.

I could see his mouth moving. I knew he was speaking, but nothing he said made sense. Left him too many times? Run away again? My God, he'd finally lost it. He wasn't just letting his anger get the best of him. He was crazy.

"And now, I'll have to kill you. Again." His face was twisted in what appeared to be lament at first, and then turned into something more like serenity as he said, "What a waste. Oh, well, there's always the next life."

I choked on my breath. "What are you talking about? Are you all right? You're scaring me. Alex?" Perspiration collected along my brow. Shit, he was really making me nervous. I tried to stall. "What do you—"

I didn't have time to finish my question. He wrapped his left hand around the back of my neck and pulled me closer, the full force of his right fist hitting me squarely in the stomach. I doubled over and choked, searching for air. Still bent over, I felt his hand on the back of my head. He grabbed a handful of hair and held me down at a ninety-degree angle as he brought his knee up into my stomach.

Any air I'd regained from the first blow was lost with the fierceness of the second. Shock ran through me, like a scalpel cutting flesh. Alex had gotten physical with me before, but it was nothing like this, nothing to what his true strength could be. My eyes rolled to the back of my head, my lungs desperately trying to pull air in. As my eyes strained to refocus, a chill ran through me and I realized for the first time that he was going to kill me. He was actually going to kill me. The words sank in and reverberated in my head like the beat of an executioner's drum.

"Alex," I pleaded when I'd finally caught some air. All that followed was a wet cough. I tasted the blood dripping from my lips.

Alex stood me up straight and pushed me up against the fireplace. "Don't talk, Katie love, it'll be easier if you just let it happen."

His hand made its way to my neck and easily wrapped around it, using the fireplace mantel for leverage as he squeezed. My hands instinctively shot up to his hand and tried to pry his fingers from my windpipe.

It was no use. He was too strong. I couldn't breathe. My God, I was going to die. Death crept around the room, circling my predicament, waiting for the right moment to pounce and take me to the other side.

"Alex . . . please . . .," I said gasping; his grip so tight tears ran down my cheeks.

"How could you? After all the work I put into you? How could you just leave? It's him, isn't it? He's what's gotten to you. I haven't sensed him, the sneaky fuck, but it must be." He was talking to himself more at this point than to me—I couldn't speak anymore.

My vision grew blurry, becoming black around the edges. Sound ceased to exist; everything was happening in silence. I felt my hands drop to my sides and knew it was just moments before the end came.

I could see white dots appear against the blackness of my vision, and in that moment, I gave up the struggle. Let him have me, let it be done.

I relaxed my muscles and felt my body droop. Soon. Soon,

it would be just seconds now. Everything was soft and warm and tingly.

And then, there was something else. Something different. I wasn't quite sure when I recognized it was there, just that suddenly it was. It was cold and hard, and just within reach of my hand.

A familiar voice in my head screamed. *Fight, Kate, fight! Grab it! Grab it and hit him! Do it, Kate! Do it now!*

Barely coherent, I grabbed the fireplace poker and with everything I had—and hadn't realized I had—I shoved the poker up into Alex's body.

Somewhere in the distance, Alex wailed in pain as he let go. Instantly, the crisp rush of oxygen flew into my lungs as I was released. My body heavy, I stumbled forward to my hands and knees, my vision still blurry, my head dizzy. I frantically grasped at my collar, trying to loosen the fabric as I gasped for air.

Get up. Even in my terror, I knew I had to keep moving. Some force inside me insisted that if I were to make it out alive, this would be my only opportunity.

The voice spoke again. *Run! Run now!*

I struggled to my feet, half running, half crawling. I didn't know where Alex was, or if he was hurt or worse, but I didn't take time to find out.

I made it to the door and flung it open. The warm autumn air filled my senses and gave me a burst of energy. I pushed myself to keep going. I was able to stand now, and I hobbled to my car, unlocking the door as I approached.

I wasted no time. I started the engine and took off, heading as fast I could away from where I'd left my husband. Was he dead? I drove for about five minutes before shock and panic began to set in.

"Breathe, Kate, breathe," I repeated over and over as I sped away. "Don't fall apart now. Just keep it together until you can figure out what to do."

I pulled the car over to the side of the road and turned off the engine. I should keep going; He might be following me. Oh my God, I could've killed him. What was I going to do? Where was I going to go? To the police? Probably, but I was too tightly strung to think clearly.

I had to get somewhere where I could think, somewhere where I knew I'd be safe, somewhere where no one would find me, not even Alex. And I had to do it fast. I saw my reflection in the rearview mirror. The left side of my face was already swollen and bruising, blood drying on my lips and chin.

"You bastard!" I screamed into the night. The noise echoed inside the car.

I brought my hands to my neck and snapped Alex's present off my neck with a violent tug. Instantly, I became calmer, more aware. It was as if the weight of the world alleviated around me as the necklace came off. I rolled down the window and chucked it as far as I could.

I closed my eyes and opened them again. I knew where I'd go, if only for a few hours, to get things straight in my head. I started the car back up and headed toward the coast.

The moon hung high in the sky. Its bright, perfect circle illuminated everything around me. I slowed when I got to the old schoolhouse, but I didn't stop. I went up another mile and pulled way off the road, my car deep in the shadows of the coastal wood. I doubled back on foot, looking over my shoulder the entire way. He'd never find me here, would he?

I couldn't relax until I entered the clearing. The full moon lit the enclave like a floodlight. I stumbled to the center and fell down on the soft, mossy carpet. The noise of the night surrounded me, the toads and the crickets jockeying for position among the loudest. An owl rustled high above my head and a small animal, probably a rodent of some sort, scurried in the underbrush.

There was buzzing and clicking and scratching all around, a reminder that life goes on while most sleep. I heard the bugs and the birds and the frogs and the wind. And above it all, closing in around my heart, I heard the rhythmic sound of the ocean waves as they crashed on the rocks below falling in time to the sound of my sobs.

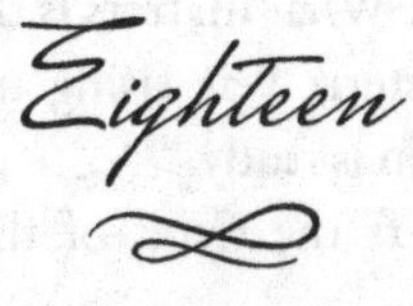

Eighteen

GIO

It was Claire's idea to keep watch at her house. I'd keep watch and the next time she left, I'd follow her until she was safe. But something went terribly wrong, and for the hundredth time in my pathetic existence, I wasn't there to protect her.

I was just coming over the hill behind her house when I saw her running for her car, frantic, scared. Alessandro was nowhere to be seen, but I knew he'd be coming soon. My heart gaped. She sped off alone. I went to follow her, but soon after, I saw him stumble out of the house, disoriented and hurt.

Shit. This wasn't supposed to happen. Not like this. I needed more time. I had to get the serum. I knew my time would be limited. I only hoped I could find Kate before he did. I hurried back to the store.

"Claire! Willem!" Sheer panic echoed in the room. "Claire! Willem!" I called again, my voice unnerved beyond comprehension. They both came running from the back room.

"What is it? What's wrong?" Willem asked.

"*He* knows," Claire answered for me. The words were choked out.

"How did this happen?" Willem stood just a step behind Claire.

"It doesn't matter. What matters is that I need to find Kate before he does." Hysteria was rising in my voice. "Willem, please tell me the serum is ready."

"Aye, it is." He left the front of the store to collect the draught.

"Gio," Claire said as she held out her hand, palm facing me, "give me your hand. Let me see if I can feel her."

"It's too risky. There's got to be another way." My thoughts immediately flew to the last time Claire lowered her guard and released her full magick. Healing Willem's hand had taken its toll on her physically, and since then, the experiments she tried when practicing her talents had always left her unconscious. I was torn. I wasn't sure if she'd be able to endure another attempt at channeling her powers without seriously injuring herself. On the other hand, she might be the only chance I had at finding Kate in this moment.

"There's no time to argue. It's my job to protect you, to guide you. I won't fail, not when there's something I can do. Kate's life depends on this."

I was no longer torn. The choice was easy. I placed my hand to hers, palm to palm, closed my eyes, and took a deep breath. Though I'd been resistant to Claire using her magick just seconds before, it was the only thing that could help me now.

Claire searched my mind for some clue as to where Kate might be. Her energy delved deep into my consciousness and beyond like long tendrils of light as she reviewed every word Kate and I exchanged over the past couple of days.

Sweat collected at my brow as Claire searched. Her pulse increased as her breathing became uneven. Her hand trembled against mine as she struggled to continue, to hold on before the magick claimed her. I fought the instinct to break the connection.

Energy built between us like two opposing forces fighting against each other, neither wanting to dominate nor submit. We struggled in this awkward dance for what seemed like eternity, time lost in the spatial shuffle of our souls.

My knees began to buckle and I brought my free hand to Claire's shoulder to steady myself. Her entire body was shaking against the magick she was calling. Together we fell to our knees, our palms fastened together by a magical glue that refused to yield to the weakness of our physicality.

When it seemed as if our bodies would implode into each other, everything stopped. Silence rippled through my mind. Everything was quiet, peaceful as I let the sensation fill my soul. I didn't open my eyes until I heard Willem's voice call out.

"Gio! Claire!"

My lids were heavy, but I managed to open them and looked around. Willem was bent over Claire, his hand caressing her cheek. Something had gone terribly wrong.

"Claire! Claire!" Willem's voice grew more panicked as Claire lay there motionless.

I got up, my body stiff and gauche from the aftermath of the magick. I crawled to where Willem hovered over her.

"What happened?" I asked, my voice hoarse.

"It was too much for her . . . too much magick. She's not like me." Tears found their way to Willem's eyes. "She's so new . . . so fragile." He bent over Claire's body, her face gently held in his hands.

"Please stay with me," he whispered as he pulled away from her, leaving a glistening trail of his tears.

Seconds dragged on as hope began to fade into the background. Suddenly, Claire's eyes fluttered. She bolted upright, gasping for air, her eyes wide with terror. Both Willem and I were instantly at her aid.

"Claire!" Willem croaked, emotion overwhelming his soul. He held her close to him as she recovered. After just seconds, she frantically looked for me.

"Gio, you have to hurry! He doesn't know where she is now, but he will. You have to get to her first or he'll kill her. I saw it."

"Where is she?"

She shook her head. "I don't know where it is, but I can describe it." She closed her eyes. "There's a schoolhouse. She's sitting on a fallen tree, where the forest ends to overlook the ocean, a field of stars blankets the sky."

I touched her arm. My pulse rang loud in my ears.

"I know where she is."

"Then go to her. *Hurry!*" She reached into her pocket and pulled out a set of keys.

I took the keys from her limp hand, stood, and ran to the door.

"Gio. Wait." I turned just as Willem tossed a small vial to me. My hand reflexively went up and caught it. It was no bigger than a domino. The liquid inside was a deep purple.

"Don't forget, she has to drink it before you're together." He paused a moment as he held Claire to his chest. "Good luck, my friend."

I nodded once before I ran out the door. I raced down the street to where Claire's motorcycle was parked. I hopped on, kicked the bike into gear, and sped off in the opposite direction.

The wind cut gooseflesh into my exposed limbs as I hit the accelerator. I envisioned the place where I knew Kate hid. It was her spot. The place where I'd been simultaneously thrilled and tortured by being so close to a love I knew so well and still having to get to know all over again. My only hope was that she hadn't told Alessandro about the place. I had to get to her first.

The town passed as a blur in my peripheral vision as I left Freestone behind, not knowing what might await me less than fifteen miles ahead. I maxed out the speed, pushing the bike harder than I'm sure Claire ever had, urging it to move as fast as my heart was beating.

As I flew toward the clearing, images of the past flipped through my mind, a grotesque slideshow of loss. I tried to push the impending doom far back into my brain, but it was persistent in its presence, reminding me of all the failures I'd accumulated over the past four centuries.

I couldn't fail Kate again. I *would not* fail again. My breath grew heavy, and I struggled to focus on the road as I left the rolling hills behind and snaked through the lush green forest of the Northern California coast.

When I saw the abandoned schoolhouse in the distance ahead, I slowed the bike and pulled off the road. I jumped off and rolled it into the forest just enough to conceal it, and then took off on foot, full speed, into the green beyond the place where I hoped to find Kate . . . alone.

"Kate!" I yelled as I entered the small clearing. The moon illuminated the grove like a soft, welcoming lantern. "Kate, are you here?"

"Gio? Is that you?" She sat on the largest fallen tree overlooking the ocean.

Relief rushed through my body, lifting fear's oppressive coat from my shoulders as I saw her for the first time in what felt like eternity. The feeling, though, was fleeting as my eyes instinctively scanned the surrounding forest, waiting expectantly for Alessandro to appear.

"How did you know I'd be here?" She'd gotten up and was awkwardly making her way down the tree's massive trunk to where I was. Was she limping? I ran to her and within seconds had her in my arms.

"Kate," I whispered in her hair, over and over, my arms wrapped around her, unyielding in their hold. She fell into my embrace.

"I left him." She struggled to speak against my chest. "I left Alex."

My thoughts, lost in the smell of her hair, snapped back to reality at the mention of his name. I pulled back from her and held her by the shoulders. Unfathomable anger welled up inside me the moment I saw her face. She flinched as my hand barely touched her cheek; my fingers traced her lips where the blood caked.

"What did he do to you? I'll kill him." Tears of rage and sorrow stifled my words through my teeth.

"I'm fine, really." Her voice was tired, and she pulled away taking a tissue out from her pocket. She carefully began to dab at her lip. "It's nothing, just a few . . ."

"No, it's not nothing." I struggled to hide the wrath that would be Alessandro's destiny behind my eyes. "Does he know where you are? Did you tell him anything about this place?" Fury leaked from my voice.

I'd known what Alessandro was capable of; I knew he was truly evil. Hell, I'd fought him for over four hundred years. But every reminder of evil he left on Kate's face only reinforced with absolute certainty my determination that he would pay dearly . . . in a very slow and excruciatingly painful way.

"Of course not. This has always been a place where I could go when I wanted to be alone. Why? What's going on?"

"Kate, please," I said softly, trying to hide the tension in my voice, "this is very important. Is there any way Alex knows where you are? Think carefully."

She was thoughtful for a moment and then answered,

"Alex has never been here, and I've never mentioned it to him, to anyone, before you. I'm sure of it." Her voice got quiet. I continued to look at her and waited for her to continue. Her face, completely focused on mine, mesmerized me. I forced myself to concentrate harder on the imminent danger, but I knew I was fighting a losing battle. She sighed.

"Gio, before I met you I . . . I . . ." She looked toward the ocean as her voice trailed off.

A slight breeze picked up and blew through her hair, lifting the ends of it gently up in all directions. She took a deep breath, taking in the warmness of the wind. She turned back to me, her eyes locked to mine, her expression a fusion of my Katarina of long ago and my Kate of present day. Two individuals melded together by one soul. I couldn't speak.

She continued, "Listen. I don't expect anything from you. I don't expect anything to change between you and me. I didn't leave him because of anything you said or did." She brought her hand to my cheek. Her skin was soft as it caressed my face. "I left him because I had to. I left him because it was the only thing I could do.

"Before I met you, I thought I was living the perfect life. A handsome husband who loved me, a career, a nice home. What else was there? But it wasn't what it seemed, you know?"

I nodded, waiting intently for the moment I'd spent an eternity hoping for, my heart now racing for a thousand different reasons.

"You must think I'm absolutely mad, I know, but it was like I was living this life without actually *living* it. Then the dream started . . . and the feeling that something was just off. Then you showed up and it was like I'd known you before, or like you were a part of me or . . . or something . . ."—her voice was almost inaudible— "like I'd been waiting for you my whole life." She laughed gently as she leaned her head against my chest.

My hands traced her shoulders down her arms. "I don't think you're crazy. You know more than you give yourself credit for." I reached into my pocket and wrapped my hand around the small vial.

This was it. This was the moment. Four centuries of pain, four centuries of guilt, four centuries of emotion amplified to a level of raw intensity that cut and bled my awareness dry were all riding on this moment.

"Kate," I said, my voice trembling. I knew what I had to ask but had no idea of how to do it. All I could do was wing it. She pulled her face away from my chest and looked up at me.

"What is it?"

"Do you trust me?"

She was silent for a minute before answering. "I do. I know that must sound silly since we just met, but . . . Why?"

I took a deep breath and collected every ounce of courage I had. It was now or never. Of all the lifetimes I'd passed through, I'd never come as close to winning her back as I was right now. Time faded into nothingness. Everything I'd been fighting for was right here in front of me, and there was nothing to stop me. I took the vial out of my pocket and placed it in her hand.

She looked down and examined it. "What's this?"

"I know this doesn't make sense, and I know I'm asking more than I . . . I've earned with you, but I need you to trust me right now. More than you've ever trusted anyone before, and I know that it may be scary and strange and— I need you to trust in me and believe I'd never do anything to hurt you."

"I don't understand." She brought the vial to eye level for closer inspection, bewilderment in her eyes. The serum was silvery purple in the moonlight. I placed my hands around her waist and pulled her close.

"I need you to trust me. If what you just said about me,

about what you feel for me is true, I need you trust me and drink it."

Kate was silent as her eyes fluttered from me to the vial and then back to me again. I died a thousand times as the seconds passed. All would be lost to me forever if she didn't drink from the bottle.

The stillness of the moment dragged on before she finally spoke the three words I'd been longing to hear.

"I trust you," she whispered removing the small cork.

I watched as she put the tiny bottle to her lips and let the purplish liquid drain from the container. When she swallowed the last drop, she dropped the small vial and stumbled back, her eyes wide, scared. I stepped toward her and wrapped my arms around her pulling her close. Her breath was fast, and she was trembling against me.

"It's okay. It's okay."

She leaned forward as she looked up at me and our faces were closer than I could resist. My hands flew to her face and pulled her lips to mine. She met my kiss with equal urgency as the passion inside me rose. My lips carefully traced every inch of her mouth, memorizing the shape of her lips as they went.

"My love," I said, no longer able to remain silent. "Please come back to me."

Four centuries of wanting, four centuries of need, four centuries of lost love came flooding back in a wave of desire so strong I knew not of anything but the softness of her body as I pulled her closer still.

Her body folded into mine, pressing against me as my muscles tensed with anticipation. My tongue licked against the inside edge of her lips. They willingly parted, opening her mouth for more exploration, though I didn't get far as she stopped my tongue with hers. It slid exquisitely into my mouth, brushing up against the edge of my teeth and into the depths beyond.

Her hands ran down my back and around my torso, caressing every bit of my body with their touch. I grew hard as she ran her hands up my chest, tracing every muscle with her fingers, and up to my jawline where she held my face fast as she continued to devour me with intense and desperate kisses.

I had to have her. I laid her down on the forest floor and hovered over her on all fours. The energy between us crackled. I pulled my mouth from hers and began working at her neck and chest, unbuttoning her shirt as I went. Her breasts were soft under her loose blouse, she arched her back until they filled my hands, and for a moment, I hesitated.

I'd wanted her for so long. Could I continue? My entire being craved her touch. Still, every minute without her, every instance I'd failed her, every memory of the pain I'd caused came rushing back and overwhelmed me with unfathomable sorrow. She sensed the change in me.

"What's wrong?" she asked through heaving breathes.

How could I explain? Where would I begin? I was falling into memories, losing myself to the past. Her voice brought me back into the present.

"Gio, it's okay. I want this more than anything I've ever wanted before."

She pulled me down to her and held my face inches from hers.

"I know it sounds insane, but I've been waiting for this moment my entire life." Her voice was barely a whisper. "It's like I've been living my life, thinking it was the right way, never knowing there was something bigger calling to me, bringing you to me. But now I know. I hear it. We're meant to be together—if only for this night. I've been waiting for you. Does that make sense?"

Emotion swelled up through my body and poured out my soul as I whispered, "More than you know."

My words were breathless. Any sorrow, any fear, any

doubt I'd had was erased and forgotten. My lips found hers again, this time with an urgency that turned into necessity. She caught her breath as she brought her hands to the front of my pants and began to loosen my belt.

My hands ran the smoothness of her legs, pulling her skirt up as they went. A small sound escaped her lips that sent me into a frenzy. She tugged at my pants with urgency as my hands finally found their way to the center of her legs.

She was hot and moist. My fingers slipped between her barely entering her molten core. She arched her back again in an attempt to deepen my touch, but I pulled my hand back. Not yet. I needed more. My mouth moved down the centerline of her body, my tongue leaving a wet line behind.

When my mouth reached her center, my lips found the upper points of her thighs and kissed them repeatedly. She hitched her hips and groaned in anticipation.

"Please, Gio . . ."

The sound of my name sparked my passion. I had to taste her. My mouth covered her center tightly and began sucking her long and hard. I flicked my tongue back and forth, her taste spilling into me, filling my mouth with its sweet pleasure.

She released a moan, her voice building upon itself, growing louder and louder, until I couldn't wait any longer. I had to be in her, to feel her around me. She was mine.

I pulled my mouth away and pushed my pants past my hips. I was rock hard. She spread herself open for me and I plunged into her depths in one smooth stroke. So deep. She threw her head back and pushed her body up to mine and I sunk further inside her. My mind went blank.

I couldn't breath. I couldn't speak. Nothing. I could only be with her in that moment, loving her with the entirety of my existence, in and out and in and out, praying with all my soul she felt what I felt. The connecting of two lost souls into one.

She wrapped her legs around my waist and tilted her hips,

opening herself up completely. My movements became wild, instinctual. We rose steadily together, building and building, our bodies pressing against each other, closer and closer, until neither of us could hold on any longer.

"Gio, I'm gonna come," she softly moaned.

And I was lost. We exploded into the other, our souls melting into one solid mass, thrusting and throbbing and pulsing. I cried out, tears spilling from my eyes with intense emotion, while her scream echoed against the canopy of trees.

Motionless in the silence, utterly spent, the heat of passion faded and gave way to a quiet peace as we lay there together, neither of us wanting to move.

When I could no longer avoid the inevitable, I slid out of her and lay half on her, half next to her. She wrapped her arms around my chest and clung tight preventing me from pulling further away. It was time. I knew what I had to do.

"Kate?" My voice trembled.

"Yes?" she said as she wrapped her leg around my leg; her head nestled against my shoulder.

This was it. The moment I'd been waiting for. Centuries upon centuries had passed and never had I gotten this far. I raised my head to look at her.

"Kate, will you look at me?"

A giggle escaped her as she pushed back from my chest. She brushed the hair out of her eyes and for the first time in lifetimes, the eyes of my lost love met mine once more.

Time froze. Everything both existed and ceased to exist as the pulse of magick built up around our bodies. It pressed down upon us and locked us together in a trance. The universe swirled, the cosmos shifted, aligning for us, and us alone.

A wind picked up and grew strong as it blew around our half naked bodies. I held out my hand and she grasped it firmly. The energy shot through from her body to mine like a bolt of lightning and then, in the same instance, everything went still.

We lay there together in silence and mortal life returned to my body once more. It was alive and active as it started in the core of my being and shot out like starbursts. My mouth became dry as emotion overwhelmed me. After four hundred years, I was alive.

Finally.

I took a deep breath, the cool coastal air filling my lungs, and examined Kate's face. Goddess above, my first real mortal breath in over four centuries, and all I could think about was how she took it away with her beauty.

A familiar smile spread across her face.

"My love . . . you found me." Tears began to fill her eyes.

"I never stopped looking for you. I would've looked for you forever. You were always my life, even before I'd known you existed." I could barely gasp the words. "I'm sorry it took so long."

"But you're here now."

"And I plan on staying for the rest of my mortal existence."

"Until death do us part."

"Forever."

We embraced and our lips found each other's once more. For the first time in over four hundred years, I was finally home.

I was home and I was alive. I'd found peace at last. It filled me slowly, warming my body as it traveled from my heart to my extremities. I couldn't believe it. Was this actually happening? It didn't seem real.

I brought my hands to her cheeks and stared into the eyes of the woman I'd spend, as a truly living man, the rest of my days with. Mesmerized by the moment, I let myself bask in the love I knew would be mine forever.

It was beautiful and compelling and lasted approximately

thirty more seconds before Kate suddenly pulled back, her eyes wide with terror.

"Gio! Look out!" Her voice was brimming with alarm.

And it was just as she had warned me all those years and years ago in that forest just outside of Rome before the word life became a four-letter insult. Before I knew anything of love or what living really meant. If I'd remembered her words before I became overcome by the glow of loving her once more, I might've been more careful. I might not have let my guard down and, perhaps, I would've been better able to prepare for my defense. Because before I knew what was happening, it was all over.

Nineteen

KATE

I saw him emerge from behind the trees before there was any sound, anger fueled by jealousy driving his soul. The horrific memories of my past lives flooded my consciousness the moment I saw him. He'd never been one to give up so easily, and as he'd proved many times over, he would've rather seen me dead than in the arms of another man.

I screamed Gio's name in warning, but it was too late. The sword blade had been run straight through his body, the tip poking out of his torso and wounding my left breast.

I looked up at Gio, his eyes wide with shock and watering as he struggled to speak. I lay there half beneath him, horror filling my soul. Everything was in slow motion. There was no sound. Alessandro towered above us, his nostrils flared as Gio's blood hit the ground.

I rolled to the side and pushed myself up to my feet to prepare for the attack I knew was imminent. My aggressor looked at me, venom spilling from his soul. Time sped up.

"No!" I screamed at him, my eyes, for the first time in centuries, recognizing him for who he really was.

Alessandro stared back at me through black and red eyes, and for an instant he faltered as he saw the true me, not the Kate he'd altered, staring back at him. As surprised as he must've been, he quickly recovered from the initial alarm and let the pure hatred return to his eyes.

"Now, is that any way to greet your husband, my love?" Venom dripped from the words like molasses, turning them sour.

My mind couldn't keep up with the images of the past nine years as they flashed through the part of me that lived as his wife.

My stomach heaved as everything I'd known to be true was revealed as false. Alessandro intuitively assessed my response. He drew his blade from Gio's body, leaving a wet, black trail along the moonlit forest floor.

"It doesn't have to be this way," he said, his voice suddenly calm. "Come with me now and we could be together still. Think back. We were happy together, once."

There was a sincerity in his tone, as if he truly believed I'd go with him. As if I could forget everything he'd ever done to me. As if I just didn't witness him kill the man I loved, right in front of me.

"Katie, come with me," he pleaded as he placed the blade on the ground and reached out with his hand. "No one knows we're here. We can forget all this mess and continue this life as if none of this had ever happened."

I stood frozen as I assessed the depth of his insanity. Continue life? As if nothing had happened? He was truly mad.

The words were out of my mouth before I had a chance to think of a more strategic plan.

"Get the hell away from me, Alessandro, you fucking murderer!"

Any chance I had of escaping his wrath vanished with the

conclusion of those words as rage instantly pulsed through his body.

"Tramp!" he screamed. "Lying bitch! I guess it doesn't matter how many lifetimes you get! Once a whore, always a whore!"

His voice was sour as he spit the words at me. He bent down and picked up his blade again.

"You're insane." My voice flirted with hysteria as terror crept up on me, illuminating the gravity of the situation.

There was no way I could win this fight if it came to blows. He easily sensed my fear, and despite his ire, this seemed to please him. He laughed menacingly as he stalked me, a predator cornering his prey.

"Do you think it matters what you think of me?" His voice was icy and calm. "That time has long past. I find pleasure in your suffering now. That's after I've had my fun with you, of course." A smile spread across his face.

"You're sick," I shot back, anger rising from deep within.

"Perhaps," he agreed as he advanced with care. I took a step back from him. "However, anything that I am today, I have you to credit, my love. After all, you are the one who started all this so long ago. You ripped my heart from my chest and danced on it with your lover."

"You knew I never loved you. It was never meant to be, you and I, don't you see?" I had to buy some time. I had to think. I'd never be able to fight him off physically. I had to stall.

"See what? Your betrayal?"

"After all this time, don't you see we were never meant to travel this path? The Goddess herself gave me a—"

"Hah! What do you know about us? We were to be married! We were to be together! Did that not mean anything to you? Did not the old Gods—" His voice cut off and he shook his head. "We were meant to be. *It* was foretold. And then, one day, *he* came along, and everything I had, *everything*, was gone! We could have had everything!"

I shook my head. "No, no. It wasn't supposed to happen."

He ignored me. "You can't imagine how I suffered when I realized you were leaving. Then to find you running into the arms of another man! An outsider! A human. The pain of having your life taken from you. I was devastated. How could you do that to me? How could you defy what was destined?" His tone turned flat as he continued, delving back to the night when I'd first tried to escape.

"I felt nothing but pain, agony. Betrayal of the worst kind. You, my love, should know about that. So that is exactly what I decided I'd give back to you. Consider it my special gift."

"Give back to me? How could you?" My voice cracked.

"How could I what? Kill you? Oh, my love, it was quite easy. Or easier, I suppose would be more accurate, the more I had to do it. The first time was a bit rough, you know, but I pulled through. You *were* coming back, after all. And then, things got quite enjoyable. Almost fun. I mean, as annoying as the Onesta were, they were quite clever with the whole reincarnation bit. And the look on his pathetic face each time I killed you—quite priceless, really." His voice sounded amused as he spoke to me.

"What've you become?" Fear had a strong hold as I fought to maintain control of myself.

"I've become what you've turned me into."

"No," I said, "you've become what you've chosen. You live now as you lived then, with a darkness lining your heart."

"How would you know what my heart is lined with?" he spewed. "You never took the time to truly know me—to love me the way I loved you."

"You loved me like a possession! Something to own! Something to control! Well, let me enlighten you, *my husband*"— the anger within me built— "one does not control his own fate. I was meant to love another. And no matter what you do to me, I will *never* love you, no matter if I live one lifetime or a thousand!" My heart ached as I glanced at Gio, just feet from where I stood, lying motionless on the forest floor.

Was he still alive? Was he dead? I forced myself to keep my eyes on Alessandro, watching his progress toward me, waiting for the moment in which I would have to defend myself to the death. He took another step in my direction, pushing me closer to the edge of the cliff.

"Now that, Katie dear, is where you're wrong. You see, I'm evidence that everyone controls their own fate. And mine was to love you." He spoke more calmly now. "After I slit your throat in front of your lover the first time, I was overrun with grief. I didn't understand why I mourned for you, as you had betrayed me."

He nodded to the shapeless mound on the ground. "He, of course, fell to your side, blubbering and begging for me to kill him as well." He laughed menacingly, his eyes rolling to the back of his head.

"Little did he know I'd other plans for him, an ingenious spell of my own creation—that he was to live forever, never aging, never able to die. I *gladly* cursed him, and then I left him crying over your lifeless body. Since being with you was what he wanted so much, I decided to give him life. Without you, of course.

"I have to admit that was my only mistake, leaving your body there with him. I should've known better."

"Known better about what?" I egged him on, though I was only half listening. I needed more time.

"I should've known those meddling Onesta would find some way to unite the two of you. Damn witches. Although now I'm glad they did. I've had a marvelous four hundred years."

A smile twisted across his face.

I listened to him as he explained how our existences had been morbidly intertwined throughout time. I shuddered as I realized this time Alessandro had gotten close to winning . . . too close. I'd never let him win. It would either be him or me. There was no way he'd let me live now, and I'd be *damned* if I was going down without a fight. Although I'd already been damned, having to live so many lives with him.

"There would've been others. You could've had love if you'd just let me go." I anxiously looked at him, my breathing heavy.

"I had love! And you took it from me! You deserve everything you've gotten."

"You'll suffer for what you've done. Such an unnatural imbalance will not go unpunished."

"By who? Your precious love?" Amusement tugged at his eyes as he looked Gio's lifeless body. "Or no, wait, maybe you? You think you can end this right now? Look at yourself. You don't have the power. Not anymore. Helpless, pathetic— you've never been any challenge for me. If I had to give my soul up a thousand times over, I wouldn't hesitate in the least to do it all over again."

"And what've you given up your soul for? For pain? For suffering? You truly are the bastard I've always known you were. No, you're worse. You're a *monster*."

His jaw got tight as he heard the finality of my assessment of him.

"You never knew me. Perhaps, if you had, you wouldn't have betrayed me."

Everything was coming to a head as Alessandro lifted his sword and pointed it toward me.

"This time, though, I think I'll take my time. I'll have my way with you, and then slowly bleed you over the body of your pathetic lover."

Alessandro lunged at me leaving me nowhere to run. I had no time to move. He threw his sword down near my feet as he grabbed my shoulders and threw me down roughly to the ground.

My punches might as well have been nonexistent. He easily deflected them with one hand as he straddled me and loosened his belt with the other.

I screamed, knowing no one would hear me, out of pure rage over what was about to happen. Tears streamed down my face as I struggled to control myself—I would not give him the satisfaction of my pain, but I couldn't let him take me without a fight.

"Don't cry, my love," he said as he brought his face close to mine, his tongue licking the salty tracks from my cheek. "There was a time when you used to like this. Very much so, if I remember correctly." A sickening smile spread across his face as I gagged on his words both physically and emotionally.

He'd gotten his pants undone and was pushing them down with his free hand. The hand that had been deflecting my punches found my wrists and pinned them above my head. I screamed in desperation.

"No!"

He spread my legs apart with his own legs as he raised my skirt and was holding himself above me, taunting me.

"If you won't love me willingly, I'll make you love me whether you want to or not."

He held his position just a fraction more before he began to slowly move toward me until I felt him press against me, stopping just before he entered.

I frantically tried to find something for my mind to hold on to, something I could grip tightly that would take me away from what was about to happen.

Tears stained my cheeks as I closed my eyes. I thought about the first time I saw Gio in the marketplace in Rome. I thought about the hours we'd spent in the bookstore. I thought about his smile. How his hair curled around his ears. My mind focused on his eyes, his smell, the sound of his voice, how he ran his hand through his hair, and the boyish way he shrugged his shoulders when he didn't know what to say. I thought about his laughter, his innocence, his honesty, his unwavering love . . .

"Alessandro, stop! Don't even think about doing it." I opened my eyes at the sound of the familiar voice.

Willem stood at the edge of the clearing, holding a gun aimed at Alessandro's head. Claire was a foot behind him, partially hidden by the trees. Alessandro froze above me. I could tell by his breathing that he was seething mad.

"Get up. Slowly." Willem's voice was steady.

Alessandro slowly pushed himself from me, his pants around his knees. His expression was a rancid mix of revenge, hate, and raw rage. I watched him carefully as he stood to face Willem.

"You really know how to kill the mood, witch," he said pulling up his pants.

"Kate," Willem called from his position, "are you okay?"

"Yes," I answered. Wanting to put as much space between Alessandro and myself as possible, I stood too quickly, and the blood rushed to my head. I lost my footing and staggered a few steps. I fell on my knees in front of him.

Alessandro, ready for the slightest opening to his advantage, abruptly knelt behind me and grabbed the sword from its resting place on the forest floor. He pulled the back of my hair and lifted me up, raising the sword to my neck.

"Take one step closer and I'll slit her throat right here," Alessandro yelled, using me as a human shield.

"Don't do this," Willem said. "Let her go. This has gone on far too long. It's over."

"Put the gun down." He gripped my hair tighter, stretching my neck.

"No." Willem was steady.

Alex pushed the tip of the sword to my neck till blood began to drip down from the wound. I gasped.

"You will do as I say or your friend here will suffer more than you can imagine." His voice revealed he meant every word he said. "Now, put the gun down and back off."

"Don't do it, Willem. Shoot him!" I was able to yell through my terror.

"Shut up!" Alessandro yelled. He pushed his sword deeper into my neck, creating a gash in its side. I brought my hands to my throat and felt the hot blood seeping out of my body. I started to feel lightheaded, and I knew if I pushed him further, my time was limited.

Willem, sensing the desperation of the situation, put his hands in the air. "Okay, okay. Slow down. Look, I'm throwing the gun." Willem threw the gun over Alessandro's head and over the cliff beyond.

Alessandro laughed as the gun fell into the ocean below. "You fool. Did you think I'd actually *not* kill her?" His eyes were glowing as he appraised the situation that had quickly turned to his favor.

"I'll admit this lifetime has been the best one yet. I'll look fondly back at it after she's dead, not knowing if I'll ever have another like it, but that's a risk I'm willing to take."

He pushed me down to my knees and pulled my head all the way back. I knelt there, helpless, thinking about what my life had been. Knowing that Gio was dead was both my worst fear and my only consolation. I'd be with him soon. I could withstand the pain and fear knowing I'd soon be with my love. The world became quiet, calm, as I welcomed my approaching death.

Alessandro brought the blade lengthwise against my neck

to make it easier to pull it through the soft part of my throat. It was cold against my skin. I waited for him to finish what he so desperately wanted when gunshots shattered the silence. The blade that'd been held against my neck just seconds before fell to the ground in front of me. I felt Alessandro's hold slacken and then let go.

I fell forward, my hands in front of me, coughing and sputtering blood. I looked up in confusion to where the shots had come from.

Claire was standing at the edge of the clearing, still partially hidden in the trees, a gun grasped firmly in her hands.

I heard staggering behind me in the soft forest brush. I looked behind to see Alessandro struggle on his feet, holding his upper chest, blood seeping through his fingers.

He looked at me, hate seething from his being. He took two more steps backward as he tried to regain his balance.

"All I ever wanted was for you to love me," he spat.

I looked at him in silence from where I knelt and watched as he neared the cliff. I didn't yell out to him, I didn't warn him, as he got closer and closer to its edge. I simply watched in hopeful silence as he neared, and then, in a flash, fell off the edge, down to the ocean below and vanished as though he'd never existed. A perforated silence ensued, before complete and total chaos snapped me back to reality. *Gio!*

Within seconds Willem was at my side. "Are you okay?"

"I . . . I think so." My hands flew to my neck. The blood had slowed and had begun to clot around the opening. It felt sticky against my fingers.

"Don't move, let me see your neck."

I pushed away from him with all the strength I had left.

"No, Willem. Gio!" I began to crawl in the direction of where his body still lay on the ground.

Claire was already kneeling next to him, her hands tugging at his shirt. I tried to stand, but my knees buckled. Willem caught me before I hit the ground. He picked me up in his arms and carried me effortlessly to Gio's side.

"Gio! Gio!" I reached for him as the burning pain in my neck disappeared to create space for a new kind of pain.

His skin was clammy and gray. I held his face gently in my hands while tears flowed from my eyes. I kissed his eyelids over and over. He couldn't be dead. He *couldn't*.

"Claire, how is he?" I could hear Willem's voice over my sobs.

"He's still alive, barely. He's so weak. He's lost a lot of blood." Claire got his shirt off and began assessing his wound.

I looked up at her and waited. She looked at me and then at Willem.

"What is it?" I demanded. "Tell me!"

"It's bad. Real bad. I . . . I don't know if I can heal him." Her voice was solemn.

Willem dropped his head, and said, "You have to try."

I held his head in my hands and began talking to him. "Don't leave me. Please, don't leave me. If you can hear me, just hang on. You can make it through this. Please, Gio, fight . . ." My voice broke off, I was unable to continue.

My eyes widened in astonishment as Claire placed her hands on the blade wound and called to her magick. A white glow emanated from her palms. The light spread from her palms to Gio's chest. The white light licked at the wound, and then entered at the opening.

Gio's skin began to glow from the inside out. Claire pushed her magick forward. It entered Gio's body and filled him up. He continued to lay there motionless, seemingly unchanged.

After a while, the white light began making its way out of the wound's opening and back into Claire's hands. When the last bit of light had left his body, Claire sat there unmoving, sweat dripping from her body.

"I've done all I can," she said, hanging her head in disappointment. Her chest heaved. "I just don't know if it's enough. We have to get him to a hospital."

I sat there frozen, shock now setting in due to both the loss of blood from my neck and the realization that Gio might be lost to me. How could this have happened? How was it I was given the most precious gift I could ever receive, only to have it torn from me in the same moment?

"Kate! Snap out of it. You have to focus." Claire's hands were on my shoulders her eyes intently searching mine.

I nodded my head. It was all I could do. If there was still a chance that Gio would survive, I'd do everything I could to make sure it happened.

"Willem, we have to get him to the car. Quick, you grab his upper body. I'll grab his legs. Kate, can you make it to the road by yourself?" Claire's voice was steady as she directed both Willem and I.

"Yes, I'll make it," I whispered, knowing there was no alternative if Gio were to survive. Of *course* I'd make it. I'd run a thousand miles barefoot over glass right now, if I thought it'd bring him back to me.

Claire and Willem carefully lifted Gio and navigated out of the clearing toward the road.

Willem's silver car was parked diagonally, half entering the forest, half on the road. I raced ahead and opened the back door.

I watched as they placed Gio into the car. Claire climbed in first, carefully positioning Gio's legs over hers. Willem slowly followed, bringing Gio's limp torso to rest across the back seat of his car.

"Kate, sit with him while I drive." Willem said.

I climbed into the backseat and struggled to hold Gio's body close to mine. His face was still gray and clammy, as if the magick had made no difference to his injuries. I began to stroke his face, my eyes memorizing each contour as my fingertips catalogued how he felt. My love, my life. Why? Why?

It's a funny feeling knowing your life is ending, holding it in your arms and feeling it slip away second by second. Try as I might, I knew I wouldn't be able to hold on to him, he'd inevitably leave me. There was just no other explanation for how he looked at that moment.

As Willem drove, the forest blur turned to rolling hills, and then into buildings as we hit the city limits of Freestone. I forced myself to look up from Gio's face as the car jolted to a stop.

The hospital.

Willem jumped out of the car and flagged down two paramedics who were walking out of the building. They came running as Claire opened her side of the car and got out, directing them to Gio.

I sat there amid the chaos of yelling and clanging and beeping, as the world seemed to continue around me. My heart still felt the connection to him, but it was weak. He was barely there. I sat there holding his head in my hands, in the horrid eye of this terrible storm committing to memory every last crease, every last eyelash, every last curve of his lips until suddenly, without warning, he was whisked from my touch and taken away into a world of artificial light and tools and tubes. Whisked into the emergency room and far away from me.

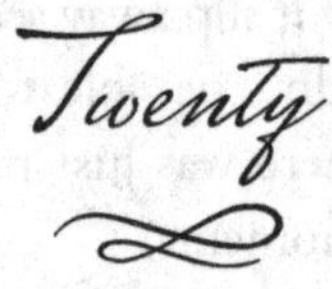

Twenty

GIO

I could feel the stiff coldness of the sword as it entered my body, and then again as he pulled it out.

I could hear her screams. *Kate! I hear you! Fight! Fight! Don't give up!*

I could smell the metallic aroma of blood as it mixed with the earthy scent of the ground below me.

I could taste the saltiness of her tears as they touched my lips; angel kisses upon my soul.

I'd almost forgotten the feeling of mortality. It was so natural, so real. Everything around me seemed to ignite all my senses. All my senses, that is, except for one.

I could see nothing. Oh Goddess, I could see nothing.

Then, without the slightest warning whatsoever, everything was simply gone.

Twenty-One

KATE

Kate

Thinking back on my life, well, my current life, it's impossible for me to overlook the fact I'd missed several early warning signs that should've told me Alessandro, my husband, was a dangerous individual.

I will always feel guilty. Gio, once so vibrant, so strong, now lay unconscious in the intensive care unit for Goddess knows how long. Will you ever forgive me?

It didn't take long for Willem and Claire to fill me in on everything I'd missed. I did, after all, retain some of my magical abilities and was able to see, with a touch, all that'd happened.

The police were trickier, but as beat up as I was and with the testimony of two eyewitnesses, they told me it would be written up as self-defense. We'd told the police the gun was Alessandro's, that he'd brought it with him along with the sword. We lied. No charges would be filed against me.

Since the moment the doctors said it was okay for us to see him, I was glued to his side. Willem and Claire were with me most of the time. They brought me food. Though I wasn't hungry, I forced a few bites. They brought me water, though I wasn't thirsty enough for more than a few sips. I didn't sleep for more than an hour at a time.

"Kate, just rest for a moment. We promise we'll wake you if there's any change," Willem implored as I continued to sit there, hour after hour.

"No. What if he wakes for two seconds and I'm not here for him? What then? I cannot bear the thought of causing him more pain."

"Kate—"

"No. I'm not moving."

It was settled. A bed was brought in for me.

After two days, they threatened to turn the doctors loose on me.

"You can't go on like this. Please, eat something," Willem pleaded.

"Just have a few bites, okay? You need to stay strong. If not for yourself, then for Gio. He wouldn't want you to do this to yourself." I narrowed my eyes. Claire's words were too rehearsed, too calculated, but they hit a nerve.

Ouch. It was a cheap shot, but I had to give her credit. Claire was incisive when it came to getting her way. But hitting my heart with such a forceful blow? Well, that was just cruel. She clearly cared about me, but it was still harsh.

"Fine," I answered taking the bagel and small cup of water she held in her hand.

I took a bite of the bagel. It was dry and chewy. It tasted like nothing. I quickly washed it down with water. I sighed. It felt good as it traveled down my throat.

The water reached out to every part of my body, its coolness filling me. I became more relaxed. Strange that water would have this much effect on me, even if I had been slowly dehydrating myself over the past few days. And then, it struck me, out of the dark sky like a flash of lightning.

My instinct was correct. I shouldn't have been so affected by water. I looked at the cup's empty bottom. My muscles became heavier and heavier with each passing second.

I flashed an accusing glare at Claire and Willem.

"I'm so sorry. It was the only way. You left us no other choice." Willem's voice was sincere as he admitted their guilt in his apology.

"What did you give me?" I slurred, though not with much impact due to my increasingly heavy eyelids.

"Don't worry. It's just something to help you rest. Just for a while." Claire's voice was thick with treachery. Traitors!

My body was heavy. I could no longer hold my head up. I struggled to keep my focus, but my eyes blurred and try as I might, I couldn't keep them open.

Fucking witches.

My eyes closed, darkness surrounded me, but I was still slightly aware when Willem picked me up and took me to the convertible chair in the corner of the room.

"She'll never forgive me." It was Claire's solemn voice I heard close to my body as a blanket covered me and my chair was reclined and pushed next to Gio's bedside.

"She left us no choice. What were we supposed to do? Let her die while she waited for him to wake?" Willem was more confident of their choice to drug me.

I heard just one or two more exchanges, though I couldn't fully comprehend their meaning as they faded further and further into the background far away from where I was going.

I slept. Goddess knows how long.

I awoke to the murmuring of voices close by. I slowly rolled my head to the side as my body came out of its stupor. The voices grew silent as I began to stir.

"Kate," a soft voice said, "how are you feeling?"

My eyes fluttered open at the touch of a hand on my arm. It took a moment to regain my composure. I glanced around the room. My eyes froze on the still figure in the bed; the oxygen tubes awkwardly crossed under his nose like a plastic snake and around his ears, flattening his perfect curls. It didn't take long to remember where I was and what had happened.

"Don't touch me!" I hissed as I recoiled from Willem's hand.

"Kate, please—"

"How could you?" My gazed moved between the two of them.

"You left us no choice. If he lives, you have to be alive when he wakes." This time it was Claire who answered. "Besides, there's been no change in his condition."

My heart stung at the implications of her words. No change. He was still unconscious. He was still . . . I pushed those feelings aside as I tapped back into the anger toward my so-called friends.

"What if he *had* woken up? What then? Did you think of that? Or let me guess, you probably had a potion for that too?" The poison fumed from my tongue, rising in curly tails of rancid smoke.

"But he didn't," Willem said.

"He could have," I shot back.

"But. He. Didn't." He said these words with a finality that made me think there was more to Gio's condition than I understood.

"But . . . but . . . how could . . ." My voice trailed off as I searched to find the right words to describe my feelings, but I had no more fight left in me as sorrow and pain flooded my heart.

"Kate," Willem said softly acknowledging he knew there would be no more discord between us, "Claire and I are both truly sorry for doing what we did. Please understand, we did it because we swore to Gio that if anything should happen to him, we'd take care of you. If he'd awakened, we would've brought you around immediately."

Sobs choked out through my throat. I let them come. What was Willem saying? Take care of me if Gio could not? Had Gio anticipated he wouldn't be able to join me in this life? Did he make it a part of his plans to leave me? Was there no hope?

I swooned, dizzy with fear and worry as Willem continued. Claire rushed to my side and wrapped her arms around me. Magick emanated from her body, soothing me.

"Please listen." Willem's voice was cautious, like he knew he had to choose his next words wisely. As if he sensed that if one word was mistaken, said in the wrong way, I might very well crumble to pieces.

"Gio is alive, but he's not conscious and we don't know why. The doctors are puzzled by it. His brain activity seems to be alert, but there is minimal evidence he can hear us when we speak. There is no way of telling if . . ." he trailed off and then paused.

I stared into his eyes. What was he not telling me?

"What? What were you going to say?"

Willem looked back at me, tears glistening in his eyes, unable to speak. Those tears meant more than tears of friendship, tears of brotherhood. They told me the extreme gravity of the situation. Of course. How could I have missed it?

I let Willem off the hook, as I whispered what he couldn't say, "*If* he ever wakes."

Willem fell to his knees, his head bent down in my lap as he succumbed to his intense grief. Claire moved to his side, holding as much of his massive frame as she could.

I looked at the man crying in my lap. I looked at my

beautiful angel asleep in the bed, just feet from where I sat. How did we get here? I couldn't think about it for too long. If I did, I knew I would curl up into a ball and wither from the inside out. I had to find something else to hold on to, something to grasp that would help me continue forward.

It didn't take long to find what I was looking for. A deep burning from the blackest part of my hate slowly began to rise. It filled my limbs with a fire that would make all seven levels of hell look like a half-empty book of matches.

I could barely control my rage.

"Alessandro."

This word grabbed both Willem and Claire's attention by the throat and forced them to look at me.

"Where is Alessandro?" I could still barely speak as the words slowly materialized on my tongue.

Willem took advantage of the distraction. His eyes flared. Claire's skin appeared to glow white hot underneath her loose cotton shirt.

"The police didn't find a body. They searched up and down the rocks the next morning after we brought Gio to the hospital, but they were unable to find anything. No body. No blood. No gun. No sword. Nothing. They concluded the body must've been washed out to the ocean and called the case closed." The irritation in Willem's voice made it obvious he didn't believe Alessandro was dead.

I called him on it. "And you believe different." It was a recognition of his thoughts, not a question.

Claire, silent up to this point, said, "I went down to the beach after the police searched the area. It was covered with some real bad magick. I felt its thorny vines scratch at my limbs as I walked to the spot where Alessandro had to have fallen. It was so strong, so powerful. At first, I couldn't breathe, it was suffocating me."

Willem wrapped his arm around Claire's waist. She placed her hand over his to comfort him as she continued.

"Then I felt the pulse. The pulse of evil, fresh from its core, and I knew he hadn't died. I don't know how, but somehow Alessandro survived, and his survival was one hundred percent dependent upon this unleashed evil."

"I've lived a long time," Willem interjected, "and I've seen many things in my existence. What Claire's explaining is something I haven't seen, haven't felt, in a very, very long time. It's something of the oldest magick."

"And what? Now it's helping Alessandro?" I said without emotion.

Claire and Willem looked at each other for a moment. It was Willem who answered my question.

"We're not sure what it means, but we both know Alessandro is alive. And, while he's still alive, you're in grave danger. You both are." His eyes flicked to where Gio's motionless body lay undisturbed. The high-pitched beeping of the heart monitor was steady in the background. Its sterile resonance was both reassuring and unnerving as it informed me Gio was still alive, but nowhere near the kind of alive I yearned for him to be.

I closed my eyes and forced myself to shove the feelings I couldn't face into the back of my brain. Right now, I had more pressing issues to attend to.

"Well, what's the plan?" My voice was resolute. And though my words were intended as a question, they sounded more like a demand. I was already nearly one hundred percent certain both Willem and Claire had already decided upon what needed to be done, and they'd just been waiting for me to ask.

The looks on their faces told me my assumption had been correct. I waited for one of them to speak.

Claire gave Willem a pointed look. He shook his head.

"The *plan* is for you to stay safe." His voice was unwavering, like he was telling a child she couldn't stay up late on a school night.

"No way, Willem. You can't push me out on this."

"Kate, I promised. I gave my word."

"I don't care. I *will not rest* until I see Alessandro *dealt with*."

"No."

I looked frantically at Claire, my anger rising rapidly. Was she in on this too? I had to hear it from her.

"Claire?"

As soon as Claire's gaze met mine, I knew she was my ally. Willem didn't miss our silent exchange. She opened her mouth to speak.

"No, Claire," Willem interjected, "we've talked about this."

"I think I'd like Claire to speak for herself." I interrupted Willem, sure she was on my side. I looked at Claire and nodded my head in encouragement.

"I'm sorry, Willem, but I can't go along with this." Her voice was soft but clear.

"Claire—" he began.

Claire held up her hand. "I understand the importance of Kate's safety. As a Watcher, I don't take it lightly." She paused. "But please also try to understand I cannot agree to keep her out of what is rightly hers. She deserves her revenge."

"No. Think of Gio. What would he want?"

"I *am* thinking of Gio. I cannot go five minutes without thinking of him—how I failed him! How he could be here *right now* had I gotten us there quicker. I think of him continuously, what I promised him and I . . . I . . . no, I won't keep Kate from what is hers." She struggled with her words.

My heart felt her guilt. This time it was my turn to interject.

"Claire, this is not your fault. Because of you, I'm alive. Because of you, I can sit here right now and say that without you, I would have nothing."

I held out my hand and she took it in hers. It was warm and soft. I wrapped my fingers around hers and let whatever feelings of gratitude I had flow freely between our touch.

"Thank you." The moment drifted into comfortable length.

Undeterred by the moment, Willem said, "Claire, you can't let guilt rule your decisions. We've discussed this. It's decided."

"No. I'm sorry, but things change. People change. And though I recognize we must do everything in our power to protect Kate, we cannot stop her from fulfilling her destiny."

"I cannot allow it." He shook his head.

"You don't *have* to allow it. I make my own decisions here." I looked at him. His face was pale and drawn. He looked tired and defeated.

For an instant, I felt the depth of his predicament. How difficult must it be to simultaneously want to keep a promise and wish to break it.

"Even if it goes against what Gio would die for?" He could barely get the last part out.

As the words hit the air, the seriousness of their meaning echoed through my soul and my body stiffened with shock. Claire was undeterred, though I could sense she felt the impact of Willem's words just as sure as I had.

"Yes, even if it goes against his wishes." She stood her ground.

"But why? I don't understand." There was desperation in his voice and I knew he knew he was fighting a battle he couldn't keep up with much longer.

Claire turned to give him her complete attention. "Willem, I remember how he looked as we drove him to the hospital. He didn't even look like the same man. He was . . . gone. For an instant, I thought *What if it was Willem?* And my world, my life"—she shook her head— "it was more than I could bear." She placed her hands on his cheeks, cradling his face.

"I can let Kate fight because if it were you, I would not *rest* until I had my revenge. It would eat me alive until I was bitter and empty—a vacant soul trapped in a shell of a body. And most importantly, I couldn't go on living, knowing I hadn't done everything in my power to avenge your death. Whether I wanted to or not, I don't believe I could go on."

"Even if I didn't want it?"

"*Especially* if you didn't want it." She brought her face close to his and barely whispered into his ear. "Don't you see? Without you, I'd have nothing to lose, nothing more to live for. There'd simply be nothing."

Willem's eyes closed as tears trickled down his cheeks. Then, in a moment of pure emotion, he pulled Claire toward him, their lips crushing together.

"I love you," he said, never pulling his lips all the way from hers.

As their kiss rose, I noticed a change in the room. A thick, mist-like fog rose from the four corners of the floor and began creeping up to the ceiling.

"Claire . . . Willem . . ." I glanced nervously around the room as the mysterious white fog appeared to collect on the ceiling just above where the two were still kissing, oblivious to their surroundings like they were under some spell.

"Claire. Willem."

I sat next to where Gio lay and threw my body over his as the two held each other closer and continued to unleash their passion completely unaware of what was happening.

I didn't know what to do as the fog began to swirl above Willem's head. It paused briefly before splitting in two. Out of the mist came a blinding, white light that shattered the prisms of human vision and pierced the space between Claire and Willem.

I sat motionless. One thing I was certain of; I wouldn't run. I wouldn't leave Gio or Willem or Claire. If this were how we died, well, I'd die with them. This time I'd die with the people I loved. I held Gio tight and waited for something to happen.

The light shot directly into Willem's body and glowed from within. His skin grew brighter and brighter until I thought he'd burst into flames. Then, slowly, quietly, just as the fog had entered the room, the light began to dim until it'd completely disappeared leaving Willem and Claire as they were, in each other's arms, and kissing.

Silence.

"Willem? Claire?" My voice was hesitant. I wasn't entirely sure if I'd imagined what had just happened.

Claire pulled away first and looked at me; a blush rose to her cheeks in a hot flurry. "I'm sorry." She was still flustered from Willem's touch.

"Did either of you see that?"

"See what?" Willem asked, confused.

I stopped to think of how I could explain what I'd just saw without sounding insane.

I didn't have time to answer Willem's question. Claire brought her hand up to Willem's head and appeared to touch the space above it, her eyes wide with disbelief.

"Willem," she whispered, "do you feel it?"

"What is it? What do you see?"

Claire looked at him with excitement in her eyes. "It's your aura. Your soul. You've been given your soul back! You're mortal again, can't you feel it?" Claire's voice rose.

"Can it be?" Willem's voice cracked, the words barely escaping his lips.

I drew in a shaky breath in disbelief. Willem had fulfilled his prophecy. He'd let love rule despite what his mind told him. He'd given into his emotion completely, and with that kiss, he and Claire excised the magick that had doomed him so many years ago. According to the Goddess he'd suffered long enough, he'd learned his lesson, paid his debt, and had been forgiven.

Understanding flooded across his face. His eyes grew wide as he looked from Claire to me and then back to Claire.

"I . . . I can't believe it," he said. "It's been so long since I was . . . living, I'd forgotten what it felt like, but I feel it now." He ran his hands through his hair. "I can feel it. So strong. Life running through me like an electric current, alive and strong."

Willem grabbed Claire around the waist and in one swift movement, picked her up and twirled her around. Her laugh was musical as they spun around together in a circle. I laid my head on Gio's chest and stroked his still hand. I watched them as a smile spread across my face.

I noticed how Willem held Claire in his arms, her body molded into his with ease. They were two souls melded into one beautiful energy, the past brought forth by the present, the future open before them.

I sighed lightly and realized I was happy for the first time since leaving the clearing. Let Willem and Claire enjoy their moment. Goddess knows they deserved it. I continued to rest my head on Gio's chest. My fingers played with his, though there was no response to my touch.

Did he feel my hands on his? Could he hear my voice when I spoke to him or feel my heart beating when I lay down next to him? Would I know the absolute and total completeness I'd felt just days before ever again?

I'd spent thirty years in this life. Thirty years of living, and I'd never actually lived until recently, when he'd found me.

But how was I to know? How was I to realize everything

I'd thought was true, everything that'd shaped my reality, was just a consequence for something that happened an eternity ago?

Still, I couldn't shake the feeling that I *should* have known better. I thought back through my personal history to all the times in which I should've been suspicious of Alessandro, times when I should've realized that somewhere, locked deep in my subconscious, I had all the answers all along. I just hadn't been listening.

Now, the people I loved the most were in grave danger. Because of me, the man I loved more than anything was lying motionless on a sterile bed, hooked up to too many machines that beeped, clicked, and stuttered.

I closed my eyes as a wave of pain rushed through my body and circled around my heart, leaving a heavy ache in its wake. I shuddered uncontrollably. This couldn't be happening, it just *couldn't*. Without Gio, nothing made sense anymore. Life didn't have purpose. He had to wake up. He just *had* to.

"Kate?" Claire's voice was tentative. Her hand interrupted my thoughts as she gently stroked my back.

I opened my eyes and looked up at her from where my head rested. I didn't have enough energy or willpower to pull it off Gio's chest.

"Hey," I answered half-heartedly.

"Are you all right?" Willem said from the other side of the bed.

"Yeah, I'm fine. I'm just . . . ."—I laughed nervously— "I don't know what I am."

"You're tired. You've been through a lot these past weeks and more than anyone should go through these past few days. You need to rest."

"What I *need*, Willem, is to find Alessandro." My voice was staunch, unyielding. I was surprised at the power it maintained, despite how very feeble I felt.

"I understand. Our first priority, however, is to keep Gio safe. At least until he's able to do so for himself," he answered. His tone was different, changed from what it had been before; it was now hopeful.

I sat up and narrowed my eyes at him, my brow furrowed. Did this mean he wasn't going to give me any more problems about going after Alessandro? When the magick released him from his curse, did he finally realize that without love, there's nothing?

He looked at Claire, and said, "How many Watchers would you say are here in town?"

Claire smiled as if instantly understanding his thoughts. "There are twelve others. Some new, some old, but all powerful . . . and available."

Willem nodded his head. "Do you think they'll help us?"

"I do, without a doubt."

"Then we'll go to them tonight. We'll ask them to protect Gio while he's here and then we'll leave. We'll find Alessandro and whatever evil he's employing and destroy them both."

Willem spoke this matter-of-factly, as if he could see the future himself.

I found it remarkable that he spoke with such confidence, since the only thing I felt confident about was that we were all going to end up dead.

But, then again, what did I know? I'd just recently woken up from a four-hundred-year nap, during which the man I loved suffered daily on my account, while the man I loathed had his way with me freely and repeatedly.

I forced myself not to be sick as the memories of my past emerged from the dark cavity of my mind which had kept my most despairing times a secret from me for so long.

I looked at Gio. He was so still, so strangely still. I reached out to touch his hand. I'd never felt so ineffectual, so insignificant, in my entire life.

I leaned over and brought my mouth just near his ear.

"I promise, my love," I whispered, "I will fix this. I will fix this and come back to you and we *will* be together, just as we were meant to be."

The crack in my heart threatened to break it in half, but I refused to let it—not yet. I had to hold it together. There were things to do.

I leaned in a bit closer and brushed my lips against his cheek. His skin was cool. I looked at him with waiting eyes, though I knew what would happen next.

He didn't move. His face was motionless. There was no flutter of eyelashes or increased beeping on the heart monitor. There was simply . . . nothing.

But somehow, in some way, I knew he had heard every word.

Chapter One
Gio

"Katarina! Katarina! Where are you?"

I ran through thick, gray fog. It hung on my skin, in my mouth; heavy and wet. Where the hell was I?

"Katarina!" I screamed. Panic ran through my veins, chilling my blood. "Katarina!"

My chest tightened, squeezing my heart as it beat at an alarming rate. This couldn't be happening. It *couldn't*. I rubbed my temples with my hands trying to remember every detail before everything went black. We were together, I had found her. She remembered me. We had won, damn it! Love had won!

No, this wasn't right. Something was wrong. What was I not remembering?

I closed my eyes and pushed far into my brain until I could

feel it. It was there, just out of reach, but I couldn't quite place it. What had happened? Just a little closer...I could almost touch it...gone.

"No!" I yelled to no one. My heart thundered in my chest, my breathing quickening to keep pace. Losing my temper wouldn't help the situation. I had to get control.

I opened my eyes and looked around. The fog was so thick I couldn't see more than two feet in front of me. Though all I wanted to do was keep moving until I had Katarina in my arms, it would be useless to continue blindly. I had to think. I stopped to regain my bearings. Taking a deep breath, I tried again. If I could just remember the last time I saw her, maybe the missing pieces would fall into place. I brought my hands to my side, closed my eyes, and let my memory take over.

It was night. Tall redwoods reached up to the sky like fingers. I remembered how the moonlight sliced through the trees, creating brilliant streaks against the forest backdrop. She was in the clearing, sobbing. Her body was hunched down on the soft ground. I could hear her pain with each sob. It broke my soul. One step. Two. I had approached her slowly. Carefully.

Oh Goddess, her face! He had hit her. Damn, bastard. A feeling of hate in its most pure, raw form oozed into my consciousness. Alessandro would *pay*. I pushed the feeling down for the moment. I'd save it for later. Right now, I needed to remember.

I took another breath and refocused. The images appeared again in my head. Fuzzy at first, then sharper with each passing second. I had shown her the serum. My stomach clenched. She had looked up at me, past my eyes, into my soul. She had *trusted* me. I watched in my mind's eye as she drank from the vial, her body doubling over as it took effect.

And then, we had kissed.

My hands pressed my chest over my heart as the next

memories danced through my mind. I gasped. She had felt...tasted...just as I had remembered. I squeezed my eyes tighter as we tumbled and turned and melded into one on the forest floor.

She knew me, had called me by name. I had called her by hers. Katarina. She was so much more than I had remembered. Every life she had ever lived, every existence she had suffered through, every experience her soul had encountered over the centuries all the way to present day, had come to the forefront of her consciousness all at once. Thousands upon thousands of memories remembered and she still had said my name. She had remembered *me*.

I took a deep breath and pushed further into my psyche. Where was she now? What had happened? The answer was somewhere inside me, I just had to think. I had to focus. If I could just remember, I could figure out what to do next. I had to find Katarina. The fog pressed in around my body and wrapped around my limbs with its wispy, soft fingers. It pulled and tugged at me gently to my left. It wanted me to follow.

Was this a good idea? Probably not, but I decided to follow the fog's lead anyway. What choice did I have? Standing around wasn't helping my situation, it wasn't putting her in my arms again. On hesitant feet, I stepped in the direction of the pulling. One step. Two. One foot after the other until I was walking steadily through the fog, quite blind to anything that lay beyond the two-foot buffer between my body and the ominous grey wall.

I continued until finally, the atmosphere thinned. With just a few more steps, I was out of the condensation and into a small forest clearing. The fog was completely cleared from the small space, only outlining its edges. My gaze combed the surrounding wall of fog. There was nothing to see, just a thick hazy gray.

But still, I recognized this place. This was the clearing

where Katarina and I were last night. I was back. I scanned the space, looking for evidence of her. Nothing. I tried to step forward but couldn't. My feet wouldn't move. Like being frozen in blocks of ice, they remained firmly planted in the spot where I had entered the clearing.

I opened my mouth to call out to her. There was no sound. The muscles in my forearms flexed. Why couldn't I speak? Fear crept around me as I realized the gravity of the situation I was in. I wasn't in the real world. What kind of magic was this? There could be no other explanation for what was happening to me.

Alessandro.

Had Alessandro somehow spelled me? Trapped me somewhere between realms of existence? And why was I the only one here? What had happened to Katarina? Was she alive? Panic squeezed my throat and I swallowed hard.

The thread. Of course. I threw my energy out and searched for the thread the Strega Onesta had conjured to tether me to her centuries ago. Frantically, I searched and searched for the invisible line that connected her soul to mine, but I couldn't find it. Had Alessandro finally figured out a way to break through the Onesta's magic? Had *he* won, after all? I clenched my jaw. No. I refused to believe that.

As I stood there, trapped inside my anatomic prison, a swift movement to my right caught my attention. My jaw relaxed as I saw Katarina run into the clearing.

"Katarina!" I tried to yell. Again, silence. Only my mouth moved.

My gaze followed as she ran to the middle of the clearing and collapsed to her knees. I watched helpless, my heart in agony, as her body heaved up and down with heavy sobs. How could I get to her? I thrust my body forward only to remain rooted in my spot. It was hopeless. I lifted my eyes to where she lay sobbing. So close. I was so close, yet somehow, she had no idea I was there. I seemed non-existent to her. A hologram of a person destined to merely stand and watch.

Her sobbing seemed to go on forever before another figure caught my attention. As the person slowly approached, I saw Katarina sit up and turn. My eyes widened as I saw that the person who approached was me. *I* was there. How was this possible? How could I be standing here, and watching myself there? It made no sense.

Every part of me froze as I watched myself take a few more steps into the clearing, Katarina meeting me halfway. This seemed familiar. Yes. Of course. This wasn't real, this was my memory. How was it possible for me to be standing here watching my memories unfold? And yet, that seemed to be the thought of least importance. Since I awoke in this place, I had been struggling to remember, and now, here was my chance. If I wanted to know what happened last night, it appeared all I would have to do was be patient and watch.

As I watched my and Katarina's interaction play out before my eyes, love filled me up like a hot air balloon and I soared. I was watching *our* movie. Our story that we wrote, directed, and starred in; the intensity of it so hot my bones ached.

I couldn't drag my gaze away as we lay on the floor of the forest. She looked up at me and smiled. Perfectly content. My heart doubled in size. Until the moment I saw it again, I had forgotten that she had smiled. How could I have forgotten such a sweet and special detail?

It didn't matter that I couldn't move, or speak, because I could see. I watched us lay there together, my hand had gently brushed a loose strand of her hair from her face. She was so beautiful, so happy.

We both were.

And then, the air shifted. Her face changed. Her eyes widened, surprise...fear? Something replaced the contentment in her expression, though I wasn't sure what. And then, I saw him. Alessandro emerged from the tree line. His right hand grasped a sword.

Two more two more easy strides. One quick thrust. He had ran the blade through my body. I lunged toward his figure, but I was still frozen, trapped on the edge of the clearing forever watching as the man I most despised made simple work of destroying me with a sick smile on his face.

The air around me pressed downward. I rolled my shoulders in a feeble attempt to shake it off. You'd think that after four centuries, I'd have been better prepared for death, but I wasn't. I never had given much thought to what death would actually look like. How *I* would actually look as I lay there on the forest floor.

Was I dead? My body was face down in the dirt. My arms splayed in awkward directions from each side of my still torso. I don't remember dying, yet, how could I deny it? I certainly looked dead. I patted my body with my hands. I didn't *feel* any different. Was this what death really was? Had I suffered for over four hundred years, waiting to be released from my curse only to be murdered by the very soul who began it all?

This can't be real. It must be a spell.

Even as the thought flashed through my head, I knew it wasn't a spell. What I was seeing was the truth. There was an ache in my body where the blade had gone through. It began to pulse. It burned my heart. With an instinctive jolt, my hand pulled at the skin where the wound should have been. I had to get out of there. Once more I tried to move but failed. It was then that I saw Alessandro take Katarina to the ground.

"No!" I mouthed, still silenced, though in my mind my voice screamed. "Fight, Katarina, fight!"

I was a wild animal, caged. I thrashed about, my soul frantic, trying to free myself from my invisible prison. It was no use. I stood planted, absolutely sickened, forced to watch the gruesome story unfold before me as Alessandro pinned her to the ground with his body and proceeded to take down his pants.

My stomach turned. I was wrong; I wasn't dead. I was alive. I was alive and living in hell.

Tears formed in my eyes and fell down my cheeks in thick ribbons. *Katarina, my love, I'm so sorry. I'm so sorry. I'm so sorry.* I wanted to turn away. I wanted to close my eyes, but something inside forced me to watch. If she had to endure the pain, then my pain in comparison would be minimal. I owed it to her to stay with her in that moment.

Then, when I was sure Alessandro would have his way, Willem appeared. Willem and Claire. At that moment, the fog began to ease its way into the clearing, obstructing my view. Everything was blurring at the edges. From my spot on the periphery, I could see Willem cautiously approach. Claire hung back in the tree line. Was that a gun? As the fog crept in more, it became a dense mist completely blocking my ability to see clearly. I saw only outlines and shadows.

My eyes darted back to where Katarina and Alessandro had been. I recognized the forms of two people, one standing and one kneeling. What was happening? What was going on? My gaze scanned the space back to where I had last spotted Willem. He stood with his hands up. In surrender? The fog pushed further into the clearing and threatened to completely cover the scene in its entirety like a grey wooly blanket.

No, not yet. I need to see what happens. Katarina!

My eyes darted back and forth between where Katarina and Alessandro had been to where Willem and Claire were. I could just see a trace of the outlines as I struggled to break free from my vantage point. A bright flash ignited from Willem and Claire's spot. Did the gun go off? Had someone been shot?

Immediately, my glance flew to where Katarina and

Alessandro had stood. Though the fog blanketed the space, I could still make out the faintest outlines. Just. A form way too big to be Katarina slowly staggered backwards with an uneven, wobbly gait, before dropping out of sight.

Had they killed Alessandro? Was he dead?

The fog rolled in with greater force, thick and efficient in its cover, and pushed the scene entirely away. I desperately scanned the area around me, trying to capture a small glimpse of my friends, of my love, but there was nothing to see. I couldn't make out anything. Then, without any warning, my feet released from their spot and I stumbled a few steps forward.

"Katarina!" I called out, my voice now back. It echoed in the mist. *Please hear me.* "Willem! Claire! I'm here! Where are you?"

Silence.

"If you ever want to see Katarina or your friends again on the earthly plane, you'll have to do a lot more than just scream their names."

I spun around and sucked in my breath and came face to face with someone I hadn't seen in over four hundred years.

About the Author

A California native turned Pacific Northwest dweller, SC Alban thrives in the moody Fall vibes and endless rainstorms that are the perfect backdrop for her storytelling. When she's not writing, she's out hiking trails, kayaking on misty waters, or chillin' at home crocheting cozy projects. Her trusty familiar and dedicated fur baby, Teo, is always by her side, making every adventure—whether outdoors or in the world of words—that much better.